Books by Gordon Ryan

Dangerous Legacy

Threads of Honor

Spirit of Union:
Volume 1: Destiny 1895–1898
Volume 2: Conflict 1898–1919

SPIRIT OF UNION

VOLUME 2 1898-1919

CONFLICT

GORDON RYAN

Deseret Book Company
Salt Lake City, Utah

Library of Congress Cataloging-in-Publication Data

Ryan, Gordon, date.
    Conflict, 1898–1919 / Gordon Ryan.
        p.   cm. — (Spirit of union ; v. 2)
    ISBN 1-57345-284-X
    I. Title. II. Series: Ryan, Gordon, date.   Spirit of union : v. 2.
    PS3568.Y32C66   1998
    813'.54—dc21   97-49436
                                                            CIP

Printed in the United States of America

10 9   8   7   6   5   4   3   2   1   49510 - 6299

For my "top-shelf" Kiwi

for three sterling women:
Michelle, Jackie, and Toni,
who have polished the silver for ten years . . .

. . . and for those who will carry on for Colleen
and for me: Cameron, Zach, Corey,
Emily, Rachel, and Kasia

Thanks to my editor, Richard Peterson, for his persistence, and to Sheri Dew, again, and yet again.

Preface

I sincerely thank the many readers who have written or E-mailed me to comment on *Spirit of Union: Vol. 1: Destiny.* Your thoughtful responses helped in the preparation of the continuing story and were most welcome.

In the creation of the manuscript for this present volume, I perhaps underwent more "conflict" as the author than the central characters do in the book. As the book was taking shape, several people with whom I consulted expressed the opinion the book needed a stronger conflict between the central protagonists, Tom and Katrina Callahan. Indeed, some suggested that the book would be more compelling if I were to put their marriage in jeopardy.

I resisted doing that. For as much as *Spirit of Union* is a story of *coalition*—of the Callahans' struggling in their marriage to accommodate their divergent religious views, of Utah's working its way to statehood in spite of national resistance, and of the effort being made by Mormons and Gentiles to find ways to live together peaceably in these fertile valleys—it is also a story about *opposition*.

Notwithstanding their religious differences, I didn't believe Tom and Katrina's marriage *needed* to be imperiled. Our prophets have told us to love our companions. They haven't said such love is to be delivered only upon conformance to our expectations. Rather, they have admonished us to love as Christ does, that is, unconditionally.

I envision Tom and Katrina attempting to do that. As many of us, they are not perfect in their efforts to love and accommodate each other. Human weakness, pride, limited understanding, stubbornness, tradition, family ties, and other things stand in the way and keep them from fully resolving their differences. But isn't that the way life is? We strive for happiness, but in spite of our best intentions, things are not always well in the garden. We aren't always able to neatly solve our problems and arrive at a point of perfect happiness. And yet, we move ahead, taking what life deals us and hoping for the best.

And so, in this volume, Tom and Katrina continue to wrestle with those things that separate them. Through the early years of their marriage and as their family grows, it is love that binds them. Whether that alone can sustain them remains to be seen. I leave it to you, the reader, to determine the validity of my premise.

Gordon W. Ryan
Salt Lake City, Utah
January 1998

The author would be pleased to receive E-mail correspondence from readers who wish to communicate. He can be reached at GordonRyan@AOL.com

Prologue

Dear Nana,

Thomas and I are finally back in Salt
Lake City, after nearly a six month
honeymoon in Europe, only to find that
Anders has gone to the war in Cuba.

Nana, I have always confided in you.
Now I need to turn to you again. You
know that I have loved Thomas Callahan,
ever since I met him on the ship coming to
America. Yet, with all that has happened
in my life these past three years, including
Thomas and Anders coming to Mexico to
bring me back home, and my marrying
Thomas in San Francisco, I feel more
confused than ever. I sometimes wonder
why the Lord preserved my life on that
desolate beach in Mexico.

Please understand, Nana, I love
Thomas. Truly I do. He stirs my heart,

1

my passion, and . . . but you know all about that don't you, Nana? Yet, since President Cannon talked with me and explained that my sealing to Harold is no longer valid, I think all the time about the things Thomas cannot provide me. My soul yearns for an eternal marriage. Oh, Nana, have I followed one foolish mistake with another?

The reasons I married Harold instead of Thomas remain valid. I love the Lord and wish to have an eternal companion. Two years ago when I was confronted by Harold and Thomas at the same time, I was intrigued by the rascal in Thomas, but I also knew that it was Harold who could provide the enduring relationship that the prophet has told us is our right, if we follow the Lord's counsel.

Papa warned me about Thomas being unable to financially care for me and especially about the Irish temperament. But during our honeymoon, I came to see how kind and thoughtful Thomas can be. Yet for all his caring and gentle loving, he cannot at present provide the one thing for which I yearn the most.

And now I carry our first child. Thomas's child, Nana. Who will bless this child? Who will baptize him or her, and who will teach the child the ways of the Lord as He has explained them to the prophet? Thomas is a good man, Nana, and I have come to understand that he would do anything within his power to care for me. (It makes me laugh when I think that Poppa once worried about our financial condition.) I believe Thomas will be a kind, considerate, loving father. But the bargain I made with him on the ship from Mexico—that I would marry him if he would not interfere with my religion or that of our children—is now concerning me.

And so, I need you, Nana. Guide me to see the way to help Thomas, as I have always asked you to help Anders. If only both of them could see the light of the gospel.

Yeg elske deg,

Your Trina

1

Far better it is to dare mighty things, to win glorious triumphs, even though checkered by failure, than to take rank with those poor spirits who neither enjoy much nor suffer much, because they live in the gray twilight that knows not victory nor defeat.

Theodore Roosevelt
Chicago, 10 April 1899

June 1898

The recruiters had lied. War was ugly.

Twenty-three-year-old Anders Hansen sat hunched over on a log next to a crackling fire. He pulled his blanket tighter around his shoulders and stared into the leaping flames that were licking at the fresh scrub brush tossed moments earlier onto the dying embers. Even in the tropical summer, high in the mountains, the Cuban evenings carried a chill that worked its way to the bone.

Anders was in Cuba serving as a hospital engineer—part of a medical contingent from Salt Lake City. The nursing sisters of Holy Cross Hospital had quickly responded to the request of the United States government to provide hospital facilities in what was projected to be a brief war against Spain.[1]

In the latest chapter in a never-ending ritual, repeated several times each century, thousands of young men across America had responded to their nation's call and pledged their allegiance to the patriotic cause described by zealous military recruiters. Their impassioned rhetoric of God, country, and duty, supported by the daily nationalistic editorials published by William Randolph Hearst's newspapers, served to move yet another generation of hot-blooded young men to enlist in this latest cause. They had been convinced that if they didn't hurry, they would miss the honor and prestige that attached themselves to the members of a military force embarked on a righteous crusade.

Far from the comforts of home, the young recruits now found themselves in a state of shock after confronting the reality of war, and seated around the campfire, they sought some respite from the horror that had so quickly and totally encompassed their lives. Anders and the others had come to understand that to the man on the shooting or receiving end, a single bullet instantly dictated the scope of war. Too many troopers, killed or maimed in this "small conflict," had already crossed Anders's path as he performed the grungy work of helping the nursing sisters maintain and operate their hospital.

Before leaving Utah, he had almost been persuaded to join the Utah Battalion, led by Richard Young, grandson of the Mormon pioneer leader, Brigham Young. For the first time since the famous original Mormon Battalion had marched two thousand miles across the great American Southwest in 1846–47, Church leaders had encouraged their young men to answer their government's call. Over eight hundred men from the Utah basin had answered the summons, and, on a bright day in April 1898, the recruits had formed up in the square in downtown Salt Lake City. Bands were playing, flags were waving, and emotions were running high. But in the end, Anders's passion to join the multitude rallying to the flag had been outweighed by his earlier commitment to Sister Mary Theophane. He had promised that he would accompany her medical detachment to Cuba, continuing the service he had provided for the previous two years as hospital engineer. That commitment had allowed him to resist the enlistment contagion that swept through the other young men in that frenzied crowd.

The Utah Battalion, with most of their horses abandoned in Florida, had arrived in Cuba some weeks after the nursing staff had already established the field hospital, and there had been little contact between the two Utah groups. Occasionally, random patients from the Utah Battalion had passed through the field hospital, a hastily assembled facility consisting of multiple tents that housed surgery, patient wards, and kitchen facilities.

Hunkered down by the fire, Anders heard the approach of a single rider, cautiously slowing his mount as he descended the hill that overlooked the medical facility. Two of the troopers reached for their weapons, but came to attention instead when the firelight reflected off the approaching horseman. They recognized the uniform and familiar face of their commanding officer, First Volunteer Cavalry Regiment, Colonel Leonard Wood.[2]

One of the troopers moved to take Colonel Wood's horse, and, dismounting, the officer stepped to the fire. The troopers stood and saluted as he approached. He took a short cigar butt from his mouth, tossed it into the fire, and returned their salute.

"The head nursing sister?" he asked, nodding toward the large tent.

Also on his feet, Anders replied, "Yes, sir. Sister Mary is in the recovery tent."

Wood pulled his pocket watch from the waistband of his military-style jodhpurs and flipped open the cover.

"Humph," he snorted. "Well after midnight. She keeps longer hours than I do."

Anders remained silent as the colonel walked to the tent, pulled back the flap, and went inside where he gazed down the rows of wounded or seriously ill troopers. Two kerosene lanterns, one at each end of the tent, gave off a dull glow and a soft, hissing sound. Recognizing one of the troopers, Colonel Wood moved to the foot of his bed. The sick trooper had his eyes closed, but was sleeping fitfully. After a moment, the semiconscious man awoke and opened his eyes. He started to lift his head from the pillow.

"Rest easy, Lieutenant," Colonel Wood said. Stepping to the side of the bed, he peered down at the sunburned, gaunt face of the young officer.

"Evening, Colonel," the man rasped.

"Just checking on the men, Lieutenant. They treating you well?" he asked, nodding toward the nurse's station at the end of the tent.

"Just fine, sir. They look after us just fine."

"Excellent. Now you get some more rest, Lieutenant. We'll have need of your services shortly. Can't do the job without good officers," Wood declared.

"Sir, some of the men have been saying the unit is moving into action. I'm not really injured. Just a bit weak. I'd sure like the chance to return to the regiment."

"That's the spirit, son. But you rest while you can," he said, bending to pat the young man's arm. "We'll be needing you soon enough."

A nursing Sister quietly walked up behind Colonel Wood and lifted the chart at the foot of the patient's bed. She quickly scanned its contents.

"Evening, Sister," Wood said, removing his campaign hat.

"And a good evening to you, Colonel," she said, inclining her eyes toward the flap of the tent.

Wood nodded his silent assent and turned his attention back to the trooper. "Eat well, Lieutenant. You'll be sitting in the saddle and back on hardtack grub soon enough," he said. "I'll be back when I can."

"Thank you, Colonel," the lieutenant said, trying once again to raise his head in a gesture of respect for his commanding officer.

"You'll be puttin' your head down now, lad, and closing your eyes," Sister Mary Theophane warned with a stern gaze.

"Yes, ma'am," he replied, surrendering to his fatigue once again.

Sister Mary followed Colonel Wood out of the tent and closed the flap behind her as she stepped out into the darkness.

"And how is Lieutenant Watkins?" Wood asked. "He's part of the 71st New York and he comes from a good, upstate New York family."

Sister Mary gently shook her head. "They all come from good families, Colonel. I'm afraid he'll not be returning to duty. His temperature has been above one hundred for three days, and the dysentery has nearly dehydrated him. Colonel, I'm afraid your young lieutenant might not make it."

The colonel nodded, twisting the end of his waxed mustache in contemplation. "War is not all strategy, field movement, or bravery, is it, Sister?" he asked.

"I wouldn't be knowing, Colonel. What I *would* know is that in the seven weeks we've been here, we've lost about nineteen of your troopers to battlefield wounds, and over *six hundred* to the diseases these boys can't seem to withstand."

"Yes. That's what I mean," Wood said, shaking his head. "Being able to adapt seems more important than having a good battle plan. The Spaniards might simply wait us out, thinking we'll die of one malady or another," he paused and looked at Sister Mary, "or go home."

"Is that being considered, Colonel?" Sister Mary asked, her interest brightening.

He shook his head. "I'm afraid not, Sister. We'll take the fight to them first, I'm certain."

"More wounded, then?" she said.

Wood nodded again. "It appears so, Sister."

"Soon?"

He nodded again. "Tomorrow."

"Aye," she replied, sighing. "I'll get the Sisters ready."

"Better you get some sleep beforehand, Sister," he suggested.

"I can sleep when we go home, Colonel."

Wood replaced his campaign hat and tightened the leather strap under his chin. He offered Sister Mary a crisp salute. "Thank you, Sister. Without your assistance and that of your nursing sisters, many more of these boys wouldn't make it home to wives and mothers. God bless you."

"And you, Colonel, and all those under your command."

Colonel Wood started to leave, then hesitated for a moment. "Sister, I get the impression all this is not new to you."

It was Sister Mary's turn to nod. "In the last one, Colonel. In Pennsylvania," she said, looking past him toward the glowing campfire. After a moment's silence, she shifted her gaze to look at Wood again. "The difference then was that Americans were killing each other."

The cavalry colonel gazed for a moment at the weary nun. "Thank you, Sister," he finally said, turning and walking back toward the fire to retrieve his horse. After mounting, he turned to face Sister Mary and politely raised his fingers to the brim of his hat. He then reined his horse around and rode up the hill he had descended, the light from the campfire reflecting off his broad back.

Anders rose from his place by the fire and walked toward Sister Mary. "Anything I can do, Sister?"

Sister Mary watched the departing horseman, silhouetted by the moonlight, until he crested the hilltop and disappeared into the night shadows. She turned to look at Anders and smiled weakly. "We can expect additional patients tomorrow, Mr. Hansen. Perhaps you should alert Stitch and the orderlies to have the ambulance wagon prepared, and I'll inform the Sisters."

"I see. Seems it never ends, does it, Sister? 'A bloody waste,' as Tom Callahan would say."

"Indeed," she said, turning and walking off into the darkness toward a small hill.

"Please, Sister," Anders counseled, "don't stray too far from the campsite."

Sister Mary Theophane raised her arm, slightly waving her hand in silent acknowledgment and continuing her climb toward the crest of the hill. Reaching the top and standing in a small copse of trees, she lifted her eyes to the brightness of the stars, struggling to control her fears and emotions.

"Mother Mary, give me of thy strength as we enter this valley of darkness," Sister Mary silently prayed. "You know the agony of this moment—caring for these poor wretched souls as they come face to face with their mortality. Bless the Sisters who will comfort and aid these needy men. Bless the officers who will lead them, and provide your blessed comfort for those who are frightened. Amen," she said softly, then crossed herself and remained still in the night. The glare from the campfire down the hill reflected off the trunks of the trees around her.

Trying to sort out her thoughts and mentally prepare for the morrow, an irony occurred to her. Here she stood, as she had thirty-five years before, awaiting the dawn of July 1st. Once again she was being called upon to minister to the wounded, the terrified, and God forbid, she crossed herself again, the dying. "Gettysburg," she whispered to herself. "Oh, dear God, not again."

Arriving in America with a small group of Catholic postulants from Ireland in 1854, fifteen-year-old Moira Molloy immediately launched into her role as a nursing trainee. By 1860, she had selected the name of Sister Mary Theophane, taken her vows, and completed her training. She began her medical practice in the Catholic hospital in Notre Dame, Indiana, the "Mother House" of her order, The Sisters of the Holy Cross. In 1861, when the Southern States commenced hostilities against the Union, plans were formulated to provide medical care to military forces, and a long-term care facility was established at Mt. Cairo, Illinois, staffed in part by Sisters of the Holy Cross.

Assigned to the nursing staff at Mt. Cairo, Sister Mary Theophane all too quickly learned about battlefield wounds and the amputations that were frequently required to save the lives of soldiers whose wounds had not been adequately treated. In April 1863, Sister Mary found herself assigned with one other sister to travel to St. Joseph's College, a Catholic school for young women in Emmitsburg, Maryland. Sent there to recruit additional nurses from among the women at the college, Sister Mary Theophane found the peaceful campus a respite from the mounting carnage she had witnessed at Mt. Cairo Hospital.

In late June, Union troops of the 1st Corps occupied the land around Emmitsburg, including much of the college campus. Sister Mary and her companion, Sister Josephina, were concerned by the reports of approaching Confederate troops, who they feared would prevent them from leaving St. Joseph's to return to their hospital in Illinois. They booked passage on the night train to Harrisburg, but were halted in Gettysburg by the news of the burning of a trestle bridge by Confederate cavalry. Disembarking the train in Gettysburg on June 30th, they were provided temporary quarters by a local Lutheran minister.

The following day, before they had the opportunity to arrange alternate transportation, they were informed of the arrival of a small contingent of Union soldiers. On the morning of July 1st, Confederate forces unexpectedly appeared to the west of town, and the battle of Gettysburg was underway.

Sister Mary soon became embroiled in what would be her most forceful indoctrination to the horrors of battlefield casualties. From late morning, when the Confederate infantry appeared, throughout the afternoon, the opening skirmish raged. Following hours of shifting advantage, and the death of one Union general, Union forces retreated from their initial defensive position near McPherson's

Ridge, toward the town of Gettysburg. In quick pursuit, the Confederate cavalry and infantry overran most of Gettysburg. By dark, Sister Mary found herself behind Confederate lines.

To her surprise, she was politely asked by Confederate general Jubal Early to help establish a field hospital to be staffed by Confederate army surgeons. Early's intent was to establish a limited field hospital at the Lutheran Seminary facilities, at the north end of Seminary Ridge, where Confederate forces were fortified on the morning of July 2nd.

After two days spent treating a constant stream of wounded, Confederate and Union alike, the relative calm of the late morning of July 3rd was shattered by a tremendous cannonade. Leaving the hospital facilities briefly and walking south down Seminary Ridge, twenty-two-year-old Moira Molloy, in full Catholic nursing habit, stood in a grove of trees. She was startled by the abrupt cessation of sound, as cannons from both sides of the battlefield almost simultaneously ceased their barrage.

She could hear horses and men moving about in the woods below the gently rising ridge where she stood. Beyond the trees lay a vast, open field across which she could barely make out the movement of thousands of distant, blue-clad soldiers, working to position their horse-drawn cannon along the elevated portions of Cemetery Ridge, which ran parallel to the Confederate positions on Seminary Ridge. Men on the Union side were taking up defensive positions behind wooden fence lines along a low, rock wall.

Suddenly, the sound of movement in the woods below her increased, and a vast army of men in gray uniforms emerged from the cover of the trees onto the open field, forming up in regimental lines. Their officers, some on horseback, moved about encouraging their men to quickly form ranks. Resplendent in his uniform, one mounted officer stood to the fore. The yellow piping on his seams and his shoulder epaulets flashed in the sunlight as he rode his skittish horse up and down the line, speaking a word here and there to encourage, chasten, and fortify his command. The muted color of the long gray line of uniforms was occasionally broken by a burst of color—the red and yellow of military sashes—as thousands of men readied themselves for battle.

Dismounting and handing the reins to an orderly, the officer strode to the head of the troop and stood facing the stationary blue line formed up nearly a mile away across the field. As if by an unseen command, a single cannon shot erupted, far to the south end of the Confederate lines, followed quickly by a second. The lone officer, who stood to the fore, raised his sword above his head and pointed it toward the distant barricade of Union soldiers, who were standing quietly, watching the massive formation develop. He shouted something to his men that Sister Mary could not hear. But it resulted in thousands of men raising their voices in unison. The cacophony carried across the field to the blue lines where a flurry of activity signaled their growing anxiety.

Over twelve thousand men, arrayed in regimental and divisional alignment below Sister Mary's position on the ridge, started forward, their line running continuously abreast for nearly a mile and a half, north to south. Slowly at first, then at a more rapid pace, the Confederate soldiers began the long, undefended march across the low-lying field. Cannons from the higher positioned Union lines on the east began to sound their call. With the burst of the first volley, dozens of gaps opened up in the gray lines that moved like a wave across the field in front of and below Sister Mary.

Horrified, she dropped to her knees in the tree line, crossed herself, and brought her hand to her mouth as she watched the carnage envelop these brave men. They continued their advance, walking steadfastly across the field, closing ranks to fill the voids left by fallen comrades. For nearly thirty minutes they went on, their numbers dwindling as they approached the intersecting Emmitsburg Road. Clamoring over fences on both sides of the roadway, they courageously followed their leaders into the hail of rifle fire being hurled at them from the Union ranks.

With the field nearly obscured by drifting smoke, a temporary silence was once again shattered by the deafening roar of cannonade. The fusillade was replaced as quickly as it had begun by the staccato of rifle fire, as one by one, Union soldiers began to find their range, targeting individuals in the ranks of the advancing Southern troops. Even through the drifting smoke, Sister Mary could see that the gray line now numbered thousands fewer as the surviving Confederate troops neared the barricade, behind which lay the might of the Union's Army of the Potomac.

After a few minutes, a light breeze cleared the field of drifting smoke, and Sister Mary could discern the carpet of dead and injured men. Bodies were strewn across the tramped-down field, from their point of origin near the tree line, to the foremost advance of the gray army, now breaching the Union rampart. Still on her knees, her rosary clutched tightly in her hands, and tears running down her cheeks, she watched as the few Confederate soldiers still advancing bravely climbed the wall. Withering fire from their enemy encased them in a volley of death. Soon, those few stalwarts who had reached their objective were sur-rounded by a horde of blue-clad soldiers, obscuring them from Sister Mary's view as they were disarmed and escorted further east off the ridge and out of sight.

As suddenly as it had begun, the battle was over. Crawling, walking, and aiding their fallen comrades along the way, the remaining gray-clad troops slowly retraced their steps, stumbling back toward the woods fronting Seminary Ridge. Further conflict ceased as the blue troops, out of respect for the valiant Confederate effort, allowed those retreating the honor of safe passage across the field.

The three-day battle of Gettysburg, defined by the most heroic yet suicidal frontal assault of the Civil War, was over. Pickett's charge would be lauded for decades to come as a moral victory, but in the aftermath of Gettysburg, although they would fight on for nearly two more years, the South would never again take the initiative.

Sister Mary recalled how, on that dreadful day, she had risen from her knees, wiped her eyes, and started on a fast walk toward the overcrowded field hospital, now preparing to receive the overwhelming and ghastly influx of wounded and dismembered soldiers.

Later that afternoon Sister Mary Theophane was sum-moned by the chief surgeon. An older man, his face drawn and haggard from hours of surgery, he steadied himself for a moment in the doorway as Sister Mary approached.

"Ma'am, I have been informed that you are from the Catholic college some ten miles south in Maryland. Is that correct?"

"I have been on assignment there for several weeks, Doctor."

"Would it be possible, ma'am, as we begin our march

south, for us to leave some of our wounded in your care? We would, of course, provide additional surgeons to assist."

"Doctor," Sister Mary replied hesitantly, "I am not in authority at the college, but I feel certain they will seek to do all they can to assist."

He nodded his head, rubbing his beard and digging at the corner of his eye with a finger. "I understand. These men will be in Confederate gray, Sister, and northern Maryland is . . ."

"Would there be any Irish among your troops?" she interrupted.

The doctor hesitated momentarily, unsure of her meaning but nodding his head in response.

"And Welsh, Scandinavian, German?" she continued.

"I believe we have them all, ma'am," he replied.

"Then, sir, the color of their clothing will not matter to our Lord. They are all His children."

The tired, old man was silent for a moment, looking down at this very young, and very small, Catholic nursing Sister, her habit stained with three days accumulation of dirt and the dark red stains of Northern and Southern blood. "God bless you, Sister," he said, his eyes moist and his voice soft.

"Aye, Doctor. If folly such as we have witnessed today is to continue, God help us all."

<hr>

The sound of Anders walking up the hill behind Sister Mary broke her thoughts of past trauma and she turned to smile at him as he approached. "Are you all right, Sister?"

"We will all have to be all right, Mr. Hansen," she said, dabbing at her eyes, a thirty-five-year-old tear rekindled. "Tomorrow will bring a test that some will not withstand."

"I've spoken with Stitch, Sister. He's seeing to the ambulance wagon at the moment."

"Aye," she said, taking one last look into the dark night, the faintest glimmer of light breaking to the east from the morning star. She turned her gaze back to Anders and offered a smile. "Are *you* ready, Mr. Hansen?"

"No, Sister," he shook his head. "In all honesty, I don't believe I am. But I *have* asked the Lord to help make me so."

"Aye. We will all need Him this day."

Sister Mary rose from her morning prayers alongside the cot in her small tent and quickly went about her morning ablutions. As she dressed, she exhaled in frustration at the state of her habit. Unable to properly launder her clothing in the rough conditions of field duty, she felt her appearance was far beneath her personal standards. On her way to her duties, she bypassed the kitchen tent, determined to continue her fast as the day commenced.

At first light, across the compound, Stitch busied himself hitching the team to the ambulance wagon, then drove to the front of the cluster of tents. Christened John Walkinghorse in 1862, the son of Ute Indian parents, Stitch grew up in the Uinta Mountains of Utah. When his mother died in his early teens, he rode with his father who served with the U.S. Seventh Cavalry on the western frontier. Stitch enlisted in the army, eventually mustering out in 1896 at Fort Douglas, Utah. When his friend, Anders Hansen, agreed to go to Cuba with the hospital contingent, Stitch had volunteered to come along, "to take care of them horses," he had said.

Anders exited the kitchen tent where he had taken

breakfast and stepped to the wagon as Stitch climbed down. Sister Mary was close behind him.

"All stocked and ready, Stitch?" Anders asked.

"Yep. I done took a ride this morning just before light. Heard some shootin' over toward Kettle Hill. Just some skirmishers, wouldn't doubt."

"Stitch," Sister Mary said, her voice reproving, "no more riding off alone until the military informs us the area is safe. I need all the help I can get here, and I can't afford to let everyone who wants, to just go off sightseeing. Now, let's get the area ready for patients. The hospital ward is prepared, and we've moved all the current patients out of the tent next to surgery to make room for newly wounded. Mr. Hansen, you and Stitch remain together today and operate the ambulance wagon. If you need additional stretcher bearers, try to get a couple of men from the security squad. Other than that, it's just . . ."

Sister Mary's attention was diverted as three riders came galloping over the hill and down the road Colonel Wood had used the previous evening. The lead rider pulled his horse to a stop, jumping down from his saddle and holding his reins. Dressed in buckskin colored trousers, dark blue shirt, and a campaign hat with the left brim pinned up above the ear, the trooper reflected the look of the Rough Riders, Colonel Roosevelt's volunteer cavalry.

"Sister, we got five wounded troopers comin' behind on a food wagon. Two bad and two light. One ain't got no hope."

"Has the fighting started for real, Trooper?" she asked.

"No, ma'am. Just some skirmishers, but it were a roadside ambush what got these troopers. Colonel asked us to git some more medicine for the shakes casin' we get bogged down out in them hills and can't get back for a few days."

"Of course. Stitch, take care of these troopers, please. Mr. Hansen, take the saddled mare and see how far behind these wounded troopers are. Be careful, Mr. Hansen."

"Yes, ma'am."

Before Anders reached the top of the road, a double-team army wagon crested the rise, two troopers on the front seat. When they drew closer, five more troopers could be seen lying in the back of the wagon. After escorting the wagon to the surgery, Anders dismounted, tied his horse, and began to help unload the wounded soldiers.

"No use botherin' *him*," the driver said with a nod of his head. "He's been dead over an hour."

The newly arrived soldiers were unloaded and quickly examined. One was immediately taken into surgery, and the other three were made as comfortable as possible in the recovery tent where several nursing Sisters went about cleansing and dressing their wounds. Stitch and Anders carried the dead soldier to a rear area designated as the morgue and located away from the view of arriving soldiers. The security detachment had also been assigned the responsibility of burying the dead before the heat could do its work.

About two hours passed before the last wounded soldier completed surgery and was moved to the recovery tent with his mates. The sound of gunfire had increased considerably as the day progressed. Individual troopers came and went, retrieving medicine and equipment, and filling water containers. Just after noon, another wagonload of troopers came over the hill and stopped in front of the main tent area.

"Colonel's compliments, ma'am," a young lieutenant with a New England accent said. Sitting astride a bay mare, he raised his fingers to the brim of his cap in a loose salute. "He asked if you could send the ambulance wagon back, accompanied by two of my troopers, to retrieve additional wounded. I've brought several lightly wounded men with me," he motioned toward the wagon, "but the more seriously wounded are waiting for the gut-wagon." He looked briefly embarrassed by his use of the troop term for the ambulance. "Sorry, Sister," he added.

Sister Mary ignored the remark. "Certainly we can help, Lieutenant. Seems a bit less shooting. Is the battle over?"

"I believe it nearly is, Sister. Colonel Roosevelt led the Rough Rider boys up Kettle Hill,[3] drove the Spanish back, and secured the top. But our regiment is scattered all over three sides of the San Juan Heights, and some mopping up still needs to be done."

"How many wounded?"

"Don't know for certain, ma'am. They gave us an artillery pounding before we commenced the attack. More than fifty at last count, but that was over two hours ago."

Sister Mary faced Anders. "Mr. Hansen, you and Stitch take the ambulance wagon and two of the Lieutenant's troopers and see if you can transport some of the wounded. We'll have to hurry now or we'll get caught by the dark." Turning back to the Lieutenant, she added, "How far away are the wounded soldiers, Lieutenant?"

"'Bout five or six miles down the road, ma'am. Troopers know where to go."

"Fine. Off with you then, Mr. Hansen," she directed.

"Right, Sister," Anders said, climbing up next to Stitch who handled the reins. Made nervous by the labored breathing and skittishness of the horses that had just arrived, the four horses in the hitch pawed anxiously at the ground and tossed their heads.

"Excuse me, Sister," the lieutenant said. "Could you direct me to the telegraph? I have dispatches from Mr. Hearst and Mr. Crane."[4]

24

"Last tent in the compound," she pointed, before lifting the tent flap and entering the recovery area.

On Anders's third trip out, having carried ten or twelve wounded soldiers per trip in the ambulance wagon that was only outfitted for six, Anders and Stitch were stopped by four galloping troopers racing toward the field hospital. Stitch pulled on the reins, bringing the wagon to a halt. The riders also reined in.

"Apparently the Spaniards have been watching your medical wagon," one of the riders blurted out. "They ambushed some of the troopers trying to get the wounded ready for your next trip. Don't be goin' up there now. They're all pinned down or scattered throughout the countryside. We got's to get word to the Colonel, but it'll be dark 'fore we can git back to 'em."

Anders looked at Stitch momentarily, an unspoken question in his eyes. Stitch just nodded and lightly slapped the reins to the back of the lead horse, who started to pull forward.

Anders called over the side of the wagon as they drove past the four troopers. "Tell Sister Mary we're going after another load, and tell her what's happened."

"You ain't got a hope," one trooper hollered at Anders, as the men spurred their mounts and started again for the field hospital.

"What we gonna do, Andy?" Stitch asked as the wagon continued down the road.

"We've got to at least look, Stitch. He said they're scattered, but maybe we can figure a way to help some of those men get out of there."

A half-mile short of where they had picked up the previous load of wounded soldiers, Stitch stopped the wagon and hobbled the lead horse. Not wanting to drive the team into a possible ambush, he and Anders proceeded cautiously on foot, slightly off the road, prepared to dive for cover into the light bush alongside the narrow dirt road that had been cut through the backwoods. About five hundred yards from where the last load of wounded troopers had waited on the road, they stopped to listen. Rifle fire was coming from off the road to the west.

"What do you think, Andy?" Stitch asked.

Anders moved off the road, stepping down into a shallow ditch running alongside, and looking up at the declining sun. "Got a couple of hours of light left, Stitch. Maybe we ought to split up and search for any remaining troopers."

"I dunno, Andy. That's risky, bein' alone in the bush and all."

"Yah, but we're running out of time, Stitch."

"Okay, we'll give it a try. Which way for you?" he asked, nodding his head in the direction he intended to go.

"I'll head east. You go off to the west, there," he pointed, "and we'll try to work our way through the brush to the point where we found those other troopers on the last trip. I think that's about a quarter mile up this road to the north." He looked at his watch. "Be back at the wagon in roughly an hour."

Stitch nodded and stepped off the road, heading toward the west. Anders moved a few feet into the brush, watching until Stitch disappeared in the overgrowth. Wending his way through the tangled low scrub brush and saw grass, Anders hadn't gone a half-mile when he heard the sound of voices. He thought they were speaking English, but he cautiously got to his knees and then crawled the remaining forty yards to a small cluster of trees where he saw three troopers lying on the ground near a tree.

"Comin' in," Anders announced loudly. Grabbing their

rifles, two of the troopers jumped to their feet, as Anders stepped through the line of brush. "Come from the field hospital, Trooper. Easy on the trigger, if you please," he smiled.

Both troopers relaxed and the taller one got down on one knee to examine the unconscious man. "He's bad hurt. Kin we git him to the hospital?"

"That's what I'm here for. Can you help carry him?"

"Yeah, I reckon."

Anders gave a quick examination to the downed trooper and saw that he had a chest wound, his breathing was slow and his color was a light gray. "Gotta get this man back to the wagon," he said. "Give me a hand." They lifted the unconscious trooper, carrying him between Anders and the taller trooper while the third man carried the three rifles and gear. In twenty minutes, they were back at the ambulance wagon where they started to place the man in one of the lower bunks for the trip.

Two shots rang out on the opposite side of the wagon. The trooper who had been carrying the rifles dropped to the ground and began to return fire. Anders fell flat in the bed of the wagon, and the trooper who had been assisting him in the carry jumped down and scrambled under the wagon, retrieving his rifle from his buddy.

"How many ya make it, Jed?" the shorter trooper asked.

"Heard three shots. Dunno how many more."

From somewhere out of the brush to the west, gunfire erupted and several rifle shots struck the wagon and the surrounding ground, pinning the two troopers beneath the wagon while Anders lay on the floor of the ambulance beside the injured man. Several shots were returned and then minutes went by as they assessed their situation. Suddenly, multiple rifle shots were heard from the direction of the enemy soldiers, and shouts in English were discernible. In a few moments, an American voice called out, "Hold your fire. We're coming out."

The two troopers under the ambulance wagon kept aim in the direction of the voice, but held fire. First one, then five other American troopers came through the brush and approached the wagon.

"Where'd you come from?" Jed asked, standing to his feet.

An older man with three stripes on his uniform spat tobacco juice on the ground and grinned. "We seen the ambulance wagon and figured the Spanerds would try to ambush the hospital boys when they brought the wounded out—like they did earlier to them wounded troopers. At least *that* bunch won't be ambushin' nobody else," he grinned, another spat erupting from his mouth.

Anders stood and jumped down from the wagon, taking in the situation. "Did you see another medical orderly off to the west?"

"Yep," he said, brown juice dribbling off his lip. "He hauled a couple'a gut-shot troopers outta the bush. They're over yonder in them trees," he pointed. Turning to one of his troopers he jerked his head toward the woods. "Git them shot-up boys over here, and let's get movin' 'fore some of their spanny cousins come lookin' for 'em," he said, hiking his thumb toward the site of the recent encounter.

"Where's the other orderly?" Anders asked.

"Back in the bush. He pulled a couple o' them troopers out, but got hisself shot on the last trip in. We couldn't see no way to get back in, and the lieutenant, he was gut-shot, so we left 'em."

Anders stared at the sergeant for a moment, startled by his callous attitude toward his fellow troopers. He turned and reached into the wagon, pulling out another aid kit and a fresh canteen of water and strapping them to his waist. "Let's go get 'em."

The older sergeant shook his head and spat on the ground again. "No sense. The other two's pinned down right proper under the guns of another bunch o' them Spanerds."

"We've *got* to reach them," Anders objected, his anger rising.

"Nope. T'other two's likely dead and that orderly's jus' an injun. Ain't goin' in *no* firefight for *no* injun, no sir."

Anders stepped toward the sergeant. "How far away are they?"

"A few hunnert yards west," he jerked his thumb. "No sense, I'm tellin' ya."

"Sergeant, my name is Anders Hansen. At the direction of Colonel Roosevelt, I carry the rank of captain when I'm in the field. I'm ordering you to remain here with the wagon and to load the rest of the wounded troopers. I'll return as quickly as I can, but you *will* wait until I return."

The sergeant's face turned bitter. Anders stared at the older man, sensing he was contemplating Anders's chances of returning alive.

"You *could* leave, Sergeant. But I might get out alive, and if I do, I will certainly report your desertion in the face of the enemy. Do you understand me?"

The old sergeant spat once more, looked at Anders and grinned, his teeth stained brown and his gums discolored. "Give ya fifteen minutes, *Cap'n* Hansen."

"You'll wait one hour, Sergeant." Anders turned to the trooper who had helped him carry the first injured man to the wagon. "Will you help me, Jed?"

The trooper nodded. He picked up an extra cartridge belt from the wounded trooper in the wagon and the two men started off into the brush while the other troopers began to load more wounded men into the wagon.

"Fifteen minutes, Cap'n!" the old sergeant shouted after them.

Anders and Jed made their way through the brush, stopping as they heard an occasional single shot ring through the trees. "Got 'em pinned down all right," Jed said. "That's their style. They like to let you know you're in their sights when they got it up on ya," he said.

The sound of infrequent rifle fire grew louder as they approached the area. Jed guided them around the woods, away from the shots, then brought them to the edge of a clearing, roughly circular in shape and about a hundred yards across. It was covered in short saw grass, one to two feet tall. Anders could see that about halfway across the clearing the ground dipped into a gully that looked like a small streambed, but the water had dried up in the heat of the summer.

Anders crept next to Jed as they watched through an opening in the bushes to see what was in the clearing. Another shot rang out and dust rose from the ground about fifty yards out. Anders saw an arm briefly raise up out of the saw grass as if someone were turning over, trying to avoid the shots coming from the far side of the clearing.

"Jed, you got any ideas? Someone's alive out there."

Jed nodded and grunted. "Be a sittin' duck goin' out there, Captain."

"Jed," Anders voiced, "he, or they, are helpless unless we try. Suppose I crawl out and see what I can do while you put a couple of shots into those woods on the other side, just to let 'em know we're here too."

Again Jed nodded. "Sounds good, Captain. Try to keep down below the grass if you can. Take a sight from here on

30

some landmark, a tall tree or somethin', and crawl toward it lookin' through the grass to keep your guide mark in sight. You can get lost on your belly in that grass if you ain't careful. And the last thing you'd be wantin' to do is go poking your head up to have a look around," he grinned.

"Okay," Anders replied. He crawled to the edge of the clearing, then looked back at Jed, giving a thumbs up, which Jed returned. Jed then fired two quick shots into the far side of the clearing, where a rustling of brush indicated that Spanish troops were still there.

Anders crawled forward through the grass, with flying insects buzzing about his face and the razorlike grass actually slicing the skin on his forearms as he crawled on his elbows. Another shot from Jed rang out, followed by two shots from the far side, this time directed at the woods where Jed was hiding, rather than at the wounded man or men pinned down in the clearing. Ten minutes into his crawl, Anders pushed aside a clump of saw grass and came face to face with the heel of a boot. Inching up alongside the man, Anders could tell from the trousers that it was Stitch. When he had reached his friend's upper body, Stitch rolled his head toward Anders and smiled weakly.

"Been thinkin' 'bout General Custer and my pappy," he mumbled, sounding delirious. Stitch had previously told Anders that in '76, when he was about fourteen, he'd been an assistant to the cook in the Seventh Cavalry and his daddy had been with Custer as a Ute Indian scout on that fateful morning at Little Bighorn.

Anders smiled at Stitch. "Not today, Stitch. We're gonna get out of here together. Where are you hit?"

"In the thigh. Got a compress on it and stopped the bleeding I think."

"Can you crawl?"

"Dunno. Them Spanish been throwing lead around every time the grass moves, so's I ain't tried yet."

Anders nodded and looked back down toward his feet in the direction he had come. A path of bent grass was clearly visible where he had crawled through the field. A small pebble bounced off Anders's shoulder and he looked off to one side, toward the direction he thought the pebble had come from. Not seeing anything, he looked back at Stitch, questioning.

"Got two more troopers over in that gully, Andy. I brought a couple out before the Spanish started shootin', but when I came back I . . ."

"I understand, Stitch. Apparently at least one of 'em is still alive."

"Crawl forward about five feet, Andy, and you can see 'em. I'll try to turn around while you do."

"Okay, Stitch. Stay low. I'll be right back."

Anders shifted his position and pulled himself through the grass a few feet until he could see through a cluster of saw grass clumps. Another shot rang out from Jed's side of the clearing, with no response from the Spaniards. Peering through the grass, Anders could make out the blue jacket of a U.S. trooper uniform, lying in the depressed area of the streambed. It was nothing more than a two-foot-deep depression in the clearing, but it afforded cover from direct gunfire of the enemy. Anders waved his fingers slightly and received a quick acknowledgment from the trooper.

"How many," Anders whispered loudly enough for the man to hear.

"Just two," came the answer.

"Right. Be back shortly," Anders replied.

"We ain't goin' nowhere," the man said.

"Hold on, I'll get you when I come back," Anders said,

slithering backward toward Stitch, who had turned around and was facing Jed's position. Passing Stitch, Anders spoke softly. "Try to crawl as best you can, Stitch. I'll keep ahead and to the side. I'll pull you when I can. It's only about forty yards."

Stitch nodded and began to crawl. His labored grunting assured Anders that the wound was painful as Stitch dragged his body over the uneven ground. It took almost twenty minutes to reach the cover of the bushes with Jed reaching out for them the final few feet and pulling them behind cover.

"Got any water?" Stitch mumbled.

"Sure 'nuff," Jed replied.

While Stitch drank and lay silently in the cover of the trees, Anders filled Jed in on the remaining troopers.

"Maybe we ought to go back and get t'others," Jed offered.

"Not enough time, Jed. Besides, the sergeant may not still be there. You help Stitch back to the ambulance and come back to this spot for me. Bring another trooper if you can so we can carry these men if we have to."

Jed nodded.

"Jed, if I'm not back here when you return . . ."

"You'll be here."

Anders smiled and nodded. "If I'm not, get back to the wagon and take those wounded to the field hospital. You'll know where to find me in the morning."

Jed just nodded his acknowledgment. He lined up his rifle again and fired another shot toward the Spanish troops. He then leaned his rifle against a tree and slung Stitch over his shoulder. Picking up his rifle, he shifted Stitch's weight for balance. "Be back," he said, grunting as he began to haul Stitch through the woods toward the ambulance wagon.

Anders drank deeply from his canteen, strapped another to his waist, and slowly began to retrace his route through the saw grass toward the two troopers in the gully. Less than five feet from the depression in the ground, Anders raised up slightly and caught sight of the trooper who had spoken to him a few minutes earlier.

A single shot from the far woods came unexpectedly, but Anders immediately felt the impact as the bullet tore completely through his left arm, halfway between the shoulder and his elbow, tearing the flesh and shattering the bone. Blood instantly began to spurt onto the ground and his trousers. Horrified by the wound, he had the presence of mind to retain his prone position, out of sight of the enemy troops, and he rolled over on his back. The sun was setting, but was still high enough in the sky to glare down on his face. Closing his eyes, he rested for a moment, gripping his arm, as yet unsure how injured he was and unable to make a thorough examination.

Just how long it was before the trooper arrived, Anders wasn't sure, but he felt the tourniquet being applied to his arm above the wound. Anders turned his face toward the man, who smiled gently at him. "Got my belt around your arm. That should stop the bleeding. If I pass out again, you've got to release the pressure every fifteen or twenty minutes to let the blood back into your lower arm," the trooper said.

"Sounds like you know your business," Anders said, handing him a canteen of water.

"I was studying to be a doctor in Utah before I joined up with Captain Young's battalion."

"I'm from Salt Lake, too," Anders grimaced as they both lay, face up in the saw grass, the sun beating down on their

34

bodies and insects swarming around their heads. "Came down with the hospital group from Holy Cross."

"Of course," he said. "Blessed Sister Mary's nurses."

"You know her?"

"Only by reputation," the trooper said. "I'm Lieutenant Anthony Richards. Friends call me Tony," he smiled, laying his head over toward Anders. "Are you Catholic, uh . . ."

"Anders Hansen. Andy," he said. "No, I'm LDS, uh, well, sort of," he wheezed, grimacing at the pain.

Lieutenant Richards let out a small, gurgling laugh. The front of his uniform was soaked in a patch of dark red blood. "No sort of to it, Andy. You are or you aren't. Doesn't depend on how often you go to church."

Anders began to cough, turning on his side away from the wound, but facing Tony. "I know. That's what my sister always told me. But how's all that gonna get us out of here?"

"I've been here about six hours, Andy. Got shot in the stomach early this morning. I saw the other fellow—the one you pulled out—rescue three of our troopers before he got shot. Glad you pulled him out. He was one brave trooper."

"He's a retired trooper, Tony. He came down with the hospital like I did."

"Umm."

"How many more in the ditch?" Anders asked.

"No more . . . now," he said. "The other man died just after you left with your friend."

"I'm sorry. Did you know him well?"

"He was my brother, Fletcher."

"Oh, I'm sorry."

"Umm. Andy, uh . . . I, uh . . . I would like to offer you a blessing if you're of a mind. Looks like we're gonna be here a while yet."

Anders shifted his head to look sideways at Tony for a

moment. "Don't know if I'm worthy of it, Tony," Anders mumbled. "Maybe we oughta just think about how we're gonna get outta here."

"Let the Lord worry about that, Andy. Do *you* believe the Lord can heal you?"

Anders hesitated for a moment. "It's not that I *don't* believe, Tony, but, you're more wounded than I am, and . . ."

Tony reached his hand inside his jacket and brought out a small vial. Unscrewing the lid and leaning over on his elbow, he placed a few drops of olive oil on Anders's forehead. The blessing was brief, but Tony's breath became labored in the process of giving it. At the conclusion, Tony fell back on the ground, exhausted, and the two men lay side by side as the sun dropped lower in the sky.

How long Anders had been unconscious he didn't know, but he woke to find two troopers reaching down under his arms to lift him up. The pain in his shattered arm was excruciating. Shaky from the loss of blood and feeling faint, Anders vaguely recognized Tony and smiled weakly at him. The sun had dropped below the treetops and clear vision of the far tree line was obscured by a low-hanging evening mist. The two troopers got Anders to his feet, and together they walked slowly toward the woods where Anders had entered the clearing. Reaching the road, Anders saw in the gathering darkness that the wagon was gone. He grimaced as Tony shifted Anders's weight and the three men began the long walk to the field hospital, with Anders being supported by one trooper on either side.

Semiconscious most of the way, Anders opened his eyes as they crested the hill above the field hospital.

"Almost there, Tony," Anders rasped.

"Andy, we'll be leaving you now. When you get back to

Salt Lake, would you please give a message to my parents and my sister, Sarah?"

"Well, you'll give it yourself," Anders mumbled, his tongue thick in his mouth.

Tony continued. "Tell them that Fletch and I are just fine and that Grandma Richards is going to take good care of us, just as she's always done. Will you do that for me, Andy?"

"Sure, Tony, but . . ."

"Just a few more yards now, Andy."

───

Sister Mary Theophane stood sick with worry outside the recovery tent, drinking from a small cup of water dipped from a barrel alongside the tent. Stitch had just been taken from surgery into the recovery tent, but had been unable to tell Sister Mary anything concerning Anders Hansen. The troopers with Stitch and the older sergeant told her that Anders had probably been killed along with the other troopers who were pinned down in the far clearing. Jed had promised her that he'd go back at first light to see what he could find.

Looking up the road toward the top of the hill, Sister Mary caught a glimpse of movement and strained to make out the shape silhouetted against the twilight sky. It was a man, descending the hill, stumbling as he came on.

She turned and lifted the tent flap, calling for one of the orderlies to come and assist her. She then started trotting toward the approaching man. As she got closer she recognized Anders Hansen. She looked back toward the hospital clearing, motioning for the orderly to hurry, and then she hiked up her habit and broke into a run. The orderly carried a stretcher, and as he ran past the center of the hospital clearing, he called for one of the security troopers to help him. When they reached Sister Mary, she was already kneeling on the ground next to Anders, who had collapsed. The men quickly lifted Anders onto the stretcher, and Sister Mary walked alongside him as they started toward the hospital tent.

"Mr. Hansen, I thought you. . . . How did you get here?" she asked.

Restricted by his position on the stretcher, Anders turned his head far enough to look back over his shoulder, trying to see past the orderly carrying the stretcher. "These two troopers carried me out," he mumbled. "They're wounded too. Hey, Tony, you there?" he called out.

Sister Mary looked back over her shoulder as they continued their descent to the hospital. "Anders, I saw no one with you," she said.

"Sure there was, two of 'em. Carried me out," he protested, his speech slurred and his voice weak.

Sister Mary stopped on the road, allowing the two stretcher-bearers to continue toward the surgery. Trained in the practicalities of hospital care and the healing art of medicine, she remained, first and foremost, a Catholic nun. She crossed herself and uttered a brief prayer of thanks—thanks for the safe return of Anders Hansen, and thanks for the miracle she had been privileged to witness.

In the morning, Trooper Jed Hastings, along with a squad of Captain Young's men from the Utah Battalion, returned to the clearing, where they found the bodies of Lieutenant Anthony Richards and Trooper Fletcher Richards, lying side by side in the dry creek bed.

Retrieving their remains and returning to the hospital, Jed found Sister Mary sitting with Anders, whose color was beginning to return. His left arm, the wound tightly bandaged and resting on pillows, had been amputated six inches below the shoulder.

"Jed," Anders said as he saw his comrade from the day before. "Where did Lieutenant Richards go?"

Jed looked at Sister Mary and back at Anders. "He's in the wagon, Andy. We found him in the clearing with his brother. I'm sorry, Andy. They was both dead."

"That can't be," Anders said. "They lifted me and they carried me here last night."

Jed lowered his head and stepped closer to Anders's bedside. "They been dead all night, Andy. I'm sorry."

"But, Sister, he blessed me, and then they carried me . . ." Anders pleaded, his eyes locking with hers, " . . . I *know* they did."

Sister Mary nodded and reached for Anders's hand. "I know they did, my son. By God's grace, I know they did."

3

Come, come, ye Saints, no toil nor labor fear . . .

Tom Callahan leaned forward, resting his arms on the polished wooden handrail, trying to find a comfortable place for his knees, which were jammed up against the balcony railing. The front row of seats in the balcony of the Tabernacle on Temple Square in Salt Lake City, with their narrow confines, had not been built for a man Tom's size. Maybe, he thought, in the old days the children had sat here as their parents watched from the rear.

From his seat overlooking the multitude on the main floor, Tom listened with awe as the Mormon Tabernacle Choir offered the music to close the final session of general conference.

Though hard to you this journey may appear . . .

Thursday, October 6, 1898, was a celebratory occasion for the Callahans. Tom admitted privately that his pride in Katrina had enhanced his enjoyment of this final session of general conference.[5] He smiled to himself. It was her first official outing as a member of the Tabernacle Choir, and he knew that behind Katrina's humble exterior, her heart was near bursting with pride. Since being accepted as a member

41

of the prestigious choir, she had hardly been able to contain her excitement.

Adding to their joy on this bright fall day was the fact that today was their first wedding anniversary. They had been married in San Francisco in a civil ceremony at City Hall on their return from Mexico, and Tom had not yet gotten over the thrill of having young Katrina Hansen for his bride. He was enormously proud of her, and as he sat watching her sing, it seemed impossible to him that it had been a year already. And could their firstborn son be six weeks old as well?

Born August 24, 1898, Patrick James Callahan had quickly been dubbed "PJ," named in honor of the first man in America to take an interest in young Tom Callahan, the late Father Patrick James O'Leary. The charitable Catholic priest in New York City had in many ways saved Tom's life, and now, in little PJ, Father O'Leary's memory was to be preserved.

'Tis better far for us to strive . . .

Only moments earlier, President Lorenzo Snow had concluded his address to this semiannual gathering of adherents of the Mormon faith. The little, white-haired, bearded man had been sustained during this session of the conference as the Prophet and President of The Church of Jesus Christ of Latter-day Saints, succeeding Wilford Woodruff who had died a few weeks previously. Four years earlier, Tom had not even heard of the Mormon Church. A Catholic, now living in a predominantly Mormon community, Tom had come to appreciate the strength and hard work of the Latter-day Saints. They had performed a monumental task in transforming the barren Utah landscape into an oasis. He admired the Mormons and counted many of them as friends. Indeed, he was married to a devout Mormon. Yet, he remained a Catholic. Upon fleeing Ireland and his abusive father, Tom had made his mother a promise—that Tom would not forsake their Catholic faith. Though he seldom attended mass and only occasionally, at the prodding of Father Scanlan, attended confession, Tom was in his mind a thoroughgoing Catholic. Abandoning his Catholic roots would be tantamount to denying his Irish heritage and dishonoring his saintly mother's memory. It was something he could not and would not do.

Katrina was equally committed to her church. Converted some four years earlier in Norway with her family, Katrina was a faithful Latter-day Saint. She attended church regularly and in her heart viewed Mormonism as not only the best but the *only* way to heaven.

Unequally yoked in this matter, Tom and Katrina avoided conflict by never discussing religion. He was tolerant of her beliefs and activities, and, in fact, often attended Mormon church functions with her. For her part, she never seemed to begrudge his occasional attendance at mass, and, along with Tom, she counted Father Scanlan and Sister Mary Theophane as dear friends. Even so, the Catholic religion, with its chantings and rituals, seemed dark and ominous to her.

Thus it was that a year into their marriage, the unspoken issue of their separate churches and differing theologies lay as a gulf between them. Up to now, it had been a chasm into which they were both fearful to peer.

Do this, and joy your hearts will swell . . .

Listening to the choir, Tom reflected on what Katrina called their "blessings." In the years since he had fled Ireland at nineteen, good fortune had followed him. Wealth had come to him almost as a fluke. Now he was engaged in a promising financial venture, they were living in a house such as he had never imagined he would ever own, and they had their little PJ—a promising son if there ever was one. Best of all, he had a beautiful wife, now a proud new mother, who was sitting on the front row of the choir seats, singing earnestly. He watched her closely, admiring her animation, her fair Norwegian features and blonde hair, and her pleasing figure.

Oh, how we'll make this chorus swell—All is well! All is well!

Tom was moved by the music and the words of the choir as they concluded the closing number, yet all was not well in his life. The birth of Patrick James had brought a significant issue into focus.

Before their marriage, Tom had made a promise to Katrina—that she would be permitted to raise their children as Mormons. Finding her in Mexico and discovering that she was widowed and therefore single and available again, had filled Tom with a sense of good fortune he had been unable to describe. And in the rush of emotion and his early passion, it had seemed little enough to enter into such an agreement. After she had become pregnant, and throughout their first year of marriage, Tom had been thrown into turmoil. He had a limited understanding of the Catholic dogma on the fate of unbaptized infants, but Father Scanlan had made it clear to Tom that it is the father's responsibility to see to it that his children are properly christened and later initiated into the faith. Damnation was the issue, and it was something that increasingly weighed on Tom's mind. The only relief available was to not think about it, something he had been unable to do.

President George Q. Cannon, counselor to Wilford Woodruff and now to Lorenzo Snow, rose to offer the benediction, and the Tabernacle fell silent. President Cannon asked God in Heaven to watch over His flock, to care for the missionaries abroad, and to take into His arms all those who were sick and afflicted, and to especially watch over the little children of His kingdom.

"Amen," Tom softly murmured in response. "Amen."

Later, outside the Tabernacle, Tom waited for Katrina beneath the gleaming granite walls of the Salt Lake Temple, recently completed in 1893. The Square still held poignant memories for Tom, of the evening he had first seen Katrina after having kept his word to make it across America and find her. On that occasion, she had tearfully told Tom that she had promised to marry another. Harold Stromberg, the missionary who had taught Katrina's family the gospel in Norway, had returned and had paid court to her for over six months. Successfully!

Unaware of whether or not Tom would make it to Utah, Katrina had gradually overcome what she came to think of as a schoolgirl's promise to Tom, to wait till the end of the year before she agreed to marry anyone. Tom *was* late, of course, by about three weeks, but that was history. Events had overtaken them, and in the end, the Lord had intervened in both their lives—Tom in his return from Alaska, and Katrina, from her harrowing ordeal following the death of her husband in Mexico. Of the Lord's intervention, Tom was certain.

The choir remained in its place to sing one additional number as the throng of conference attendees was departing the Tabernacle. Temple Square was full of people, strolling through the grounds, admiring the last of the fall flowers before the advent of winter snow.

Recognized as a prosperous banker, albeit in truth a newly prosperous and a "not-quite-yet" influential one, Tom found himself tipping his hat to many well-wishers who passed by as he stood waiting for Katrina. Eventually, the multiple exits to the Tabernacle dislodged fewer and fewer occupants. Finally, members of the choir began to emerge from one of the west entrances of the oval-shaped building. Katrina was walking with several members Tom recognized from the soprano section, and two men. Upon seeing Tom, she hurried to him, anxious to introduce him to her new musical associates.

Tom removed his hat once more, and Katrina stood on her toes to kiss his cheek.

"Oh, Thomas, it was so thrilling! Could you see me?" she gushed.

He smiled broadly and hugged her. "Was there anyone else singing?" he teased.

Katrina punched him on the arm as her friends arrived, three steps behind her.

"Thomas, may I introduce you to Sarah Conners, Abigail Matthews, and Martha Young." The three ladies curtsied slightly and smiled at Tom. "These gentlemen," Katrina continued, "are also members of the choir—John Templeton and Geoffrey Masterton."

"A pleasure, sir," Masterton said with a pronounced British accent. "Captain Geoffrey Masterton, late of Her Majesty's Welsh Color Guard," he said, offering his hand to Tom. "It's an honor to meet you, Mr. Callahan, and might I say, this lovely young woman who seems to fancy you so, has the voice of an absolute angel. A wonderful addition to the Lord's choir."

Tom smiled at the man, his distinctive British upper-class, public school accent so familiar to Tom's ears. Tom reached out to accept Captain Masterton's outstretched hand. "Thank you, sir, but I'm the one who fancies *her*," Tom said, winking his eye.

"Ah, then both of you are indeed most fortunate, eh, what?"

Tom smiled again at the man, whom he took to be in his late twenties or early thirties, his sandy-colored hair a bit unruly in the breeze. He stood eye level with Tom and had a similar build, his posture straight and formal, combined, however, with a pleasant, warm smile.

"Thomas, I have a surprise for you," Katrina laughed, an impish gleam in her eye. "I know I didn't have a party for your birthday yesterday, and you probably think I forgot, but, well, I do have a small party arranged. I've invited some of our friends to come to our home this evening. Is that all right with you?"

Tom's eyebrows went up slightly, and he smiled at his wife's girlish enthusiasm.

"I've also invited my new friends," she said, gesturing toward Masterton and the others. Taking Sarah Conners by the arm and linking her other arm in Tom's, she led the group toward the south gate exiting Temple Square.

"Who else have you invited to this *small* party?" Tom asked.

"Of course, Robert and Alice Thurston will be there, along with some of our new neighbors," Katrina said. She fought to contain a smile, and Tom could see that something else was in the works.

"And is that all, for this *small* birthday party?" he queried, turning the group left as they exited the temple grounds. Katrina pulled at his arm, turning Tom to face her.

"No, Thomas, that's not *quite* all," she said, once again reaching up to kiss his cheek. "Captain Masterton," Katrina said, looking toward the immaculately attired man, possessed of a military bearing, who was also smiling, "could you possibly tell me the time?"

Masterton made a show of retrieving his pocket watch from the vest of his suit, releasing the catch, and holding it at arm's length to read the dial. "Sister Callahan, I make it to be two twenty-seven, exactly," he said, snapping the case and replacing the watch in his pocket.

"Well, then," she said, turning back to Tom and squeezing his arm, "in exactly thirty-three minutes, if the telegram I received last week was correct, and the train is on schedule, we will have two more persons to attend your birthday party." Katrina's joy was so apparent to Tom and to the five choir members gathered that Tom had no choice but to capitulate to the drama of the moment.

"And who, pray tell, will . . ."

"*Anders!*" she practically screamed, wrapping her arms around Tom's neck and hugging him tightly. "And Sister Mary! They telegraphed last week to advise of their arrival. Tom, they're *home* and they're *safe*. Our *family*, Tom. Our family is back together."

Tom looked at the small cluster of people, their faces reflecting their joy at being able to participate in this small conspiracy. Captain Masterton stepped forward, again offering Tom his hand.

"My heartiest congratulations, Mr. Callahan. And may I offer my sincere best wishes on the advent of your birthday, sir. With your permission, we'll take our leave now, and join you at your residence this evening." Masterton reached for Katrina's hand and kissed the back of it, nodding his head and smiling at her as he turned to leave.

"Thank you," Tom responded, somewhat overwhelmed by the turn of events. "Thank you all," he continued, looking around the group. "Please, please be sure to come this evening. It seems Katrina has once again completely bamboozled me. To my delight, I might add," he laughed, taking her in his arms and spinning her around on the footpath. "May you always hold such sway over my heart, Katie, m'darlin'," he said, kissing her lips boldly, to her embarrassment and the delight of the others.

"Till this evening then, sir," Masterton said, tipping his hat and turning to walk east with his companions, tapping his walking cane rhythmically on the footpath.

Tom and Katrina gazed after them for a few moments, then Tom turned Katrina in the opposite direction. "Best we walk the other way, I suppose, out to the train station."

"Henry will meet us there with the buggy and will see to the luggage."

"Always good to have a carriageman handy," Tom allowed. "It seems you've got it all arranged," he said, smiling and striding off toward the station, Katrina's arm linked in his. "Who exactly is this Masterton fellow?" Tom asked.

"Oh, he's a wonderful man, Thomas. The ladies in the choir think he's quite charming. He was with General Kitchener in the Sudan during the campaign to capture someplace called Khartoum, I think. I understand he was wounded there, and returned to England where the missionaries met him. I heard he was engaged to marry an Earl's daughter, but when he joined the Church, she called it off."

"I see," Tom said, continuing to walk along the footpath, Katrina's arm linked with his.

"Oh, Thomas, I'm so happy today. I can't think of a *thing* that could make my life more blessed. Our anniversary; little PJ healthy and growing so fast; singing in the choir; and Anders coming home. And you, Thomas Callahan," she said, stopping him and standing to face him directly. "I love you so *very* much."

The same thought Tom had while sitting in the conference session quickly crowded his mind again. He knew the one *other* thing that Katie desired—the thing she prayed for but that continued to elude her. It was something he had the power to grant, yet he couldn't. It pleased Tom that Katie worked so hard to be a loving and caring wife, and in return, he felt he had tried to be a good husband. *We are happy,* he thought. But he knew that the difference in their religions must nag at her, as it had nagged at him. He knew there was an empty longing in his wife, and reflecting on how she never voiced her fondest desire and deepest concern filled him with a sudden feeling of love and gratitude.

Stopping their walk and turning her to face him, Tom looked deeply into her green eyes and said, "Katie, m'darlin', *you* are the one who has made our life so blessed."

His expression was serious, and he gently stroked her cheek with his fingers as they stood outside the wall on the southwest corner of Temple Square, people milling about and the crowd of conference attendees just beginning to diminish.

"But just to show that you're not the *only* one who can plan surprises," he said, reaching into his inner coat pocket, "I'll take this moment, since my planned, quiet anniversary dinner at home has now become a public affair," he laughed, "to try to express the depth of my feelings for you."

He tilted his head back and looked up toward the sky for a moment, then took a deep breath. "In Ireland, Katie, we have a saying for some *thing,* or some *one,* who is very special. We call that thing or that person, 'Top Shelf,' and you, Katrina Hansen Callahan, are the most 'Top Shelf' person I have ever known. This," he said, revealing a long velvet case, "is my feeble attempt to honor your value."

Katrina looked down at the case for a moment, then raised her eyes to meet Tom's, causing him to smile broadly.

As she opened the case, her slightly moist eyes began to flood, and her vision of the beautiful object blurred.

"Oh, Tom," she whispered, raising a finger to wipe away her tears. The velvet-lined case contained a slender, golden chain, to which was attached a gold, one inch by three-quarter inch miniature kitchen cupboard. The cupboard had three shelves, and on the top shelf, a magnificent solitary diamond had been set, resplendent in its brilliance. A quarter inch below, the next shelf had two asymmetrical stones, and the third shelf, three. All six diamonds were brilliant and glistened in the bright October afternoon sun. The size and placement of the stones drew the eye upward, toward the "top shelf." Katrina snapped the case closed and laid her head against Tom's chest, her voice absent and her heart pounding within her breast.

"Happy anniversary, Katie, m'darlin'. You'll always be my 'Top Shelf' girl," Tom said, his arms enfolding her.

⸺∽∾∽⸺

At 3:12, its engine venting steam, the train pulled into the Union Pacific station at the west end of South Temple. As the train jostled to a stop, Tom and Katrina waited excitedly for Katrina's brother, Anders, and for Sister Mary Theophane to appear. Today, their circle of family and friends would once again be complete.

Katrina had found it difficult to honor her brother's request that she not inform their parents of his arrival. Why he wished it so, she would have to wait to hear, but she had controlled the urge to tell them—to have a Hansen family reunion at the station.

Anders's father, Lars Hansen, had opposed him going to Cuba. But then, Lars had opposed most of the things Anders had ever attempted. Only when Anders had taken

51

the position of hospital engineer and moved into Tom's old quarters in the basement of Holy Cross Hospital, had the young man found any peace.

Sister Mary's letters to Mr. and Mrs. Hansen, and the separate letter to Tom and Katrina, months earlier, had informed them of the necessity of amputating Anders's left arm. It had come as a shock, but once the initial impact wore off, Katrina had thanked God that her brother's life had been spared.

Now he was home. In time for Thomas's birthday, she thought. If the windows of heaven, as President Snow had said, furnished no further blessings, her family had already filled their baskets and had more than enough to spare.

Tom and Katrina stood anxiously watching as people began to exit the train. With her arm locked into his, Katrina felt Tom's body brace slightly, and she turned her head to follow his gaze. There, in full habit, looking tired and drawn, stood Sister Mary Theophane with several other nursing Sisters gathered behind her. Tom and Katrina watched as Bishop Lawrence Scanlan, Archbishop of the Salt Lake Diocese, stepped to greet them. Sister Mary leaned forward slightly and reached for Father Scanlan's hand, kissing his bishop's ring. The senior prelate took her by both shoulders, and modestly, but firmly, embraced the chief administrator of Holy Cross Hospital. She thanked him respectfully, then, from the corner of her eye, caught sight of Tom. Her warm smile quickly acknowledged his presence and Tom's mind flashed back to an identical smile that had greeted him in the foyer of Holy Cross Hospital, when, freshly arrived in Utah, he had made his own intro-duction, cap in hand, nearly three years past.

Also spotting Tom, Bishop Scanlan raised his hand to invite Tom and Katrina to join them in the welcome of

Sister Mary. As Tom was guiding Katrina through the crowd on the platform toward the pair, Katrina's hand flew to her mouth and she uttered a small cry of joy. Stepping down from the train was Anders Hansen, followed by his friend Stitch. Anders immediately saw Katrina and moved in three quick strides to greet his sister.

For long moments Anders held Katrina tightly in his good arm. Tom took note of Anders's empty left sleeve, which was pinned to the shoulder of his jacket, representing to Tom's mind a badge of honor reflecting the sacrifice he had made in Cuba. Sister Mary's letters had been full of praise for his brother-in-law's contribution to the medical mission. Her rendition of Colonel Theodore Roosevelt making a special trip to visit Anders and Stitch in Tampa, Florida, on his way back from Cuba, had brought tears even to Tom's eyes.[6]

"You've done a bully job, you have," Roosevelt had ebulliently announced to all in the hospital ward. "And these two lads have saved many a desperate trooper to return to their family, a life yet to pursue," the former Assistant Secretary of the Navy had extolled.

Sister Mary had explained in her letter that Roosevelt had personally informed Anders that if he could be of any help—anything at all—in the future, Anders Hansen was a name that would cause his door to open. Anders had failed to mention the incident in his personal letters to Tom and Katrina, but Sister Mary had filled in the missing parts.

"Aye, so here they are, all together," Bishop Scanlan professed. "And well they should be, too, eh, Sister Mary?" he laughed heartily.

Her eyes glistening from the sight of Anders and Katrina embracing, Sister Mary simply nodded her head. Katrina pulled from Anders's grasp and moved to greet the elderly woman. As they hugged, Katrina whispered in Sister Mary's ear, "Thank you, Sister. Thank you so much for caring for my brother." Sister Mary just gave a small squeeze to Katrina and remained silent.

Tom shook Anders's hand, then Stitch's, and finally Bishop Scanlan's. "Father Scanlan, with your permission, sir," Tom said, reaching to wrap his arms around Sister Mary and holding her silently for a moment. The fullness of her habit hid her frailty, but Tom took note of how thin she'd become, and as he held her in his arms, he looked over her shoulder at Katrina and winced. His wife acknowledged him with her eyes, but they said nothing.

"Well, then," Tom said loudly, "I have been informed, that as of six o'clock this evening, at the home of Thomas and Katrina Callahan, a slightly belated birthday party will be held in honor of some Irish larrikin who has seen the error of his ways. If all those present would care to partake of the refreshments, which, I am certain, Mrs. Callahan has taken great care to arrange, we would be pleased to have your attendance. It is, in fact, a 'command performance,' in honor of this wonderful reunion of friends and family. Please come, one and all," he laughed.

The buggy carrying Tom, Katrina, and Anders pulled away from the train station and headed up South Temple. Henry had been left at the station to arrange transport of the luggage, and Sister Mary had gone with Bishop Scanlan, after promising to attend the birthday party.

South Temple, or "Brigham Street" as it was more often called for the first several blocks east of State Street, was a divided boulevard, with separate pathways for carriage and foot traffic. A two way trolley track ran down the middle of the dual carriageway.

Enroute to their home, Katrina sat holding tightly to Anders's arm, while Tom drove the buggy.

"Anders, you'll just love our new home. It's wonderful, and we've fixed a bedroom and a sitting area for you."

"I saw the initial construction before we left," Anders replied, "while you were in Europe. It seemed awfully large."

"Oh, yes," Katrina laughed. "I thought so too when I first saw it. On paper it looked . . . well, it looked large, but when I first saw it—oh, my, was I surprised."

Completed on time and ready for occupancy when Tom and Katrina returned from their honeymoon the previous April, the elaborate home had been made ready by Alice

Thurston. With her husband, Robert's, help, she had stocked the food larder, filled the coal bunker, assisted the small staff in assuring the home was clean and tidy, and made certain plenty of wood was stacked out back in the shed and near each of the four fireplaces, even though spring had already graced Utah.

The day Katrina got her first glimpse of the completed home, she was so taken by its appearance that she was unable for a time to step out of the carriage. She leaned against the cushioned backrest and, from the circular driveway, admired the exterior of her new home for several minutes. By the time she set foot on the ground, Henry, the butler and carriageman, and Tom had practically completed unloading the luggage from the wagon that had followed them from the train station.

The architectural drawings had been nearly worn out by Katrina during her romp through Europe. The real thing, magnificently displayed before her eyes, surpassed anything she might have imagined.

The five-story residence, four above ground and one below, was the equal, with only a few exceptions, of any other house on South Temple. The architect had employed all the latest innovations from East Coast builders, including electrical fixtures that were designed to receive the electrical current, which was soon to be extended the length of South Temple. In the interim, gas-fired lighting fixtures graced the walls and tables.

The five stories included a full basement divided into shelf-lined rooms that remained at a fairly constant, cool temperature. Vegetable storage was planned for one of these rooms, and another had been designed as an insulated ice-block storage area, served by a ground level delivery chute.

The English Tudor exterior, then so popular in the

British Isles and in some places on the Continent, had been one area where Tom and Katrina had immediately agreed. Thereafter, Tom had limited his involvement to choosing the wood paneling for what would become his top floor study and library.

The rooms on the main floor and all family quarters were furnished entirely with furniture built by Scandinavian craftsmen who worked in Katrina's father's factory. As she had ascended the stairs that April day, briefly walking through each room, Katrina had immediately seen the loving care Lars Hansen had lavished on each of the exquisite pieces. Even Tom, whom Lars had yet to fully embrace as a son-in-law, had to admit that the elder Hansen had taken this opportunity to express his love for his daughter and his pride in his work.

Seen from the outside, the fifth floor appeared as opposing towers of a great castle. It was occupied by a vast library and by a massive fireplace that dominated the center of the room. In each of the corner alcoves, tall windows opened onto a majestic view of the Wasatch Range to the north and east. Positioned between the fireplace and the eastern alcove sat Tom's new desk. Ornately carved and hand polished, again by Lars, the magnificent desk was obviously a first peace offering from his stubborn father-in-law—a gesture Tom immediately recognized as such. Richly appointed with floor-to-ceiling bookshelves, a thick carpet, and comfortable leather chairs, the study was by any standard a princely or presidential retreat.

The house provided the overall personal effect that Katrina had desired—crowned by a massive ballroom, furnished with a grand piano and located on the third floor. An elaborate circular stairway led to an expansive landing, guarded by an oak railing and overlooking the main entrance and foyer below.

A formal dining room occupied the rear of the first floor. The centerpiece of the immense room was a huge, European style, dark walnut grained dining table, with seating for twenty-four in deep-cushioned, high-backed chairs. An Old English C was carved into the topmost back piece of each chair. In the front of the home on the ground level, a large, gracious parlor adorned one side, and a smaller library/combination meeting room, with a more formal business atmosphere, sat opposite.

The home, then as yet unveiled to Salt Lake society, presented a masterful work of architecture, rivaling the grandest homes on Brigham Street. During a weekend-long Pioneer Day celebration party in July, the Callahans had finally opened their home to friends, neighbors, family, and society reporters from the *Tribune* and the *Deseret News*. Editorials in both newspapers had appeared, lauding, in addition to the grandeur of the home, Tom Callahan's no-longer-secret philanthropic gifts to the Holy Cross Hospital.

A week after the Callahans got home, Henry picked up Katrina from her shopping downtown at ZCMI and drove her home. She arrived to discover a massive wooden placard that Tom had ordered attached to the wrought iron entrance, which brought a lump to her throat. Without consulting his wife, Tom had named their home "*Valhalla*," in honor, he said, of "those ancient Viking warriors who had raided Ireland for centuries." Having won the love of such a beautiful Norwegian woman, Tom, as a modern-day Irishman, wondered why those seafaring Vikings had ever left home. Perhaps that was why they were often called "squareheads," he had thought. *Valhalla* was now *their* home, and if Tom had his way, it would ever be so.

New *mansion* might have been a more accurate description, Anders thought as he stepped from the buggy. His balance was still shaky as he continued to adjust to the loss of his arm. Katrina resisted the impulse to offer her hand, but once he had alighted from the carriage, she led him through the double-door entry.

"Welcome home, Anders," she said with a little cuddle. "Tom and I hoped you'd stay with us for awhile. At least until you get your feet on the ground and decide what you intend to do."

Anders smiled and stepped quickly through the ground floor rooms. "You haven't lost your touch since marrying an Irish ruffian," he smiled. "It speaks of love everywhere, Klinka."

Hearing her nickname, first applied by Anders when she was born and he was four, Katrina felt a pleasant chill rush through her body.

"Anders, I have missed you so. I hadn't realized how important my brother is," she said, sitting on the divan and patting the seat next to her. "Come, sit down and tell me about your adventures."

"Hold on, lass," Tom said, coming through the parlor door. "Maybe the returned brother would like to see his room, wash his face and hands, and, well, you know," he laughed.

"Of course," Katrina said, blushing. "How insensitive of me. Excuse me, Anders. I'm just so happy to have you home safe and sound," she said, hugging him yet again. "You clean up and have a rest if you'd like. I'll have a sandwich and a cool drink sent to your room. Remember," she pointed her finger, "it's your brother-in-law's birthday party at six."

"I didn't know, Tom, uh . . . and I didn't get . . ."

Tom wrapped his arm around Anders's shoulder and started to lead him from the parlor. "Yes, you did, Andy. Just look at Katrina's beaming face. That's present enough for me. We've put you on the far side of the second floor—our family floor. It's a nice room with eastern exposure and a small sitting room off to the side with a fireplace."

"It's not covered by a tent, is it, Tom?" he laughed.

"Those days are over, Andy."

"But first," Katrina interjected, "*Uncle* Andy needs to peek in and see little PJ."

"Oh, yes. The next generation. What kind of child comes from an Irishman and a squarehead?" he teased.

"We'll leave that to the uncle to decide," Tom rebutted. "But, I can assure you that those who don't appropriately ooh and aah, get no dinner."

While Anders was resting, Katrina sent a message to her parents, asking them to come early to the birthday party. When they arrived and discovered that Anders had returned, Mrs. Hansen nearly fainted. In a tearful reunion, Anders hugged his mother and gracefully accepted his father's awkward embrace.

By six-thirty, most of the guests had arrived and Katrina was entertaining them in the ballroom on the third floor. The Tabernacle Choir's assistant organist had agreed to play for the gathering, and soft strains of some of the popular tunes of the day drifted from the grand piano situated in the western alcove.

As Katrina had promised, the affair was small, with less than two dozen people in attendance. Since receipt of the telegram advising of Anders and Sister Mary's return,

Katrina had decided to limit the party to family and close friends. The neighboring residents, invited to previous functions, had been advised through the informal network of household staff that this was to be a family affair to welcome Katrina's brother home from the war. The Callahans had quickly learned that feelings were easily hurt when status was involved. To not be invited to one of the soirees on Brigham Street was tantamount to a snub. However, private family affairs enjoyed an unspoken exemption from such societal rules.

The last to arrive were Bishop Scanlan and Sister Mary. Downstairs on an errand for Katrina, Tom saw their buggy approach and met them at the front door. He watched as Father Scanlan physically helped Sister Mary climb the polished granite stairs to the entrance. When she observed Tom at the door, her countenance brightened, and she tried to pretend that all was well.

"I'm glad you could make it this evening," Tom greeted the two clergy. "What good's a party without my two closest Catholic associates?"

"Don't forget, young Thomas, that ye also be me cousin," Father Scanlan said, speaking in the Irish brogue he had mostly eliminated many years earlier.

Tom laughed and offered Sister Mary his arm as they ascended the stairs. Father Scanlan paused at the downstairs library entrance. Climbing the spiral staircase, Tom noticed he was not following and stopped to look back.

"Not to worry, Tom," he said with a wave of his hand. "I'd just like to browse your book collection for a minute, if I may. There's something I believe I've seen in here that I'd like to review. If that's all right with you, of course," he smiled.

"Certainly, Father. Join us when you're ready," Tom said,

continuing the climb. On the second floor landing, Tom gently ushered Sister Mary into a small room, off the stairs. Immediately they began speaking in the thick, Irish brogue both of them enjoyed using in the privacy of their conversations, a sort of humorous way of reclaiming their origins.

"And would you be abducting an elderly nursing Sister now, Thomas?" she grinned.

"No, Sister Mary, but I'll be havin' the truth, if you please."

"The truth?" she hedged.

"Aye.

"And what would you be meanin', Thomas Matthew Callahan?" she said, tilting her head downward to peer over her glasses at him.

"Aw, c'mon, Sister. You're in desperate need of some rest. It's clear to all who know you, you've worn yourself out in this bloody war."

"I've a touch of the malaria. Just a bit short of breath, Thomas. Nothin' a'tall, lad."

"And that's how you'll be havin' it then?" Tom questioned.

"Aye, Thomas, and you'll be keeping your mouth shut, as I have for you these past years."

"Aye, that ye have, Sister. That ye have. And can I be of no help then?"

Reaching past Tom to open the door and taking a step toward the stairway, Sister Mary took Tom's face in both of her hands. "You've been of more help to me than you'll ever be knowin', Thomas Matthew," she smiled.

"If that's the way you'll have it, Sister, we'll be goin' upstairs then and to the party. But you'll be takin' a seat in the corner, and I'll have refreshments brought to you. And that's an order from the master of the house."

"Between you and Father Scanlan, all I've been getting is orders, but that sounds lovely, yer honor," she replied.

Katrina saw them enter the ballroom and came straight to greet them. "We are so honored to have you in our home, Sister Mary. Tom was disappointed when Father Scanlan came to bless the house after we returned from Europe and you were not here to participate."

"'Tis a lovely home, too. What an exquisite pendant, my dear," she commented, noticing Katrina's necklace.

Katrina fingered the small golden cupboard and glanced up at Tom. "Thank you, Sister. I doubt it shall ever come off," she said. "It's my anniversary present from Thomas."

"I see," Sister Mary replied, glancing quickly at Tom and then taking a closer look at the unique design. "That would be a thoughtful Irishman's way of telling his lass she is 'Top Shelf,' I presume."

"Oh, Sister, then you know the saying?"

"Aye, although I've never seen it so lovingly represented before."

Tom nodded toward the corner and from behind Sister Mary pointed his finger at a chair and mouthed the words "sit down" to Katrina. Catching on, she took Sister Mary's arm and moved her toward the grand piano and several chairs lined against the wall around the alcove. "To be sure you get close to the music, Sister Mary," she said, offering her a seat. "Can I get you anything?"

"Perhaps a wee cool drink, if you please."

"Certainly. I'll be right back." As she walked toward the sideboard and the Waterford crystal punch bowl, Tom fell in alongside Katrina.

"She's very ill, Katie," he whispered as they walked.

"She certainly is. Is there no way to keep her from returning to her job immediately?"

"I'll have a word with Father Scanlan before he leaves this evening."

"Good."

The sonorous baritone of Captain Masterton echoed through the ballroom as he took a place next to the grand piano and called for attention.

"Ladies and gentlemen, if you please." Assuming the role of master of ceremonies, he waited for the guests to give him their undivided attention. "In honor of the host for this splendiferous occasion, I, together with three of my associates, will be pleased to provide some light musical entertainment." He arched his eyebrows and feigned a mournful expression. "It pains my Welsh heart to render such atonal sounds." He paused and then sighed, holding the small gathering in rapt attention. "We have specifically been requested to perform a medley of," again he paused, shaking his head dramatically and looking toward the ceiling, "dare I say it, *Irish ballads*." His listeners caught the drift of his taunt and broke out in polite laughter.

"It is my sincere hope," Captain Masterton continued, "that you will find no insult in the delivery of this, shall we say, *music*, but given my regard for the gentleman to whom we pay respectful homage, and my even higher regard for his lovely and musically talented spouse, we shall try to overlook the geographical origin of our selections."

He broke into a broad grin, and the assemblage began to laugh even louder. Katrina clapped her hands, looking shyly at Tom who stood quietly, shaking his head in mock disapproval, his face reflecting disdain in response to the Welshman's slander.

Father Scanlan slipped into the room during the second selection and quietly moved next to Tom, both men applauding as the group concluded "Mother McCree."

"Might I have a word with you, Tom, before we leave this evening?"

Tom nodded. "Certainly, Father. I was going to ask you the same."

Father Scanlan also nodded, and they both stood quietly as the quartet continued through the program. After the group sang another three or four songs, Captain Masterton once again addressed the audience.

"Thank you. Thank you for your kind applause. It is my understanding that there is some special significance attached to our final number, for which we will be joined by the beautiful lady who is our gracious hostess at *Valhalla*. In her performance, I am certain you will agree with my earlier comments about her angelic voice. The Tabernacle Choir is most fortunate to have discovered such a talent. Ladies and gentlemen: Mrs. Thomas Callahan." He bowed toward Katrina, and stepped back into the quartet as she approached the piano.

Katrina came forward to the light applause of her guests.

"Captain Masterton, thank you so very much for your entertainment tonight, and to you, Sarah, Martha, and John," she addressed the quartet. "It was so kind of you to come and participate." Katrina turned to face her audience, just over a dozen people, not counting the musicians behind her.

"My heart is so full tonight," she said, struggling to control her rising emotions. "The Lord has blessed Thomas and me with so many close friends—people who have chosen to serve Him and to allow us to participate. To my brother, Anders," she said, smiling at him as he stood by a few of the guests, "and our dear friend, Sister Mary Theophane—how much we owe you and how blessed are those fortunate soldiers whom you so lovingly nursed back to health." She took a deep breath, her composure faltering.

"Three, no, almost four years ago I met a young man on my family's ocean voyage to America," she began, looking at Thomas. "I took a liking to him, in spite of his brash attempt to speak to me without introduction, *and* my father's warnings," she laughed. "The evening before our voyage concluded, I was asked by the ship's first officer to entertain the dinner guests with a few songs. Little did I know that Thomas would be among those present, but my brother, Anders, had invited him to join the family at dinner our last evening at sea. You see, at that time, Thomas was *not* traveling first class," she laughed again, as did those in the room.

"One of the songs I had chosen that evening has become a favorite of ours. I suppose it always will be, won't it, Thomas?" she asked, smiling at him as he nodded. "And so, tonight, on our first anniversary, and in honor of Thomas's twenty-third birthday yesterday, and of course, in celebration of the safe return of Anders and Sister Mary, I would once again like to tell Thomas of my love for him and to thank him for the blessings he has brought into my life."

She nodded to the piano player who commenced the introduction, and with the quartet providing a muted harmonic background, Katrina began to sing the strains of "Sweet Rosie O'Grady."

As Katrina sang, Tom gazed at her fondly, scarcely able to believe his good fortune in having such a beautiful and talented young woman for a wife. He had thought when he first saw her on the dock in Cork that he had never seen such a face. Now, nearly four years later, and after having been married to her for a year, he was even more taken by her appearance. Following the birth of little PJ, her girlish face and figure had given way in a breathtaking manner to those of a woman in the prime of her life. Her eyes, still an arresting green in color, shone with love and contentment, and as she sang the familiar tune, she used those eyes to flirt with her husband. Tom met her gaze, and they exchanged the silent signals they used to communicate with each other in public. He was delighted to have his friends gathered in his honor, but at that moment, he began to wonder how soon he might graciously bid them good night.

When Katrina finished singing, several of the female guests in the room dabbed at their eyes, moved as much by the open display of adoration as by the beauty of Katrina's soprano voice. Standing with her arm entwined in Robert's, Alice Thurston had tears on her cheeks. Captain Masterton stepped forward and put his arm around Katrina's shoulder, giving her a gentle squeeze. Tom observed Masterton's action and immediately stepped toward his wife, surprising himself by the involuntary jealous reaction to another man handling his wife.

Seeing Tom emerge from the gathering of people, Masterton whispered to Katrina and then looked back toward the guests. "Perhaps," he said, "it would only be fitting if we were to hear from Thomas Callahan himself," he invited. The guests applauded as Tom continued to walk toward Captain Masterton and Katrina.

Joining Katrina at the head of the ballroom, Tom gave his wife a kiss on the cheek and drew her close with a hug. Then he looked around the room, making eye contact with each of his friends.

"Father Scanlan," Tom began, "being just a mortal man myself, of the heaven you preach, I can only surmise. But if it is anything like my current condition on earth," he smiled, drawing Katrina closer, "then I'd like to be considered a candidate for admission. And as to you, Captain Masterton," Tom said, intent on maintaining his public decorum, "in spite of the geographical error of your birth, you've done well this evening with the Lord's own music."

Captain Masterton accepted the rejoinder and, smiling broadly, applauded Tom's comments.

"And lastly," Tom continued, "not wanting, of course, to correct my wife, at least in public," he laughed loudly, "I do have *one* small point from her comments that I must contest. It's true that when we first met I was traveling steerage with the others, like so many cattle. But since the first moment I laid eyes on ye, Katie, m'darlin' . . . " he grew silent, taking Katrina's face in his hands and kissing her lips, " . . . I've been traveling first class."

Later in the evening, seated upstairs in Tom's study, Father Scanlan swirled a snifter of brandy and leaned comfortably back into one of Tom's leather chairs. In a concession to Tom's business affairs, Katrina had agreed that liquor would be available, but only in Tom's upstairs study. Rarely would anyone be present in their house who would be offended by the lack of available alcohol downstairs. Katrina's Mormon standards dictated liquor not be served generally, but, in the sanctity of the upper den, Tom was able to indulge his guests who were so inclined. As for himself, Tom had kept his vow, made in the confines of a cold, drafty railway cattle car on the Kansas prairie, that he would never again imbibe—a promise he had made to God long before he came to know anything of the Mormon's Word of Wisdom.

Tom waited for Father Scanlan to speak. Several

moments passed while the Father sipped his drink, sitting with his eyes closed and resting his head on the back of the tall chair. As the prelate's first cousin, once removed, Tom had come to know and to love Father Scanlan. He had also come to appreciate, given the overwhelming size of his diocese, how rare it was for the archbishop to actually find a few moments in which he was able to achieve solitude.

The prelate had left the ballroom shortly before other guests began to leave. Tom knew he was going upstairs rather than down, and with prearranged approval from Father Scanlan, Tom had asked Sister Mary if she would mind Henry driving her back to Holy Cross Hospital.

"Tom, it's a fine home you've built here," the Father said. "I'm quite shocked and must offer my apologies for the leak to the press with regard to your most generous offerings to the hospital. I did so want to respect your anonymity."

"I understand, Father. It's no problem," Tom said, taking a seat across from the priest. "I'm starting to discover that the newspapers have a nose in everyone's tent, it seems."

"Quite so." Scanlan paused again, took another sip of his brandy, then set the glass down on a teakwood chess table alongside his chair.

"Tom, surely you've noticed Sister Mary's condition. Her health is appalling. I must move immediately to restore her well-being or we will likely lose our friend, not to mention the best nursing administrator Holy Cross has ever had, or is ever likely to have, for that matter."

Tom nodded agreement. "I tried to speak with her while you were downstairs in the library, Father. She'd have none of it."

Father Scanlan nodded. "Right. I stayed in the library to check your medical text on malaria. From the signs, that's what I believe is ailing our dear friend. But she'll jump right back into her duties and her fourteen-to-sixteen-hour days if no one takes charge of the situation."

Father Scanlan rose and moved to stand in front of the unlit fireplace. An oil painting of the River Shannon flowing through the Irish countryside hung prominently above the mantle. He turned back to face Tom.

"Fortunately, I *am* in a position to disallow such devotion to duty."

"That's good, Father," Tom said. "What will you do?"

"Within an hour after meeting her at the train, I telegraphed Sister Mary's mother superior at the convent in Indiana. I have requested permission for Sister Mary to return to the cloister and to take a minimum of six months convalescent leave, with no duties assigned."

Tom stood and moved to stand beside the priest. "Sister Mary won't take kindly to that, but God bless you, Father. She is my dearest friend on God's earth, and anything I can do, you need only ask."

"I know, Tom. And so does she," he smiled. "I should have an answer soon and then I'll speak with her. Above all, Sister Mary is obedient to her superiors. Until then, let's keep this between ourselves."

"You have my word, Father."

Archbishop Scanlan smiled at Tom, and gestured for him to retake his seat. "Please, Tom. Have a seat. There's one other thing I'd like to discuss with you."

Tom resumed his seat and crossed his legs, waiting for Father Scanlan to continue. Sitting back down in his own chair, the priest took a final sip of his brandy and leaned back.

"Thomas, I well remember our discussion last year shortly after you and Katrina were married. My thoughts about the sanctity of your marriage . . . well, you'll recall I tried to fulfill my responsibility to the church and . . ."

"I recall, Father," Tom said, apprehensive now about the coming sermon.

"That decision, although I must say once more, in the eyes of the church . . ." He paused again, looking first down and then directly across at Tom.

"Father, you must see that I have a marriage to protect, regardless of what church we were married in. Good grief, Father Scanlan," Tom said, leaning forward in his chair and wringing his hands, "didn't you see that Masterton fellow downstairs? *That's* the kind of person Katie wants. She talks about having the priesthood in her home and an eternal marriage. I can't give her those things," he said, a tone of despair in his voice.

"They don't matter, Tom," the priest declared.

"What do you mean they don't matter? Of course they do."

"Not in God's eyes, Tom," Father Scanlan said, shaking his head. "Look, Tom, in spite of the respect I have for the Mormons, I must confess that I've never understood their preoccupation with marriage in heaven. In keeping with my priestly vows, I've never married. Under their system, what's to become of me? Or of Sister Mary, for that matter?"

Tom nodded his head. "That's true isn't it, Father?" he said.

"Of course it is. I don't mean to be unkind, Tom, but since you brought it up, the Lord himself said something on the topic that the Mormons might do well to consider." The old priest reached into his vest pocket for a small Bible, flipping quickly through the pages.

"Right here, Tom, in Matthew, the scriptures say that in the resurrection there is neither marrying nor giving in marriage. Tom, the Mormon concept of eternal marriage is fallacious."

"But Katrina doesn't see it that way," Tom pleaded.

"I respect yours and Katrina's decisions, Thomas, because you are both adults and responsible for your own actions. I'd be happy to talk with both of you about this issue, but my current concern is even more urgent. Patrick James is what, about six weeks old?"

"Aye," Tom replied, quickly standing and holding his hand up, his palm open in a gesture of restraint. "Father, please," he said, "this is all too much for me. I've given Katrina my word. I understand the church's teachings on this matter and the importance of baptism. My mother explained it to me fully as I grew into manhood and we talked about marriage. I agree with you on the problem our marriage presents in God's eyes, but, Father, I also have come to understand," he paused, rubbing the back of his neck, and then exhaling deeply, "and even to *agree* with Katrina's beliefs concerning young children.

"Truly, Father, I cannot comprehend that God would do other than embrace these little ones in His arms, even if they die without being baptized. In light of my *Catholic* beliefs, though, I know I will have to take the judgment upon my own head. Should I be wrong in my desire to honor my promise to Katrina to respect her religion, I pray God He will take the judgment on *me*, and not on my innocent child. This *is* difficult, Father," Tom said, beginning to pace, "and more than likely, it will always be so. I have come to love you, Father Scanlan, and even to think of you as a cousin," he smiled. "I love Holy Mother Church as well, but I'm firm in this commitment and will support Katrina in all that she desires for our children regarding religion."

"My son," the priest said, his voice now stern. "I must

warn you. You say you have come to *believe* in the Mormon concept of baptism. Next, you'll be embracing the eternal marriage concept. You are on a disastrous path if you seek to balance the two beliefs. As good a people as the Mormons are, they have left their children unprotected in the sight of the Lord. In this area, our beliefs are most definitely not compatible. We are talking about Patrick James's *immortal soul*, Thomas. You *cannot* take such a thing lightly. And you are correct, Thomas, God *will* hold you responsible as the child's father."

"I gave my word, Father," Tom said softly. "It's not so much a belief of faith, as it is an understanding of the logic that a benevolent Lord would not condemn little children to hell."

Father Scanlan mulled over Tom's words for a few moments before answering.

"Thomas. It is true that we don't understand *all* God's ways, but he has made this matter very clear." He hesitated, then said in a softer voice, "Tom, as PJ's father, and a good Catholic, it is your responsibility—"

"No, Father. I gave my word," Tom said, shaking his head. "And I intend to honor it."

Father Scanlan stood and reached for Tom's hand. As they shook, the priest said, "My son, you must follow your conscience, I understand that. But you also have a responsibility as father to this child, and to those who will follow. You must *lead*, Thomas, and determine the future of your family. I will be there to support you and to discuss it with you and Katrina, if and when you so desire."

"Thank you, Father. It will not be an easy path, as they grow."

"That's correct, my son. Think on what I've said. I've learned much here among the Mormons, Tom. As I've told you before, they are good people, and they practice what they believe, perhaps better than some of our own Catholic parishioners. But that does not make their doctrine right in the sight of the Lord. Ah . . ." he said, raising his hands above his head, ". . . enough. You are most kind, Thomas. But you understand my concern . . ."

Tom extended his hand once again to Bishop Lawrence Scanlan, recently turned fifty-four, with a thick shock of hair turned fully gray. "And you fulfill them with great dignity, Your Grace. As one of your flock, I confess my weaknesses before you, but beg your indulgence in these matters. Pray for me, Father, that our God will look down on me, and upon my children, and bestow His grace upon us. I tell you this, Father—the day I left home, my mother extracted a promise that I would remain true to the faith. It is my intention to do that, *within*," he raised his finger to make a point, "the bounds of *my own* authority, and not so that I interfere with my wife or the children I promised her could be raised in her belief."

"So, then," Father Scanlan said, "we understand one another."

"Aye," Tom nodded.

"I'll notify you the moment I hear from Mother Superior. It's not pleasant, thinking about spending another six months without Sister Mary, but the alternative is less pleasing."

"I support you fully in this decision, Father. Just ask if you need anything."

Together they descended the stairs and found Katrina at the front door saying good-bye to Robert and Alice Thurston.

Father Scanlan took Katrina's hand and said, "I'll take my leave now. Katrina, it was a decided pleasure to attend your lovely party this evening. If I might be so bold, I would like you to consider performing for our Christmas pageant this year. I know your schedule with the choir must be demanding, but just give it some thought."

"I would be honored, Father Scanlan. Thank you for asking," Katrina said, taking Tom's arm.

"Can I have Henry drive you home, Father?" Tom asked.

"No, thank you, Tom. I think I'll take a bit of the night air. It's quite lovely outside just yet, and soon we'll have plenty of the white blanket to comfort us."

"Indeed. Good night, Father."

As Father Scanlan left the doorway, Tom turned a bright smile toward Robert. "What say ye, Mr. Thurston?"

Robert smiled back. "I think you're a year older, Mr. Callahan."

"Barely, Robert. And a lot younger than you, I might add," he laughed. "I'm going to take Friday off and settle a few details with Andy. Robert, do you remember that attorney who came to us a few weeks ago? Something about his being on call for contractual needs of the bank?"

Robert nodded his head. "I do, Tom. Evanston, I think he said. Gerald Evanston."

"Right. See if you can contact him tomorrow and set up an appointment for Monday afternoon. I've got a proposition involving the two of you."

"Any clues you might offer?" Robert probed.

Tom just shook his head. "No, not tonight. But I'll explain it all Monday. Good night, Alice," Tom said, kissing her on the cheek. "Thanks for coming."

Robert embraced Katrina and the Thurstons left. Tom waited until they were away from the house, then closed and bolted the door. As they reached the second floor, Tom turned toward their bedroom suite but Katrina hesitated. "I think I'll see Anders for a couple of minutes before I turn in. Do you mind?" she smiled.

Tom kissed her cheek, gently swatting her as she stepped across the hall. "Don't be too long, Mrs. Callahan," he said, raising an eyebrow to her.

Katrina lightly tapped on Anders's door and received a muted, "Come in." She opened the door, then closed it behind her. Anders was sitting in his chair, reading. Wearing the new silk pajamas and robe that Katrina had purchased for him, he patted the right arm of his chair and took her hand as she neared. She sat on the cushioned arm of the lounge chair, and Anders looped his arm around her waist.

"I was hoping you'd drop in to say good night."

"You knew I would," she laughed.

Squeezing her waist, he said, "Yah, that I did. I have a story to tell you. A remarkable story. First, I must say, Klinka, that you were right all along."

"Right? About what, Anders?"

"About all of it, Klinka. The story I have to tell you will take some time, but the end of the story is what you really need to hear." He exhaled, and then took in a long, deep breath. "The gospel, my wonderful, loving sister, is true. It's *all* true, Klinka. Everything you ever told me is true. The Lord has shown me."

Katrina sat speechless for the next several moments as Anders struggled to control his emotions. In the end, she simply slid into his lap and held his head while he cried.

Finally he said, "It had to be *you*, Klinka. I had to tell you first," he whispered, embracing her tightly. He gently pushed her to a sitting position and wiped at the tears on his face. "Sit across from me, here," he said, pulling the adjacent chair up close to his. "This story is long, and I've not yet told anyone, although Sister Mary knows most of it."

Until the light began to creep through the eastern window, Katrina sat enthralled, occasionally laughing through her tears as Anders Hansen, reluctant Mormon, described his rescue in Cuba and the very real way in which the Lord had reached down and cared for him.

Tom had at first waited for Katrina to come to bed, anxious to be with her. In time, he grew a little impatient, then began thinking about Father Scanlan's admonition. He waited for a long time for Katrina to return—to discuss the issues with her—but had finally fallen asleep alone, oblivious to what kept brother and sister together through the night.

Shortly before dawn, Katrina left Anders's room and closed his door softly. Tiptoeing to a small desk in the corner of her dressing room, off the main bedroom suite, she got to her knees, and for the remaining time, until the sun broke through the light cloud cover hanging over the tops of the Wasatch Range, Katrina spoke with Heavenly Father, who already knew more of the incident than she was able to recount. It was not in the telling, but in the thanking, that Katrina spent this time praying. There *was* more than *one* thing for which she had often pleaded. And if God could provide fulfillment to *that* prayer, then he could, in time, provide all.

Rising, she opened a small drawer in her desk and removed a well-worn, leather-bound book. Quickly flipping to a blank page, she hesitated briefly, thinking, and then picked up her pen and dipped the nib in the inkwell.

October 7, 1898

Dear Nana,

Anders believes! You knew he would, didn't you? And I am filled with the

Holy Ghost. The Lord's blessings are so abundant, I feel certain you must have asked Him to watch over your Anders and to answer my prayers. Please continue to help me with Thomas. I know it is possible. Thank you, Nana.

Yeg elske deg,

Your Irina

5

Tom and Anders were both breathing heavily when they reached the rocky outcropping and found a suitable flat rock to sit on and look down over the entire Salt Lake Valley. The first light snow had dusted the peaks of the mountains surrounding Salt Lake, but their observation post was several hundred feet below the snow line.

"I found this place when I was working at Holy Cross," Tom said. "After Katrina married Harold, it became a favorite place of mine."

Anders remained silent, looking over the valley floor and chewing on a stalk of dry grass. Tom held his peace and shifted his position to provide a backrest against a large boulder. Finally, Anders spoke.

"There were a few moments, Tom, back there in Cuba, I mean, when I thought I might never see all this again. There's beauty all over the world, especially in Norway, but I guess we take it for granted until the day . . ." He grew silent again, spitting out the grass and sliding back against the boulder that supported Tom.

"You've been good for Katrina, Tom. Considering her condition when we found her in Mexico, she's recovered well."

"Aye, she has. But, of a night, she sometimes wakes up, and I know it's all still there. Less than at first, but there, all the same. We don't speak of it. She just slides up closer, and I hold her till she falls asleep again."

"That's what I mean, Tom. You've been good for her."

"Thank you, Andy. I know how much she loves you, and it means a lot to hear you say that."

"I mean it, Tom. I *really* mean it. You saved me from a beating on the ship, bore the brunt of Harold's false accusations, and assisted me in finding Klinka in Mexico. You've become my brother," he said, looking directly at Tom.

Tom laughed to make light of the matter. "Sure now, I've got a paddock full of brothers in Ireland, Andy, and at least one more somewhere else in the world, but I reckon you can never have too much family."

They heard a bird screech and both looked up to watch a golden eagle swooping down the face of the mountain in the sky above them.

"What will you do now, Andy? Back to Holy Cross?"

Anders thought for a moment and slowly shook his head. "No. I want to go back to the university. I thought about it in Florida while I was . . . uh, adjusting to my new dexterity," he laughed.

Tom glanced at his brother-in-law's empty sleeve and winced. "Actually, Tom, it's not so bad. Once I learned to button my shirt and tie my shoes, I became practically independent again. But you don't want to wait too long, or be in too much of a hurry, to go to the toilet."

Tom laughed out loud. "What will you do at the university?"

"I'm not sure. I met a fellow in the hospital in Florida. He was a lawyer from New York and a captain in the cavalry regiment. He'd been temporarily flash-blinded when some gunpowder went off in his face. I kind of liked what he said about the law."

Tom's ears perked up and he leaned forward. "Andy, now *that*, interestingly enough, is *exactly* what I wanted to talk to you about."

"Oh?"

"Absolutely."

Anders listened as Tom explained his concerns over his lack of knowledge about banking and mining, and his limited ability to manage Utah Trust Bank. "In truth, Andy, I kind of sit at Robert's feet and, together, we meet with other bankers and mine owners and work on joint contracts with them. I've learned a bit, but no one takes me seriously as the chairman of the board of a bank. I need to correct that weakness, Andy, and from what you're saying, we might be able to go down this road together."

"I'm listening."

"Well," Tom laughed again, "it's not quite that simple, or," he paused, looking up again at the eagle, "maybe it is. I want to go to the university and also apprentice with a lawyer. I want to gain a lawyer's credentials, Andy, with economics and mining knowledge as well. I thought perhaps I could do both together. In fact, from what you've said, we could *both* do it together."

"I'm still listening," Anders smiled.

"Well, I'd need your help. I propose that you come to work for the bank. I could put you in charge of the front office, the tellers and all. You can attend classes as required, work the other time, and," he grinned, "here's the good part. I'm going to retain the services of a young lawyer who came to the bank a few weeks ago looking to represent us. If I retain him, then you and I can apprentice ourselves to his office. I can enroll in the university with you, take my economics and mining classes, and together we can spend part of the day in the lawyer's office."

"That's pretty sharp, Mr. Callahan. You've thought this through," Anders said.

"Aye, ya got that right, mate. So then, we're agreed?"

"And, Tom, I'm sharp enough, too, you know."

Tom tilted his head slightly, questioning.

"Thank you for the job, Tom. However neatly it was packaged."

Tom smiled. "Andy, as I said earlier, you can *never* have too much family, eh? It's actually an important job, and I really need someone to brighten the front office, train the tellers, and provide a pleasant atmosphere. I'm counting on the training you got working for your father in the furniture store. I want that kind of helpful attitude toward our customers."

"Yah, Tom, I can do that. But thank you, anyway."

"Well," Tom said, standing. "What say we hike back down for a bite of lunch? Maybe we can take Katrina down to the Knudsford House tonight. They've got a dance band in from California, and we haven't been dancing for quite a while."

"Thank you, Tom, but I have another engagement to arrange. Maybe another time."

"Sure, Andy."

"Tom, do you know a family named Richards? The father would be Albert Richards, I think."

Before beginning their climb off the rocky point, Tom said, "I've heard that name, Andy, but I don't think I know them." He paused. "Wait a minute, Katrina may know them. I think she's in the choir with Albert's wife. Who are they, anyway?" he asked.

"A final piece of the war, Tom. A promise I gave."

"I see. Anything I can help with?"

"Thank you, Tom, but no. It's a personal errand. But there is one other thing you should know, Tom. I explained it to Katrina last night. The details are unimportant at the moment, but, Tom, I've had . . . well, I've changed since we last spent time together."

"I guess war does that, Andy."

"It's not the war. Well . . . perhaps it is. But I've come to believe in the teachings of the Church, Tom. I actually still don't know them very well, but I *know* the gospel is true. I intend to follow it as best I can."

Tom's eyebrows raised. "I'm glad you found something so important in your life. That's something Katrina and I are going to have to face. Religion, I'm finding, can be a problem. To tell you the truth, Andy, I'm worried about living up to the promises I made to your sister. Ah," Tom said, raising his hands toward the sky and exhaling, "but that's another discussion." Tom grinned, clapping his hands on Anders's shoulders. "I must admit, though, I haven't had much luck with Mormon lawyers over the past several years," Tom said, chuckling at Anders as he jostled his shoulders.

"It'll be a long time before either of us is a lawyer, Tom, but I'd say you won out over both of the Strombergs, if that's what you're talking about," Anders replied.

"Hmmm, I suppose I did," Tom said. "I'm still hungry, Andy," he laughed. "Stop all the jabbering and let's go eat."

"It's beautiful up here, Tom," Anders said, taking another look around.

"The Mountain of the Lord, some call it."

"Yah. I can see why."

Anders Hansen rapped the bronze door knocker twice and waited in the crisp, October night air. A tall, balding man opened the door and smiled at Anders.

"Please excuse the interruption, sir. I'm looking for the home of Albert Richards."

"You've come to the right place, young man. I'm Albert Richards. How can I be of service?"

"Sir, my name is Anders Hansen, and I knew your son, Anthony Richards, briefly . . . in Cuba. I wonder if I might have a moment of your time, sir?"

The older man's face turned solemn, and he opened the door wider.

"Please, come in, Mr. Hansen."

Inside, Richards assisted Anders to remove his overcoat and hung it on a coat hook in the entranceway. An awkward moment passed as Mr. Richards noticed Anders's empty sleeve pinned to his shoulder. "My family is in the parlor, Mr. Hansen. Please, come and join us," he said, leading Anders through the archway.

In the parlor, Anders quickly scanned the room. Two young boys, one about twelve and the other perhaps nine, were lying on a rug covering the polished wooden floor. A woman Anders took to be Mrs. Richards sat on the sofa, and a man about Mr. Richards's age sat in an overstuffed chair. A young woman was seated on a divan. The group sat silently as Mr. Richards escorted the unknown guest into the room.

"This is Mr. Anders Hansen," Richards announced to all. "Mr. Hansen, this is my family. This is my wife, Althea, our daughter, Sarah, and our two sons, Phillip and Nephi. And this is one of our family friends, Reed Smoot." Richards motioned toward a seat across from the divan and invited Anders to sit down.

The size of the family gathering caused Anders some distress and he took his seat awkwardly.

"Mr. Hansen knew Tony in Cuba," Mr. Richards announced, taking a seat by his wife. Mrs. Richards covered her mouth with her hand, then glanced at her husband and back at Anders. She leaned against her husband, and he took her hand as he settled into his seat. All were silent as Anders sat on the edge of his chair, gathering his thoughts.

"Mr. Richards, I apologize for coming without prior announcement," he said, fear beginning to override his determination to fulfill this mission. "Perhaps," he continued, glancing at Smoot, "in light of your visitor . . . I mean, if this is an inconvenient time . . ."

"Mr. Hansen," Mr. Richards said softly, his kind, but sad eyes encouraging Anders, "as you can well imagine, this has been a very trying time for all of us. We've lost our two oldest sons in one sudden instance. Their bodies," he paused to compose himself, "were returned to us just over a month ago, and since the funeral, we have tried to adjust to their absence. But sir, . . . we have not spoken with anyone who knows anything substantive about what happened. Captain Young, their battalion commander, has not yet returned, although he did write and inform us the boys had . . . died, but if you know any of the particulars, we would be most grateful to hear what you can tell us. Please, you are most welcome here."

"Mr. and Mrs. Richards, I, uh, I . . ." Anders lowered his head and stared at the rug for a long moment.

"Mr. Hansen," a gentle voice said. Anders looked up at Sarah. She was in her late teens and had auburn hair which she had piled in a becoming way up on her head. A pair of ringlets framed her pretty face and Anders could see tears in her eyes. She struggled to speak.

"Anthony and Fletcher were my heroes, Mr. Hansen. They were my friends and my guardians, as well as my brothers. Please, Anders," she said, using his first name. "If you can tell us *anything* about them we will be so grateful to you."

Anders looked back at Sarah's parents, both of whom were looking directly at him, tears also rising in Mrs. Richards's eyes. He glanced quickly at Mr. Smoot, who gazed at him with interest, but held his silence.

Anders nodded, and took one further glance at Sarah, who was trying to smile through her tears.

"Brother Richards," he started, establishing his church connection, "I knew Tony very briefly, and I was not blessed to, uh . . ." he stumbled, "I did not actually *know* Fletcher. Sir, Tony asked me to deliver a message to you when I returned, but I find it very difficult to deliver that message without explaining how I . . .—Sir, I need to tell you the story behind the message and that may take some time."

Mr. Richards slid back into his seat, and placing his arm around his wife, he nodded his head toward Anders. "Please go on," he said. "We have plenty of time."

Anders took a deep breath then leaned forward in his chair. "Sir, Tony asked me to tell you that Grandma Richards is taking good care of him and Fletcher, and that you are not to worry or grieve for them." Anders exhaled slowly, his breath coming more evenly now, the message having finally been spoken.

Mrs. Richards gasped at the words, burying her face in her hands and allowing an audible sob to escape. The two young boys on the floor looked to their mother, and slid closer to the sofa at her feet. The older boy reached for her hand. "It's all right, Momma. I told you they were all right. I knew they were," the young lad said.

Sarah Richards had taken a handkerchief from her sleeve and was blowing her nose and wiping at the tears on her face. Gaining strength from his vision of this family's grief and compassion, Anders continued. "Lieutenant Richards and I met when I was on a medical team out to recover wounded soldiers and return them to the hospital area. Perhaps you know that Holy Cross Hospital here in Salt Lake sent a medical and nursing detachment to aid in the war effort. I was a part of that detachment. On that particular afternoon . . ."

Near midnight, with the younger lad asleep on the floor at his mother's feet, Anders completed his story—including the loss of his arm and the message Tony had delivered just before Anders had crossed the ridge and begun his descent toward the field hospital. Sarah's tears had ceased, and her acceptance of the incredible story was evident in the radiance that encompassed her face. Throughout the telling, Anders had found himself moved by her obvious love and concern for her brothers, while he was at the same time confused by the instant attraction he felt for her. Her face, so reminiscent of the young lieutenant's who had given him a blessing over three months before, provided for Anders a possible explanation for his otherwise unusual affinity toward this beautiful stranger.

"Mr. Hansen," Brother Smoot spoke for the first time during the evening, "what are *your* plans now that you've returned?"

Anders looked directly at Reed Smoot, segueing his thoughts to the unexpected question. "Well, sir, I will take a position with my brother-in-law's bank, and attend the university to study the law."

"Your brother-in-law works in a bank?"

"Yes, sir. Thomas Callahan, sir. He is the owner and chairman of Utah Trust Bank."

"Of course," Smoot acknowledged. "I know Thomas Callahan. Fine young man. And the law, you say?"

"Yes, sir."

"Good. Very good," he said, standing. "Albert, I'll take my leave now. I've stayed far longer than I intended. Althea, thank you for your hospitality, and Mr. Hansen," he said, stepping toward Anders's chair, from which Anders rose, "it has been an honor to meet you, sir. You have been privileged to partake," he said, grasping Anders hand in both of his, "of a witness from the Lord, the likes of which most mortals will not experience in a lifetime. Take it to heart, son, and learn from it. These were two fine men who came to your aid. Whether in this life or from the spirit world, they came to assist you. For the rest of your life, Mr. Hansen, you will have the solemn duty to extend similar assistance to those in need."

Brother Smoot looked into Anders's eyes and smiled at him. "We'll be seeing one another, Mr. Hansen," he said. "Sarah," he called, reaching for her hand as everyone but the sleeping boy took to their feet, "you've understood this all along, haven't you?" She remained silent, her eyes speaking volumes. Brother Smoot patted her hand, then took his coat from the hall rack. With a brief nod to the family, he opened the front door and departed.

"Well," Anders said, "I, too, must be going. Thank you for allowing me to visit with you this evening."

Albert Richards walked with Anders to the door, Mrs. Richards at his side. "Young man, you have been a blessing to our house this evening. You are forever welcome in our home, Anders, if I may call you that, and we both hope you will take advantage of our invitation."

"Thank you, sir. That is most considerate. But actually, it is *I* who should be thankful to you, for the two sons you raised and trained in the gospel. Except for them . . ." he paused.

"I understand," Richards said.

"Good night, sir," Anders said. Sarah stepped forward and handed Anders his overcoat. She stood only a couple of inches shorter than Anders.

"Mr. Hansen . . . Anders, I . . ." She looked into his eyes for a long moment as her parents stood quietly alongside. Without warning, she raised up on her toes and kissed his cheek, then turned quickly and disappeared into the next room.

Mrs. Richards looked shocked. "She was very close to Anthony and Fletcher, Mr. Hansen. Please excuse her. She is not usually such a forward person," she explained.

Anders buttoned his coat, his hosts observing his single-handed dexterity, and then he took Mrs. Richards's hand.

"Thank you, ma'am. Thank you both for your kindness." With one final glimpse toward the room where Sarah had gone, Anders stepped through the front door and walked down the path into the night.

His mind reeled with the events of the evening, and he inwardly chafed at the fear he had felt when first confronted with the actual fulfillment of his promise to Tony. But Brother Smoot had said it to Sarah. *"You knew, didn't you?"* he had said.

And Anders knew even more. As surely as if he had been tapped on the shoulder, the still small voice spoke to him. The message was suddenly as clear as if Tony, once again, had delivered it in spirit.

The walk up South Temple, the only sound a soft wind rustling through the few leaves remaining on the trees, was peaceful to Anders and gave time for thought. Quietly climbing the stairs toward his room, Anders was startled by Katrina opening the door to her bedroom, her robe wrapped around her as she smiled at him.

"Anders, I'm so glad you're home. I was worried. Tom told me about . . ." she started.

"Klinka," he kissed her in passing. "There's no need to worry, little sister. Oh, and you should know one other thing. I'm going to marry Sarah Richards," he said casually, walking toward his room.

"*What?* Anders, what do you . . ."

"Good night, Klinka," he smiled, closing his door.

Katrina stood in the hallway for several moments, half-in and half-out of her room. Tempted to barge into Anders's room, she decided instead to return to her bed. She shed her robe and slid between the covers. "Thomas! Wake up, Thomas!"

"Ummm?"

"Thomas, Anders said he's going to marry Sarah Richards."

"Ummm," Tom said, rolling over on his side to face her. "I wouldn't bet against him," he yawned, fluffing his pillow and closing his eyes.

"Thomaaas!"

———— ✀ ————

Tuesday afternoon, Tom, Anders, and Robert Thurston walked several blocks to the office of Gerald Evanston, Attorney-at-Law. Having obtained Robert's support for the would-be students, they now explained the proposition to Evanston. Wholeheartedly in support, Gerald Evanston quickly agreed to the proposition, acquiring in the process a retainer from Utah Trust Bank, first stock options on future UTB joint ventures, and two able and willing apprentices. The only stipulation that Tom placed on their apprenticeship was that their assignments and their law training be related to the nature of the business UTB intended to pursue. All parties were pleased with the arrangement, and Tom hosted the newly formed group at a celebratory luncheon.

Anders Hansen, having slept but little during the previous two nights, drifted mentally during lunch and privately celebrated his own personal conspiracy. With the aid of his sister, Katrina, who was as yet unaware of the forthcoming request, Anders intended to pull out all the stops in arranging the courtship of his future bride. Sarah Camellia Richards had been chosen.

Anders, however, was not the only one who had forgone sleep the previous evening. Following Anders's departure from the Richards's home, Althea Richards had gone to her daughter's bedroom intent on advising her daughter of the impropriety of having kissed Mr. Hansen after barely meeting him. As soon as she entered her daughter's bedroom, the mother was greeted by a smile from her daughter, who patted the side of her bed for her mother to sit.

"It's all right, Momma," the beautiful young woman said, her tears gone and her eyes bright.

"But, Sarah, it's not proper for a young lady—"

"Momma, I'm going to marry Anders Hansen. The Lord told me so tonight."

"But, Sarah . . ." her mother exclaimed, her eyes now wide and her mouth open.

Young Sarah just smiled and hugged her mother. "It's all

right, Mother, truly. You tell Daddy. The Lord will tell Mr. Hansen."

December brought heavy snows to the Salt Lake Valley, and also the first major row between Tom and Katrina. It had begun innocently enough, from Tom's point of view. The baby had kept Katrina up nearly all night with an earache, and Tom had slept soundly through the whole, miserable time of it, as she walked the floor, trying in vain to comfort the wailing PJ and get him back to sleep.

Tom got up in the morning to find an exhausted Katrina dozing in a chair with the baby asleep on her lap. When he awakened her, she was tired and irritable. And when he suggested that it might be well to hire a children's nurse to help care for PJ, he had been astonished by her reaction.

"You don't think I'm capable of taking care of my baby?" she had asked.

"I didn't say that," he said. "It's a lot of work to keep up the house. I just thought it might be easier on you to have someone who could help."

"Have I neglected the house in some way?" she asked.

"No," Tom laughed. "It's been fine, only . . ."

"Only what?" she demanded, glaring at him. Struggling unsuccessfully during the night to comfort PJ and get him to stop crying, Katrina had grown as frustrated as she was tired. She had yearned to have Tom's support and thought several times of waking him, not that he would have known any better than she what to do. It had also occurred to her during the long hours that if he had held the priesthood and was the kind of father she wished him to be, he might have given PJ a proper blessing.

"Nothing," Tom said. "I don't have any complaints."

"Complaints! Well, I hope not. I work hard to keep the house up and take care of PJ. It's not easy, you know."

"I know that. That's why I suggested we hire someone to help with PJ," he said, wondering why she was so angry.

"I'll not have some other woman caring for my baby," she said.

"Katrina, that's not what I'm suggesting. It's just that you're always so tired. Half the time when I reach for you in bed, you're not there. Besides, it's not like we can't afford it. Why don't you see if there's someone you can bring in."

"That's your solution to everything, isn't it?"

"What is?" he asked, now completely perplexed.

"Just throw money at the problem," she said, irritated for the first time since their marriage by his insensitivity to her feelings. She was thoroughly exhausted and feeling overwhelmed and strangely alone, and this unshaven man, standing there in his wrinkled pajamas and provoking her, was suddenly a stranger to her.

"Oh, I don't want to talk about it," she said, turning away.

"Katrina! I don't understand you," Tom said.

"Obviously!" she said, gathering up PJ and walking away.

The disagreement had not immediately gone away. Tom hadn't known what to say to smooth things over, and Katrina had remained aloof and moody until the next day. They never really resolved the problem, but Tom finally cornered his wife and took her in his arms. At first she resisted his holding her, but she finally relented, and they both ended up saying they were sorry, though Tom didn't know for sure what he had done wrong.

In an effort toward conciliation, a week later Katrina did hire a cook who would also help out with light housekeeping and who, together with their houseman, Henry, filled out the Callahans' small household staff.

Katrina's stubbornness was a wonder to Tom and helped him understand the strength that had enabled his petite and generally even-tempered wife to survive her ordeal in the Mexican jungle when she had cared for a dead woman's baby and eventually found her own way to safety. *Katie, I don't always understand ye, lass,* he had later thought, *but you're sure some kind of woman.*

A week before Christmas, Katrina was in the nursery, giving young PJ his morning bath and talking with her middle sister, Sophie. Henry, whose duties had grown over the past year of his employment to range from carriageman, to butler, to occasional baby-sitter, ascended the stairs and knocked lightly on the doorjamb.

"Excuse me, madam, but a gentleman has arrived and has asked to see you."

"Do you know who he is?" she asked, as PJ splashed her with warm, soapy water.

"He is an older gentleman, Mrs. Callahan. He said his name is Magnus Stromberg."

Katrina was stunned. Her thoughts raced wildly. *Hadn't Magnus been killed in Mexico with Harold?* she thought.

"Henry, please tell the gentleman I am, uh . . . I am involved at the moment. I will join him in the parlor, presently."

"Yes, ma'am."

Ten minutes later, having straightened her hair and removed the apron she had adopted as protection from PJ's bathroom antics, Katrina descended the stairs and entered the front parlor. The elderly gentleman, into his early seventies, Katrina surmised, rose, smiled, and nodded his head in acknowledgment.

"Thank you for seeing me, Sister Callahan." He remained standing as Katrina took a seat opposite.

"I must admit, sir, it was, well, it was a shock to hear the name again. I thought . . ."

"Certainly," he said, resuming his seat. "Sister Callahan, I am Magnus Stromberg, *senior*. Magnus was my son, and young Harold was my only grandson. I know," he smiled and nodded his head, "not the size of most Mormon families of that era. My wife died a few years after we entered the Valley, and, in spite of the advice of the Brethren, I could never bring myself to . . ."

Katrina sat with her hands folded in her lap, beginning to understand. "I'm certain they were hard times, Mr. Stromberg. But I don't recall having met you, sir. Were you . . ."

Again, Stromberg nodded his head. "We would not have had that opportunity during your brief . . ." he hesitated, "during your brief stay in Salt Lake following your marriage to Harold."

"Yes," she acknowledged, "we did depart the Valley within several months of our marriage."

"Sister Callahan, during those months and in fact for the past several years, I have been serving as a mission president in the southeastern United States. I was slow to learn of your marriage, and due perhaps to strained communications between my son, Magnus, and myself, was quite unaware, until after your departure, of the new colony in Mexico. President Cannon wrote to me and explained." The elderly gentleman sat forward on the edge of his seat and looked earnestly at Katrina.

"Sister Callahan . . . Katrina, if I may call you that. I

have come to formally extend my sincere and humble apology for the treatment you received at the hands of my family. I can offer no excuse," he shook his head. "Our free agency, a gift from our Lord, has always provided for choice, however opposed that choice may be to the will of the Lord. President Cannon has explained to me the circumstances under which you followed your husband, my grandson," he smiled sadly, "to Mexico with the intent of restoring the 'Principle.' It was appalling and quite unchristian for them to have misled you by such a deception. I was pleased to see how understanding Brother Cannon was, and even more pleased, my dear," he smiled kindly, his face drawn and wrinkled, "to learn of your testimony and subsequent good fortune.

"Katrina, the Stromberg name has been prominent in this Valley since three months after Brother Brigham led us west. When my mission was concluded last summer, I returned to our ranch. Perhaps you didn't know, but we run cattle on several thousand acres located just beyond Hidden Valley, about twenty miles south, near Draper. It was there, just a few weeks ago, that I learned of your presence in Salt Lake City.

"I have prided myself that the Strombergs have always stood among the faithful members of the Church. This action on the part of my son has blemished our family name, but that is not what is important. What I believe *is* important, is that you can find it in your heart to forgive an old man, whose progeny have gravely offended you, and, if I understand correctly, placed you in danger of your life. Sister Callahan," he said, lowering his head, "I apologize for the injuries you have suffered. If there is anything, *anything* . . ."

Katrina rose from her chair and moved to sit next to the

old gentleman. Taking his hand from his lap and holding it tightly, she said, "Brother Stromberg, perhaps you will never know how grateful I am for your visit and for your obvious concern. I would like you to know that I am now well and happy. The Lord has provided a wonderful husband, and as you have indicated, President Cannon has assured me that I may retain my Church membership. As for your grandson . . ." she stopped mid-sentence, glancing toward the stairs.

"Upstairs," she said, raising her eyes toward the stairwell, "is my firstborn . . ." she stopped, thoughts of the loss of her first child, Harold's son who died in childbirth, rushing to her mind ". . . is my son, barely four months old. I will teach him, Brother Stromberg, of the Lord's love, of the correct principles, and of his duty to God, as I'm certain you did your children. But the time will come, sir, when he will grow into manhood, and then, as you have said, he will exercise his agency. We can only hope, Brother Stromberg, that our children will have listened and learned."

Magnus Stromberg patted Katrina's hand, and looked into her eyes. "For one so young, Sister Callahan, you have learned much," he said.

"Perhaps, sir. But what I *have* learned is that young or old is more a matter of experience, than of years."

"Hmmm," he nodded. "Truly the Lord *has* blessed you, and I would like to leave my blessing with you as well. God's good graces on your family, Katrina Callahan," he said, standing. "And now I must go, and leave you to your chores. Thank you again for seeing me. My heart is lighter as a result."

"And mine, Brother Stromberg," Katrina smiled. "Are you back in Salt Lake permanently then?" she asked, also standing.

He laughed. "Well, the cattle business is certainly

keeping me busy, after being gone for so long, but I suppose the Lord will tell me what He has in store for me, in His good time," he said.

They walked toward the front door, and he reached for her hand at the entrance. "Katrina, if it will ease your mind further, it is my firm belief that young Harold was only following his father's direction. I know the boy had a strong testimony, and, according to his mission president, he served with distinction in Scandinavia. Now, that does not excuse his actions, but his father was adamant about the political expediency of the Manifesto. That was the source of our strained relationship as I tried to redirect him to understand the will of the Lord."

"Thank you, Brother Stromberg. I know Harold tried to be a good member of the Church. In fact, you may not be aware, but he was the one who taught and baptized my family in Norway. But events just . . . they, just overtook him, I believe."

"I understand. Then perhaps," the older man smiled kindly, nodding his head, "in your family's membership, some good did indeed come from his short life. A good day to you, Sister Callahan."

"Thank you for your visit and for your blessing, sir."

Magnus Stromberg nodded once more at Katrina and walked slowly down the circular drive, turning west on South Temple and stepping carefully through the drifts of snow. Katrina watched him for a few moments until he disappeared behind the trees lining the street and then she closed the door and ascended the stairs.

Re-entering the nursery, she found PJ had been dried, dressed, and was kicking his arms and legs, cooing all the while to his young Aunt Sophie. Katrina lifted her son and held him close to her chest.

"Grow strong, young PJ Callahan," she whispered in his ear, rocking him gently. "And listen with your heart as well as your mind. The world is difficult, my son, but I will guide you until you are old enough to see for yourself," she said, tears beginning to form in her eyes.

"Are you all right, Klinka?" Sophie asked.

"Yah, Sophie, I feel just wonderful."

"Thomas, is that you?" Katrina called out as she heard the downstairs door close. Moving to the top of the second floor landing, she leaned over the railing and smiled as her husband came into view.

"I understand a man can get a free meal here, if he plays his cards right," Tom said, looking up the stairwell.

"I'm certain we can rustle up something," she said descending the stairs. "I didn't expect you home for lunch."

Tom stood at the foot of the stairs as Katrina reached the ground floor. "Robert and I concluded the negotiations for UTB to purchase twenty-five percent ownership in the *Ontario* mine today. I decided I had earned the rest of the day off," he laughed, picking her up and twirling her around.

"Would you like me to fix you something to eat?" she asked.

"No. I'd like you to fix us *both* something to eat, in a basket, if you please. I think we should take the buggy for a ride up the canyon."

"Thomas, there's snow in the canyon."

"So! We'll take the sleigh."

"It's too cold for a picnic and I just got PJ down for a nap."

"Well, we'll take blankets, and Sophie's still here, isn't she?" he said, fending off her objections as if they were serves in a tennis match. "Can't she watch PJ for a few hours while I whisk my wife out into the brutal, cold wilderness?"

"Well, I suppose . . ."

"Hey, Sophie," Tom called out. Sophie came to the second floor landing and smiled down at Tom. "Katrina has a desperate need to see the cottonwoods up the canyon," he laughed. "Would you mind staying through till dinner and watching PJ for us?"

"Yah, Tom. I'd be happy to," the young girl said.

"Thanks," Tom replied, looking again at Katrina. "That settles it, Katie. Just a few sandwiches, some hot drinks, and we're off. I'll hitch up the sleigh."

"Thomas, you're always so impetuous."

"And that's why you love me."

"Oh, go get the buggy ready, Mr. Mine Owner. And don't forget blankets and our heavy coats. I'll get the food."

The argument flared just as they passed the university grounds, before either of them realized what had happened. Katrina's simple pronouncement, that Magnus Stromberg Sr. had paid her a visit earlier that day, brought a sharp response from Tom.

"Haven't we had enough of the Strombergs?" he asked.

"He was most courteous, Thomas."

"And well he should be. His son and grandson led you a merry chase through the jungle, or have you forgotten?" Tom pressed.

Katrina didn't respond immediately, and they rode in awkward silence for another few minutes till they reached the plateau Tom had chosen for their impromptu picnic. The blanket spread on the ground and the food basket arranged, Katrina took an extra blanket from the buggy. She sat down next to Tom and snuggled up against him, pulling the blanket across their shoulders. Ignoring the food, they sat in silence for several minutes before Tom wrapped his arm around his wife and pulled her closer.

"It's not really Brother Stromberg, is it, Thomas?"

He remained silent another few seconds, looking out over the valley below.

"I suppose not," he said, a resigned tone in his voice, "even though it gets up my nose that he would choose to come by during the day while I was gone."

"I understand that," she replied. "Perhaps he never even gave it thought. He was very kind and apologetic. Did you know he has a big ranch down near Draper?"

"Hidden Valley is *Stromberg's* ranch?" Tom said, surprised. "UTB loaned the Hidden Valley spread fifteen thousand last year for winter feed. The owner was gone, and the ranch manager applied for the loan. Come to think of it, George Cannon co-signed the loan, or I wouldn't have been able to approve it. Robert knew the owner, he said, and felt it was a good risk."

"Was it?" Katrina asked.

"Ummm," Tom mumbled, nodding his assent. "Paid in full last month, but I was in Denver when the owner . . ." Tom paused and looked at Katrina, "that would be Stromberg, I suppose, came in and paid the loan in full."

Katrina nodded. "But it isn't Stromberg that's worrying you, is it, Thomas?" she asked again.

"As I said, I suppose not. Are you happy, Katrina?"

She thought for a moment, and responded without looking at Tom. "I have a lot of blessings, Thomas. Much to be happy for."

"Aye. We're both blessed with worldly things. But are you *happy?*"

"Has Father Scanlan been at you again?" she smiled, pausing for a moment.

"Is there someone else, Katie?" he asked, reluctant to voice the words.

"What!"

Tom turned to look down at his wife seated next to him on the blanket. "Do you care for someone else?"

"Thomas, how could you ask such a question? You know that I love you."

"Aye, but I also know that you are sad that I can't or . . . that I haven't provided the things that you really seek. And Captain Masterton can," he added.

"How did Geoffrey Masterton get into this conversation?" she said, bewildered.

"Katie, I . . ."

"What, Thomas? You what?"

"I read your journal."

Katrina sat quietly for a moment, her expression one of disbelief. "I would never have thought, Thomas, that you . . ."

"Katie, I'm sorry. I truly am, but I was worried about us, and frightened about our marriage. You wrote that Masterton had all the qualities you admired in a man."

"Thomas, my personal journal is just that—*personal*. I resent you invading my privacy."

"Do you love him, Katie?" Tom asked, his voice lowered.

"Yes," she replied, "I do love him and all his qualities . . . just as I love Anders, the same way I love Brother McKay and Robert. But *you* are my husband, Thomas, and I have never taken our marriage vows—even without the sanctity of the temple—never taken them lightly. I'm hurt and angry that you would ask such a question."

Tom just sat silently, his chin practically resting on his chest.

"Seriously, Thomas, this talk is long overdue, isn't it?" Katrina said.

"Aye," he nodded again. "But I'm torn apart inside, Katie. I love you with all my heart, but my whole family history is . . . well, it's just going against everything I've ever been taught."

"Our spiritual paths, you mean?"

"Aye. The men you admire, the things you seek for our family, and the path we're trying to provide for our son."

"Yes. We've placed quite a burden on ourselves and any children we might have, haven't we? Have you reached any conclusions?"

He shook his head. "That's just it, Katie. I have no answers. My spiritual leader tells me that my son is in danger of losing his eternal soul, while *your* spiritual leaders tell you to rest easy, that if anything happens to our son, he will be in heaven. Father Scanlan also tells me that eternal marriage is a mistaken notion, according to the scriptures, and *your* church teaches that families will be together in the hereafter. How can a God be so different in His teachings?"

"I know," she agreed softly.

"But that's not all, Katie. We travel different paths sometimes, you and I. Oh, we're always together, holding hands, sharing our love, but I can tell sometimes that you're far away, sort of wistful, and the family prayers you always want—well prayer has not been a common factor in my life, other than the book prayers I learned as a child."

The afternoon was brilliant and clear, with a light breeze playing through the canyon. Notwithstanding the blanket of snow, the early afternoon temperature had risen to the mid-fifties and the view of the valley from the mountainside was as magnificent as ever. Katrina let Tom's questions hang in the afternoon air, while they both gazed out toward the Great Salt Lake, mentally wrestling with their differences.

"Katie, it's not as if we can go to someone for answers. We *know* what my priests and your bishops believe. It's how *we* come to terms with it that eludes us. For me," he said, pulling her closer and burying his face in her hair, "the *problem* is simple. If there is but one God, he wouldn't give such diverse instructions to the various churches. The *solution* however," he laughed out loud, "is another matter. Whose God is right?" he asked, throwing his hands up.

"*The* God is right, Thomas. It's mankind that's wrong. Our interpretations of God's teachings. We've had centuries of men, some good, but others bad, seeking to use God's word to their own purposes. But only in your own heart can you come to hear the whisperings of the Spirit."

"That's even more frustrating," Tom fumed. "Take Anders for instance. Why do some receive such a powerful, spiritual witness, while others,—and believe me, I *have* prayed for guidance, Katie—why do others receive no direction?"

She looked up and smiled at him and kissed his cheek, then laid her head back on his shoulder. "I don't know, Thomas. I truly don't." She lifted her head to smile at him again. "And I *do* know that you've prayed to find the answers. I'm very thankful to you for all you've tried to do to honor your commitment to me, and to our family. I know it hasn't been easy."

"I love you, Katie m'darlin'. *That* has made it much easier," he smiled.

"Thomas, would you like Father Scanlan to baptize PJ?"

"That would be easiest, wouldn't it? Cover both requirements. Believe me, I've thought of it. But what would I tell PJ when he's eight, and your Bishop asks about getting him ready for baptism. 'Hey, PJ, your Mom and I wanted to be sure you could get to heaven, so we . . .'" He stopped as Katrina began to laugh at his mimicry.

"We've paved a hard road, Thomas."

"Aye, we have. And PJ's baptism is only the current problem, isn't it, darlin'? You say you know that I've prayed for guidance. Well, I know a bit about your prayers, too, sweet Katie," he said, taking her face in his hands. "Alice and Robert have spent hours trying to help me understand the complexities of eternal marriage. They've not pressured me, of course. Robert is too loving for that, and he cares very much about both of us. But Alice knows what's in your heart, and Katie, I'll tell you God's truth, that it pains me to know there is something in this world that I can't provide for you. Sure, I could just join the Mormon Church and go to the temple with you, but I love you too much, and if I look into my own heart, I respect the God we both love too much to fake such a commitment."

Katrina laughed and stretched her legs out, leaning back to look upward toward the sky. "Thomas, believe it or not, I've entertained thoughts about becoming a Catholic. I even had a brief conversation with Sister Mary some months ago."

"You did?" Tom asked, incredulous.

"Yes. But I came to the same conclusion you did," she said, shaking her head. "Thomas, I have a testimony that I'm where the Lord wants me to be. I cannot turn my back on Him."

"Nor would I allow it, Katie. But thank you for the thought."

They sat for a few moments in silence. Finally, Tom sighed and said, "So you really *don't* love Captain Masterton?"

"Oh, Thomas, don't be silly."

"He cares for you, Katie. I've seen it in his eyes."

Katrina nodded. "I know. But he has always been a complete gentleman, Thomas. Absolutely proper."

"So, where do we go from here?" Tom asked.

"First, we go home. I'm cold, Mr. Callahan. What a day for a picnic," she laughed. She got to her feet and reached for Tom's hand, pulling him to his feet and wrapping the blanket around both of them.

"Then, my loving husband, we continue to ask the Lord for His guidance. His ways are not our ways, Thomas. All I know is that He loves us. Somehow, someway, we'll find the answers. In the meantime, Mr. Thomas Matthew Callahan, Irish larrikin of the first order, I will love you with all my heart."

"Ah, you Scandinavian girls sure know how to win a man's heart, don't ya?"

"And, Thomas, you have all the qualities that I want in a man. I trust you, I love you, and when the Lord sees fit to reveal his truths to you, then the Brethren better look out. The stake president will have just gained himself another bishop."

The New Year's Eve party at the Hansens' was to be a private affair. The Brigham Street neighbors of the Callahans had planned for weeks to stage a progressive dinner party, with a scheduled stop at each of the magnificent homes along the street. But Tom and Katrina had accepted her parents' invitation to spend a quiet family evening in the Hansen home on Third South and had sent their regrets to the Brigham Street gentry and removed *Valhalla* from the list of intended stops.

The only two people attending Lars and Jenny Hansen's party who were not directly related to the family were Henrick Jensen, seventeen-year-old Sophie's new boyfriend, and an absolutely beautiful Sarah Richards. Tom and Katrina watched as Anders helped Sarah out of her coat. Dressed in a dark green, velvet gown, with gold braid looped throughout the sleeves and bodice, she was a stunning young woman to whom Anders was obviously devoted.

"Ah, Katie. She reminds me of a young lass I met in Ireland once," Thomas said, his eyes riveted on Sarah.

"Oh?" Katrina tugged at his arm.

"Aye," he said, looking down into Katrina's green eyes. "There is *one* difference, however," he said, smiling at her.

"And what would that be, Mr. Callahan?" Katrina asked, aware of Tom's keen sense of the tease and trying to keep a straight face.

"Well," he continued, looking back at Sarah and Anders walking toward them, "this lass I'm speaking about, she was just about as beautiful as young Sarah there, but she changed over the years."

"Over the *years*," Katrina exclaimed, her eyes now wide.

"Aye," Tom laughed softly, "as she grew older, and became a mother, her beauty also changed." His face became serious now, and he held her eyes in check as he completed his thoughts. "Her beauty became . . . well, one day I noticed it came from within, if you know what I mean. She *was* beauty, whereas young Sarah there," he said, nodding toward the approaching couple, "*has* beauty."

A delicious shiver ran up Katrina's spine as Thomas's meaning unfolded. He was not one to praise on every occasion, and she had learned that he had this knack, when she least expected it, to make her heart flutter. "Oh, Thomas, I—"

"So, how's my baby sister and her Irish hooligan?" Anders said, breaking the moment and leaving Katrina to simply squeeze Tom's arm in loving reply.

Throughout November and December, in full view of the Salt Lake community and with the full support of Sarah's parents, Anders had paid continuous court to Sarah Richards. Tom and Katrina had enjoyed watching the relationship develop. Sarah was not only a beautiful young woman, she was refined and loving too. And it was wonderful to see the change she made in Anders. Previously shy and withdrawn with regard to women, he had become confident and even witty with Sarah as a companion. He was devoted to her, and he beamed with pride as he escorted the young woman to public functions during the holiday season.

Though only nineteen, Sarah was a remarkably mature young woman. As the only daughter in a family of four boys, she had been pampered, but she had also been well trained by her mother in both domestic duties and social arts. The tragic deaths of her two brothers was the first real adversity she had experienced, and dealing with the grief and adjusting to the loss had created in her a sensitivity and depth of character unusual in such a young woman. Anders was eight years her senior, but he had a young-looking face, and being in love had transformed him into a near giddy young swain. The couple presented a picture of mutual devotion and contentment, and their engagement was accepted in the community as a happy event.

Theirs was seen as an almost "arranged" marriage, with both young people accepting their role in the matter. The two were content in the understanding that they had indeed found their respective soul mate and that the Lord, who had confirmed His intentions to each of them, was pleased. For Anders, who had found it painful to even ask a young woman like Martha Young for a dance at Saltair, this new relationship with Sarah Richards was comfortable because it had been confirmed by a spiritual experience. It didn't hurt either that he was near breathlessly in love with the strikingly beautiful young woman. As for Sarah, she never lost the starry-eyed attraction she had first felt for Anders.

Anders had become something of a hero. The story of his daring rescue of Stitch Walkinghorse and the even braver attempt he had made to rescue the two Richards brothers had become well known in the Valley. Public knowledge of the spiritual experience he had had in his deliverance by Tony and Fletcher Richards was limited, however, to the Richards family and to Reed Smoot. Anders's stock in the community had risen rapidly. Prior to her departure to convalesce in Indiana, Sister Mary had granted an interview to the *Salt Lake Tribune* regarding Holy Cross Hospital's participation in the Cuban campaign. Her description of the valor of young Anders Hansen and John "Stitch" Walkinghorse left no doubt as to their heroism.

That Anders had only one arm became an accepted fact, and his empty sleeve served as a reminder of his valor and as a badge of honor. As for Sarah, her intended's missing arm seemed not to be an issue.

The dinner table at the Hansen's was overfilled with food and the excellent Norwegian delicacies Tom had come to love. Nana Hansen, as Katrina had taken to calling her mother since the birth of PJ, with the assistance of her two as yet unmarried daughters, had prepared for days, and the Norske "Jul kake" lavished throughout the house bore tribute to the effort.

Two enormous turkeys graced the table, along with a fifteen-pound ham. Steaming bowls of potatoes, corn, and vegetables of all sorts filled the long dining table as the family members gathered around the early evening dinner. Lars Hansen remained standing at the head of the table as his family and guests took their seats. Finally, a silence came over the assemblage as they turned their attention to Poppa Hansen.

Speaking English, but with a strong Norwegian accent, he began, "We have much to be thankful for this year. Anders, by the grace of God, has been returned to us," he said, nodding toward his eldest son. "Katrina has given us a fine new grandson, and Sophie and Hilda have finished their schooling and are becoming fine young women," he said to his two younger daughters. "Yah, yah, the Lord is good," he said, holding up his glass to frame a toast. "To our family," he said raising the glass, "and to the fine young man and young woman who have become," he said, looking at Tom, "and who are becoming," smiling at Sarah, "a part of it. As we enter the last year of this century, may we continue to deserve our blessings. *Skoll,*" he announced, raising his glass to his lips. Those gathered around the table raised their glasses and joined him. Seated next to Nana Hansen at the far end of the table, Tom also stood as the toast concluded, and remained standing as glasses were refilled.

"Father Hansen . . . Poppa," Tom said, smiling. "May the Lord bless this house and all those who dwell herein."

"Yah," Lars nodded. "May it be so, Thomas. May it always be so," he smiled.

———

Ten months later, at nine A.M., on 1 November 1899, Anders Lars Hansen and Sarah Camellia Richards were married. In the presence of their parents; Anders's sister Katrina Callahan; Tom and Katrina's friend, newly returned Scottish missionary David O. McKay; and a host of Hansens, Richardses, and other family and friends; the two young people were sealed to each other in the Salt Lake Temple.

Though she was delighted to be there, Katrina was also very uncomfortable. Now seven months pregnant, she fidgeted and shifted her weight, seeking respite from the intense pressure on her lower spine. That relief came during some brief moments spent in the celestial room of the temple, where she sat alone on a cushioned divan. Young Elder McKay, who, through Tom and Katrina, had become friends with Anders and Sarah, came to stand near the very pregnant woman. Sitting alone, Katrina had taken an opportunity to pray silently. Respecting her privacy, McKay waited until she looked up, then sat down next to her.

"It's a happy day for your family, Sister Callahan," he said.

Katrina nodded and smiled. "Are you glad to be home, Brother McKay?"

"Aye," he replied. "Yet, not all of me returned."

Again Katrina nodded. "Perhaps we all left something back there in the Old Country, but in its place, brought something with us."

"President Cannon advised me you were a woman beyond your age, Sister Callahan. Much has transpired since we first met, I understand. And I haven't forgotten our wee dinner in Scotland," he said, a soft Scottish burr accenting his voice.

"Yes," she said, looking upward to admire the pastels of the tastefully elegant room, her face serene, yet contemplative.

Young McKay leaned slightly forward. "Do you know your husband to be a good man, Sister Callahan?" he asked.

Katrina looked briefly startled. "I do, Brother McKay, by any man's standard," she stated firmly.

"Aye," he said, an understanding smile crossing his face. "Perhaps by any of *God's* standards also," he said. "Truly, I do understand, Sister Callahan. I suspect though that you'd as soon have him here with you as to have all the material blessings that have entered your life these past years. Yet, here you sit, alone. Is that possibly your thought at the moment?" he asked gently.

Katrina allowed a small smile to play on her lips. "You're not so young for your age either, Brother McKay."

"That really *is* the question, you know," he continued.

Katrina's quizzical look was attended by silence.

"God's standard, I mean. If Thomas is a good person by any *man's* standard, then perhaps he's a good man by God's standard. Then, in His own good time, and if it be His desire, Thomas *shall* sit here in this room by your side."

Before Katrina could reply she looked up to see the newly married Sarah Camellia Richards Hansen make her way into the room, accompanied by the beaming Anders. Katrina looked back briefly at David McKay. "Thank you, Brother McKay, for your kindness. I pray God the Lord *will* make such a decision, but this is Anders's and Sarah's day, is it not?"

"Indeed it is," he said, standing. "I hope we can remain in touch," he smiled, taking her hand.

"So do I, uh . . . D.O., I believe is what Thomas calls you."

"It is, and I'd be pleased if you, too, would use the name."

"Klinka," Anders said as he reached the divan, "may I present your new sister-in-law, Sarah Hansen?" he said, smiling broadly.

Katrina stood with McKay's gentle assistance and placed her hands on Sarah's shoulders and pulled her as close as Katrina's physical condition would allow. Laying her cheek alongside Sarah's, Katrina whispered. "Although I didn't know who you would be, I've always known the Lord had you in hiding for Anders. I *will* be your sister, Sarah, always."

"And I, yours, Katrina," Sarah replied, her voice soft.

On New Year's Eve, 1899, a small, family dinner was held at *Valhalla*. Anders and Sarah had arrived home only three days before from their extended honeymoon, after taking the train to San Francisco and then an ocean steamer to Vancouver. The return train trip down from Seattle through the Northwest had filled Sarah with the magnitude of the country and the beauty of God's creations.

Among the guests were Father Scanlan and Sister Mary Theophane. The Sister's health had been considerably restored during her recently ended convalescent leave, but she was still subject to recurrent bouts of malaria. Lars and Jenny Hansen; Sarah's parents, Albert and Althea Richards; Katrina's sister Sophie and Henrick Jensen, to whom she had become betrothed at Christmas; Robert and Alice Thurston; and David O. McKay and Emma Ray Riggs McKay, his lively new bride, were also present. Captain Masterton attended alone. Rumor had it that he had recently broken off an unofficial engagement to Martha Young some weeks earlier. Tom had continued to be wary of Masterton, and it still rankled him that Katrina was as friendly toward the captain as she generally was. Masterton had never again placed his hands on Katrina, even in a friendly hug, almost as if someone had warned him of Tom's feelings. But Tom noticed, or as he sometimes thought, or imagined, that Masterton continued to have eyes for Katrina.

The dinner was held upstairs, and the third floor ballroom was beautifully decorated for the occasion. After dinner and some light conversation, musical renditions were required by all attendees, to the amusement of many. Sister Mary found Tom avoiding Captain Masterton by hiding in a corner alcove. Masterton was serving as emcee and cajoling couples to perform their favorite numbers.

"I don't think you'll have to hide any longer, Thomas," she said, tugging at his sleeve. "You've duties elsewhere."

Tom's quizzical look brought a smile to Sister Mary's face. "No, Thomas, we'll not be singing, nor will we be about delivering food to the needy tonight," she laughed. "But you *will* be needed. I've asked Father Scanlan to make your apologies to the guests, and Henry has the buggy ready. Katrina is highly desirous of your company at the moment."

His attention was instantly riveted. "Is . . ."

"Yes, Thomas. You're about to be a father again, and we'd best be going quickly."

Tom bounded down the stairs, inadvertently leaving Sister Mary to carefully traverse the circular stairway by herself. Katrina was already being assisted into the backseat of the buggy by Henry and by Robert Thurston, who had been downstairs in the library.

"Deserting your own New Year's Eve party, Tom?" Robert laughed.

"I'm sorry, but I've got to go, Robert. See everyone is taken care of, please," Tom called as he boarded the buggy with Katrina.

"No worries, Tom," Robert called out. "All the best."

"Aye," Tom replied. Sister Mary appeared at the side of the buggy, and Tom realized that he had left her on the stairs. He jumped down and assisted her up into the seat next to Katrina. Tom then quickly stepped up to sit next to Henry, who nudged the horse forward. It was crisp and cold, but only a skiff of snow remained from the Christmas storm that had blanketed the valley several days earlier, and the short ride to Holy Cross Hospital took only a few minutes. Tom helped Katrina dismount as Sister Mary entered the hospital and reappeared in moments with two attendants and a wheelchair. Katrina took her seat, and they entered the foyer of the hospital, moving immediately toward the surgical unit. Sister Mary stopped in front of the entrance to the labor area and smiled at Tom.

"We'll prepare her for delivery, Thomas, and then you may see her again for a few moments, if there's still time. She's about ready, I'd say. Lovely dinner wasn't it?" she smiled.

Tom tried to see over her shoulder as she disappeared into the room and the door closed, then he walked a few steps back down the hallway and sat on a solitary bench against the wall. In the emptiness of the hospital corridor on New Year's Eve, Tom was suddenly engulfed by concern for Katrina's safety.

Forty minutes later, at eight minutes to midnight, Sister Mary opened the door to look out into the hallway where Tom sat with a fresh cup of coffee, courtesy of Sister Jude. He set the cup down and stood to walk toward the door. "You've another fine son, Thomas, but we're not quite through yet," she said tersely, immediately closing the door.

"Sister Mar—" he called out as the door closed. Taking his seat again, Tom finished his coffee as the time dragged slowly on. Shortly after midnight, Father Scanlan appeared and joined Tom on the hallway bench.

"Any news, my son?"

"Aye, Father. A son, according to Sister Mary."

"Wonderful. And Katrina?"

"I don't know, Father," Tom said. "Sister Mary was just—"

The door opened again and Sister Mary came to stand before the two men, her face drawn. Tom stood to face her.

"The young lad's fine, Thomas, and you have a new daughter as well, but Katrina is . . ."

"Is what? Sister Mary, tell me!" Tom said.

"She is hemorrhaging, Thomas. Severely. I won't mislead you. She is in serious trouble, but the doctor is with her, and he has called for Dr. Carmady to assist."

"Will she be all right, Sister? Can I see her?" Tom said.

"I'm afraid not, Thomas. The doctors are going to be with her for some time. Perhaps, Father Scanlan, if you would . . ." Sister Mary asked, looking to the priest for assistance.

"Of course, Sister," Father Scanlan said.

Sister Mary put her hand on Tom's shoulder and smiled weakly at him. "She is being well taken care of, Thomas. I assure you." The nursing sister looked briefly again at Father Scanlan, took a deep breath and exhaled, looking back at Tom. "She has asked for a blessing from her church. Could you arrange for that, Thomas?"

"Uh, yes. I, uh, I'll get someone."

"Good, Thomas. Father, if you would come with me, please," Sister Mary asked.

As the two Catholic ministrants left the waiting area, Tom suddenly found himself alone in the hallway, the silence more overwhelming than during his previous wait.

Unaware of Katrina's condition beyond the brief explanation given by Sister Mary, Tom instantly felt helpless, unsure what to do. Then, Katrina's request for a blessing returned to his thoughts. In three great strides, he was out the front door of the hospital and down the steps. Henry had returned home with the horse and buggy, and Tom ran the three blocks to the house, where most of the guests had departed. He burst through the front door, nearly colliding with Captain Masterton who was donning his overcoat.

"Have you seen Dave McKay?" he asked frantically.

"I'm afraid he left much earlier, Thomas. Is there something I can do for you? Is everything all right?"

"No, it's not. I need . . ." Tom paused, his breath coming in short, ragged gasps.

"Thomas, please, calm down for a moment. Is Katrina all right, and the baby?"

Suddenly, Tom looked directly at Masterton as if seeing him for the first time. "Geoffrey, I need your help. Katrina needs a blessing. She's having trouble. She's asked . . ."

"Tom, perhaps we could find Brother Thurston. I'm not . . ."

"Masterton, you're qualified to give a blessing aren't you?"

"Why, yes, but—"

"Look, Masterton, I know how much you care for Katrina. I haven't liked it, but I know. Now I need your help. *Katrina* needs your help."

"Say no more. Henry," Masterton called out toward the kitchen area. The butler stuck his head through the doorway and walked toward the two men.

"Yes, Captain?"

"Henry, Mrs. Callahan is having a spot of trouble and

has requested a priesthood blessing. Are you prepared to administer with me?"

"Indeed I am, sir," Henry replied.

"Fine. Get your coat and join us at the hospital."

"Certainly, sir. I'll just see that the cook can stay with Master PJ, and I'll be right along."

Masterton turned his attention back to Tom. "I think we should go straight back to the hospital, Thomas. Henry will follow."

As the two men entered the hospital, two nursing sisters exited the delivery room, walking quickly down the hallway. Tom called out after them.

"Sister Thomasina, could you please tell Sister Mary that I'm back and that Captain Masterton is here to bless Katrina?"

"Certainly, Mr. Callahan," the elderly sister said.

In a few moments, Sister Mary came through the double doors and stepped toward Tom. "The hemorrhaging has been stopped, Thomas, but she has lost a lot of blood and she's not out of danger yet. She'll need much rest now. Captain Masterton," she said, looking toward the sandy haired man, "are you here to offer the blessing Mrs. Callahan has requested?"

"I am, Sister. And Henry will be along presently."

"Fine. Follow me and we'll go to her before we move her to a private room. If you'll excuse us, Thomas."

"Oh, Sister, please . . ." Tom pleaded.

She looked at him for a moment, and nodded. "Yes, Thomas, I understand. You may accompany us."

Just as they turned to leave the waiting room, Henry came into the hallway and followed the small group into the delivery room. Upon first seeing Katrina, Tom was stunned. He grasped the railing at the foot of her bed. She was completely pale, nearly chalk white. Her eyes were closed and beads of perspiration covered her forehead. Her damp hair was matted against her head, and a pile of blood-soaked sheets lay on the floor next to her bed. A nursing sister quickly picked them up and whisked them away. Tom moved to stand by Katrina's side, taking her hand in his. Father Scanlan stood across the bed, also at Katrina's side. As Tom patted her hand, she opened her eyes.

"Just rest, Katie. Geoffrey has come with me to bless you."

Katrina smiled tiredly. Tom looked at Father Scanlan, who nodded and offered a small smile of assurance. Finally, Tom moved aside as Captain Geoffrey Masterton and Henry Murchinson, the Callahans' butler, came closer to the bed. Father Scanlan stepped back against the wall.

Masterton took Katrina's hand and spoke softly. "I understand you would like a priesthood blessing, Sister Callahan."

Katrina gave a strained smile. "Yes, please," she whispered.

Masterton nodded to Henry who opened a small vial of oil and commenced to anoint the exhausted woman. Then, Captain Masterton, together with Henry, laid his hands on Katrina's head and pronounced a blessing, while Father Scanlan, Sister Mary, and Tom watched.

A while later, Captain Masterton and Henry having left some time before, Tom sat with Sister Mary and Father Scanlan over coffee in the basement cafeteria. Tom listened as his nursing friend recounted the events of the evening, assuring Tom that Katrina was recovering well.

"And the babies?" he asked.

"Thomas, you have a new son, born last night at 11:48, December 31, 1899, and a beautiful new daughter, born this morning at 12:17, January 1, 1900. Katrina has given birth to twins—a century apart," she laughed, the first happy sound of the evening.

Tom looked at both of his friends and smiled his recognition of the event and his relief that all was now going well. "Some New Year's Eve, eh, Father?"

"A beautiful start to a new century, Thomas. Just beautiful."

"How long will it take Katrina to regain her strength?" Tom asked.

"Go home, Thomas, and get some sleep. She'll be conscious when you return this evening. We'll talk more later."

"Thank you, Sister," he said, reaching across the table for her hand. "Thank you for everything." Tom stood, shook Father Scanlan's hand, and departed the room.

After Father Scanlan had poured himself another cup of coffee and retaken his seat, he said, "There's more, isn't there, Sister?"

"Aye. It's unlikely, Father, that Katrina Callahan will be having any additional children. When I explained to Dr. Carmady that she'd lost her first child during a breech birth, under primitive conditions in Mexico, he said he was surprised that she'd been able to have little PJ without difficulty."

Father Scanlan nodded his understanding. "And will you tell Thomas?"

Sister Mary hesitated for a moment. "I'll speak with Katrina first," she said.

In the morning, when Tom returned to the hospital, Sister Mary escorted him to the door of Katrina's room, opened it, and ushered him inside. "Ten minutes, Thomas. That's all."

"Right, Sister." He walked to the side of the bed where

Katrina lay, one child tucked up under each arm beside her. He could see that she was still exhausted, but her color was better.

"Oh, Thomas, aren't they beautiful?" Katrina whispered.

"Aye."

"Thomas, I'd like you to meet your second son and Irish namesake, Thomas Matthew Callahan III."

Tom's eyes widened, and he peeked inside the blanket that Katrina pulled aside to reveal a dark-haired, sleeping baby.

"And your new daughter," Katrina beamed, as Tom leaned over her to the far side of the bed. "Teresa Moira Callahan." When Katrina pulled back the blanket, the tiny, fair-haired infant screwed up her face. She blinked her small, unfocused eyes, and her bottom lip quivered.

Tom was silent as he looked back and forth between the two helpless infants, now added to the growing family the Lord had placed under his protection. His gaze finally fell upon Katrina who had watched his face as he observed his two new children. PJ was now sixteen months old, and the coming of the twins had nearly doubled the size of their family. Tom reached out and stroked the side of Katrina's face, loving her with his eyes.

"You don't mind, Thomas? Calling our daughter Teresa, I mean? She *was* my friend."

"I understand," he said, bending over to lightly kiss her forehead. "And Sister Mary will be pleased at 'Moira,' too." Tom looked once more at each infant, kissed Katrina again, and lifted a strand of hair away from her eyes. The thought of the horrible possibilities of the previous evening was foremost in his mind. He dropped to his knees beside the bed and buried his face in the blankets at Katrina's side.

"I'm so sorry, Katie, that I wasn't able to be there for

you," he stammered, "to provide the blessing you needed. Oh, God, please forgive me."

Katrina remained silent and stroked her husband's hair as he poured out his grief, sobbing into the bedclothes.

"I love you, Katie. I do *so* love you."

Tom had not gone straight home from the hospital after the births, but had walked for several hours down the length of Brigham Street and then back home through the lower Avenues. Walking alone, that time of night, Tom was stopped by the police department foot patrolman with whom, once he was identified, he had shared a few moments. Emotionally ragged, he had spent the time pondering his life and his relationship with Katrina, his growing fatherly duties, and the place of religion in their marriage. His thoughts ran wild, and he was filled alternately with a sense of well-being and anxiety that bordered on despair. He raged inwardly at the idea of having to call on Geoffrey Masterton to pray for Katrina, assisted by his *houseman*. He considered such options as offering Katie a divorce, renouncing his Catholic faith, and even surrendering and joining the Mormon Church. By four o'clock in the morning he had dismissed each of these thoughts and found himself standing, cold and emotionally spent, in front of Robert Thurston's home.

Robert answered the door wearing his robe, his hair disheveled.

"Tom, is Katrina all right?" he asked.

Tom stepped inside, brushing past Robert as Alice came down the stairs, tying her dressing robe around her as she descended. Tom walked, as if in a daze, into the living room and sat down in the darkness. Alice turned on the light and stood close to her husband, the fear showing in her eyes.

"Tom?" Robert said, hesitantly.

Tom looked up at his two friends, waiting fearfully for the impending news. "Katrina's all right. And the twins are both well."

"Thank God," Alice exhaled, covering her mouth with her hand.

"Katrina hemorrhaged, badly," Tom continued, now staring at the floor. "She nearly . . ." He looked up again, holding Robert's eyes as he spoke. "Geoffrey Masterton and Henry, our *butler*, gave a priesthood blessing to her. Robert, our *butler* gave my wife a blessing while I watched, helpless." Tom stood, his hands outstretched toward Robert. "Why can't this God you all love show me? SHOW ME SOME-THING!" he pleaded.

News of the mine disaster at Winter Quarters Coal Mine, near Helper, Utah, in May of the new year, swept through the Salt Lake community like a wind roaring out of the canyons.

The afternoon of the day following the explosion, Anders recognized Reed Smoot when he came through the door of the bank. The thirty-eight-year-old friend of the Richards family had been sustained as the newest member of the Council of the Twelve Apostles at the just concluded April general conference, and Anders wondered what the newly appointed Church leader might want.

"Elder Smoot. How nice to see you in Utah Trust Bank," Anders greeted him.

"Thank you, Brother Hansen. I actually came to see you, if you have a moment?"

"Certainly," Anders said, quickly scanning the lobby. "Jean, will you watch the front please, for a few minutes?" he asked one of the tellers.

"Of course, Mr. Hansen."

"Brother Smoot, let's step into our conference room. We can have a bit of privacy in there."

Seated at the oblong table, Anders waited for Smoot to initiate the conversation.

"So, how are you and Sarah doing?" he asked, smiling.

"She's made me a very happy man, Brother Smoot."

"Yes, I can see that. And you've done wonders for her, too, Anders," Smoot said. The Apostle adjusted his spectacles and leaned forward. "Of course you've heard about the mining disaster down in Helper?"

"Yes, sir."

"An awful thing. I've been instructed by President Snow to attend along with several of the Brethren to conduct a general funeral service. I'll be driving down tomorrow. I stopped in to ask if you could possibly accompany me. We'd be gone two or three days."

Anders rested his arm on the table and nodded his head thoughtfully. "Well, I could talk with Robert about . . ."

"You're wondering why I'd like you to come along. All I can say really is that I'd like to talk with you about a few important things and thought this might provide the opportunity and the time. It has nothing to do with the mine episode or the bank."

"I see," Anders replied. "Well, then, Brother Smoot, I guess I'm up for a brief visit to Southern Utah."

"Good. I'll pick you up at your place tomorrow morning about nine. Be sure to dress warmly," he laughed. "I've just purchased a new Packard and it's apt to be a bit chilly in the mountains."

"All right, sir. Thank you for the invitation."

Smoot stood and his expression became serious. "The visit itself, Brother Hansen, will be quite sorrowful. First reports indicate nearly two hundred miners are dead. We will be in a dire situation down there."

"I understand, sir. I'll be ready at nine."

Later that day, Sarah greeted Anders with a kiss and a lingering hug when he arrived home.

"When I think of all the time we wasted, waiting nearly a year to get married . . ." he joked as she walked back toward the kitchen.

"I had a visit from Reed Smoot today, Sarah," Anders said while hanging up his overcoat. "He's asked me to go down to Helper with him. He's been assigned to conduct a funeral for the miners."

"Why does he need you?" she called from the kitchen.

Anders entered the kitchen and sat at the table. "I don't know. He said he just wanted to talk to me. It has nothing to do with the mine incident."

Sarah stirred the pot of soup, then came to sit at the table. "He's one of the Twelve now, Anders. Do you think he could be calling you on a mission or a church assignment?"

Anders shook his head. "I wouldn't think so, Sarah. More likely, if that were the reason, he'd have me come to his office in a more formal setting. I just don't know."

"Father says Brother Smoot will likely stand for political office in the near future. Maybe it's about that."

"I don't know how I could help him there, either," Anders said. "Well, some dinner would be great and then maybe we can walk over to Tom and Katrina's. He's got a good sense about these things."

"That's great. I'd love seeing the twins."

"But first," he said, pulling her to him, "another kiss from the cook is overdue."

⁓

By the time Smoot had driven the forty miles to Provo, Anders had a much better understanding of the reason he'd been invited to make the trip. The open-carriage Packard rumbled along the main road smoothly at about twenty-five to thirty miles an hour, although Smoot seemed unsure of the controls.

"That's a pretty big step, Brother Smoot," Anders said, shaking his head. "I mean no disrespect, sir, but what brings you to the conclusion that I'm electable?"

"Anders, the story of your heroic efforts in Cuba is well known. You have that certain demeanor that allows people to trust you. A presence—a confidence if you will. I trusted you immediately, or I'd never have permitted you to continue to see Sarah," he laughed. "Although, Brother Richards may have had something to say about that also. But seriously, Anders, running for Utah's congressional seat will be a hard job. If elected, filling it will be even harder. How soon could you complete your law apprenticeship?"

"Well, Tom's course will be much longer, since he can't attend as frequently, but I think it will take only another year or so to complete my degree and law training."

"That's fine. It's not necessary, of course, but a handy credential for lawmakers. Now you'll want to talk this over with Sarah, of course, because if you're elected, you'd have to move to Washington D.C. She might be concerned about leaving her family."

Anders nodded. "She's quite a levelheaded woman,"

he laughed, "but of course, you'd know that already. I appreciate your confidence, Brother Smoot. It's just that I really hadn't thought of my future in terms of political office."

"Anders, Utah needs dedicated leaders who understand the Church's position. There are opposing views on most things we believe in, and we need to assure our support is strong. Since statehood, the First Presidency has made a concerted effort to withdraw from government issues and to expand the Lord's missionary work throughout the world. That's why the Brethren have begun to counsel new members to remain in their own countries and build up the Church there. Still, we need to be sure that everything we have worked so hard to achieve in these valleys is not dissolved by several years of unopposed Gentile leadership. We need to accommodate one another, to be sure, but each perspective should be viewed in light of how it will impact other perspectives. I trust your instincts, and I believe our people will, too."

"Again, sir, I'm flattered. I would like to discuss it with Sarah, and my sister and her husband. Then, of course, I'd like to pray about it."

Smoot looked across at Anders and smiled. "That's the right path, Anders. And I'm sure you'll find the answer. Now," he said, pulling off the main road and crossing to a smaller, rougher road, "it's a long, slow climb up into the mountains. Might as well lay your head back and take a nap."

"Maybe I will, sir, but the countryside is quite beautiful at the moment," Anders said as they entered the canyon.

"Ever get homesick for Norway?" Smoot asked.

"Yah. And the fjords. But the mountains here are a constant reminder of home. And Sarah is here," he smiled.

Tom, Katrina, Sarah, and Anders sat in the parlor following dinner. Katrina was discreetly nursing three-week-old Teresa while Tommy slept in a cradle at her feet. The discussion of Katrina's health had by Sister Mary and Katrina had resulted in Katrina promising to tell Thomas, "when the time is right." Sister Mary had raised her eyebrows, hesitant to let the issue slip away, but in the end, she had agreed that it was Katrina's decision.

"He must know, my child. Your life could very well be at risk, and I'm quite certain that Thomas values your health more than he does a larger family."

"I promise," Katrina had said, but as yet, the issue had remained unspoken between husband and wife.

Anders was shaking his head as he recounted his trip with Elder Smoot. "Tom, the scene was almost unbearable. Literally hundreds of children stood with their mothers, brothers, and sisters while rows and rows of coffins lay stretched out in the field. All those children without fathers," Anders said. "You can't imagine the sorrow."

"A tough thing, Andy," Tom said.

Sarah sat next to Anders and linked her arm in his while he spoke.

"It's not just tough, Tom. I think it's criminal, and so does Brother Smoot. The safety conditions in those mines are appalling. If something happens, the miners literally have no chance to get out. Tom, I don't mean any offense, but as one of the owners, can't you do something about it?"

Tom nodded. "We've discussed it, Andy, and the owners agree in principle. UTB has only an eighteen percent interest in Winter Quarters. We *are* one of the three largest shareholders though."

"Tom, you know *in principle* sounds good, but it doesn't result in any action."

"I know, Andy. I'll bring it up again, and the newspaper accounts will likely force the Board's hand. We'll have to take some action. We've already decided to compensate the miners' families with approximately a year's salary."

"Well, that will be appreciated and needed, I'm sure. So," Anders said, his face brightening, "what is the family consensus on the other matter up for decision?"

Katrina leaned down and tucked the blanket tighter around little Tommy and continued to nurse Teresa. She gave Anders a bright smile and nodded in the affirmative. Tom saw her signal and also turned toward Anders. "I'd be proud, Andy."

"Well, then I guess the final support has to come from the most important person, eh?" he said, patting his wife's knee. "What does the lovely Mrs. Hansen have to say?" he asked.

Sarah looked at Tom and Katrina then turned to face Anders. "Whither thou goest, I go. Thy people shall be my people," she said. "I think I left something out there," she laughed, embarrassed. "But, you do understand, don't you, darling? I will support you in all that you do in righteousness."

Anders kissed Sarah lightly and patted her hand. "Well, that settles it. Now starts the hard part. Brother Smoot advised me of this as well. I need to get a campaign manager and to start raising some funds. I thought I might find both right in my own family," he laughed out loud. "Ever managed a political campaign, Tom?" Anders said.

"Is that an offer or an honor, and how much is it going to cost me?" Tom said, straight-faced.

"Tom, all joking aside. I'd be honored if you would side

with me in this run for office, but you should know about one important issue and where I stand."

Tom nodded his head again. "From where I sit, Mr. Would-Be-Congressman, the hot topic is mine safety. You can hammer that subject all you like, Congressman Hansen. I'll support you."

"Thank you, Tom. Thank you very much."

PART TWO

8

In the years 1900 to 1906, Katrina filled two volumes of her personal journal. Her periodic jottings were those of a woman who loved her family and was superficially happy, but who was spiritually unfulfilled. Giving birth to the twins had nearly proved fatal, yet in the experience she had drawn closer to God. Though she had never discussed it with Tom, she kept in constant remembrance the priesthood blessing she had received at the hands of Brother Masterton and Henry. She knew it had preserved her life. That and a hundred other daily occurrences had bolstered her faith in the priesthood and the gospel she had so happily embraced as a young woman in Norway.

There were times, while singing in the Tabernacle Choir, attending church, or reading the Book of Mormon, that her testimony burned within her. What she had verbalized only to her sister-in-law, Sarah Hansen, was her sadness that Thomas was as yet unable or unwilling to embrace the truths she cherished. He was a good man—a loving husband and kind father, to say nothing of his performance as a generous provider. After two years of marriage, and without formal declaration, they had reached an accord with regard to Mormonism. He never stood in the way of her activity in her church and in fact sometimes attended with her. He gave his approval to the children being raised in his wife's faith. Yet they remained unequally yoked in the matter, and Katrina's heart often ached to have Tom join with her in worship and attend the temple with her. For her, it was all they were lacking in their life together, but it was something for which, privately, Katrina could not help constantly yearning.

As for Tom, his personal accord eventually came in the form of a reluctant acceptance that other men whom he admired and respected, yet resented, including Captain Geoffrey Masterton, would provide the spiritual guidance and occasional blessings his wife and children would need. When Robert Thurston was called to serve as bishop of their ward in 1903, he became a more frequent visitor in their home. Having his partner and friend serve as a spiritual adviser to his family was less embarrassing to Tom than if some other man had intervened in their personal lives. Tom had such a respect for Robert that it was impossible to view him in his role as bishop as anything other than a welcome member of the Callahan family, rather than merely Tom's financial partner and president of Utah Trust Bank.

Katrina's inner accord was different. With the help of those whom she loved, her mother among them—a woman who had wrestled most of her life with a domineering, albeit Mormon, husband—Katrina tried to be grateful for the fact that she had a good husband, and, seen in the broader light her mother presented, often a far better companion than some husbands who were already members of the Church. It helped that she loved Tom passionately and couldn't even imagine life without him. That was the problem. She believed in, and longed for, a celestial marriage, but for now she had no assurance her husband would ever join her in that union.

Her fear of the fact that perhaps Tom would never be able to fulfill her fondest wish, that of a temple marriage, caused her to spend long hours in prayer and to seek out several private sessions with Bishop Thurston, including one at which David O. McKay, high councilor in his stake, as well as a family friend, was also present.

Once Robert had changed roles and become her bishop, she found that he had always been aware of the inner conflict with which she wrestled. An added benefit was that Robert himself had come to love his business partner and to admire the policies Tom had established for the bank—policies that reflected Tom's own character and integrity, and, as the name of the bank implied, trust. Had it not been so, Robert had told Katrina, he would not have been able to continue as Tom's partner.

"How then," she had asked him, "do we get Tom to take the final step?"

"We don't," he had replied. "Tom has to find his own way on this."

Katrina had nodded her assent. They both realized that such a decision would depend on Tom's ability to respond to the Lord's promptings. Katrina could only hope the man she loved would one day embrace the truths of the gospel. Until then, she would continue to pray for him and try to be patient.

She sometimes felt guilty because of her feelings of discontent. She lived a life of relative ease and comfort. Her days were filled with joy, service to many other families, and above all, a deep and abiding love for her husband and four children. Yes, four. Katrina had not heeded Sister Mary's nor her doctor's warnings to avoid another pregnancy following the birth of the twins, Tommy and Teresa.

She had in fact not shared her medical prognosis with Tom. Not wanting to concede her inability to bear another child, Katrina hadn't even detailed her condition in her journal. Instead, she agonized alone over her condition. Given the doctor's warnings, she was fearful she might not be able to bring a baby to term or even to survive another pregnancy. Still, as the twins grew to become toddlers, she found herself desperately wanting another baby. Struggling to know what to do, she had an experience that convinced her to get pregnant again.

After lying awake through much of one hot summer night, listening to Tom's snoring and fretting yet again about his refusal to embrace the gospel, she had at last fallen asleep. She dreamed about a blond, fair-skinned, green-eyed young boy. He said nothing, but stood silently at the foot of her bed, gazing at her with a warm, laughing smile. And when she awoke in the morning, and in the days that followed, she couldn't get his innocent face out of her mind.

When she finally became pregnant, Katrina sat in Sister Mary's office at Holy Cross Hospital and delivered the news. Sister Mary lowered her head, looked over her glasses at Katrina, and slowly shook her head.

"There's no turning back now, my child," she said.

"I know, Sister," Katrina had smiled, knowing of this one concept where Catholics and Mormons were in total agreement. "I'll just trust in the Lord."

And so it was that on February 13, 1905, Benjamin Lars Callahan became the fourth child and third son of Thomas and Katrina Callahan. With three doctors, Sister Mary, and several nursing sisters present, Benjamin appeared, as Katrina knew he would, without incident. To the medical staff, he was a miracle baby. To Katrina, he was a gift from God.

By 1906, Katrina's brother, Anders Hansen, had been serving in the United States Congress for two years. Acting on Reed Smoot's suggestion, Anders had in fact become a candidate for Utah's congressional seat in 1900, but had withdrawn his bid for office in favor of another party selectee. He had instead stood for and been elected to the Utah Legislature where he was serving in 1903 when President Theodore Roosevelt visited Utah. Upon being introduced to the one-armed assemblyman, Roosevelt instantly recollected the service the young medic had rendered to the Rough Riders in Cuba in 1898. Armed with the popular president's endorsement and a generous campaign contribution provided by Tom, Anders had been elected to Congress in 1904.

Viewed as an up-and-coming political figure, things had gone well for Anders and his beautiful wife. Except for one thing. They had remained childless during the six years of their marriage. If passion and longing could have produced a child, the couple would have had a quiver-full, but they had not succeeded in the one area that Utah society viewed as most vital, and it had created a sadness in their marriage.

On a cold, early spring day, during one of Sarah's increasingly rare visits home to Utah, Katrina and Sarah were working in the Callahan's big kitchen, preparing food to take to the home of a woman in the ward whose young husband had died suddenly of pneumonia. Chopping vegetables for a pot of soup, Katrina watched the industrious Sarah as the younger woman rolled out pie crusts on the kitchen table. The two had found themselves remarkably compatible. Sarah especially loved helping Katrina with the children, and the three older children—PJ, Tommy, and Teresa—had responded lovingly to their aunt.

"Oh, Katrina," Anders's pretty and enthusiastic wife had exclaimed one day, "you're the sister I never had!"

Her hands and wrists now covered with flour, Sarah blew ineffectively at some loose strands of auburn hair that had escaped their pins and were dangling in front of her face. Katrina reached to brush the hair back, and in that small act felt again the joy of having such a friend. As Sarah smiled her thanks, Katrina inexplicably began to cry, and she turned quickly away to hide her tears.

From the day they were first introduced, they had been drawn to each other and had almost immediately fallen into the pattern of sharing their innermost thoughts and feelings. Katrina had spent countless hours consoling Sarah over what had become a constant heartache—her inability to conceive—a painful fact that she was reminded of each month. After a time, Katrina had even confided in her sister-in-law her own sadness over Tom's unwillingness or inability to embrace the gospel—going so far as to allow herself to wonder out loud if she had done a prudent thing by bringing children into a marriage not sealed by the priesthood.

Isn't it ironic, Katrina thought, watching Sarah work with the pie dough, *that Sarah should have the priesthood in her home but no children, while I have children but no priesthood?*

Later that day, after attending the heart-wrenching funeral and helping afterward to serve dinner to the deceased man's extended family, the two emotionally spent sisters-in-law collapsed for a moment on the couch in Katrina's parlor. Recalling the grief-stricken young widow and her sorrowing children, Katrina said to Sarah, "I guess we don't need to look very far to find those who are in more pain or difficulty than we are, do we?"

"How true," Sarah agreed. "But God is good. Perhaps all we can do is trust that he cares for us, and that things will work out for the best."

Too tired for the moment to offer any other solution, Katrina could only smile and say, "I suppose you're right, Sarah. I suppose you're right."

———⊙⊙⊙———

And so 1906 moved on toward summer. Utah Trust Bank was continuing to prosper; Tom was providing everything possible for his family, save one thing; PJ was growing strong, dependable, and righteous—"an ambassador of goodwill," grandfather Lars called him; and although younger, Tommy was already showing a rebellious streak, "somewhat like myself," Tom allowed. Teresa—"Tess" to everyone by now—was becoming more winsome and coy; and baby Benjamin was willing to cuddle with anyone who would hold him.

Certain issues beyond religion occasionally cropped up to hinder the tranquility of their lives, but, on the whole, Katrina thought that Tom had become a fine father and husband. There was one incident, however, that had required her to adamantly oppose Tom and, as a result, they hadn't spoken for days.

In September, 1906, young Tommy had entered first grade and had come home from his third day of school with a small cut over his eye. Immediately, Katrina had questioned him about what had happened. When he didn't respond, PJ had spoken up. Tess, also in first grade, entered the room and took a seat, listening to the story.

"He got in a fight, Mom," PJ had said with a semblance of pride in his younger brother. "And he won, too."

"A fight?" Katrina asked. "Why?"

"It's not Tommy's fault, Mom, really," PJ continued. "Butch Tully tried to take his money."

"Who's Butch Tully?" Katrina asked.

"He's in the third grade with me. He always picks on the smaller kids. Can we have some milk?"

"Later, PJ," Katrina said, becoming exasperated at trying to pull information out of her sons. "Did you see this fight, Tess?" she asked.

"Nope. I walked home with Rachel."

"Well, will someone *please* tell me what happened?" Katrina said.

"Mom, nothing happened," Tommy said.

"Sit right down on the couch, young man," she said to Tommy. "You too, PJ, while I send for your father. Perhaps you'll answer *his* questions."

The boys fidgeted for several minutes while Katrina asked Henry to drive to the bank and ask her husband to come home. Tommy sat uncomfortably in the parlor for the thirty minutes it took his father to arrive. He was at first afraid of how Tom was going to respond, but as they talked about what had happened, Tommy could see his father was actually proud of him for standing up to the older boy. Of course his dad wasn't able, in the presence of Tommy's mother, to actually praise his son, but the man and boy nevertheless communicated.

Most of the description of the school-yard scuffle came from PJ. Shocked by her young son's behavior, Katrina alternated between asking for additional information and saying she didn't want to hear any more about the incident.

"Dad, Butch is a bully. He's too chicken to take on

anyone bigger or older, but he's picked on the first graders every day since school started and made them give him their lunch money or something. Tommy said no, and Butch hit him."

"And then what?" Tom asked, trying to keep from smiling in the face of the "emergency" Katrina had described when she had sent Henry to ask him to come home.

"Then I showed him the left jab and the right hook you taught us, Dad. It really works," Tommy said, smiling, but quickly regaining a straight face as his mother frowned at him.

"Seems he handled it well, Katie," Tom shrugged. "What can I say?"

"Thomas, I will not have fighting promoted among my children."

"Would you rather your son was beaten up?" Tom said, taking his handkerchief and kneeling in front of Tommy to wipe the cut on his forehead.

Before Katrina could respond, Henry stepped into the room. "Mr. Callahan, there is a Mr. Tully asking to see you."

"Ask him to come in, Henry."

"Excuse me, sir. Mr. Tully specifically asked that you come out on the front steps to speak with him."

"All right," Tom said, rising and tousling Tommy's hair and giving him a quick wink that was hidden from Katrina's view.

"That'd be Butch's dad, I bet," PJ said.

"Well, let's see what he wants," Tom said. The children scrambled off the couch and followed their father to the front door. Katrina followed closely behind.

"Mr. Tully," Tom said as he stepped out onto the porch and offered his hand. "How can I be of service?" Tommy stood next to his dad while Katrina, PJ, and Tess remained just inside the door.

Ignoring Tom's offer to shake hands, Tully said, "For one thing, you can control your brat."

Tom raised an eyebrow and smiled at the other father.

"Ah, Mr. Tully, it seems our lads just had a misunderstanding. Isn't that right, son?" Tom said to the young boy standing behind Tully.

"I wouldn't call a chipped tooth and a black eye a *misunderstanding*, Callahan." Mr. Tully reached down at Tom's side and grabbed young Tommy's arm, shaking him. "You, young man, need a good hiding," he said loudly.

"I think you'd best take your hands off my son, Mr. Tully," Tom said, his smile now gone.

"I suppose you support his behavior, Callahan. No wonder the kid gets in fights," Tully said, continuing to shake Tommy's arm.

Tully was bent over slightly, holding on to Tommy. The quick, downward punch went unseen by Katrina who had been reaching for Tommy to pull him away from Mr. Tully's grasp. Suddenly, Tully was stretched out, face down, on the steps in front of her home, and his son, Butch, was wide-eyed and backing away.

"Thomas!" Katrina shrieked.

By then, Tom was bending down to help Mr. Tully regain his feet. "Perhaps we can discuss this some other time, Mr. Tully," Tom said.

Tully regained his feet, rubbing his jaw and scowling at Tom. "You ain't heard the last of this, Callahan," he said. As the Tullys were leaving, young Tommy called out, "Hey, Butch. See ya tomorrow," just before his mother grabbed him more roughly than Mr. Tully had, moments earlier.

"Inside, and up to your room," Katrina commanded.

For three days, Tom endured the absolute silent treatment from Katrina, until, finally, he had pleaded with her to forget the incident. She had extracted a solemn promise from him that he would never again strike another person. None of the exceptions Tom tried to add to the bargain, such as self-defense or danger-to-the-family situations, were acceptable. The boxing lessons Tom had been giving to Tommy and PJ were also ended, and any further discussion of the incident was avoided. Tommy's comment to his father one evening, a couple of weeks later, that Butch wasn't bothering any of the younger kids anymore, brought only a quick wink, a smile, and a nod of the head.

Teresa, at six, and also in the first grade, provided a completely different sort of challenge to Tom. Almost since birth she had known what most little girls discover if they are observant—that their fathers will do whatever they want if they present their case well. While reading the newspapers in the evening, Tom would often only grunt in response to his sons' questions and even to Katrina's attempts at conversation. They all knew that their father was not paying any real attention to their entreaties.

Tess, however, would worm her way up under his newspaper, take her father's face in both her little hands, look him straight in the eye, and make her case. As she perfected the maneuver, she added a kiss on the cheek and a wink of her bright blue eye. Tom would lay the paper aside and listen with full attention to his pretty daughter's prattle. She discovered early that her father could be cajoled in this way to giving into just about anything she asked. As young as they were, her brothers weren't blind to their sister's ability to get what she wanted. In fact, they had watched their mother use a similar version of the same technique to get around Tom and get what she wanted. It was a strategy they could never use and something they understood was simply a female privilege.

Before his children were born, Tom had assumed that being married to Katrina would be the greatest pleasure he would enjoy in life. Fatherhood, however, had opened up a whole new set of perspectives. Watching his children at play, he often thought of his own childhood in Ireland. He had loved his mother, but his father had been a tyrant who bullied Tom and the other children and made life miserable for the whole family—especially when he came home drunk. Remembering, Tom was grateful for the influence of Father O'Leary, who, shortly after Tom's arrival in New York, had pointed out to the young brawler the frightening direction alcohol was taking him.

While eating dinner with his children or watching them seated around their mother as she read to them in the evening, it made him happy to be able to provide them a safe place to grow up, where they could live without fear of him. Being a father had brought out a gentleness in him that often surprised him, and he was enormously protective of his children. It was true that he still had a temper, and his children could provoke him, but he always felt bad after raising his voice to reprimand them or following the occasional spanking he administered. By and large, it pleased Tom to treat his children in a kindly way.

The circumstances of Benjamin's birth helped Tom understand the premium that Katrina placed on her own parental role. He hadn't known, until the doctor made a remark about Katrina's good fortune, following the successful delivery of Benjamin, the danger Katrina had put herself in by becoming pregnant again. Learning the truth about her condition and realizing how near he had come to losing her had shocked Tom to the core. It had also increased his admiration to say nothing of his love for her.

While discussing the birth of Benjamin with Robert Thurston a few days later, Tom's business partner observed that there was a biblical precedent.

"Jacob and Rachel's last-born son was also named Benjamin, but unlike Rachel, who died giving birth, Katrina had been spared. You're a lucky man, Thomas. God has given you one final child to care for, and has seen fit also to permit you to continue to love and care for Katrina as well."

Apart from any specific religious feeling, Tom found himself awed by the responsibility involved in being a husband and father. He never confronted Katrina with his new-found knowledge regarding her medical condition, but was privately pleased when both Katrina and the doctor informed him, together, that she would be unable to have any more children and that medical procedures had been effected to assure her health.

As 1907 approached, Katrina continued to write in her journal, to pour her heart and soul out to Nana, the one confidant who was privy to all the things, or at least most of the things, that occurred in Katrina Callahan's life. At twenty-eight, with Sarah Hansen a couple of years younger, she hoped there was yet time for both of their desires to be fulfilled—children for Sarah, and Tom's Church membership for Katrina.

The convocation hall was filled with family members, friends, and neighbors, gathered to watch the commencement ceremonies for the University of Utah, class of 1906. Seated with Robert and Alice Thurston and Anders and Sarah Hansen, Katrina wondered where her husband was and what was taking him so long to arrive. She was visibly nervous and glanced again at her pendant watch, an Easter gift from Tom. The Callahans and Hansens were home less than a week from a hurried trip to Europe, where on May 17, 1906, they had participated in independence day celebrations in honor of Norway's new nation status.

The collective buzz in Salt Lake City and in the convocation center still revolved around the disastrous earthquake in San Francisco that had occurred a few days after the Callahans and Hansens had left for Norway. Upon arriving home, Tom had learned from Robert that Gary Simonsen, the San Francisco attorney who had originally purchased Tom's Alaska gold claims, had been killed, along with over five hundred other people in the catastrophe.

Katrina looked again at her watch. "I don't understand it, Robert. He's never late for such events. I hope nothing's wrong."

"Don't fret, Katie," Sarah said, "I'm sure he'll be right along, or that he'll have a reasonable explanation, and if he doesn't make it in here in time, he'll probably be with the graduates as they form up outside."

"I attended the choir's practice last week, Katie," Alice said, trying to divert her attention. "The rendition of Bach was overwhelming."

"Thank you, Alice. I so love that number. We're going to sing it in October conference."

"That will be lovely," Alice added.

The university orchestra began to play, and quiet descended over the auditorium. After several minutes, the orchestra commenced to play "Pomp and Circumstance," and the graduates of 1906 began to file into the auditorium. Katrina scanned the two lines of gowned graduates, watching for Tom to appear.

"Surely he wouldn't miss this moment, after all these years of effort," Katie said. "He always likes to be on time, and if I'm a minute late, with my hair or something, he's pacing up and down the hall."

"I declare," Anders said, "you're more nervous than Tom, Klinka. You'd think you were giving the commencement address."

"Ladies and gentlemen," the officiator began, "tonight we are honored to . . ."

Finally Katie relaxed and began to take interest in the proceedings, content to allow Tom his awkward entry should he arrive during the ceremonies. Following the commencement addresses, and presentation of special awards, the president of the university instructed the graduating class to rise, and the faculty and administration prepared to present the diplomas. The first row of students began to file toward the stage, waiting for their names to be called.

"Wilson Talmage Addison, Bachelor of Science, Astronomy," the announcer called. A smattering of applause rose from the audience.

"Henry Madison Baker, Bachelor of Arts, Music." More applause, from a different section of the audience.

Katie studied the graduates again, frustrated by the uniform look the caps and gowns gave their appearance. She caught Robert's eye for a moment, and he smiled at her, giving her a quick wink. He whispered, "They all look alike in their robes, Katie. He'll be all right."

"Geraldine Marie Brubaker, Bachelor of Science, with honors in Mathematics," the officiator continued.

"Thomas Matthew Callahan, Bachelor of Science, Economics," the announcer called. Katie's head jerked upright, and she looked toward the podium as Tom made his way down the aisle toward the stage. Under the mortarboard, there he was, the University of Utah's latest graduate in economics. Tom bounced up the stairs, his black gown flowing, then walked briskly across the stage to shake the university president's hand and receive his parchment scroll.

Katie beamed as if her firstborn were graduating. She had a quick, fleeting thought of her long-ago dream of attending the university and becoming a teacher. She smiled to herself, quickly dismissing the thought. She looked over toward Robert and Alice who were smiling and clapping enthusiastically. On her other side, Anders and Sarah were likewise engaged. As Tom descended the far side of the stage, filing back along his row to resume his seat with his classmates, Katie took a moment to review the printed graduation program. She traced the names alphabetically down the list and paused as her finger came to the name, Callahan, Thomas Matthew, Bachelor of Science, Economics. Sure enough, after nearly nine years of marriage and seven years of intermittent study, Tom was listed with the other graduates.

Katie's tears appeared as she reached for Robert's hand. "It is a fine evening, Robert. I'm so proud of him."

Afterward, during a late supper at the Knudsen House, Tom explained how his punctured tire had forced him, in cap and gown, to scurry up Second South, all the way to the university, arriving breathless and sweaty underneath the robe. He was in fine form and kept the six of them laughing through the evening as he parried the good-natured teasing he took from the other five about his advanced age among so many young college students. Finally, as the evening got late, the couples said good night and went their separate ways.

Later, in the privacy of their bedroom suite, Tom lay

propped up on his pillow watching Katrina brush her hair. After a time, she turned out the light and joined her husband in bed.

"So, Mr. Callahan, newly possessed of a university degree, has it made you any smarter?" Katie laughed as she snuggled up to him in the moonlight that was coming through the east window.

"I think not, Katie. The smartest decision I ever made is still the one I made while an ignorant Irish lad, running away from the law—the one I made on the *Antioch* when my heart sang out to me, 'She's the one, Tommy, me lad.'"

"Mr. Callahan," she said, rolling closer to kiss his lips. "I think the Irish were born with a degree in linguistics. It's genetic, I believe."

"Why thank you, lass," he laughed, and pulled her into his arms.

April conference, 1906, caused quite a stir in the Salt Lake community. In October of the previous year, two of the members of the Twelve had resigned their positions on the Council. When newly called Apostles were read into the record for general membership sustaining vote, thirty-two-year-old David O. McKay was among those sustained. Tom and Katrina were not in attendance, having already left Utah for Norway and the celebrations.

Now, at the October conference, Tom smiled as he looked down from his seat in the Tabernacle balcony at his old friend sitting on the dais with President Joseph F. Smith and the other General Authorities. Katrina, as usual, held her place on stage with the choir. Tom's increasing family, however, had added to his space requirement, since PJ,

Tommy, and Tess usually accompanied him. Young
Benjamin was left at home under care.

Following the session of conference, the children left
the temple grounds with Aunt Sarah who agreed to take
them home for the evening, and, if they were good, she had
said, to freeze some homemade ice cream. Tom waited as
usual for Katrina to arrive following her appearance with
the choir. He could see small groups of well-wishers gathered around Elder McKay and his tiny wife, Emma. Since
their marriage, the McKays had been occasional guests in
the Callahan home, and vice versa, but Elder McKay's
increasing church responsibilities had often taken him over-
seas for weeks at a time. Those responsibilities, Tom surmised, would only increase with his new calling.

Katie arrived just as the small gathering around D.O.
began to disperse, and the young Apostle started to walk
toward the south gate. Catching his eye just briefly, Tom
nodded and tipped his hat toward Emma. D.O. walked
straight over toward Tom and Katrina.

"Good day to the Callahans," McKay said.

"And a very good day to you, D.O., Emma," Tom said,
once more tipping his hat.

"I've been meaning to catch you one fine day, Tom. I've
just been carried away with duties abroad and elsewhere in
the States. I was present at your graduation, but was unable
to find you in the crowd after the ceremonies. My sincere
congratulations on a well-deserved honor. I know you
worked long and hard on that degree and on your legal
training. A lawyer *and* a banker—a formidable combination," McKay smiled. "This man is just full of surprises, isn't
he, Katrina?" he laughed.

"My life has been one *big* surprise since he came along.

A *pleasant* surprise, mind you," she added, slipping her arm into Tom's and smiling warmly.

"And it seems a measure of honor has developed in *your* life while we were in Europe," Tom offered.

McKay cocked his head sideways and clicked his lips. "Well, I imagine it seems that way to some, Tom, but it is in fact a very humbling experience. There are so many worthy men who—"

"David," Tom said, reaching for his hand. "Bishop Scanlan himself has told me on many occasions that the Lord doesn't always call the most worthy, or the best qualified. But, and this is where I believe both your religion and mine concur, the Lord *always* qualifies whomever He calls. I think He made the right choice, *Elder* McKay," Tom smiled brightly. "And now, if I remember it right from our early-morning walk in Scotland some years ago, '*What 'ere thou art, act well thy part.*'"

David smiled, nodded his head, and clasped Tom's hand in both of his. "It seems that perhaps we both have a mission to accomplish in this world, Mr. Callahan. In that regard, perhaps I could come and speak with you at your bank one day soon. President Smith is preparing to clear the final bond indebtedness on the Church. I'd appreciate the advice of Utah Trust Bank's chairman," he smiled.

"My door is always open to you, Brother McKay. Please come at your pleasure."

"Thank you, Tom, and thanks for your kind words. Emma and I would love to have you and Katrina join us some evening for dinner, if that would suit your plans."

"We would love that, Elder McKay," Katrina said.

"It used to be D.O.," he teased.

"Yes, it did . . . *Elder* McKay," Katrina repeated.

"A lovely day to you both," McKay said, as he and his wife continued toward the south gate.

Tom and Katrina watched the couple walk away, and Katrina waved to several other choir members who were also leaving Temple Square.

"Thomas, did you enjoy the choir?" Katrina asked as they began to stroll toward the exit.

"Were there others singing?" he laughed.

"Thomas," she laughed, "you need a new scriptwriter. You've been saying that since the first conference you attended."

"Aye, and you've been asking me the same question, knowing well the answer," he said, holding on to her arm.

Katrina blushed slightly. "I'm sorry we missed the April conference. It would have been thrilling to have been here for the announcement of D.O.'s calling. What do you think of it?" she asked.

Tom thought for a moment as they exited Temple Square and began the walk up Brigham Street toward home. "It's as I said to him, Catholic or Mormon, the Lord chooses the right men it seems. D.O. has impressed me as a fine man since the day he pulled me out from under the hooves of a wild horse, right over . . . *there*," he pointed.

"Well, Thomas, if Brother McKay is the Lord's appointed, and if he saved your life so long ago, perhaps the Lord used Brother McKay on *that* occasion also," she beamed. "Maybe, as Brother McKay said, He has a purpose for you, too."

"Let's not be stretching the meaning, Katie," he chuckled.

"We shall see, Thomas. We shall see."

"You may well be right, as you often are," he smiled. "For now, let's go home and have some of that fine roast beef. Robert and Alice should be over in an hour or so."

"What was it Robert wanted to talk to you about?"

"I don't know, actually. He's always got some scheme or another afoot."

"I'll see the roast beef is rare enough for him," Katrina laughed. "He practically likes it to walk in from the kitchen."

"That he does," Tom laughed.

"But, Thomas, I don't want to go without you."

"Katie, we've been all through this several times. Please understand. I *need* to be here. The union issues are extremely volatile right now. In fact, they have been for some time. The bomb explosions at the Hotel Utah construction site last year were no accident. I'm afraid we can expect more of the same, if the militants have their way. Robert and I need to work closely with the other mine owners, and the governor, if we're to bring some sanity to these issues."

"I do understand that, Thomas," she said, cutting a sandwich in two and putting the plate in front of him. "But why must *I* go with Momma and Poppa back to Norway?"

"You know your parents are going anyway. It's 1911, Katie. Your father hasn't seen Norway since he first came to America in 1895. Lars . . . well, Lars has made it plain that he thinks he hasn't got much longer, and, from what your mother says, his doctor agrees. He wants to see Norway again before it's too late. And your mother, bless her heart, will be by his side every step of the way, but she can't really take care of him. She's not all that well herself."

Katrina sat down across from Tom, put her elbows on

the kitchen table, and, resting her chin in her hands, she stared at her husband.

"Thomas Callahan, who do you think you're *really* fooling? Not since you bought me that new car for my birthday, and told me it was for the bank, have I let you mislead me so," she smiled. "But this is serious. You want us out of the way because of the danger. Some of the other mine owners' wives have been talking. Their husbands feel the same way."

"And rightly so," Tom said, standing and filling his glass with milk, then setting it next to his plate. "Katie," he said, moving to stand behind her, placing his hands on her shoulders, and rubbing her neck. "*Please* do this for me. I'll feel so much better about what needs to be done if I know you and the children are safely away from Salt Lake and any possible trouble."

Katrina leaned her head back and looked upside down at Tom. "You know PJ can't, or more likely, won't go. He's determined to stay and keep his place in the bishop's new Boy Scout program."

"I know. I can deal with PJ, if the rest of the children are with you. He's thirteen, quite sensible, and he can pretty well take care of himself. Besides, he'll spend some of his time with Anders and Sarah while they're home from Washington. But if Tommy, Tess, and Benjamin are with you, I'll be able to relax a bit more."

Katrina stood up, turned around, and put her arms around Tom's neck. "The *last* thing you'll be doing, Mister Callahan, is relaxing. If no one is here to demand that you come home, you'll spend twenty hours a day at that bank. And what about Robert and Alice? I suppose you'll make him work long hours, too."

"Alice is probably having this same conversation with

Robert right now. He wants her to go down to St. George and stay with her sister."

"Fine," she growled. "Get all the women and children out of town and fight it out with the union. That's no answer."

"No, it's not," Tom said, exasperated. "But what choice have we got, Katie? We've put a lot of effort and years into this enterprise, and I don't intend to see it frittered away because a bunch of immigrants want to drag us down."

"Thomas, I'm surprised at you," Katie exclaimed. "We're *both* immigrants. You know that."

"Of course we are, Katie," he replied, his voice softer, "but we've tried to *contribute* to our world, not just demand that everything be given to us."

"In all fairness, Thomas, you have to admit, the Lord has blessed us greatly. There are some appalling conditions in those mines, and in the homes where those poor mothers have to raise their children—it just makes me want to cry."

He nodded and resumed his seat. "Indeed. They remind me of the coal mines in Ireland and the shacks throughout the village. But I'm *only* one man, Katie, and I'm not the sole owner of any of the mines in which UTB has an interest. I'll try, but if we give these union people an inch, the negotiators will rip our hearts out."

Katrina picked up Tom's plate and placed it in the sink. She leaned on her arms, hanging over the sink for several moments while Tom remained silent, watching her and knowing her thought process. Finally she turned around and leaned back against the sink, her arms folded across her chest.

"All right, Thomas. I'll take the children and go with Momma and Poppa. They'll be leaving in October, Momma said. But we'll be gone six months, Thomas. *Six* months.

They aren't planning on coming back until April. That's next year. Think about it. You're going to miss us, Mr. Banker."

Tom stood and stepped to the sink, where he took his wife in his arms. "I miss you already, Katie, just thinking about your not being here. But thank you, darling. Thank you. I know it's for the best."

"I hope so, Thomas. I sincerely hope so."

"Oh, by the way, Katie," Tom said as he started to exit the kitchen, "did you get a chance to visit Stan Telford's wife?"

"I certainly did," Katrina said, brightening. "It was such a moving experience. You didn't tell me that you had arranged for her to stay at Mrs. Brown's Rooming House, Thomas."

"Well, she had no way to get back and forth between the hospital and Park City. The company is taking care of it, Katie."

"Right," she said, grinning at her husband. "Anyway, I caught her in the foyer of the hospital and she invited me up to Mr. Telford's room. It was interesting. She went immediately to the window and pulled the drapes all the way back so her husband could see."

"Could see what?" Tom asked.

"That's just it, Thomas. As you know, he broke both his legs in that accident and is in traction, so he can't get out of bed. He was straining to see his son."

"Why didn't the boy come in with his mother?"

"He's only nine. Holy Cross rules prohibit children under fourteen from visiting the patients' rooms. Mrs. Telford told me that young Robert is staying with her at the boardinghouse and attending school here in Salt Lake. Every day, after school, he comes to the hospital and waves to his dad from outside."

Tom laughed. "That's great, Katie."

"Thomas, *that's* not the story."

"Excuse me?" Tom said, a puzzled look coming over his face.

"Sister Mary walked in while we were helping Mr. Telford lean forward so he could wave to his son."

"What did she say?" Tom asked.

"Nothing, but she saw what was happening and immediately left the room. In a few minutes, we saw her talking to little Robert. The two of them went into the ground floor of the building and to our surprise," Katrina said, clasping her hands together, "she appeared in the room a couple of minutes later."

"So?" Tom said.

"*So*, she had Robert hidden under her habit. She'd snuck the young lad into his father's room! Thomas, it was wonderful. Mr. Telford had tears in his eyes and hugged his son for a long moment. Sister Mary winked at me and left us alone for a while."

"Aha, the infamous 'rule-maker' and 'rule-breaker,' Sister Mary Theophane," Tom said.

"That's exactly right. I've never met a woman like her, Thomas. And I probably never will."

"One of God's true servants," Tom agreed.

"I'll bear witness to that. It was a fine moment," Katrina said.

Tom took the boys to Lake Blanche in Big Cottonwood Canyon—one more fishing trip before the voyage to Norway. This time, young Benjamin was included, his first venture into the mountains with the "men" of the Callahan family. Katrina had objected, but finally gave in at the pleadings of PJ and Tommy. Tom had simply sat in his parlor chair before the open fire and watched his sons cajole their mother into relenting. Tess had opted out of fishing, deciding instead to remain at home and have the run of the house without interference from her brothers.

With the tent set, dinner disposed of, and their other foodstuffs stacked off the ground, "to keep the bears away," the older boys had warned Benjamin, the Callahan men sat around the fire the first night out, listening to the fire pop in the stillness of the night. Seven-year-old Benjamin nestled on the log close to his dad, watching with big eyes as his older brothers played with sticks, pushing the burning embers around and jumping back as the sparks flashed upward.

"Dad, tell Benjie about the bear that ate the two boys up here last year," Tommy taunted.

Tom smiled and put his arm around Benjamin. "Better we send *you* out into the woods to look for that bear, Tommy," Tom replied.

PJ laughed and pushed his younger brother. "Yeah, Tommy, you're so brave, go find that bear and skin it," he challenged.

The bantering, ghost stories, and teasing continued through the evening until Tom finally thought that Benjamin had earned his place and put a stop to it. Long before nine o'clock, Benjamin had fallen asleep on the ground, wrapped in a heavy woolen blanket, and PJ had gone to the tent and curled up in his bedroll. Only Tom and eleven-year-old Tommy remained, sitting next to each other by the dying campfire.

"Dad, why are there so many more stars in the mountains?" Tommy asked, looking upward into the sky.

"There are the same number as in the city, Tommy,"

Tom replied, "but with fewer city lights to block our vision, we can see them better."

The boy accepted the answer and sat quietly beside his father. Tom's thoughts drifted to the one and only time his father had taken him and his older brother, John, to fish and camp out overnight on the Shannon River, a few miles from Limerick. He had few such memories of Ireland and fewer still of good times with his father.

"Why can't I stay with you, Pop?" Tommy asked, breaking the silence.

"What do you mean, Tommy?"

"When Mom takes Tess and Benjie to Norway with Grandma and Grandpa, why can't I stay? PJ's staying home."

"PJ's entering the Boy Scout program, Tommy. You know that. He's actually going to stay most of the time with Uncle Anders and Aunt Sarah. I think he'd really like to go on the trip, but he wants to become a Scout."

"Well, I do, too."

Tom smiled and pulled his son closer to him, hugging the lad. "You're not old enough, Tommy. Besides, Mom will need you to help with Benjamin and to carry luggage. You know that Grandpa is getting along in years."

"I know, I know," Tommy sighed. "That's what Mom said when I asked her. But I still don't see why I can't stay home with you and PJ."

"There's always got to be a man in charge of the family, Tommy. On this trip, that's you. I'm counting on you to take care of your mother and Tess and Benjamin. But speaking of being in charge, what's with the letter from your principal the other day? Mom said you got in trouble for fighting at school."

"Aw, it's nothin', Pop. We were just foolin' around, and

Eddie Ward started crying when he got pushed down. I wasn't fightin'."

"You know, Tommy," Tom laughed, "of all my sons, you remind me the most of myself at your age. And *that's* not a compliment. Of course, there *are* some differences. When I was your age, I was already working in my father's store. You, on the other hand, seem to take life as a lark. I don't see you taking much responsibility."

"PJ does all that stuff, Pop," Tommy said easily, standing up and picking up another stick, poking it into the fire.

"Well, PJ's not always going to be part of your life, Tommy. You've got to accept some responsibility for yourself. You're part of our family, and you have to carry your load."

"But you said I was like you, Pop," Tommy smiled at his father.

Tom nodded and smiled back. "*That's* what you've got to watch out for, son. Well, how about some sleep? Big fish are out there in the lake shaking in their boots 'cause we're gonna get 'em tomorrow."

"I *always* get 'em, Pop. PJ might as well keep sleeping," Tommy laughed.

The two rose and Tom picked up little Benjamin, carrying him to the tent and laying him beside PJ under the multiple woolen blankets Katrina had insisted they bring. As Tom and Tommy settled down into another set of blankets, Tommy pulled off his boots and bunched up his jacket for a pillow.

"*I'm* the man on Mom's trip to Norway, right, Pop?"

"That's right, son. Only don't step on your grandpa's toes in the process."

"And Pop . . ."

"Yeah, Tommy?" Tom said as he pulled the blankets up around his neck.

"I like being like you were."

"Ummm," Tom mumbled as he smiled to himself. "I like it too, Tommy. Good night."

"Night, Pop."

—⊗—

Even before Katrina, the children, and the Hansens left Salt Lake City for Norway, union problems mounted, plaguing mine operations. Utah Trust Bank and the other mine owners found themselves locked in a war of wills with their hired labor. The *take-it-or-leave-it* approach that had previously kept the miners in line was no longer working. The miners were sticking together, and production had come to a standstill. In previous times one mine owner would simply import additional labor, or offer a few pennies more a day to some other mine's workers. But shortly after the turn of the century, mine owners had formed an association that precluded such plundering of another man's workforce. Additionally, the miners had banded together to present a united front in their demands for increased wages and improved, safer working conditions. Times, the mine owners had discovered, were changing.

The Alta Club, on Brigham Street, was the assembly point for a cluster of cigar-smoking men who gathered together of an evening to proclaim their rights and grumble about the ignorant immigrants who had the gall to call a halt to work. Nevertheless, the union movement continued to make a significant impact on mine activity, and consequently, on mine revenues. Utah Trust Bank, holder of multiple notes on many of the area mines, as well as many minority share positions, found itself in a cash flow dilemma. Clearly, a crisis was brewing.

William Spry, a moderate Republican in the Reed Smoot camp, was elected governor of Utah in 1908. He had worked tirelessly to bring some reform to the mining industry, including the safety issues—the same issues over which Tom and Anders Hansen had conferred so many years earlier. The truth was that during the intervening ten years since that discussion, few improvements had actually been made.

But mine issues and labor union issues were not the only problems on Governor Spry's agenda. A weak and ineffective system of health laws existed in Utah, and people by the thousands were routinely sick and many died as a result of food poisoning or water contamination. The demand for improved and expanded water and sewer systems had long since outstripped the development and available funding.

At the same time, costs of medical care were increasing, principally in the area of doctor's surgical fees, which were on the rise. Sister Mary Theophane and Holy Cross Hospital struggled to maintain their high level of service, while retaining the dollar-a-week insurance plan that had been implemented many years earlier when the miners were fewer and the range of diseases was limited. Fighting against the misleading cry of physicians to control costs, with the finger pointed at hospital fees, Sister Mary and several of her associates took the battle seriously and confronted the physicians in public meetings. Long a proponent of order and respect for the medical profession, Sister Mary nevertheless understood that the cost of a three hundred dollar surgical procedure, which lasted an hour or two, was certainly more responsible for the high cost to the patient than the hospital's charge of ten to twenty-five dollars a week, depending on one's room, with food and care provided. This message she intended to make public, and she did so at a meeting of the State Medical Society, earning condemnation from those physicians who felt threatened by her description of the relative costs.[7]

Under the guidance of Tom Callahan and Robert Thurston, Utah Trust Bank continued during these hectic days of growth in Utah to make its way successfully through a morass of financial dealings. Robert Thurston's son, Mark, had returned from his education at Harvard in 1908, and he immediately assumed responsibility for managing most of UTB's stock investments. His economic instincts and his understanding of the need to diversify the bank's holdings was perhaps the only thing that kept UTB prosperous during the disruptive mining strikes and high costs associated with keeping the mines open, even in the face of lost revenues.

The biggest challenge to UTB holdings, at the time Katrina Callahan took the children and left for Norway, was an impending problem with Utah Copper and a threatened strike by workers at the company's Bingham Mine. For most of 1911, management and the miners had been jostling for position. What made matters worse was that several factions were vying for the right to represent the miners. Perhaps the only advantage held by management and mine owners was the fact that the mine workers were comprised of several ethnic groups that didn't always agree on strategy. The discord among the miners had worked to the advantage of mine owners. Yet, there were some among the owners and management, notably Tom Callahan and some who sided with him, who felt that labor relations needed to be improved and that a place needed to be made on the governing boards for the workers' representatives.

All owners and management, however, were in agreement that resisting the outside union agitators, who seemed satisfied only when they had stirred discontent among the already frustrated miners, was the single most important objective.

As Tom, Robert, and Mark rode toward a meeting with Governor Spry, the issues had reached a boiling point. Shots had been fired in Bingham Canyon, and armed Greek miners had taken up defensive positions on the canyon walls. The situation had already resulted in the deaths of several participants, and both sides were quickly becoming callous to the injury and insult to their opposite number.

Ushered into Spry's office, Tom shook hands with the governor.

"It's good to see you, Tom," Governor Spry said. "And you, Robert."

"Thank you, Governor. I don't know if you've met Robert's son, Mark Thurston. Mark is Vice President of Investments at UTB."

"Welcome, son. Please have a seat. Thanks to all of you for coming. I wanted to talk to you before meeting with the larger group this afternoon."

The group took seats around a small conference table, and the governor's assistant placed a silver coffee service in the middle of the table. Tom poured himself a cup and sat back to listen to the governor.

"So, Tom, Katrina and the children have gone abroad?"

"Yes, Governor, she's accompanying her parents on a trip to the Old Country. I think you know Lars Hansen, Katrina's father."

"I do, indeed," the governor said, turning in his chair to point toward his desk. "The workmanship that man has accomplished on my desk is nothing short of artistry. I admire his skills."

Tom nodded and sipped his coffee. "He's made his mark in this valley all right. They'll be in Europe till next spring, Governor."

Governor Spry looked at Robert, a question in his eyes.

Robert nodded. "Yes, Governor, Alice is down in St. George with her sister."

"So then," Governor Spry commented, "we've circled the wagons, gotten the women and children to safety, and are prepared to deal with the attack, so to speak." The governor rose and started to pace the room. "Right. Let's put the cards on the table, gentlemen. Utah Fuel broke the back of the United Mine Workers in Carbon County back in '04. Now, some of your group would like to do the same thing to the Western Federation of Miners up there at Utah Copper. That's *not* what I'm after. I want a fair and impartial settlement of this thing," he said, looking directly at Tom as he paced by. "No shenanigans. Now before you get your nose in a knot, I know that you aren't a lone voice in the wilderness, and that you can't commit the consortium to which you belong, but you *have* spoken in favor of improvements, and for some reason," he smiled, "it's my understanding that profit is not the *only* consideration of UTB. Am I correct in that assumption?"

Tom smiled and took another sip of his coffee.

The governor held up his hand. "Don't answer that, Tom. It was unfair of me to ask. I'm just frustrated over recent developments and the way we seem to be going. We're not a frontier any more, gentlemen. We need to recognize that the safety and security of our base working force is vital to our economy and to the future of our state. I don't oppose a profit motive. That's what made America great.

But in Europe, for centuries, that profit has been taken at the expense—at the health, mind you, and often the lives as well—of the workers who bring in the product. That needs to change, and you, Tom, and the other owners like you, need to come to the table and accept the necessary changes."

Robert shuffled in his chair, and Governor Spry halted his pacing. "Mr. Thurston? You have something on your mind?"

Robert shook his head. "Governor, I've sat in a few meetings where Tom has been roasted by his fellow mine owners. It seems from my perspective that he's being pummeled by both sides."

Governor Spry paused for a moment, and then laughed out loud. "I'm certain he has, Mr. Thurston. Perhaps that alone would qualify him to run for governor. But, look, gentlemen," he said, standing behind his seat, "we *must* find a way to resolve these issues. Many more important things need to be done if we are to bring Utah into the twentieth century—taxation, health, sanitation, employment, housing—all these issues will result in a public mutiny if we can't, as elected and community leaders, find answers for our people. Even Senator Smoot has seen the need and expressed his concern. If he hadn't been battling for so long, just to be seated in the United States Senate, he might have made some headway on these issues." Governor Spry continued to pace the room, pausing to occasionally make a point, and to jab his finger into the air.

"Tom, your own brother-in-law, Congressman Hansen, has worked wonders in the Utah delegation since his return from Norway. And now talk has it that Roosevelt intends to run for president again in 1912. You know, of course, how he broke with tradition back in '02 and intervened in that coal strike back East. He even threatened to have federal troops take over the mines. If he's elected again next year— well, I needn't tell you what he might think to do with our mines out here. Times are changing, I'm telling you, and we need to move with them."

Tom nodded his acknowledgment and leaned forward, resting his arms on the table. "We get the picture, Governor. What would you have us do?"

Spry also nodded. "First, Tom, please understand that I know you're at the forefront of change within your economic peer group. That is admirable. And I am well aware of your philanthropy. But, all that aside, I want to resolve this Bingham issue a different way than hammering it out around the bargaining table."

"I'm listening, Governor," Tom said.

"I've asked Father Vasilios Lambrides of the Greek Orthodox Church to join us in a few minutes. I want him to use his good offices to find common ground."

"You think the church can play a role?"

"These Greeks are very spiritual, respect their religious leaders, and need someone whom they can trust to mediate. If my sources are right, they don't even feel they can trust the union negotiators who have come in to represent them."

"Well, surprise, surprise," Tom said sarcastically.

"I know, I know," the governor replied, his arms raised in supplication to the ceiling. "But what do you say, Tom? Will you lend your support to this proposal when the other owners arrive for this afternoon's meeting?"

Tom looked at Robert who nodded slightly, and then turned his gaze back toward Spry.

"Governor, Utah Trust Bank will do all we can to support your initiatives to resolve this strike. If Father

Lambrides can be of assistance, he'll receive all the support we can give."

"Thank you, Tom," the governor said, rising. "Then I'll see you back here at three this afternoon. That meeting should be a *real* donnybrook," Spry laughed.

"Aye," Tom also laughed.

"And, Mark," Spry said, clapping him on the back, "you've got two fine men to emulate. Your father and Mr. Callahan are held in high esteem in this community. You'll do well to follow their lead."

"Thank you, Governor," Mark replied as he exited the office.

In the car, heading back down State Street toward UTB, Tom was silent as they drove.

"Tom?" Robert asked, "a penny for your thoughts."

"He's right about one thing, you know. Utah, America, the world for that matter, is changing considerably. We have a telephone and telegraph that tell us instantly what happens halfway around the globe. Somehow we need to find ways to come to grips with conflict other than by pounding our fists on the table and presenting a take-it-or-leave-it stance."

"Do you have the answers, Tom?" Robert smiled as he turned the car onto Second South.

"Robert, you and I are eating quick bites at the hotel, running home for a few hours sleep each night, and thinking about our wives and families hundreds and thousands of miles away. And you ask me if I can solve the world's problems?"

Robert turned the corner, pulled into the bank's parking lot, and turned off the engine. "Well, not this week, I suppose," he laughed, getting out of the car.

The striking Greek miners were deployed throughout the canyon, positioned in strategic places on the walls, rifles prominently displayed as several police and government cars slowly made their way up the canyon road.[8] Management had sought to break the back of the strike by the use of temporary miners—"scabs" the strikers called them—brought in from outlying areas of the state.

Throughout the narrow approaches to the canyon, armed men could be seen kneeling or crouching behind rocks and bushes high on the canyon sides. Tom Callahan rode in Governor Spry's car, along with Sheriff Joseph Sharp. Earlier, representatives of General Wedgewood, National Guard Commander, had informed representatives of the striking miners that National Guard troops would be called upon to storm the canyon if reason could not prevail and the strike brought to an end. Father Lambrides was carrying Governor Spry's last offer of conciliation.

Exiting his car, the elderly priest gathered the skirts of his robe about him and, without waiting for escort, began to ascend the hillside toward a group of men standing partway up. Shouts echoed throughout the canyon, as leaders of the striking miners warned their men not to react and accidentally injure the priest. Finally, Father Lambrides came face to face with two of the miners, and requested that their leader descend to speak with him. One of the men relayed the information, and three men made their way down the hillside and approached the priest. In several minutes of conversation, during which Greek miners at first rejected, then considered, the priest's advice, a compromise was reached and the miners agreed to meet with Governor Spry at the Bingham Opera House the following day.

Attending the negotiations in the Bingham Opera House, Tom Callahan, silent during the entire proceedings, recognized that once again the mine owners and management had won the day, notwithstanding the few concessions granted the miners during the negotiations. Public support had swung against the miners during the strike, and Father Lambrides had been able to convince the Greek community that the governor would have no choice but to call in the National Guard, which would inevitably bring about further violence and death. The miners accepted a small hourly increase in wages and a promise that safety measures would be adopted in return for their going back to work. Several weeks of confrontation, accompanied by the deaths of striking participants and the beating of several others, came to an end.

Riding home from the meetings, Governor Spry was contemplative as they drove. Tom, again invited to ride with the governor, finally broke the silence.

"You've done a good job, Governor. Bringing in Father Lambrides was an excellent move."

"Humph. It appears so now, Tom, but we haven't seen or heard the last of the issues. Somehow, during the hopefully quiet period this will give us for a few months or, if we're lucky, a few years, you've got to convince those entrenched owners that these miners are people. They've got families, too. Is there *really* that much difference if the owners make twelve percent instead of fifteen or eighteen? The numbers don't matter, Tom. But something has to be done to better the conditions those men talked about. That one Greek fellow—the spokesman—I'd have joined him myself if I hadn't been the governor."

"Aye. He was eloquent all right. But, as you say, more importantly, he was right about much of what he said. The irony, Governor, is that one of their major complaints is the extortion required to obtain work in the mine. That, I'm sure you noticed, was extracted by one of their own—the Greek foreman Skliris. Certainly it didn't go unnoticed that they agreed to return to work under the prevailing wage, if the company would just fire Skliris. And then Jackling—I'll be looking to have a word with him, I can tell you—defends Skliris in his telegram. I don't know, Governor. It's a convoluted situation all right, but at least we've calmed the issue down and there should be no more killing."

"Humph," Spry grunted. "Perhaps not in the open. Well, anyway," he said, looking out the window of the car as they approached Temple Square, "I didn't have to send in the Guard."

"Aye," Tom nodded. "We can be grateful for that."

10

Tom's telegram made Katrina's heart race a little faster.

"HMS Oceanic *voyage canceled—Stop—New bookings arranged—Stop—Tickets at White Star Office, Southampton, departing 10 April—Stop—I leave Utah 12 April to meet you in NY—Stop—Children to Utah with Lars—Stop—You and I for a fabulous week in NY—Stop—Hurry, KMD—Stop— Love, Tom.*"

Katrina smiled at their secret code—KMD—Katie m' darlin'. She lay back on the bed, staring at the ceiling in her upstairs bedroom in Horten, Norway. After six months of touring Norway, seeing parts of it she had only studied as a child before they left for America, Katrina had gained a deeper appreciation for her homeland and the struggles of many generations of Norwegians who had learned to terrace-farm the hillsides to provide sufficient crops to survive.

Lars and Jenny Hansen had taken one more three-day trip, taking the ferry from Horten across the fjord to reach Moss, Sweden. One of Father Hansen's schoolmates was the headmaster at a school there, and Lars wanted to see him again.

Katrina had been pleasantly surprised at her father's stamina during the trip, and under her mother's watchful eye,

Lars had done much of what he had intended. As a tourist, he had seen more of Norway than he ever had before they emigrated to America.

Tom's letter of the previous week told how much he missed her, and how pleased he was that their return voyage would start the following week. As a present to Lars and Jenny, he had rebooked their reservations on a new ocean liner in First Class accommodations. His letter caused her thoughts to return to Utah, her husband, and her American life. It was as Tom had once said about Ireland. Norway would always be her native country, but Utah was where her family was and that was home. Norway was in her heart, as Ireland was in Tom's, but Utah—Salt Lake City—was now their home, and almost instantly she longed to return—to have Tom take her in his arms again and to call her 'Katie, m'darlin', as he always had.

Tommy and Tess, now eleven, and young Benjamin, barely seven, had not really posed as much of a problem as Katrina had imagined they might. The twins' dark hair, blue eyes, and ruddy complexions stamped them as Tom's children as surely as if a mold had been cast. Tess actually acted like quite the young lady with her Norwegian cousins, and Tommy, as the man of the family—a title Grandpa Lars had given him—had been quick to assume the role. Benjamin had been totally taken over by his Norwegian relatives. His fair skin, blond hair, and green eyes, so much like Katrina's, had assured him acceptance in the Hansen homestead.

In the morning, they would begin the journey home. They would take a short ferry ride to Copenhagen and then passage on a small coastal freighter to Scotland. Then once again, as they had so many years before, there would be a train ride through Scotland and England to Southampton. There they would board yet another British White Star liner. A brand-new vessel, she was of immense proportions and reputed to be the finest ocean liner in service.

Katrina read Tom's telegram once more, folded the paper, and tucked it into a side pocket. She stood, smoothed the front of her pinafore, and went downstairs, prepared to assist with dinner for the family. Lars and Jenny were due back in Horten on the afternoon ferry, and the whole Hansen family was gathering again this evening for a farewell party. The trip had been pleasant enough, and it was certainly rewarding to see the children take an interest in her homeland. But on the morrow they would leave. Katrina Hansen Callahan was ready to go home.

The size of the ship was overwhelming. Comparing this vessel to the *Antioch*—the ship Katrina had first taken to America—was like comparing a hotel to a tent. Her suite, one of twenty-eight exceptionally elaborate suites located on B Deck, consisted of a sitting room and two smaller bedrooms, one off each side. Tommy and Benjamin were assigned to one room with twin beds, and Katrina and Tess took the other. Lars and Jenny Hansen were several doors down the passageway, also in a First Class suite.

Departing Southampton proved to be a noisy affair, with official proclamations, traditional British pomp and ceremony, and representatives of the Crown making speeches about the maiden voyage of the new ship. The band stood on the Promenade Deck and played "Rule Britannia," as the harbor tugs pulled and pushed the great vessel clear of obstacles. Katrina and the children remained on deck to watch the proceedings and the myriad of smaller vessels in the harbor for the occasion.

Precisely at noon on 10 April 1912, under the control

of six harbor tugs, the great ship was pulled from the pier and moved into the channel, where it began a slow journey down the River Test.

Passing two vessels idled by a local coal strike—the White Star's *Oceanic*, the ship on which they had originally been booked, and the American Line's *New York*—she glided on, through a channel passage made considerably narrower as a result of the two smaller vessels being warped side by side, with the *New York* on the outside. Suddenly a succession of sharp cracks rang across the water, as one after another the gigantic ropes securing the *New York* to the *Oceanic* snapped, and the *New York* began to drift out into the channel toward the larger vessel that was moving to reach the open sea. Quick thinking by one of the tug captains enabled a line to be secured to the stern of the *New York*, and the episode passed without incident.[9]

That evening, following a brief stop at Cherbourg, France, the ship passed Fast Net and began to parallel the coast of southern Ireland. Katrina was exploring on deck with Tess, and Tommy had taken Benjamin to the gymnasium where a swimming and diving instructor had scheduled a program to entertain the younger children.

"You all right, Mom?" Tess asked, sliding closer to her mother as the cool April evening breeze blew across the deck.

Katrina wrapped her arm around her daughter, tucking Tess's shawl closer around her neck.

"I'm just fine, darling. I was just looking at the land your father loves so much."

"I'd like to see Ireland one day, now that I'm grown," Tess said.

Katrina laughed. "You'll see Queenstown this evening, my sweet, but it won't be hard to convince your father to grant that wish and show you the rest of the country," Katrina said, hugging her daughter.

"Is that where you met Dad, Mom?"

Katrina nodded silently. "Over . . ." she hesitated, trying to discern exactly where they were in relation to land. A junior officer of the deck walked close behind and Katrina saw him approach.

"Oh, excuse me, sir. Would you be able to point out where Cork might be?"

The man tipped his cap and stepped beside the two women at the railing. He scanned the darkening horizon off the starboard side of the ship for a moment. The light was beginning to wane, and visibility was poor.

"Ah, yes, there she be," he said, pointing. "We're going to enter that small estuary in about an hour, Mum, up the channel to Queenstown. Cork is actually out of sight now, but that soft glow of lights just off the starboard bow—that'd be Cork, Mum."

"Thank you, sir," Katrina replied as the man again tipped his hat and left.

"Did you meet Dad in Cork?" Tess asked.

"Well, I did, but I didn't know it," she laughed.

"What?"

"I know that sounds funny, dear, but your father was . . . well, he was sort of a brazen lad. He found a way to bump into me one day when your Uncle Anders and I were out for a walk. I don't actually remember the meeting, but your father has described it to me several times. But then," Katrina continued, her gaze turned forward toward the setting sun off the bow of the ship, "we were underway about a day when he once again, very brazenly mind you, took it upon himself to speak to me, alone on deck, without even being introduced."

"What did you do?" Tess asked, her eleven-year-old eyes growing wider.

"I spoke with him," Katrina admitted.

"*Mother*, you've told me never to—"

"I know, dear. And I didn't stay long speaking with your father. But something about him . . . something just . . ." Katrina grew silent again, her thoughts racing to a far distant time and the unknown future that had lain ahead of her. She thought of the sixteen-year-old girl whose heart had been taken by a brash, Irish lad who, following their meeting, had made his way halfway around the world to claim then eventually lose the girl. And of how he had challenged the wilds of Alaska in search of his future, only to return to the woman who had captured his heart.

"Mom?"

"I'm all right, dear, I was just remembering."

The dinner arrangements in First Class were exquisite. Several groupings of passengers were seated around Katrina's table, along with her parents. Both Hansens were quiet. They had usually traveled First Class on their voyages, but First Class on *this* ship was, indeed, *First Class*. As the waiter unfolded her linen serviette and draped it across her lap, Katrina thought for a moment that her parents would feel somewhat out of place among the wealthiest of the passengers and that Tom's present of exchanging their reservations for the more elaborate accommodations could become troublesome. She quickly dismissed the idea, however, and tried to open a light conversation.

Seated directly across from her was a woman slightly older than herself, dining alone. From the drift of her conversation with others, the woman was already acquainted with most of the people at the table. Katrina smiled at her when their eyes met.

"Evening," the woman smiled. "My name is Abby Pearson, from Chicago. My father is Hermann Pearson, of the meat-packing Pearsons," she laughed. "And the steward told me that you are Katrina Callahan from Salt Lake City."

Katrina cocked an eyebrow.

"Yes, well," the lady laughed, "I like to know who I'm dining with. And these are your parents?" she said.

"Yes," Katrina replied, "please excuse my manners. These are my parents, Lars and Jenny Hansen, also from Salt Lake City. We've been on an extended trip back home to Norway."

"Magnificent country, Norway. I love it," Mrs. Pearson said. "It reminds me of New Hampshire, up in the Green Mountains. Actually, Mrs. Callahan—may I call you Katrina?—actually, I believe I've met your husband. He was in Chicago once, meeting with my father, and dined in our home."

"Oh, how lovely. You must come to Salt Lake and return the visit," Katrina offered.

"That would be my pleasure. Did I see you on deck with your daughter?"

"Very likely," Katrina said. "I have three of my children on this trip. My twins, Tommy and Teresa, the young lady you must have seen, and my youngest, Benjamin. My oldest son, PJ, stayed in Utah with his father."

"Quite the family. Still, it's nice the children have their own dining accommodations. Our talk can be so *boring* to the young ones, can't it?"

"Oh, yes, I certainly agree with that," Katrina replied politely.

Abby Pearson leaned slightly over the table and winked

at Katrina. "Actually, Kate, it can be pretty boring to me, too."

"Yes," Katrina laughed, "I can *also* agree with that."

"I think we're gonna be friends, Kate Callahan," Abby announced.

"I'd like that, Abby," Katrina smiled.

By the third day of the voyage, Katrina and Abby Pearson had established a routine of meeting about mid-morning in the *Café Parisien*, aft on the Promenade Deck. The café was a new idea for a British vessel, attempting to bring a bit of French atmosphere to the voyage. It quickly became very popular.

On Sunday, April 14, Katrina was invited by Mrs. Pearson and several of her friends to dine in the *A la Carte* restaurant, the most posh of the First Class facilities. Lars and Jenny had taken their meal earlier and had decided to retire to their cabin for a night's rest. Tommy, Tess, and Benjamin attended a puppet show early in the evening and then Katrina got them settled in their cabins prior to leaving for dinner.

At dinner, Katrina was introduced to Captain Smith, in command of the vessel, who made the rounds of each table politely, and then joined in a small dinner party given in his honor by the Widener family of Philadelphia. After the course of filet mignon *Lili*, Abby suggested they all attend the Sunday evening band concert, which lasted until around ten-thirty. Finally, after drinks and late-evening refreshments, Mrs. Pearson excused herself for the night, and Katrina quickly followed.

Rather than head straight for her cabin, Katrina wrapped her shawl around her shoulders and took a walk outside. It was immediately evident that she was inadequately dressed for the brisk temperatures, and she quickly returned to the warmth of the dining room. Most passengers had already departed, but a small group of men and one woman sat laughing and chatting. As Katrina descended the stairs toward her cabin, she felt a slight shudder from the ship, and heard a distinct scraping sound that lasted nearly thirty seconds, seeming to emanate from the starboard side of the vessel. The noise progressed along the right side of the ship, finally ceasing altogether.

Although the jolt wasn't abrupt, she briefly lost her balance and held onto the railing for a moment. Another passenger, coming up the stairs, commented on the noise and the jostling. Katrina turned to look up the stairs and saw the group of men she'd noticed earlier emerge from the dining facility and head for the outside deck. She retraced her steps up toward the door leading outside and joined the small group of passengers, which now included several women.

"Did you feel something, too?" one of the ladies asked.

"A slight shudder with a scraping sound," Katrina responded.

As the group came out onto the ship's deck, once again the extreme cold of the night air hit Katrina, and several of the ladies complained of the chill. It took a moment for their eyes to adjust to the darkness but then one of the men pointed aft on the starboard side.

"My word! Would you look at the size of that iceberg?" he exclaimed.

The people in the group all looked in the direction he pointed and as their eyes continued to adjust they were able to discern the ghostly shape of a monstrous iceberg, fading slowly into the night as the ship continued on course away from the obstacle.

"Do you suppose we brushed it?" one of the ladies asked.

Another gentleman, somewhat forward of the group,

returned with chunks of ice in his hands. "I'd say that was likely," he laughed, as he put a piece of the ice on his companion's shoulder.

"*Albert!*" she screamed.

"I'm sorry, dear," he laughed. "It is cold, isn't it?" he said, throwing the remainder of the pieces over the side. "But now, my darling, you've seen an iceberg and had an authentic piece of North Atlantic ice on your person."

"A dubious honor, I should think," she rebutted, irritably.

A uniformed crew member walked quickly toward the bridge, but he was stopped by the group.

"I say, old chap, have we had a mishap of sorts?"

"Nothing to be alarmed about, I assure you. Captain Smith will be in full control of the situation."

"Ah, yes, of course," the man replied. "Shall we go in, ladies? It's frightfully chilly out here this evening."

"That is an excellent suggestion, sir," the officer said. "Perhaps if you all returned to your cabins, you would be much more comfortable."

"Certainly. Ladies, if you please?" he said, holding open the door to the dining salon.

The group of passengers turned in different directions as Katrina resumed her journey down the inside stairs toward her cabin. The clock on her nightstand read a few minutes before midnight as she entered the cabin and checked on the children. Tess woke up as her mother began to undress for bed.

"Did you have a nice evening, Mother?" she asked.

"I did, dear. Thank you. Try to go back to sleep now," Katrina whispered.

Before Katrina was fully undressed, she heard a growing commotion in the hallway outside her cabin, but remained inside. A knock on the cabin door surprised her, but she threw on a robe and went to see who was there.

"Yes?" she said through the doorway.

"It's Poppa, Katrina. Are you all right?"

Katrina opened the door to admit Lars Hansen and noticed people milling about in the hallway.

"It's a bit late for so many people to be up, isn't it, Poppa?"

"The stewards want us to go to the Boat Deck, Katrina. It's just a precaution and they say they're sorry for the inconvenience. Momma is getting dressed, and I came to see if I could help. Are the children asleep?"

"The boys are, Poppa. I hate to wake them unless you feel it's essential."

"Well," Lars said, trying to sound reassuring, "maybe we better do what they say. Just to be safe. I'll go roust Tommy and Benjamin, and you help Tess. And, Katrina, they've asked us to wear our life jackets."

"All right, Poppa, if you think so."

"Dress her warmly, Katrina. It's bitter cold out tonight."

A mere twenty minutes passed between the HMS *Titanic* striking the iceberg and Captain Smith, fully apprised of the severity of the damage, giving the order to take to the lifeboats. Refusing to believe there was any real emergency, many passengers ignored the order in the following hour, and, in fact, more than half the early lifeboats left the *Titanic* filled well below capacity. The most telling statistic was the one possessed by Captain Smith as he gave that fateful order to abandon ship: the *Titanic* had 2,201 passengers and crew, but lifeboats for only 1,178.[10]

On deck, First Class passengers milled around on the

Boat Deck, uncertain which lifeboat was theirs or what the procedure would be should it become necessary to board the small wooden craft. Second Officer Lightoller was in command of the lifeboat stations on the port side and commenced loading boats immediately after Captain Smith gave the order. When the first boat actually took on passengers, and the divots swung out, lowering the smaller craft to the ocean below, passengers began to sense the reality of the situation. Almost concurrent with the first lifeboat's departure, passengers began to notice the great ship's list to starboard, and the forward tilt to the deck as, unknown to most, the bow began to fill with water. Still, no member of the crew had informed the ship's passengers of the fact now clearly evident to the complement of the ship's senior officers: the *Titanic* was sinking!

As they left the cabin, Katrina took Tess firmly in hand and instructed Tommy to take Benjamin's hand and not to let go. Lars stayed with his family as they ascended the stairs toward the Boat Deck. Now, outside, with the earliest of the lifeboats departing, Lars' chest began to constrict, and he quickly grew short of breath.

Second Officer Lightoller continued to exude confidence as he calmly directed the loading of additional lifeboats, calling for women and children first and often having to cajole those women who had not yet grasped the idea they were in a life-or-death situation and that it was necessary for them to leave their husbands.

Early lifeboats departing on the starboard side of the *Titanic*, under the command of First Officer Murdoch, actually did contain some male passengers since the departure of a lifeboat half-empty made little sense to him. Second Officer Lightoller, however, determined that "women and children first," actually meant "women and children *only*."

For many on the *Titanic*, living or dying became a matter of which side of the vessel one was assigned for emergency departure.

The crowd grew larger and a bit more unruly as Officer Lightoller approached the boat closest to where Katrina stood with her small cluster of children. When Lightoller called for her to board, she hesitated, looking to her mother who was clinging to Lars' arm. Katrina offered her place to another woman with two children and then stepped close to her mother.

"Please, Momma, come into the boat with me and the children. I'm sure the men will come later."

"You go, Katrina," the older woman said softly. "I will stay with your father."

"*Please*, Momma," Katrina cried, her anxiety growing.

Lars, now breathing heavily and leaning up against the outside bulkhead, attempted to disengage Jenny's arm. "You should go with Katrina, Jenny," he said, laboring to speak.

"Lars, we have been married for over forty years, and I have never disobeyed your voice. But I *will* stay with you this night."

"Jenny, *please*," he pleaded.

Jenny Hansen raised her hand to the side of Lars' face and smiled at her husband. "Lars, after all these years, would you refuse me this one request?" she said.[11]

"Oh, my darling, Jenny," he whispered. Lars turned his face toward Katrina. "Take the children, Katrina," he said, his arm around Jenny. "We shall be together again soon," he smiled gently at his daughter. "Do not fear for us."

"Oh, Poppa," Katrina cried again, and embraced both of her parents. Tess was crying as she watched the emotional scene develop between her mother and her grandparents. Tommy stood slightly off to one side with Benjamin, as the crowd began to lean against the forward tilt of the ship and gradually accept the inevitable need to enter the lifeboat.

Again Lightoller called for more passengers to board, and Katrina started for the lifeboat. Suddenly Benjamin jerked his hand from Tommy's, crying something about his airplane and darting away between two male passengers standing behind the group that was waiting to board.

"Benjamin!" Katrina screamed.

"Please, ma'am, come aboard," Lightoller said firmly.

"My son! My son!" she screamed again.

"I'll get him, Mom," Tommy hollered, ducking through the crowd in pursuit of his brother.

"*Tommy,* wait!" Katrina screamed even louder, as both her sons disappeared into the crowd of passengers.

Lars stepped forward, his voice now commanding. "Katrina, take Tess and board the boat. I'll find the boys. Please, go *now!*" he said, motioning for Officer Lightoller to assist. Grabbing Katrina's arm, the second officer practically lifted Katrina over the railing and inserted her into the lifeboat, now almost full. Tess followed her mother and shortly the lifeboat began to descend. Katrina was panic-stricken as she watched her mother and father disappear above the Boat Deck railing, the lifeboat swaying slightly as it dropped toward the icy waters below.

———

For several hours the lifeboats drifted on the ocean. At first, occasional cries of swimmers were heard in the distance. But after the great vessel had finally lifted her stern and slid beneath the calm, flat waters, the screams of swimmers diminished and, then, after a while, ceased altogether.

The cessation of human cries was at first comforting to those in lifeboats. But as the realization of the fate of those who had floundered in the freezing waters began to coalesce in their minds, most passengers responded to the horror with silence. Fears for their own safety were overshadowed by the loss of their loved ones who had remained on board the ship.

Before dawn, rocket shells could occasionally be seen in the night sky to the southwest, and the ship's officer in Katrina's lifeboat said that was a sign that a rescue vessel was coming to their aid. With the first rays of light breaking to the east, the lights of another vessel could be seen on the horizon, growing larger as the day broke. Finally, the first rescue vessel arrived on the scene and, one by one, began plucking survivors from lifeboats and collapsible life rafts. Eventually the rescuers reached Katrina's lifeboat.

Numb from the cold, Katrina had clung throughout the night to Tess, wrapping her daughter in her own coat and trying to shield the young girl from the spray of the freezing waters. A light wind and the absence of waves throughout the night had been a blessing the passengers had not taken the time to notice. As the ropes were attached to the lifeboat and the occupants began to be assisted up the ladders, Katrina looked up toward the main deck, lined with passengers from the *Carpathia*. One face, pushed between two male passengers, jumped out at her and she cried out.

"Tommy! Tommy!"

"Momma?" the young boy cried.

Katrina reached the deck of the *Carpathia* and Tommy lunged into her arms. Katrina dropped to her knees, hugging her twins, her tears flowing freely.

"Momma, I couldn't find him. I couldn't find Benjamin. Momma, Momma, I couldn't find him," the boy sobbed.

"How did you get off the ship?" Katrina asked.

Tommy continued to sob, the tears streaming down his

191

face. "Mrs. Pearson, Momma. She saw me on deck looking for Benjamin, and she grabbed me and told the officer to put me in her boat. I didn't want to go, Momma. I wanted to find Benjamin. Oh, Momma, I couldn't find him."

Katrina pulled the boy closer, hugging him tightly, and pulling Teresa into her arms. "I know, Tommy. It's all right. Maybe he's here somewhere. We'll find him, Tommy. We'll find him."

The crewmen from the *Carpathia* wrapped more blankets around the survivors as they continued to rescue additional *Titanic* passengers from the few remaining lifeboats. About midmorning, another ocean liner appeared on the horizon, and the *Californian* joined the rescue. As the *Carpathia* departed the scene, Abby Pearson appeared in the dining room, also wrapped in a blanket and, without words, wrapped her arms around Katrina.

"Abby! Oh, dear God, Abby, thank you for helping Tommy."

"He was a brave boy, Kate. I had to force him into the boat. He wanted to continue looking for his brother."

Katrina buried her head in Abby's shoulder and cried, the emotion of the moment completely draining her body of strength and will. Tommy and Teresa sat silently in the corner of the dining room aboard the *Carpathia*, sipping hot chocolate as the vessel steamed for New York.[12]

11

Tom's train rumbled through the eastern Pennsylvania countryside. When the porter knocked on his door at six-thirty, as prearranged, Tom acknowledged him and turned over for another five minutes of slumber. The repetitive sound from the wheels crossing each intersection of railing reminded Tom of his location, and his soon-to-be-arrived-at destination, and the five minutes' delay disappeared.

Clean-shaved, dressed, and packed, with the train's arrival in New York only about one hour hence, Tom headed for the dining car and breakfast. Notwithstanding the early hour, the car was nearly full as the train continued to traverse the rural countryside of Pennsylvania.

" . . . absolutely horrible, Henry. Can you imagine it? Oh, those poor people," Tom heard someone say as he walked down the aisle. The steward seated him in a forward-facing seat across the small table from an older woman, who was having her breakfast alone.

"I hope you don't mind company," Tom said as he took his seat. "We seem to be quite full this morning."

The well-dressed, silver-haired woman looked up from her newspaper and smiled. "Not at all, young man. I'm glad for the company."

"Thank you, ma'am."

"Sir?" the waiter asked.

"Umm," Tom replied, "just some toast, coffee, and perhaps a small order of bacon, please."

"Right away, sir."

"Now your Irish mother didn't teach you to skip breakfast, did she?" the lady smiled over her newspaper.

Tom shook his head. "No, ma'am."

"I didn't think so," she replied, folding the newspaper and placing it on the empty chair beside her. "And what part of Ireland might you be from?"

"The part in Utah, ma'am," Tom laughed, "but some twenty years ago, I came from Tipperary."

"What a beautiful country, Ireland," the lady commented.

"Thank you, Mrs. . . ."

"Mrs. Virginia Van Brocklin. VeeVee, to my friends, Mr. . . . ?"

"Well, I certainly get low marks for my manners this morning, Mrs. Van Brocklin," he laughed. "I'm Thomas Callahan, from Salt Lake City. I'm enroute to New York to meet my family returning from a trip to Norway."

"It's very pleasant to meet you, Mr. Callahan. I've been out to Indiana to visit my daughter. I live in upstate New York, in Hyde Park, near Poughkeepsie."

The waiter arrived and placed a pot of coffee next to Tom along with a small plate of toast, butter, and several strips of bacon. "Thank you," Tom offered.

"My pleasure, sir," the man said.

"How long till we arrive at the station?" Tom asked.

"Just under an hour, sir. We're right on time," he smiled brightly. "Should be in at 8:12, sharp."

194

"Thank you," Tom repeated. He placed his napkin across his lap and began to spread butter on a piece of toast.

"Just a dreadful story in the news this morning, Mr. Callahan," Mrs. Van Brocklin said. "Have you seen the papers?"

"No, ma'am. I was preparing my luggage for our arrival. Was there some accident last night?" he asked, stirring his coffee.

"Oh, yes, but the details are very sketchy. Only the wireless reports so far. The porter provided the paper as we passed through the last town, about twenty minutes ago. All they know is that hundreds, perhaps thousands, of persons may have died last night in a catastrophic ocean tragedy."

"Ma'am?" Tom said, his interest rising.

"A British vessel, I think, the name . . ." she hesitated, reaching for the paper and turning to the front page. "Ah, yes, here it is, 'Hundreds Perish in Sea Disaster.' The Titanic was her name. On her first voyage. Dreadful news, I'm afraid," she said, shaking her head.

"May I, please?" Tom asked, reaching for and grabbing the newspaper.

"Yes, of course," Mrs. Van Brocklin said, startled at Tom's abruptness.

He quickly scanned the headlines then hurriedly read several paragraphs into the story. "If you'll excuse me," he said, rising and stepping into the aisle. "May I?" he asked, holding the paper up and asking to retain it.

"Yes, certainly. Is something wrong, Mr. Callahan?"

"My family are, uh . . . are on the Titanic, Mrs. Van Brocklin. Please excuse me," he said, turning quickly away and walking down the aisle.

"Oh, my Lord," Mrs. Van Brocklin exclaimed, covering her mouth with her hand. "Oh, my dear Lord."

Quite literally, hundreds of people milled about outside the White Star Lines' office in New York City. The lobby of the building was jammed to capacity, and once Tom exited the taxi, he was unable to force his way into the building. He retreated across the street into a small café and asked to use the telephone.

"Won't do no good, sir. The line's been jammed all morning."

Tom nodded and left the building, once again crossing the street to join the press of anxious, desperate relatives pleading for information about possible survivors of the *Titanic* disaster.

Jostled by the crowd and waiting impatiently for definitive news, Tom was both sick with fear and angry at himself. If only he hadn't changed their booking. It was his fault they were on the *Titanic* in the first place.

Tom could see into the lobby of the building and the crowd that was being held in the main foyer by six police officers stationed at the bottom of the stairs. Shortly after noon, a man leaned out of an upstairs window and called to the crowd that a list would shortly be posted in the foyer, and that if people would cooperate, he would send someone down to distribute four carbon copies of the list, and that they would try to keep everyone updated as quickly as they received word.

"Where are the survivors?" someone shouted.

"The *Carpathia* has picked up *hundreds* of survivors," the man yelled back. "They expect to reach New York by Thursday."

"*Thursday!*" the same man responded. "Surely you don't

expect us to wait until Thursday to find out if our family is alive or not!"

"Sir, please," the man pleaded. "We *are* doing our best. I will post names on the board as quickly as we receive wireless transmissions." He shut the upstairs window.

A young boy came down the inside stairwell and tried to shove his way through the unruly crowd to post his document on the bulletin board. An elderly man grabbed one of the sheets from his hand and tried, against the press of those surrounding him, to scan the list for names. Several people reached for the list, resulting almost immediately in the paper being torn in pieces, rendering it useless to anyone. Finally, the man who had leaned out the window appeared at the top of the stairs and leaned over the railing.

"Ladies and gentlemen, please, if I may have your attention. Please!" he shouted.

Someone in the crowd yelled, "Shut up! Be quiet!" and the noise began to slowly subside.

"Ladies and gentlemen," he said, shaking his head. "This is a disaster of unprecedented proportions. We understand your anxiety and your need to know the fate of your loved ones. This is not the way. Please allow us to try to provide you the information you need as quickly as it comes to us. I assure you, we will distribute information as soon as it becomes available."

"Wilson," a man in the crowd shouted. "Do you have any Wilsons on your survivor list?"

"Sir," the man responded, "can you not see the hundreds of concerned people who all wish to know if their families are alive? We have alphabetized the names we've received. We'll continue to add names as quickly as they come in. If you'll just let the lad post the list and allow all to have a few seconds to review it, we'll be able to assist you much faster. Now, if you'll all just try to form some sort of line . . ."

The young boy struggled again through the crowd, attempting to reach the board, but once again, a hand grabbed the list the lad carried, tearing the paper as the boy held on to its end. Finally, the man at the top of the stairs leaned over to the police officer standing on the top step and said something to him. The officer handed the man his baton, and with short raps, he banged the baton on the railing, obtaining quick response from the crowd.

"This is not going to work unless all cooperate. If I may have your attention, I will try to read the names we've received. We have over five hundred names so far, and more are coming by wireless, so this will take some time. It would be far quicker if you allowed us to post a list and scanned it as you walked by, but for now . . ."

The crowd surged forward, toward the stairs, with several shouts for quiet, as the man at the top of the stairs began to read out the names.

"Addison, A., Addison, R., Altheimer, P., Brubaker, L., Brubaker R., . . ." He continued for some time, with each movement from one letter of the alphabet to another bringing desperate cries of anguish from the crowd as the name they anxiously awaited was not read. Several women fainted in the press of the crowd at the news, or absence of news, regarding their particular family member.

Having squeezed his way into the building, Tom stood toward the back of the crowd. After a time, screams and sighs of relief alternately coming from the crowd, the man at the top of the stairs reached the Cs. "Cagney, H., Call, P., Call, S., Callahan, K., Callahan, T., Cordova, C., . . ."

Tom leaned against the wall of the lobby, thoughts racing through his mind. *Only one "T" and no "B." Maybe the wireless operator thought it was a duplicate. But the lists were incomplete, the man had said, and Tommy and Teresa both start with "T."*

Clearly it would be hours, if not days, before the lists were sorted out completely, and, in fact, not until the rescue vessel actually arrived in New York would they know for sure. Tom waited until the man reached the I's, and then the J's, without hearing any Hansen name called.

The lobby began to clear somewhat as the reader progressed through the alphabet. People in the crowd reacted with jubilation or grief and despair, based on the names that were read. For the next three days, however, until the actual arrival time of the *Carpathia* was determined, the offices of British White Star Lines continued to be besieged by relatives, press corps, and friends of those known, or thought to have been, on the *Titanic*.

The *Carpathia* was warped into her berth at Pier 54 on Thursday, 18 April 1912, shortly after dark. Coming up New York harbor, the ship had been surrounded by dozens of smaller craft filled with reporters and family members, holding up signs and placards bearing the names of relatives. Finally, the ship was secured to the pier, and the passengers began to depart, with the *Carpathia* passengers, for the most part, giving way to the *Titanic* survivors. Bedraggled and confused, some of the survivors needed to be assisted down the gangplank, not so much because of physical injuries as from the shock of the disaster. Hardly a survivor had not left other family members at the scene of the sinking, and during the intervening four days on board the *Carpathia*, they had time for their loss to settle into their subconscious, bringing some to an emotional state of mental withdrawal.

Cries of anguish were heard as survivors met with waiting family members who were then told of others who had perished. Each with his or her own fears in their heart, they waited, clinging to the hope that somehow their loved one had been spared. Even those for whom personal family was not involved, such as reporters, police, and medical personnel, the sights and sounds occurring along the length of the pier spawned open displays of emotion.

Tom's first view of Katrina was as she descended the gangway, Tommy and Teresa close by her side. He pushed his way through the few people standing in front of him and jostled the gate guard to one side as he stepped onto the pier. The guard tried to restrain him, but with Tom's entry, several other people clambered through the gate, and instantly, the guard had more than he could handle.

Katrina saw Tom in the rush of people and ran the last few steps down the gangway, collapsing in his arms, weeping and unable to speak. Tom held her tightly as the children burrowed in as closely as they could to their father. They were bumped back and forth by other families, meeting or seeking their loved ones. Yet, each family gathering assumed an aura of privacy amid the collective chaos.

Without words, Tom knew from his absence that something dreadful had happened to Benjamin, but until the moment when Katrina would mouth the words, he dared hope and pray that Benjamin would be carried off on a stretcher, or that perhaps he was on another rescue vessel. Deep in the bowels of his being, Tom knew that his hopes were fallacious. Word had come two days earlier that the *Californian*, the second rescue vessel on the scene, and all other subsequent rescue craft, had failed to find another living person from the tragedy. The *Carpathia*, the newspapers had said, carried over seven hundred survivors. Seven hundred out of over two thousand.

"Benjamin's gone," Katrina sobbed in Tom's ear. "Our baby's gone. Oh, Thomas—and Momma and Poppa. It was awful, Thomas, just awful. All those poor people . . ." she whimpered.

The children were crying as well, and Tom sought to remove his family from the pressure of the crowd. He had paid a taxi driver to wait near the entrance to the terminal, and slowly he maneuvered his family through the crowd toward the street. Once in the taxi, Tom ordered the driver to go directly to the Waldorf-Astoria Hotel.

It was well after ten before the family was settled into the hotel suite. Both children were bathed, fed, and put to bed by hotel staff who were gracious in their solicitations to the Callahan family. In all, nineteen survivors of the *Titanic* disaster spent their first night on dry land in the plush surroundings of the Waldorf-Astoria, protected from and oblivious to the throng of reporters that filled the lobby throughout the night, clamoring for a response from the survivors and their families.

Sometime after midnight, Katrina woke from a fitful sleep and found Tom's side of the bed empty. She rose, threw on a robe provided by the hotel, and walked into the sitting room where Tom sat in the dark, muted somewhat by the glow of light coming through the window from the streets of New York below.

"Thomas?" she said.

At the sound of her voice, he rose quickly and stepped to take her in his arms. She laid her head against his shoulder, and he stroked her hair, neither speaking. Tom gently urged her toward the couch and both sat, Katrina leaning against her husband with her feet curled up under her. The deep, welling sobs had been expended hours earlier, and the quiet mourning was just beginning. Till nearly daylight they sat together on the divan, few words exchanged other than when Katrina asked for a glass of water.

"Your mother was a brave woman, Katie," Tom eventually said. "And I understand her desire to remain with Lars. I know it must have been difficult for you to watch them together, but they're *still* together now."

Katrina nodded her head slightly, and slid her hand behind her husband's neck. She raised her face from his chest and looked into his eyes. "And Benjamin *will* be with them, Thomas, won't he?"

"Yes, my darling, he will be, and they'll love him until we can see him again."

"Will we, Thomas? Will we see him again?" Katrina whispered.

"Katie, you know the Church's teachings about children, and—"

"But *you*, Thomas. What about *you*? I've heard Father Scanlan talk to you about infant baptism. He's asked you many times to reconsider your decision about baptism for the children."

"Katie, I—"

"Thomas, I know that what you have done all these years was for me. But I'm asking now about you. What do *you* believe?"

Tom was silent, standing to pour himself another glass of water and pausing by the window, looking at the streets below, just beginning to come awake with morning traffic. People were starting to go about their business, yet up here, in a suite in the Waldorff-Astoria, Tom's family had been diminished by one precious son and two grandparents.

Where was *Benjamin*? Tom thought as he stood,

contemplating Katie's question. Was he condemned to Purgatory as Father Scanlan had so often said was the fate of unbaptized children, and had that happened because he, himself, hadn't had the strength to go against his wife's wishes in these matters? Had Father Scanlan been right that as head of the household, Tom should have taken the lead and *demanded* the Catholic baptism of his children? He shook his head and turned to face Katrina, waiting quietly on the divan for her husband's response.

"Katie, I've told Father Scanlan several times that I do not understand a God who would be so cruel as to damn innocent children, especially if omission of their baptism was a result of their parents' actions. No loving God could do such a thing. I must believe—in fact I *do* believe that Benjamin *is* with his grandparents and that God will take him to His bosom. I cannot . . . no, I *will* not admit any other possibility."

"Come, sit by me, please," Katrina said, patting the seat next to her. "I want you to know that I believe what you say is true. It *is* by the grace of Christ that these little children return to His presence. Still, I've thought for the entire four days on the *Carpathia* about this question. I have prayed for assurance, and I have besieged God with my pleadings to show me that Benjamin is with Him."

"And did He answer you, Katie?" Tom asked, retaking his seat next to her.

"I don't know, Thomas. I just don't know. He doesn't always work so directly as we would like. Elder McKay has told us that many times."

Tom nodded. "Yeah, D.O. seems to be perplexed himself at times, yet he always seems to have this quiet assurance that what he does is right."

"It's not so much that what he does is *right,* Thomas, but

perhaps . . . well, perhaps it's his knowledge that the Lord he believes in will not let him stray far from the truth. Elder McKay told me himself that he knows he has been wrong on some occasions, even since being called as an Apostle, but that he feels certain the Lord allowed him to have those learning experiences for a reason."

"Oh, Katie, this Catholic-Mormon thing has stood between us for so many years now. How could they *both* be right? How could a loving God allow such confusion to exist on earth? It's at times like these—when people need Him most—that the confusion between churches hinders rather than helps us to sort out the problem. I just don't understand."

Katrina again laid her head against Tom's chest, and they remained close together, the question hanging in the air, unanswered.

"How did he get away, Katie?" Tom asked. "I mean, how did Benjamin get separated from the rest of you?"

"He was with Tommy, and I had Teresa. Momma and Poppa had helped us come up to the Boat Deck, but Benjamin jerked his hand free from Tommy and ran back toward the cabin. I think when he realized we were going to leave the ship, he wanted to get the model airplane Poppa had bought for him in Norway."

"And Tommy had hold of Benjamin's hand?"

"Yes. I told them to stay together, but . . ."

"Then Tommy let him get away. He lost him in the crowd?"

"No, Thomas, it wasn't like that," Katrina said, her eyes now once again focused on Tom's, the dim light barely sufficient for her to see his expression.

"Katie, there were ship's officers and your parents to

assist. You told me earlier that you had told Tommy to keep watch over Benjamin. He didn't listen, did he?"

"Thomas," Katrina said firmly, "you've got to stop this train of thought. You weren't there. It was utter chaos with people screaming and running all over the place. Benjamin had no idea that we were going to actually leave the ship until we came on deck and he saw people getting into the lifeboats. He loved that silly airplane, and he probably thought it was going to get lost if he left it behind."

"Katie, you gave Tommy the responsibility for his brother."

"Tom, stop it. He's only twelve years old. He's just a boy. And besides, how could you expect a twelve-year-old to control a seven-year-old?"

"But he was supposed to do a man's job, Katie. I was doing a man's job at twelve. He failed. It's as simple as that. And his brother is dead. Gone. Never to return."

The tears had returned to Katrina's eyes as she saw the anger beginning to form in Tom's.

"As God is my witness, Thomas, he is not to blame for this tragedy. You *must* understand that."

"What I understand, Katie, is that I sent my family to Europe intact, and that you gave instructions to Tommy to watch his brother. He didn't do that, and now Benjamin is dead. That was a cowardly act, no matter how old he is. *That's* what I understand," Tom said, standing again, and picking up the telephone.

Katrina rose to come and stand by his side, trying to convince him of the error of his position. As she started to speak again, Tom raised his hand, the palm facing toward Katrina.

"Yes. Room Service, please—Room Service? Breakfast for four in the Constitutional Suite, as soon as possible."

He hung up the phone, and Katrina could see that her husband had taken on the intransigence she had so often observed in his decision-making process. Tom walked to the bedroom, toward the lavatory, while Katrina stood by the telephone table, tears blurring her vision. She heard a sound behind her and turned to look. For an instant, she locked eyes with Tommy, who stood behind the slightly ajar bedroom door, tears running down his cheeks. Then the young lad silently closed the door.

Salt Lake City
May 28, 1912

Dear Nana,

By now Momma and Poppa will have been rejoined with you and you will have welcomed my youngest son, Benjamin. My heart is broken. I do not understand the ways of the Lord sometimes, Nana. I can only trust in His judgment and pray that He gives me strength to survive this agony.

Thomas has not spoken to Tommy since New York. On the train trip home, he comforted Teresa and gave instructions to Tommy through me. He blames Tommy for Benjamin's death. In truth, Nana, he blames himself for not being there. But if he had, then he would have gone down with the ship like Poppa. Perhaps, if he had . . .

Nana, Benjamin was not yet eight years old, so I know that he is with you, but I am afraid that since he is not sealed to our family, I may not see him again. President Thurston has explained that when Tom joins the Church, we may complete the sealing. But when might that be? My heart cries out for Thomas to see the truth of the gospel and to take his place as the true head of our family. It has been almost fifteen years now, Nana, and he is still stubborn in his refusal to believe. Is this my destiny? Will the Lord not provide an eternal companion for me? Would I not be better off on my own than with a man who cannot believe through faith?

Jeg elske deg,

Your Trina

PART THREE

12

On Tuesday morning, the second week in February 1916, Tom began a solitary drive from Salt Lake City to Price, Utah, a mining town located high in the southern end of the Wasatch Mountains. Hoping that snow would not block the mountain pass at Soldier's Summit, he drove down the valley, through the small towns of Murray, Sandy, and Draper, toward Utah Valley and Daniel's Canyon. The newly graveled road was fairly smooth, and Tom was enjoying the sense of speed provided by the steady thirty-five miles an hour he was able to achieve in his new 1915 Pierce Arrow touring car. The day was clear and mild, and it would have been a pleasant drive except for his concern over continuing labor troubles at the Winter Quarters Mine, located near the coal mining town of Helper. Strikes had plagued the Utah mining industry for nearly ten years, and if the prognosis from the majority of mine owners was to be believed, it was only going to get worse.

It was ironic that many of the mine owners were first- or second-generation Americans themselves, yet to a man, they resented and mistrusted the immigrants who made up the work force and who had banded together to demand concessions from management.

211

Tom's bank's investment holdings in coal had increased sharply two years earlier, following Tom and Robert's correct analysis of the potential to be gained from the outbreak of war in Europe. Steel, the lifeblood of any modern war, was badly needed. Steel mills required coal, and so, UTB had moved thirty-five percent of its investment capital into steel mills and coal mines.

As a result of several timely business opportunities, Robert Thurston's astute management, and Tom's instincts and increasing knowledge of the business, Utah Trust Bank had, in the nearly twenty years since its founding in 1897, increased its assets from approximately five million dollars to roughly two hundred million dollars. Tom held sixty-five percent of the stock, which included the one-third interest he had long-since repurchased from Gary Simonsen, the man in San Francisco who had bought Tom's Alaskan gold claims and become his initial partner in UTB.

As President of UTB, Robert Thurston had exercised share options to acquire an eight percent ownership over the preceding eighteen years. Tom had privately donated five percent of UTB stock to Holy Cross Hospital. He had also set aside ten percent in Katrina's personal account under her direct control, and had established four percent custodial accounts for each of his children, to be held in trust until their emancipation at age twenty-one. All in all, Tom had long since personally passed the hundred million dollar net worth mark, and each of his children had trusts worth several million dollars apiece, although only Katrina, and Robert as executor, knew of the arrangement. Tom and Katrina had agreed to keep their children's personal wealth a secret from them until they had shown they could handle the money properly.

UTB and the Callahan family had come a long way

since Tom's runaway journey up the mighty Yukon River in the summer of '96, and his trip back down that same river in '97, bearing crates of Alaskan gold dust.

The war in Europe had created a situation where fortunes could be won or lost, practically overnight—a situation, Tom understood, that made it imperative to make sound and timely economic decisions. With more at stake, effective management was more critical now than it had been in the early days of the bank's existence. America had gotten her nose bloodied on a couple of international issues, and it was becoming more and more apparent that some U.S. involvement in the European war would be required. Coal would become all the more important. If the flow to the steel mills were to be interrupted, Tom could foresee military intervention to ensure the mines kept operating. That meant government involvement and a variety of inspectors sticking their noses into operations. The meeting of the major shareholders of Winter Quarters Mine, held the day before in Park City, was called to forestall any such government action and resulted in Tom being asked to travel to Price to sort things out.

Tom pulled his new sedan off the main road and drove into Provo. Katrina had tried very hard to get Teresa to attend the church college there, but she had insisted instead on entering the University of Utah, just up the hill from their home on South Temple. It was hard for Tom to imagine Teresa in college. Barely sixteen, she had overshadowed both her brothers in academics and extracurricular activities, finishing high school at fifteen.

Thinking about the difference between Tess and Tommy, Tom shook his head. Tommy was just as bright as his twin sister, but he seldom applied himself, except in planning mischief. Getting by on his native intelligence and

213

doing just enough at critical times, Tommy had also finished high school at fifteen. But his was not an unblemished record. Sprinkled with some outstanding marks, it was also tarnished by notations of more than a few visits to the principal's office. Tommy applied himself all right, but not always in the right direction.

Tom and Tommy had never spoken directly about Benjamin's death, but a barrier had been erected between father and son. Tommy's ability in sports, academics, and even troublemaking, demonstrated that he was a leader, yet from the time the family returned from the fateful trip to Norway, the young lad had never really regained his father's approval. As a friend and business partner to Tom, as well as a member of the stake presidency following his release as their bishop, Robert Thurston had tried to talk to Tom, but to no avail. Katrina was acutely aware of Tom's resentment of Tommy and had also tried to talk to him about it, but to no greater effect than Robert. It was as if Tom had built a wall between himself and his youngest son.

Tommy's single attempt to cross the breach had actually brought more agony to him. Thinking, perhaps, that he could align himself with his father, when he was thirteen, Tommy had approached Father Scanlan, asking for permission to join the Catholic church. The kindly old archbishop, then nearly seventy years old, understood young Tommy's desire and counseled the lad to confer with his father. But Tom had taken umbrage when the boy summoned the courage to speak directly with his father about the matter, further widening the gulf between them.

"Your mother and the Callahan children are LDS," Tom had said, "and that is how it is going to be." End of discussion. Tommy's refusal to attend the newly founded LDS seminary program associated with area high schools had only served to widen the chasm between father and son.

PJ was a different story. He had it all, Tom knew, but somehow he'd not found a reason to put any of it to good use. All his teachers said he had a good mind, attention span, and conceptual ability, but unlike Tommy, for whom the wayward side presented a challenge, PJ had found no such challenge worthy of his attention, good *or* bad. While Tom and PJ shared a good relationship, and indeed PJ and Tommy frequently enjoyed each other's company, it was Tess and Tommy who formed the bond so common to twins. As they moved into their teens, their frequent horseback riding excursions up in the canyons provided Tommy his only outlet for his frustration. He was never able to confide in Katrina his longing for his father's acceptance, and so Tess became his sole confidant.

But Katrina knew. Ever since that awful moment in the hotel in New York, when she had met Tommy's eyes, she had known. And she was certain that Tommy's decision to attend George Washington University in Washington, D.C., where he could be near his Uncle Anders, was partly motivated by his desire to strike out on his own and prove something to his father. Katrina's brother, Anders, had often proven more of a father to Tommy than Tom, and Katrina had thanked Anders more than once for his sensitivity to her son's needs. Aunt Sarah, with two miscarriages and an empty household, was more than happy to have Tommy close by and to have her nephew and his friends stop by on weekends to visit Tommy's uncle, Congressman Anders Hansen.

With regard to family loyalty, the three Callahan children were as similar as the three leaves in the clover the parish priest in Ireland used to explain the Holy Trinity. But as the years progressed, it became apparent to Tom and Katrina that their children were as different as possible in their outlook toward life.

And then, notwithstanding Tom and Katrina's long-standing accommodation, there was the issue of the LDS Church. For nearly twenty years, Tom had stuck to his bargain with Katrina. He often thought of how close he had come, back in 1900, to joining the Mormon Church, immediately after Katrina's close call at the birth of the twins. Through the intervening years, the children had been fully exposed to the daily and weekly activities the church provided to retain the interest of its youth. PJ, nearly eighteen, was committed, or professed to be so, although his activity level had decreased as he got older. At sixteen, Tommy, following his abortive attempt to join the Catholic church, wanted nothing further to do with any religion. Tess had been her mother's constant companion through the years at church meetings and socials. Secretly, Tom hoped that attending the University of Utah might broaden Tess's horizons and that she would come to see the world a bit more realistically. He had, in fact, wanted to talk to her about attending Stanford or UCLA, but Katrina had quickly vetoed the idea.

Even though the Callahans lived just a short distance from the University of Utah, Teresa had chosen to live at her sorority house. The first weekend she had come home with a few new friends from the university, Tom thought he saw the first hint of change, but he had not been pleased with certain intolerant attitudes he saw displayed. When he stopped by the parlor, where the latest grammies were playing, he said, "So, how are the college girls today?" Teresa had responded stiffly, "Father, we prefer to be called university *women*, if you please." "Well, pardon me," Tom had laughed, and departed. Later, when he returned, he encountered the cluster of girls sitting in the yard, under the sycamore trees. Two of the girls were smoking, which Tom asked Teresa about that evening, after her friends had departed.

"Kind of flaunting custom, isn't it, Tess, for young girls to be smoking in public?" he asked.

"It's 1916, Father. It's considered chic."

"And you?" he asked.

"I obey the Word of Wisdom, Father, but I don't condemn those who don't."

"And who was the girl you were all talking about? I hope she isn't aware of your friends' opinion of her."

"Good grief, Dad. Patty Johnson's grandfather was a polygamist, and her father was excommunicated for continuing to practice polygamy long after it was outlawed. She tried to get into the sorority. Can you imagine? I'd just die if my friends thought I'd come from a polygamist family. I don't know how Patty had the nerve to try to join."

"You sound like a bit of a snob, Tess. It's a whole new world you're entering. I hope you can discern its rights and wrongs and understand that people have different lives and we have to try to understand," he added, and no more had been said about the episode.

It wasn't that he thought her strong belief in Mormonism, so much like her mother's, was wrong. In fact Tom had often thought that if his had been a Catholic family, Tess would have been the one to go the way of Sister Mary and join the convent. Not that she didn't like boys. *Valhalla* had seen a constant stream of would-be suitors during her high school years. Tommy and PJ had taken great delight in heckling the long line of love-sick swains who longed after their pretty and popular sister.

217

Sister Mary had seen the divine spark in the girl and had encouraged her to nurture it, whatever religious leaning she practiced. How the thought amused Tom. Katrina had learned long ago that Sister Mary, a Catholic nursing Sister of the highest traditions, nevertheless always took the opportunity from those brief teaching moments to expound to the Callahan children a broader concept of love and Christianity than the specific definitions taught by either Catholic or Mormon. And in the process, Katrina and young Teresa had come to love Sister Mary, much as Tom had learned to do, years earlier.

For over twenty years, ever since he first met her in the lobby of Holy Cross Hospital, Sister Mary Theophane had been for Tom the personification of Christlike love. Whomever, wherever, and whenever, she had never thought to ask from whence a man's religious beliefs derived. "We are all God's children," had been the basic philosophy of her life, and no one Tom had ever known had practiced that belief as decisively as Sister Mary.

As Tom drove south through Provo, his thoughts segueing from one subject to another, his memories of Sister Mary and concern over her current health brought an ache to his chest. She had never fully recovered after Cuba. Father Scanlan, until his own death the previous year, had required her to take on an assistant director and actually threatened her with a forced retirement if she didn't allow her assistant to assume much of the work load. Now, at seventy-seven years of age, Sister Mary was well advanced in years, and her body was simply worn out. Tom knew her time was not far off. For him, the pain of losing Sister Mary Theophane would exceed even the loss of his mother, gone also these past seven years.

Tom pulled into a gas station on the south end of Provo

and watched as the young man pumped the gas up into the clear glass cylinder on top of the pumpstand, measuring the gallons before draining the fuel back into the car. Three times he did that while Tom wiped some of the dirt from the windshield.

"It's a real snapper, Mister," the young man said, using his rag to polish the chrome headlamp housing.

"No, actually it's a Pierce Arrow, son," Tom replied.

The kid looked at Tom like he'd stepped out of a history book and just shook his head. "Whatever you say, Pops. That'll be $1.40," he said, holding out his hand.

"Right," Tom replied. He knew he'd said something wrong, but what it was eluded him. How was one to keep up, anyway? Katrina's understanding of the slang used by the younger set was amazing to him. As the kids had grown and times had changed, she had practically learned two or three additional foreign languages as far as Tom was concerned. Tom shrugged his shoulders. Impressing *university men*, or *university women*, with his bilingual skills didn't come easily to an old man of nearly forty-one.

Pulling out of Provo, Tom began the drive into the mountains toward Helper. Even the Pierce Arrow labored to climb the graveled road and steep grades cut through the mountain passes to the east-southeast of Spanish Fork. About three hours, Tom figured. He'd check into his usual room at the hotel, get cleaned up, and meet with mine management for dinner. What excuses would they have this time, Tom wondered? The constant tug-of-war between foremen, managers, and general miners went back as far in Tom's mind as he could remember. Even his father had told him that he was lucky he was working in the family store in Tipperary, because if he'd had to go down in the coal mines in Ireland, he'd be no better off than any other "Paddy." He'd escaped that life and was grateful to have done so.

Tom's new automobile climbed smoothly as the scenery changed above the snow line. Running away from Ireland as a youth, Tom had never given thought to how his parents viewed life. Maybe they expected acceptance of responsibility from their kids—as he did now, from his. But all three of his children seemed set on individual paths.

And now PJ was having a look at the old Irish sod—a trip Tom thought might help the young man to sort out his life and perhaps give him some direction. Convincing Katrina to let the lad go had been hard at first, but once she saw the merit of allowing him to meet his aunts and uncles in Ireland, she relented. Only the danger of the war remained a concern, and, so far, the European conflict had not yet threatened Ireland, although many Irish were serving in His Majesties forces. PJ had been gone only three weeks when the first telegram arrived to say he was safe and rooming with Tom's youngest brother, Seamus, in Dublin.

Seamus, who had only been three when Tom left Ireland in 1895, was just six years PJ's senior. Tom really didn't even know his youngest brother, although the entire American branch of the Callahan's had gone to Ireland for a visit in 1905. The trip could certainly do PJ no harm, and Tom, who was beginning to wonder which of his children would eventually take an interest in UTB and seek to come into the firm, thought maybe seeing Ireland would give PJ a different perspective. His kids didn't seem to grow up quite as fast as he had, Tom thought, but times were indeed different.

Tom was pleased with the performance of his new car on its first outing into the mountains. He crested the climb at Soldier Summit and entered a brief level plateau. Pulling off to the side of the road and exiting the car to stretch his legs, he found himself staring at the snow-covered mountains above him. In the twenty-odd years that Utah had been his home, he had come to love the mountains, the high valleys, and the stillness found in the back country. Camping and fishing trips with the boys, sometimes including the adventurous Tess, had been such a joy when they were younger. They had not gone since Benjamin's death. Indeed, the young lad's tragic passing had been a watershed emotional event in the life of the Callahan family.

Arriving in Price, Tom checked into the hotel and was given a message sealed in a small envelope. His luggage was attended to by an old Mexican porter who greeted Tom by name.

Tom opened the envelope and unfolded the piece of paper.

Seven-thirty in the hotel dining room. Be prepared, Dickson's got his lather up and the union wants blood. J. Milner.

Tom pulled his pocket watch from his vest and flipped open the cover. Five-twenty. Time enough for a quick change into some old clothes, a casual visit to a tavern where he might ascertain the local mood, and then back to the hotel for a bath before dinner.

"Can we be of any assistance, Mr. Callahan?" the desk clerk asked.

Tom looked up from studying his message, folded the paper, and put it in his shirt pocket. "Just luggage to the room, please. Oh, and the latest edition of the local paper, if you have one."

"Certainly, sir. We've got one right here," the clerk motioned to the old Mexican porter.

"It's nice to have you with us again, Mr. Callahan," the clerk said.

221

"Thank you, Horst. And how's your oldest?" Tom asked.

"Growing, Mr. Callahan. Always growing."

Tom nodded as he accepted the newspaper from the elderly Mexican. Tom gave the man a quarter and asked him to knock on his door at seven.

"Certainly, Mr. Callahan. Would you like us to care for your shoes before this evening?"

Tom looked down at the accumulated dust and nodded. "They could use it, couldn't they? Thank you. Seven, sharp."

"Yes, sir." he replied. "Just leave the shoes in the hall."

———

About thirty people were seated at various tables in the hotel dining room when Tom entered at seven forty-five. John Milner, General Foreman at Winter Quarters Mine, the man who had left the note, rose to greet him, stepping to shake his hand before he arrived at the table.

"Evening, Tom," he said quietly. "Dickson's got his nose all out of joint. Claims you're late and he's not standing for it."

Tom nodded and kept walking toward the table. Two men sat at the four-person table. Neither stood as he approached.

"Evening, gentlemen," Tom said, coming around the table to shake Dickson's hand. "It's good to meet you, Mr. Dickson," Tom smiled.

"Cut the malarkey, Callahan. You're late—you're wasting my time, and it's gonna cost you plenty," Dickson snarled. Dressed in a rough weave, western-cut shirt with a colorful Indian bandanna tied around his neck, Erik Dickson fully played the role of roughneck to the members of his union, and a tough, hard-boiled negotiator to management who had to meet his demands.

Tom made a show of pulling his pocket watch from his vest pocket and looking at the time. He shook his head, mumbling to himself. "I've been meaning for some time to replace this watch. Just that it's sentimental to me."

"But," he said, looking back at Dickson, "you're exactly right. I've wasted your time and I apologize. Thank you for coming," he continued, once again offering to shake Dickson's hand. "Perhaps we can spend a few minutes together tomorrow, that is, if you can come out to the mine for a while."

Dickson stood, throwing his table napkin down on the floor. "I came out here to meet with you, Callahan. What's this nonsense about meeting tomorrow? I got some demands to make to you, right now!"

Tom looked quizzically at John Milner. "Didn't Mr. Dickson get my message, John?"

"Well, sir, I'm not actually sure what . . ."

"Oh, of course. It's our new gal in Salt Lake." He turned back to face Dickson again. "I am really sorry, Mr. Dickson. This has certainly inconvenienced you, I'm sure. I sent, or at least I thought I sent, a message to Mr. Milner to be delivered to you yesterday. I've only come down for a couple of days to make arrangements to close down the Winter Quarters Mine. For the rest of the year that is. The owners, well, they, uh, they met a few days ago and considered your demands. Frankly speaking, Mr. Dickson, I'm having trouble understanding their intractability, but, well, there you have it. Most of 'em, like me, are just immigrants themselves. I'd still be glad to meet with you tomorrow, but, well, we're just going to kind of tidy up the place, and give the workers a week's notice."

Dickson stood open-mouthed as Tom's words sunk in. It was all Tom could do to keep a straight face, and Milner, to whom this was all news, stood quietly by.

"We'll see about that. I know your type, Callahan. Been dealing with 'em all my life. You'd bleed the men dry, if you could."

"I'm sure I've been misrepresented to you, Mr. Dickson," Tom said calmly, his ever-present smile glowing. "Still, in all," he nodded, turning to Milner with a question, "John, have you actually canceled your supply contracts yet?" he asked.

Milner was, by now, fully appraised of the game. "I've drafted the contract cancellation letters, Tom, but I was waiting for your visit to wrap it up."

"I see," Tom said, looking back at Dickson, whose face reflected a glimmer of hope. "Well, sir, perhaps tomorrow, that is if you're available, we could give it another shot. I really don't know. I'm only a minority share holder, and the major stockholders were quite adamant about closing it down."

"Let's get out of here," Dickson said to his companion. "Tomorrow, Callahan," he said, pushing his chair back and stepping away from the table. "Ten o'clock."

Tom quickly nodded, submissively. "Ten seems fine, doesn't it, John?"

"That'll be good, Mr. Callahan," Milner said.

Dickson started to leave and Tom moved from behind the table to stand in his way. "Mr. Dickson, about my *type*. I'm a bit confused. You don't like the Irish, or what?" he asked, still smiling.

Dickson glared at Tom. "We're all Irish here tonight, Callahan. But some of us were mucking out stables before we learned to stand up for the men in the mines."

224

"Oh, I see," Tom slowly nodded. "And that would make me . . ."

"That makes you the enemy, Callahan."

Tom continued to smile at Dickson, an affectation that he could see was getting on the heavier man's nerves. Finally, Tom stepped a bit closer to Dickson's face. "You still gettin' a dollar a month 'employment fees' outta these poor, mistreated miners, Dickson," he said with sudden grit.

"I, uh, well, the union . . ."

"C'mon out tomorrow, Dickson, and let's allow the men to see who the enemy is. Oh, and Dickson, I came over steerage, just like you did. And what would you be knowin' about the working man. You've been a bloody Dublin Jackeen all yer life." He leaned into Dickson's face, inches away. "And what I've *got*, Dickson, I didn't get from bullying everyone and sucking the life out of my fellow workers. I think it's time I see what the other men have to say about it."

"We'll see who runs these men, Callahan," Dickson shouted.

The growing confrontation had drawn stares and mumbling from some of the dinner guests in the hotel dining room. Now, with Dickson's outburst, all heads turned in their direction.

"Ten o'clock, Callahan. And be on time," he said, poking his finger at Tom's chest, before storming out the door.

Tom watched him leave and smiled at Milner. "How about a nice quiet dinner, John?"

"Suits me, Tom," he grinned.

"Aye," Tom said, taking a seat and unfolding his napkin. The waiter approached and asked if they'd like a drink before dinner.

"Coffee for me," Tom replied, "and there'll be just two for dinner," he smiled.

"I'll have the same, please," Milner said.

"What's his story, John?" Tom asked, nodding toward the departed Dickson.

"He's one of the shift leaders and supposedly the main spokesman for the miners. Fact is, it's like you said to him. His thugs are just tougher at the moment, than the other ethnic groups. His bullies have won the day."

"Is there opposition?"

"Sure. Plenty of it."

"Think we can find a couple of their leaders tonight?"

John Milner flapped his napkin open, laying it across his lap, and looked up at Tom, smiling. "They'll be at my house at eleven."

Tom leaned back in his chair and laughed as the waiter returned with a pot of coffee. "Two steaks, please," Tom ordered. "And make his rare," he gestured, pointing to Milner. "I think he could eat it on the hoof," Tom said, continuing to laugh.

About three hundred angry and perplexed men were gathered at Winter Quarters Mine early the next morning when Tom and John Milner arrived in Tom's car. A visible division was apparent in the clusters of men standing in what appeared to be, from the looks of their clothing and features, ethnic groupings of Greeks, Irish, and Mexicans. At the head of the Irish group, Erik Dickson stood with several cronies gathered around him. A few men carried ax handles. Tom cut the engine and exited the car, walking straight to the platform surrounding the mine office. He climbed up on the porch then turned to face the crowd. The men were silent, waiting to hear what he had to say.

"I'm Tom Callahan from Salt Lake. Now, if some of your mates don't understand English, I'll speak slowly so you can translate for them. I'm told we have a bit of trouble here at Winter Quarters Mine. From what I can gather, there is no clear-cut consensus on the issues. I'd like to hear from a spokesman from each of your groups so that all get a fair chance to speak."

Dickson stepped forward and shouted, "*I* speak for these miners, Callahan. And *I'll* be the one to negotiate with you bloodsucking owners." A murmur of assent arose from the three groups of men forming a semicircle in the area in front of and below the office porch.

"I said I'd like to speak with a representative of *each* different group of miners who have concerns. And *that*," he said looking directly at Dickson, "is exactly what we're going to do." Tom looked away from Dickson, glancing at the other two groups. "If you have a spokesman in your group, let him step forward now, and we'll take some time together in the office." Tom paused while several men turned back into their respective cluster of miners and began to translate. In a few moments, the men grew silent again.

Tom stepped down from the porch and approached the crowd of men. "Now, who speaks for the Mexicans?" Tom asked, turning to look at the smallest of the groups of men.

A tall, muscular man stepped forward. "I will speak for my people, *Señor*," the young man said. Tom estimated him to be only eighteen or nineteen—*a bit young for a spokesman*, Tom thought.

Dickson stepped between Tom and the young Mexican

man. "I said *I* speak for these miners, Callahan," he spit out. "Not some baby-faced, wet-nosed greaser."

Tom eyed Dickson and, from the corner of his eye, saw a couple of his Irish supporters move forward.

"What's your name, son?" Tom asked, looking past Dickson at the young man.

"Raul, *Señor*."

Without warning, Dickson whirled and whipped a pistol he had drawn across the side of Raul's head, knocking the young man to the ground. As Dickson turned back to face Tom, the banker stepped in close and grabbed the back of Dickson's head, pulling him even closer. Tom's right knee came up into Dickson's groin, causing the heavier man to double over. Clasping his hands together in a double fist, Tom brought his full force down on the back of Dickson's neck, dropping the man to his knees. With his back now to Dickson's group, Tom didn't see one of Dickson's men raise the ax handle, but Raul was on his feet in a flash. He grabbed the length of wood just as the man was starting to bring it down toward Tom's head. Jerking the wooden handle out of the man's hand, Raul turned it sideways and jabbed him hard in the ribs, driving him backward, away from Tom.

Tom heard the scuffle and turned quickly to see what had happened. Dickson got to his feet, but missed in his attempt to grab Tom's shoulder. As the dazed man stumbled by, Tom landed a right fist to the man's temple and Dickson sprawled on his face, dropping the pistol and lying still on the hard, bare ground of the compound. Tom sprang for the pistol and fired two rapid shots into the air. The report of the gunshots stopped Dickson's supporters, several of whom were moving to the aid of their leader.

When the confrontation began, John Milner immediately left Tom's side and moved to the rear of the office building. He now reappeared with about fifteen men, all armed with shotguns. They stood lined up in front of the office, facing the miners.

With the new men to protect him, Tom stepped over to the Mexican man who was leaning on the ax handle. "You all right, son?" he asked, keeping his eyes on Dickson's crowd.

"*Si, Señor*," he said, taking a rag from his pocket and wiping blood from the side of his head.

Dickson slowly regained his feet with one of his gang assisting him up.

"Now I said once," Tom hollered, "and I say again, *each* group will have the opportunity to express their concerns, including the Irish," he emphasized, looking toward Dickson. "Now back off and let's not get anyone seriously hurt." Tom motioned for Milner to come and take the young Mexican into the office. "We'll take care of your injury, lad, and then I'll talk with you," he said.

"Do the Greeks have a spokesman?" Tom shouted toward the group.

Two men stepped forward. "We do," one said.

"And when I've heard their concerns, Dickson, then I'll listen to you," Tom said, moving closer to the bigger man. Dickson stood quietly, his head bowed, rubbing the back of his neck. When he was within close speaking range, Tom lowered his voice so that only Dickson could hear.

"Now, Mr. Dickson, you've caused me to break a promise. It's been ten years since I've struck another man, and I promised my wife it wouldn't happen again. Got to admit, that angers me some. And I don't exactly know what to do about it," he said, pulling the hammer back and spinning the revolver cylinder. "But," he continued, looking into Dickson's face, "if you *ever* bring a firearm onto my property again, Mr. Dickson, you'll be fired." Tom stood his ground quietly, waiting for Dickson's reply, but the man remained silent.

"Look, Dickson, I'm here to listen to you and if what you say is indeed the consensus of all, then I'll listen more carefully. But you're through forcing your leadership on these immigrants. They may be new to America, Dickson, but so were we once. You seem to have forgotten that, *Mick*." Tom lifted the pistol again, the barrel pointed toward Dickson, whose eyes grew larger. The point of aim slowly passed Dickson's body, then his head, as Tom continued to raise the pistol toward the sky. He fired the remaining four rounds into the air, then flipped the pistol to hold the barrel and shoved the butt end toward Dickson. "*This* will be gone before your turn to talk, Mr. Dickson." Tom turned his back on Dickson and his men, motioned for the two Greek spokesmen to wait, and then he stepped into the office.

Two days passed while Greek, Mexican, and Irish miners aired their grievances. As Tom anticipated, pay and working hours were of concern to all, but the fact that all the shift foremen had been picked by Dickson proved to be one of the primary concerns. From talking with other Irish miners, Tom discovered that not even all the Irish were in support of Dickson's demands.

By Thursday afternoon, Tom had worked out an arrangement with all three groups, one that satisfied Milner's production schedule. Each group was assigned to work one of the three shifts, independent of the others, with shift foremen chosen from within their own ethnic group. Shifts would rotate each three months to equitably distribute the undesirable work times. Tom promised the Mexicans that he would seek additional Mexican workers to fill their crew requirements, inasmuch as they were the smallest ethnic group.

The Irish miners under Dickson at first balked at the solution, since all of the previous foremen had been chosen by Dickson from among the Irish. But Tom's threat to close the mine, or to import more Greeks and Mexicans to replace the Irish, forced Dickson to concede. Retention of some of his power, at least on his own shift, allowed Tom to mollify the hefty Irishman, but Tom could see he'd made an enemy for life. Thursday evening, Tom prepared to leave the mine office for another night at the hotel prior to returning to Salt Lake.

"Tom, about this young Mexican boy, Raul. He's challenged Dickson's lads now, and he's gonna have an 'accident' in the mine if he stays," Milner said.

"Aye, I've been concerned about that. Can you spare him?" Tom asked.

"Better to spare him, than to bury him, Tom."

"Aye! Well, tell him if he's interested, I'll take him back to Salt Lake with me tomorrow morning and help him find something at Park City or Utah Copper."

John nodded. "That's good, Tom. You're probably saving the kid's life."

Tom got in his car, slammed the door and smiled at John. "Tell him to meet me at eight o'clock tomorrow morning in front of my hotel. And John, try to keep these guys apart, eh?" he laughed. "We've got guaranteed contracts for delivery of this coal."

"And what would you have done if they'd called your bluff about closing the mine?"

"Bluff?" Tom replied.

"You were *serious?*" Milner blanched.

"Well, I'd have called Robert first and had him sell my stock," he smiled.

John threw his head back and laughed, then patted the hood of Tom's car.

"Want to change jobs, Paddy?" Milner quipped.

Tom smiled broadly as the engine roared to life. "I've swirled a few gold pans around, John. It's your turn now," he laughed. "See ya."

"Till next time, boss."

"Let's not have a next time, John," Tom called out.

13

By mid-March, 1916, it seemed even more certain that the United States would eventually become embroiled in the war in Europe, although many antiwar groups were even protesting the aid being provided to the combatants by the United States. Mine orders for both coal and iron had soared and, smelling blood, union leaders had held the knife to management's throat. Concessions in the form of higher wages and safer working conditions had been given and production continued.

Teresa was in her second quarter at the university, and Tommy was continuing to attend college near Washington, D.C. where Uncle Anders had helped him obtain a part-time job in the Department of the Treasury. Although only sixteen, Tommy was already over six feet tall, handsome, and solidly built. Uncle Anders's chief legislative assistant noted to the congressman that as a result of the time and attention Tommy was receiving from the secretaries in the government office, the lad had demonstrated an unusual willingness to work extra hours.

With the Callahan brood away on their adventures throughout the world, Katrina had the house to herself once again. Her spiritual resilience and depth of belief had sustained both herself and her marriage following the loss of Benjamin and of Katrina's parents. When Tom had withdrawn into silent anger, frustration, and, known only to himself, fear, Katrina had carried on raising the children, tending to household duties, and trying to support her husband, for whom work and the next bank deal had become paramount.

It was not that Tom didn't show love for her or his family, but his priorities had changed, and it was as if work were the only way he could mitigate the agony resulting from the loss of his youngest son. The one discussion Katrina had been able to generate, late one night in the quiet darkness of their bedroom, had consisted of a terse exchange.

"Do you still believe that Benjamin is with Momma and Poppa, Thomas?" she whispered in the stillness.

Tom lay quietly, causing Katrina to think he had gone to sleep. Then he moved, slightly. "I know that believing he is has made your life more bearable. And I am grateful for that. But the fact that I *don't* know, and that God has not chosen to speak to me, has put me through a hell on earth."

Tom had then rolled away from his wife and gone to sleep without another word.

Thoughts about his comment to Katrina occupied Tom's mind for some time following his cynical response, and after several days, he had found the courage to take her in his arms one morning before leaving for work, to tell her that although his confusion was real and disturbing, it in no way diminished the love he felt for her, or the joy his life otherwise brought to him. Somehow, he sighed, they would all find their answers, and he asked her to continue to be patient with him.

"Thomas, after nearly nineteen years being married to you, do you think I haven't learned patience?" she smiled.

"You are the very soul of patience, Katie, m'darlin'," he laughed, relieved that she had forgiven him in her continuing way of loving him unconditionally, as she had been advised to do by David O. McKay so many years before.

As Tom arrived for work later that morning and entered the lobby of the bank, the head teller smiled and gestured to him for a moment of his time.

"Good morning, Albert," Tom said.

"Good morning to you, sir," he said. "Mr. Callahan, a Mr. Antonio is waiting to see you if you have a few moments."

"Certainly. Please show him into my office. I'll be with him shortly, after I speak with Mr. Thurston."

"Yes, sir."

Mr. Antonio rose as Tom entered the office through the side door that connected his office with that of Robert Thurston's. "Good morning. Mr. Antonio was it?"

"*Si, Señor.* Sebastian Antonio."

Tom extended his hand. "Care for a cup of coffee, Mr. Antonio?"

"*Gracias, Señor,* that would be most kind."

Tom stepped to his doorway. "Janice, would you be so kind as to bring a couple of cups of coffee?"

"Right away, Mr. Callahan," she said.

Tom walked back to his chair, smiling at the younger man seated in front of the carved, walnut desk, another gift from Lars Hansen prior to his departure for Norway. "How may Utah Trust Bank be of service, Mr. Antonio?"

"*Señor* Callahan," Sebastian started, "can you tell me

the current condition of this account?" he said, leaning forward and providing a slip of paper with an account number written on it. "You will see, *Señor*, that the account is under the name of Sebastian Cardenas or Sebastian Antonio."

"I see," Tom replied, accepting the slip of paper. Janice entered the room with a coffee tray and placed it on the side of Tom's desk.

"Tilly brought some wonderful Danish rolls this morning, Mr. Callahan. I've placed several on your tray."

Tom smiled at the young woman. "Mrs. Callahan will be in to see you, Janice, about my weight, if you keep taking such good care of me," he laughed.

"Yes, sir," she smiled.

"Janice, would you please bring me the file for this particular account?" he asked, handing her the slip of paper.

"Yes, sir. Right away."

"Mr. Antonio, Janice will have those records in just a moment. Are you from Utah?"

"No, *Señor*, I come from Mazatlan, Mexico."

"I see," Tom stalled, his face expressing some recognition of the name and place.

"*Señor*, it is not my intent to deceive. My full name is Sebastian Antonio Cardenas . . . Stromberg," the young man said, drawing out his Anglican surname.

Tom nodded, recognition dawning. "I thought there was something familiar about the name. It's been a long time, Mr. Ant . . . uh, Mr. Stromberg, since I heard the two names connected."

"*Si, Señor.*"

Janice returned with the account records and placed them on Tom's desk, smiling politely at the visitor as she left, closing the door behind her. Tom quickly scanned the records, his eyebrows rising slightly, while Sebastian waited quietly in front of the desk.

"Opened in August 1914, with a deposit of $500,000," Tom reiterated softly, perusing the records, "with three additional deposits totaling, let's see, just over two million dollars. No withdrawals, or deposits since the last, which was November 1915, some four months ago."

"Si, Señor. My grandfather, Don Sebastian Antonio Cardenas, suffered a fatal heart attack in December of last year."

"I'm sorry to hear that, Mr. . . . uh, Stromberg. I met your grandfather. As I recall, he was a most gracious gentleman."

"Thank you, Señor. I believe some explanation is in order."

Tom poured Sebastian a cup of coffee, took one for himself, and sat back in his chair, sipping slowly. He gestured for the young man to continue.

Some two hours, three cups of coffee each, and four Danish later, the story of the Mexican revolution, the destruction of their hacienda, Don Sebastian's death, and the earlier death of Don Sebastian's only son, Miguel Antonio, killed while riding with government forces against the rebels, had been revealed.

"You're lucky to have gotten out, Mr. Stromberg. And it was very wise of your grandfather to have secreted some of his fortune in this country. But why Utah Trust Bank?"

"Señor, my grandfather told me the story of the brave Yanqui woman who saved my life when my mother died in the buggy accident. He kept track of her, and her marriage to you, as best he could. He knew of your banking ventures, and felt that, should the situation worsen, he and I—that is until his death—that we could move north to re-establish the Cardenas estate. At least until Mexico is able to determine her future."

"As I said, Mr. Stromberg, a most wise gentleman. How can we help?"

"I would be honored, *Señor,* if you would call me Seby," he smiled.

"Seby, it is," Tom laughed. "Where are you staying?"

"I am presently at the Peery Hotel."

"Well, I'm sure this will be quite a surprise to her, but Mrs. Callahan—Katrina—will not allow the grandson of Don Sebastian, or," Tom hesitated, "the son of Teresa Cardenas Stromberg, her best friend in Mexico, to stay in a hotel. Let's see what we can do to have your things moved to our home."

"*Señor,* I wish to cause no disruption of your family."

"Seby," Tom said, rising, "we have enough of our own, as do most families. But your presence will greatly brighten Mrs. Callahan's day, I'm quite certain."

"You are most gracious, *Señor,*" Seby said.

Tom noticed immediately that as they entered the foyer and looked around the downstairs area, Seby accepted *Valhalla* in stride. But, as he thought back, Tom remembered Don Sebastian's palatial Mexican hacienda where he and Anders had stayed for several days following Katrina's jungle ordeal. Clearly, Seby was used to fine surroundings. Henry met Tom and Seby downstairs.

"Henry, is Mrs. Callahan or Teresa home?"

"No, sir. Mrs. Callahan has gone out to Sugar House with the Ladies Guild. She advised that she would be home about six. Miss Callahan left just a couple of moments ago. She intended to run up to her sorority. She said she'd be back in about thirty minutes and certainly before dinner."

"Fine. Thank you, Henry. Mr. Stromberg will be staying

with us for the weekend. Please show him to the guest room."

"Certainly, sir. Right this way, Mr. Stromberg."

Seby carried his own suitcase, a hand-tooled, brown leather piece, with silver buckle straps. As he started to follow Henry up the stairs, Tom called out after him, "Oh, Seby, I've got a few errands to run. Please make yourself at home. There's a library in here," Tom indicated, "or you can take a walk around the neighborhood if you'd like. We'll have dinner at seven. Informal dress is fine," Tom thought to add.

"*Si, Señor,*" Seby smiled and continued to follow Henry.

Shown to his room, the same small suite of bedroom, sitting room, and toilet facilities that Anders had occupied during his stay so many years earlier, Seby splashed water on his face, laid out a fresh shirt and trousers for dinner, and descended the stairs. He lingered for some moments in the library, considering Tom's extensive collection of literature, and then departed the house.

The homes on South Temple were impressive, and as he strolled through the neighborhood, he saw several people who were quite well dressed. His thoughts flashed to his boyhood in Mexico and the privileges and prestige he had enjoyed as a consequence of his birth and upbringing at the hacienda. But the destruction of the ranch, the loss of the family assets, and his grandfather's death, had brought about more Spartan living conditions for the better part of a year.

He returned to the house about six-thirty and went immediately to his room, where he washed up for dinner and changed clothes. As he left his room, Seby hesitated on the second floor landing before descending the stairs. He could hear music wafting up the stairwell from the front parlor—a popular tune of the day. Reaching the main floor, he stood just outside the entrance to the parlor. Teresa was lying on the divan, her feet dangling over the end of the armrest as the gramophone cranked out one of the latest songs. Teresa noticed Seby in the doorway and sat up, smiling at him.

"Pardon me, *Señorita*. If I am not intruding?" Seby inquired.

"No, of course not, please come in. You just startled me," Teresa replied. "I'm Teresa. Teresa Callahan," she added, waving for him to take a chair in the parlor.

"Thank you, *Señorita*. My name is Sebastian Antonio Stromberg. Seby, if you like," he smiled, taking the seat. "I am a guest of your father's, although perhaps I should have waited until he was able to introduce us properly."

"Nah, we don't stand on such formality around here, Mr. Stromberg."

"Seby, please."

"Okay, Seby. You know this song?" she asked, gesturing toward the Grammy and bobbing her head to the tune.

He nodded. "I've heard it since coming to Utah."

"How long have you been in Utah?" she asked, continuing the conversation.

"I came into Arizona nearly a year ago with a small group of immigrants, and my friend and I came further north to Utah last August."

Teresa got up and cranked the gramophone, then replaced the needle against the roll. As she turned, her mother entered the room and Tess quickly stepped to give her a kiss.

"So, home for the weekend is the college girl," Katrina teased. "As I came in, Henry said we have a guest for dinner," Katrina said, looking over toward Seby and smiling. "Welcome to our home."

Seby immediately stood and bowed slightly to Katrina.

"Mom, this is Seby, uh, Stromberg is it?" she asked.

"*Si*, Sebastian Antonio Cardenas Stromberg," he said softly. "It is most gracious of you, *Señora* Callahan to have me in your home."

"*Stromberg!*" Katrina exclaimed. "*Sebastian?*" Katrina stared wide-eyed at the handsome young man.

"*Si, Señora.* I am sorry for the abrupt introduction. I think that *Señor* Callahan had planned to meet with you first."

Katrina sat down on one of the hassocks, and let out a deep breath. "My goodness, Tess, this is, uh . . . this is quite a surprise."

"Do you know Mr. Stromberg, Mom?" Teresa asked.

"If I'm correct, I think I did—once—" she laughed. "Your grandfather was Don Sebastian Cardenas, of Mazatlan?" she asked, turning to look at Seby.

"*Si, Señora,*" he smiled.

"My goodness, Seby," she laughed, tears brimming in her eyes. "I had no idea I would ever see you again."

"Nor I, *Señora,* but again, I appreciate your hospitality and I hope not to intrude. I was at the Hotel Utah, but *Señor* Callahan, well, he offered . . ."

"And rightfully so, Seby. This is your place to stay, if I have any say-so, for as long as we can be of assistance. As your grandfather said to me, once upon a time, Mi *casa es su casa,*" Katrina offered.

Seby's head lifted and he smiled. "*Se habla Español, Señora?*"

"No, Seby, I'm sorry for the pretense," she laughed. "But I did learn a few phrases many years ago, and your grandfather, a most wonderful gentleman, taught me the meaning of 'my house is your house.' We try to practice that

241

wonderful Mexican tradition here and make our guests feel welcome."

"Thank you, *Señora*. It is a wonderful home."

Scarcely able to comprehend who this young man was, Katrina stared at him for a long moment. She had often wondered what might have happened to Seby, and to have him standing in her home as a grown man was quite overwhelming. Gathering her thoughts, she said, "Well, I think dinner should be ready. Shall we go to the dining room?"

Tom came through the front door just as the three exited the parlor and were crossing through the foyer into the dining room.

"I see you've met our guest, Katie," he said before Katrina had a chance to speak.

"Thomas Callahan, you scalawag. How dare you pull such a surprise without warning me," she scolded.

"Hey, when Seby walked into my office this morning, I was just as surprised, and, in my defense, I did try to tell you first, but Henry said you'd gone out to Sugar House."

Katrina smiled at Tom, taking his arm and walking toward the dining room. "My heart nearly stopped when he said his name," she said, turning to smile at Seby.

Tom laughed. "I'll bet it did. A ghost from the past."

Teresa took her seat at the side of the table, unfolding her napkin and placing it on her lap. "What are you guys talking about, Mom. How do you know Seby?"

"Oh, my goodness, Tess," Katrina stalled, looking furtively at Tom. "That's such a long story, sweetheart. Perhaps we can talk about it after dinner."

Tom interjected. "Seby, you sit here on my right if you will."

Seby continued to stand behind his chair while Katrina moved to the far head of the table. She noticed Seby's exaggerated Mexican formality, and quickly took her seat, followed by Seby. Katrina gave Tom a sort of, 'did you notice that, Mr. Callahan?' look, smiled, and rang a small bell for the cook to serve.

"Seby, I'm dying of curiosity. Tell us about yourself and what brought you to America," Katrina said.

"There is not much of a story, *Señora*," Seby evaded. "I merely came looking for work."

"Actually, Katie," Tom interrupted, "young Seby here came into the bank today, to transact some business," Tom said.

Katrina's eyes opened wider and she nodded appreciatively at Seby. "And why Utah Trust Bank, Seby?" she asked.

"Well, thank you very much, Mrs. Callahan," Tom said. "We are, in my humble opinion, the *only* choice in the Salt Lake Valley, for the smart businessman," he boasted, winking at Seby.

"With a very humble management, Seby, present company excepted," Katrina said.

"Well, I have some ideas that I think Mr. Stromberg will like, and over the next several days, I will offer to show him around the valley and discuss some prospects," Tom added.

"Not before he shows me how to ride Mexican style," Teresa added. "Dad and I are going riding in the morning, Seby, would you like to come?"

"That's a rather presumptuous invitation, young woman," Tom said.

"*De nada, Señor*. It would be my pleasure to join you on your ride. And I would be most pleased to show you how Mexican women ride."

"Seby's mother was an expert horsewoman, Tess," Katrina added.

"Seby," Tom said, leaning toward him and pointing with a bread roll, "have you ever broken a wild filly?" he laughed.

"*Si*," Seby answered hesitantly.

"Well, when I tried to teach Tess to drive the car, it was worse than that. I hate to imagine how she might react to a new riding instructor. What do you think, Katie?" Tom asked, grinning.

Katrina had watched the interplay between Tom, Teresa, and Seby and was instinctively aware of Teresa's interest in the handsome young man. Katrina could see, however, that Seby was unaware, or indifferent, to Tess, at least at present, perhaps seeing her as yet a child.

"I think she needed a *different* driving instructor as well as a *different* riding instructor. You didn't last long teaching *me* to drive either, Thomas Callahan," she teased. "Thank goodness for Henry's patience."

"Aye, he earned his pay that week, that's for sure," Tom rejoined.

"So, Seby, tell me, do you still have family in Mexico?" Katrina asked.

Seby was silent for a moment, reaching for another piece of bread and tearing it in half before answering. "No, *Señora*. You know, of course, that my parents died. My grandfather and uncle are also dead now."

"I am so sorry, Seby. I greatly admired your grandfather."

"How many brothers and sisters, Seby," Teresa asked.

"I am an only child, *Señorita*."

"How about that, Mom? He's breaking *all* the traditions," Teresa laughed. "I thought that only the Catholics could surpass the Mormons for large families. He's got blue eyes and is an only child. That must be a Mexican record," Tess added glibly.

"*Teresa Callahan*," Katrina scolded.

"Aw, Mom. I didn't mean any disrespect. You didn't take offense, did you, Seby?" she asked, taking a fork full of dinner into her mouth.

Before Seby could respond, Katrina spoke again. "That's not the point, Teresa, and you well know it. We've taught you that it's impolite to ask personal questions beyond what someone is willing to reveal. Maybe your father and I could give Seby a few hints about what to ask *you*," Katrina teased.

"Mommmm, I get the point. Okay?" she said, her eyebrows raised and her voice sharp.

"Good. Now where were we?" Katrina said.

Seby smiled at Katrina and looked back at Teresa who was grinning.

Tom stepped into the fray. "Seby, the gentle Mexican civility that I have known, limited as it was, leads me to believe that you may find a weekend in an Irish-Norwegian home a bit unsettling. May I offer my apologies in advance? Especially for any difficulty your riding student may present tomorrow."

"What is this . . ." Teresa asked, " . . . get Tess day?"

"Not at all, my adorable 'university woman,'" Tom teased. "You've done well enough on that score all by yourself."

Teresa looked at the broad smile that covered Seby's face as her parents continued to impale her with wit.

"Perhaps it's just as well you don't have to put up with this from *your* parents, Seby," Teresa blurted out.

"*Teresa*," Katrina warned sharply. "Thomas, I think this has gone just about far enough. Please, let's bring some decorum back to the dinner table. We *do* have a guest in our home."

Teresa looked sheepishly across the table at Seby.

"I'm truly sorry, Seby. I forgot about your parents. Really, please . . ."

"*Señorita*," he said, his face calm and friendly. "I took no offense, truly. But I *will* say, that you are quite fortunate to have two parents who so obviously care about you."

"Well, I can see whose side you're on, Mr. Stromberg," she laughed. "So, to change the subject and save myself further humiliation, how about some music after dinner. I brought home some new Grammies."

"Wonderful idea, Tess," Katrina said. "Do you sing, Seby?"

"I believe I ride better, *Señora*," he laughed.

"Good," Teresa interjected. "Maybe there is *something* I can do successfully tonight."

Teresa's songs and the duet by Katrina and Teresa filled the evening as the four people sat in the parlor, enjoying a blazing fire, which was kept stoked by Tom. Again, Tom took note of Seby's gracious behavior and the ease with which he blended into the setting. Immigrant miners who had occasionally passed through their home had often given the appearance of being ill at ease, although Katrina had always tried to make them as comfortable as possible. Seby's upbringing clearly had taught him all the social graces, and he was a pleasant guest.

After a time, Katrina interrupted Tom's thoughts as she stood and moved toward the door. "Thomas, could you help me with a small chore in the kitchen?" she asked.

"Certainly," Tom said, rising and passing by Teresa, tousling her hair. "Tess, we've covered riding and singing, but nothing about dancing," Tom said as he walked toward the door. "I've a feeling Seby might have developed other social graces we've not discovered yet."

"Don't pay them any mind, Seby," Katrina offered.

"We'll be right back with a bit of dessert. Please excuse us for a moment."

Seby rose as Katrina left the room, and she hesitated for just a moment, briefly startled by his courtesy. In the kitchen, Tom wrapped his arms around her and kissed her forehead. "Couldn't wait to be alone with me, eh, Katie, m' darlin?'" he said quietly.

"Thomas, this is an unbelievable night. I'm scared. When we get around to telling Tess how I know Seby . . ."

"Teresa will be surprised, no doubt. But she's not naïve about life, Katie. She'll be all right."

"I hope so, Thomas. But I'm still scared."

"Tess likes him, that's certain," Tom added, "but I'm not sure I'd like to promote *that* idea. She's far too young."

Katrina laughed out loud. "Two months older than the young woman you pursued on board the *Antioch*."

Tom grinned. "That was different," he said.

"Right," she said. "Do you think *our* parents would have agreed?" she teased.

"Certainly not your *father*," he said, "but Tess has never really expressed interest in a particular boy, Katie. Have you watched her? I think she's keen on Seby."

"Good grief, Thomas, they've only just met. I don't think they're quite ready to marry," she laughed.

"Aye. But I've seen that look before," he smiled at Katrina, hugging her again. "And, like the fool I am, I've already introduced them," Tom added.

"That will sort itself out, Thomas, and he's going away again on Monday, you said."

"I don't know exactly how long he'll be around. I do have some business prospects for him," Tom replied, "but I want to be certain he doesn't get *too* familiar."

"Thomas, you just stop it. We've raised a proper daughter and from what I can see, he is a most proper young man."

"And you were a most proper young lady, Miss Hansen," Tom, said, continuing to taunt.

Katrina smiled at him and reached up in the cupboard for saucers. "What prospects are you talking about? For Seby, I mean."

"Katie, he came into the bank today, and presented an account number. When I reviewed the account, it had four deposits over the past two years, totaling just over two million dollars."

"Goodness. Then he's a very wealthy young man."

"It would seem so. His grandfather saw the revolution coming his way and tried to prepare another life for them outside the country, but then the old man had a heart attack."

"How dreadful. Thomas, I don't have the slightest idea of how to present this to Teresa. And what about PJ and Tommy?"

"We'll deal with them later, Katie. But for now, just try to summarize what happened in Mexico. I'll support you."

"I'm shaking," she said, leaning against the kitchen counter and cupping her face in her hands.

Tom stood behind Katrina at the counter, and wrapped his arms around her. "You have nothing to be ashamed of, Katie."

"I know, but . . ."

"Let's just go back in there and see how it goes. I'll be there to help."

Katrina finished cutting the cake, prepared a tray, and handed it to Tom. She lead the way back to the parlor. Distributing the cake, Katrina resumed her seat beside the fireplace. All four were silent for a few moments as the cake consumed their attention. Katrina broke the silence.

"Seby, how long did you say you've been in the United States?"

"Not quite one year, *Señora*. I was attending the university in Mexico City. Don Sebastian suggested I come to the States and prepare a place for us. I came first to Arizona, but then he wrote and explained about the bank account he had established in Utah."

"Mom, you were going to tell me how you know Seby," Teresa said.

Katrina took a deep breath then said, lightly, "I knew Seby as an infant, in Mexico."

"You lived in Mexico?"

Katrina glanced at Tom, a brief flicker of fear in her eyes, and in that instant, Seby discerned that Teresa did not know the story of the two marriages, the polygamous colony, and the part Katrina had played in his birth. He had himself learned the whole of it only after his Uncle Miguel Antonio's death, when his grandfather disclosed the details of Seby's childhood. It had been as shocking to him as he was sure it would be to Teresa.

"I did, Teresa, when I was a young woman not much older than you," Katrina responded.

"How? I thought you came to Salt Lake from Norway?" Teresa pressed.

Tom was standing in front of the fireplace, near Katrina's chair. "Tess, your Mom lived for a period of time in a Mormon colony, partway down Mexico, near Mazatlan."

"A Mormon colony? I've heard about those. Weren't they polygamous?"

Seby noisily set his plate down on the side table, his

249

action briefly drawing attention away from the conversation.

"*Señora* Callahan, perhaps you would like to see a picture of my mother?" He pulled a small, leather wallet from his pocket and removed a well-worn, wrinkled photograph. "This is a picture of my mother about the time of my birth, *Señora*. Her name," he said, smiling at Teresa, "was also Teresa. Teresa Maria."

Katrina took the picture and reached for her reading glasses on the table next to her parlor chair. She adjusted the glasses and angled the picture to reflect the light from the small lamp next to the chair.

Teresa looked curiously at her mother whom, she could see, was quite moved by the picture.

"That picture was given to me by my uncle some years after her death. I actually did not know the full story," he paused, glancing at Teresa, "until after my uncle was killed fighting the rebels. My grandfather told me the story of the colony, my father, and the death of my mother."

Teresa sat quietly on the divan, unsure of what was happening between her mother and this new visitor.

"Katie," Tom said, "I think it was a difficult time for Seby and his family. The revolutionaries were not too pleased with the upper classes. When Seby came into the bank this morning, his account was under the name of Antonio. Sebastian Cardenas and Sebastian Antonio."

"*Señor*, and *Señora*," Seby said, looking toward Tom, "I meant no harm, but when I left Mexico, I took my uncle's name. The revolutionaries were, uh . . . they were seeking persons from the . . ." he paused, looking again at Tom.

"Seby . . ." Tom said, moving to stand beside Katrina's chair and gently patting her shoulder and nodding in support to ease the boy's frustration, ". . . as we all know, you come from a prominent family, and in light of the revolution against the upper classes, I presume you felt it necessary to change your name until you came to the States. Is that correct?"

Seby nodded. "*Si, Señor*. The *patrons* were not in good favor."

"I understand," Tom said. Katrina lifted her hand to cover Tom's, which rested on her shoulder.

"Sebastian," Katrina said, "your mother was my dearest friend—my sister, in fact," she added, her voice cracking.

"I have wondered if I would ever meet the *Yanqui* woman who my grandfather said was so brave and cared for me when my mother died."

"Well, I don't understand *any* of this," Tess finally blurted out. She saw that her mother's tears had begun to flow, causing her more frustration at her ignorance—frustration that was beginning to turn to anger. "Will someone *please* tell me what's going on?" she pleaded.

Katrina cupped her hands over her face, crying softly as the picture of Seby's mother lay in her lap. "Oh, Tess, I don't know how to tell you."

"Tess," Tom said gently, "your mother was married before our marriage. She married Harold Stromberg, the young man who baptized her family in Norway. When he came home from his mission, they courted and eventually married. His father, Magnus Stromberg Jr., started the colony in Mexico."

"*Stromberg!*" Teresa gasped."

"Just listen, Tess—"

"Seby is my *brother!*" she cried.

"No, Tess. Let me explain," Tom continued.

"I'll do it, Thomas," Katrina said, rising from her seat and moving to sit next to Teresa on the divan. "Tess, at

251

seventeen, I married Harold, as your father has said. His father, unknown to me, was at odds with the Prophet's Manifesto on polygamy. He had purchased a large section of land in Mexico and was determined to start a new colony, 'in the Lord's way,' he later said. Harold told me none of this, Tess, and we prepared to move to Mexico."

"Mom, I don't . . ."

Katrina took Tess's hand and tried to smile at her. "Tess, I know this is hard for you. Please, let me explain. We moved to Mexico, and on the ship, just before we arrived, Harold said that I should pretend to be his sister, since my name was now Stromberg. I didn't understand, but he said his father needed to arrange land purchases, and everything would be better if they did not know his son was married. It didn't sound right, but I agreed. Eventually, Tess," Katrina said, tears again flowing, "I discovered that he had also married Seby's mother, Teresa Maria Cardenas, on a trip to Mexico some months after he had married me in Salt Lake. I was devastated. She thought I was Harold's sister, and Tess . . . we were both pregnant."

"You have another *child?*" Tess wailed.

"No, Tess, he died at birth. Teresa and I became very close friends. Like I said, almost sisters. We had both been betrayed by Harold. Eventually an uprising of local villagers destroyed the colony, and Seby's mother, a very brave woman," Katrina added, smiling through her tears at Seby, "was killed that evening just as she gave birth to Sebastian. Seby's uncle, Miguel Antonio, took me and the baby . . . she hesitated, looking again at Seby, "I don't think he knew you were Teresa's baby, Seby. Anyway, he took us to a remote shack on the beach, on the edge of the jungle. I lived there for nearly four months, alone with Seby. Finally, I felt if we remained there, we would both die, and I hiked a very long way through the jungle to Don Sebastian's ranch. Your father and Uncle Anders came for me after that."

The room was silent except for Tess's labored breathing, and Katrina's sniffles.

"You were in a polygamous marriage, Mom? A colony of Mormon *polygamists?*"

"Yes, Teresa," Katrina answered softly.

"Tess," Tom added, "your Mom didn't know about any of this until it was too late for her to escape. And she was married, to Harold, in the Temple."

"What did the Church say about all of this?" Tess asked.

"Harold and his father were excommunicated," Katrina said.

"And you?"

"No. When I returned, President George Q. Cannon interviewed me and, bless his heart, understood much more about the situation than I did. He blessed me with the strength to overcome and later, well, later he said I bore no responsibility and wasn't guilty of any wrongdoing. He counseled me to love your father until he saw the light and joined the Church," she said, smiling at Tom and sniffling.

"How could you do this to me, Mom?" Teresa said, standing up to look down at her mother.

"What do you mean, Tess?" Katrina asked.

"Why didn't you *tell* me? How can I face the girls at school? They all make fun of Patty because her grandfather was a polygamist. They refused to let her into the sorority," she cried.

"Maybe she's better off without them, Tess," Tom said sternly. "You might find it easy to look back and judge your mother, but it was—"

"It's all right, Thomas," Katrina said, her control returning. "Tess, I am truly sorry for the way this came to your attention. That is my fault. I should have told each of you years ago. For that I offer my apology."

"*Señorita*, it was your mother who saved my life on that beach," Seby interjected.

Katrina shook her head, her hands folded in her lap. "No, no Sebastian. It was *you* who saved me. If you had not been there, I would have given up and . . . I lived because I had to care for you. I am indebted to *you*, Sebastian, not you to me."

"Mom, what are you saying!" Tess shouted. "I can't believe you were a polygamist. And you, Dad, you knew this too, didn't you?" she accused.

"I did, Tess," he nodded. "And although I already loved your mother, I became very proud of her once I knew what she had endured."

"*Si, Señorita*, your mother is a very brave woman," Seby added.

"Oh, you all just don't understand," Tess screamed, running from the room.

Katrina looked at Tom and quickly followed her daughter. Tom and Seby remained in the parlor until long after midnight, talking about the events of the past as well as future business opportunities in Utah.

"Maybe we better turn in, Seby. It's been a long and eventful evening," Tom said.

"*Si, Señor*. Perhaps in the morning I should return to the hotel?"

"No, that's not the answer."

"I think your daughter is not pleased with the story. I am sorry for her distress, but I know from my grandfather that *Señora* Callahan is an honorable and brave woman."

"Thank you, Seby, but Teresa's just confused. She's got

her mother's toughness. Don't worry about her, she'll be fine."

"Good night, *Señor*," Seby said. "And, *Señor*, thank you for your hospitality and your concern. I apologize again for deceiving you upon my arrival at the bank."

"Think nothing of it, Seby. You had good reasons. Get a good sleep, and I'll see you in the morning."

Tom found Katrina already in bed and as he slid between the sheets, she turned over and moved close to him.

"Oh, Thomas, I'm so ashamed about all of this. I've kept it hidden for so many years. Teresa is very angry. She told me she could never face her friends again, and hollered at me to leave her room."

"She's not angry, Katie. She's hurt, but she'll come around."

"But, Thomas, such a shock all at once. How could I have not confided in her years ago?"

"Aye. Perhaps we should have told her—told them all, long ago."

Katrina succumbed to another flood of tears—silent tears—as she lay in Tom's arms.

"It *will* be all right, Katie. I promise you. And, Katie— Sebastian has come back to you after all these years."

She raised her head and in the dim light from the waning moon, Tom could see a slight smile cross her tear-stained face. "I will never understand the workings of the Lord, Thomas."

"Nor I, Katie, but He'll tell us what He wants us to know . . . in His own good time."

14

Teresa did her best to keep her mount well separated from both Tom and Seby as they worked their horses in and out of the twists and turns of Red Butte Canyon. Her voice cold and aloof, she had told her father earlier in the morning that she would not be riding that day.

"We have a guest, Tess. You *will* accompany us. It was *your* invitation, if you recall."

"Fine, but it won't be pleasant," she said, slamming her bedroom door.

Tom noticed that almost no conversation ensued between Seby and Tess, but Seby rode beautifully. Tom's good-natured reminder about Tess wanting to learn to ride Mexican style brought a terse rebuttal that she had decided she had no need for *foreign* riding instructions.

Tom's look of displeasure at her conduct did nothing to deter Teresa's disdainful treatment of Seby throughout the day. Tom found it admirable that Seby was able to ignore her rude behavior and refrain from being equally caustic.

Returning to the stables, Tom left the horses in Seby's care and went to speak with the manager of the stable. Seby took the opportunity to ask for Teresa's help.

"*Señorita* Callahan, could I ask for your assistance with unsaddling the horses?" he smiled politely.

Teresa gave him a disgusted look and instead of moving to assist, began dusting off her trousers. Finally, her personal grooming accomplished and Seby patiently waiting, she stood erect and glared at him.

"We have stable hands for that task, Mr. *Antonio*, or whoever you're calling yourself today. Besides, since you are obviously working to become my father's *lackey*, I don't want to stand in your way."

"*Señorita*, you have misjudged . . ."

"Mr. *Antonio*, or *Cardenas*, or *Stromberg*, or good grief, whoever you are, as far as I'm concerned, Monday will not arrive soon enough. Until then, please have the decency to avoid me whenever possible. You've brought quite enough disruption to my family for one weekend."

Holding the reins of the three horses, Seby held her stare. Teresa snorted a last humph, and spun on her heels to walk away.

"*Señorita* Callahan," Seby called out, his voice resonant and demanding. Teresa stopped and turned in her tracks, angry that he would have the insolence to speak to her in such a tone of voice.

"Further communication between us is not necessary, but know one thing: According to my grandfather, your mother acted in the best interest of all concerned. But you are young and perhaps shouldn't be expected to possess her strength and understanding. Good day, *Señorita*," he said, turning his back.

Seething, but at a loss as to know how to reply, Teresa watched him as he led the three horses further into the stable and began to unsaddle one of the mounts. Then she turned and stomped off.

Tom passed Teresa as she headed for the car and turned his head to watch her bristle. Entering the stable, he saw Seby working with the horses.

"Lucky she didn't set the hay on fire," Tom laughed.

"*Señor?*" Seby questioned.

"Nothing, Seby. Poor humor. Let me help you and we'll get through quicker."

"*Señor,* if you please. I will finish with the horses. Please return to your home, and I will follow when I am finished."

"That's quite a walk, Seby. You sure you don't want to ride with us."

"*Gracias, Señor. Por favor,*" he smiled. "And, *Señor.* If you would be so kind as to have your houseman put my few things together in my bag and have it ready. I am most grateful for your hospitality and that of *Señora* Callahan, but I wish to cause no further distress in your household."

"But, Seby, you didn't . . ." Tom could see the pleading in the young lad's eyes and nodded, understanding the request. "Seby, about two blocks west from our place and two blocks south, there is an excellent boarding house. Mrs. Wilson's, it's called. There's a sign out front. I'll arrange for a room there and have Henry deliver your things."

Seby brightened.

"On one condition," Tom said.

"*Señor?*"

"On condition that you promise to come back to my office at the bank on Monday morning at about nine o'clock, *and* that you make me a firm commitment that you will do just that. I have a couple of ideas I think might be of interest to you. Agreed?"

"*Si, Señor.* Thank you for your understanding."

"I think I do understand, Seby. I'm sorry for my daughter's behavior. She is completely out of place."

259

"No, *Señor*. It is *I* who is out of place."

Tom nodded his understanding. "Monday morning, Seby."

"*Si, Señor Callahan*. You have my word."

"That, *Señor* Stromberg, is good enough for me," Tom said, leaving the stable.

The ride home was accomplished in silence. Tess looked out the window, refusing to make contact with her father. When they turned into the driveway in front of the house, she quickly opened the car door, but before she could get out, Tom spoke to her.

"Tess," he said firmly.

Her face was an angry mask and she stared straight ahead, listening resentfully.

"It strikes me that a certain *university woman* has a lot to learn about life. You've been acting like a child, and, frankly, I'm embarrassed for you. What you learned last night may have come as a shock, but you're in no position to judge your mother. She went through a very difficult time in Mexico. If she had been less of a woman, she wouldn't have survived. But she did, and in the process saved the life of a helpless baby whose mother died during his birth.

"As to how and why she was in Mexico and how she came to be in a plural marriage is not yours to question. She trusted a man who took advantage of her, and she suffered because of him. She's never offered you anything but uncon-ditional love, and if what your friends might think is more important to you than the feelings of your mother, well, . . . I feel sorry for you. I suggest you go upstairs and think about how you are behaving."

Without looking at him, she said, "Is that *all*, Father?"

"I hope not, Tess," he said, exhaling in his frustration. "I sincerely hope not."

Tess got out of the car and started to leave, but hesitated. She turned back as Tom exited his side of the car and glared at him over the hood of the Pierce Arrow.

"This *unconditional love*, Father. Is that the kind of love I've watched you withhold from Tommy since we returned from Norway—since Benjamin's death—and since you drove Tommy to leave home?" she said, spitting the words out of her mouth.

Teresa spun on her heels before Tom could respond and quickly entered the house, her angry attack on her father already bringing tears to her eyes.

For nearly four years, the subject of that night on the *Titanic* had never been directly addressed in their home, but once Tommy had finished high school, his decision to attend college out of state had come to him easily and was not a surprise to Teresa. Only to her had he revealed his resentment and personal agony, and the two of them had often talked of his anguish.

Tom watched Teresa disappear into the house, his chest aching from her stinging rebuke. The thought flashed through his mind that Tess and Tommy were nearly as old as he and his brother John had been when they had decided to leave Ireland. Forever!

<hr />

Magnus Stromberg Sr. bent painfully to slip on his white buckskin shoes, then lifted his tall, slender frame from the bench in the dressing area. He looked briefly in the mirror, adjusted his white tie, and straightened a wisp of hair that had fallen over his glasses. Nearly ninety, and newly called as second counselor in the Salt Lake Temple presidency, he still possessed a shock of thick, silvery hair. He stepped through the doorway, out into the open area, and walked the several steps to the temple administrative office, smiling pleasantly as he entered.

"Good morning, President Stromberg," a young man behind the desk said. "Two sealings this morning," he added, handing the elderly man two sets of papers in manila folders. "The Debbins family, President, has specifically requested that you perform their sealing."

"I see," Stromberg said. He opened the first folder and quickly read the particulars. Harrison Debbins was to be sealed to Alicia Evanston. Witnesses were also named. The ceremony was scheduled for eleven-thirty. He glanced at his pocket watch, which read eight-fifteen. As he started to open the second folder, the young man spoke again.

"I almost forgot, President Stromberg. A sister came in earlier and asked to see you briefly, if you have time before the sealings. She's waiting in the foyer, just outside your office."

Stromberg closed the second folder and looked down the hall toward his office door. A woman sat alone, dressed in white, her hands folded in her lap.

"Thank you, son," Stromberg said and turned toward his office. Some feet short of reaching the woman, Stromberg recognized her, and his face brightened as he approached.

"Sister Callahan! What a pleasure to see you in the House of the Lord. Please, come into my office," he said, extending his hand. "How can I be of assistance this morning?"

"Good morning, President Stromberg. Thank you for taking the time to see me."

"Not at all, Sister Callahan. It's my pleasure. In fact," he smiled, "at eighty-nine, it's indeed a pleasure to see a lovely young woman at *any* time," he laughed. "Please, have a seat here," he said, ushering her into his office and to a soft, woven cloth chair in front of his desk.

"Thank you, President. I'll try to make this brief, but it is . . . perhaps I should start at the beginning."

Stromberg laughed again. "As good a place as any, usually."

"When I read of your calling to the Temple, I was *so* pleased, President," Katrina smiled.

"Sister Callahan, seeing you again makes me very happy. How have you been?" Stromberg said, resting against the back of his chair, his fingers interlaced and locked under his chin.

"I've been well, President. I know I have not communicated since your kind note some years ago, following the death of my youngest son. It was most comforting."

His expression grew serious and he leaned forward, taking Katrina's hand and holding it tenderly. "Sister Callahan, I was *devastated* by the news of your son's death and that of your parents'. A tragic, tragic event," he said, shaking his head.

"You were very thoughtful to think of us at that time, President. Thank you."

"Is your family involved in one of this morning's sealings?" he asked, picking up the folders.

"No, President," she said, "I came about another matter. When you visited with me, those several years ago, there was something I didn't tell you. I didn't know how to, actually, and didn't know if it would ever become, well . . . become known."

President Stromberg sat quietly, a compassionate look gracing his face.

"President, a young man recently came to Utah, to visit Thomas at the bank. He stayed at our home overnight and

263

is now at a boarding house. He is a fine young man, President. A credit to his family. He is from Mexico, President Stromberg. His name is Sebastian Antonio Stromberg—Seby we call him—and he is your great-grandson," she said, a slight glistening in her eyes.

President Stromberg looked confused. He questioned Katrina with his eyes.

"He's Harold's son, President. Born in Mexico to my friend Teresa Cardenas Stromberg. He came to America something over a year ago, escaping the Mexican Revolution."

The old man leaned back in his chair, removed his glasses, and with a fresh handkerchief taken from his vest pocket, wiped his eyes.

"The President of the Church himself called me to this position some months ago, Sister Callahan, and I told him I was *far* too old to be of service. He put his arms around me and said, 'Brother Stromberg, your work is not finished.' Evidently, that's the case. Please, you must tell me this story, Sister Callahan."

"It will be my pleasure, President," she nodded, patting his hand. "My *great* pleasure."

15

The two young men leaned against the granite pillars at the end of O'Connell Street Bridge, casually watching the people pass. One smartly dressed fellow across the street stopped at the corner, removed his bowler hat and picked at a piece of lint. Replacing his hat, he crossed the street toward the Four Courts Building, one of the most prominent public buildings in Dublin.

"That's him, PJ. I'll go first, then you come along behind in about a minute. Be careful, now."

PJ stayed at the end of the bridge as his uncle, Seamus Callahan, darted between cars on the bridge and scurried off toward the impressive building two blocks down, its granite facade facing the River Liffey. When Seamus had disappeared from sight, PJ stepped off the footpath, finding his way among the light traffic on a Sunday morning and following after Seamus.

Across the street, two men sat behind a window covered by sheer curtains on the second story of an office building from which one could see all activity on the O'Connell Street Bridge.

"Patrick, I say it's late to be lettin' a new lad in," the man said.

"Aye, but this isn't just some new lad. He's Seamus' nephew, actually. They look more like brothers, don't they?"

"I still say it's too late," Patrick complained.

"It's my decision, Paddy, lad. He'll not be told much. Do ye not know who his Da is?"

Patrick shook his head.

"He's Seamus' older brother, Thomas, gone from Ireland these past twenty-odd years. He's a bleedin' millionaire in America."

"Yer daft, man," Patrick said.

"Perhaps," he replied, his eyes following young PJ as he, too, disappeared into the Four Courts Building. Robert Lynn, Commander of Central Brigade, slid his chair back from the window and stood. "But now we're about to find out, aren't we?"

"And if he is?" Patrick asked.

"Patrick," Lynn said, taking his friend by the shoulders. "Let me do the thinking, lad. If his Da is who we think he is, then the kid will find himself in a spot o' trouble with the Brits. When word gets home to his Da, he'll be here on the fastest steamship there is, even if he has to buy the bloody thing. But first, Patrick . . ." Lynn said, taking his coat from the clothes hook and throwing it over his shoulder, " . . . Mr. Thomas Callahan, late of County Tipperary, will telegraph the American Ambassador in London, and the bloody Yank will jump through fire to reach His Majesty's bloody Irish Office and demand young Callahan's release," he smiled.

"Robert, how will that—"

"My dear, Patrick. I know you're all fired up about the rising, but it won't succeed, lad."

"What," Patrick exclaimed. "But you said—"

"Aye, lad, I said we were going to finally free Ireland. But it won't happen next Sunday—next bloody Easter

Sunday. But the message will have been sent, and if young Callahan down there," he nodded toward the river front, "has a concerned father, with millions, who thinks the bloody Brits have done his son wrong,—well, ye *do* get me point now, don't ye, Patrick?"

"We can get his money?"

"Ah, Patrick. There's hope for ye yet, lad. Now, let's go meet young Mr. Callahan and help him to find his destiny."

Robert Lynn, Commander of Central Brigade of the Brotherhood, referred to later as the Irish Republican Army, had underestimated the influence of Thomas Callahan, Irish-American. The original notification process did indeed follow the formal and interminable British protocol. The British Foreign Office notified the American ambassador in London that several Americans had been taken into custody following the abortive attempt at a rebellion in Dublin, during Easter weekend, 1916. When the list of American detainees was telegraphed to the State Department in Washington, a mid-level functionary reviewed the list, and attempted to obtain next-of-kin information to advise the respective families. When the telegram arrived at the home of Thomas Callahan in Salt Lake City, the bureaucratic process abruptly ended.

After calming Katrina and telling her not to worry, Thomas went upstairs to his private den, sat at his desk, and lifted the receiver from the telephone. His call to Anders Hansen, United States Congressman from Utah, at his home in Alexandria, Virginia, set in motion a flurry of transatlantic cables. Congressman Hansen called the Speaker of the House, and within one hour, they met in the Speaker's office. Together they telephoned the president and asked for an immediate audience, which, favors owing, was granted forthwith.

President Wilson's telegram to Winston Churchill was acted upon with unusual expediency, exceeding that of traditional British procedures. Executions had begun in Dublin of those found guilty of treason against the Crown during a time of war. Churchill's orders to retain in custody, but not to harm anyone holding American citizenship, saved not only young Patrick James Callahan, but also the primary leader of the rebellious Irish contingent, Eamon de Valera.[13]

Tom's arrival in Dublin, slightly more than three weeks later, was met with appropriate protocol by the governing British officials. Tom declined the government proffered hotel accommodations and demanded to immediately meet with key officials. He was taken directly to Dublin Castle and presented to the commander of British forces in Ireland.

"Mr. Callahan," the officer said, extending his hand, "we are most—"

"I'll see my son now, sir, if you please," Tom said curtly.

The officer, a Brigadier, and a veteran of the ill-fated campaign at Gallipoli, tilted his head back slightly, unaccustomed to being interrupted by others—especially Irish others.

"As I was saying, sir," Brigadier Sir Edmund Hillcrest continued, "this most unfortunate incident—"

Tom stepped forward to the edge of the desk, coming face to face with Brigadier Hillcrest. "I said, sir, I will see my son, *now!* If that is not possible," Tom said, reaching into his inner coat pocket, "I will lift *that* telephone receiver and will connect with *this* number," he said, handing the slip of paper to the Brigadier, "which, I am advised, will get me directly to Mr. Churchill's office. Have I made myself perfectly clear, Brigadier?" Tom demanded. "I *will* see my son, sir, and I will see him *now.*"

"Mr. Callahan," Hillcrest said, moving back behind his

desk to take his seat, "surely we can reach some accord, can we not?"

Tom turned around and lifted his briefcase from the side table where he had placed it upon entering the office. Reaching inside, he removed a newspaper and slammed the paper down on the desk, the masthead facing the Brigadier.

"Have you seen this edition of the *New York Times*, sir? It *is* a couple of weeks old now, and from what I understand the latest editions have begun to use *red* ink for the headlines. This, sir, is what America thinks of the bloody executions you've been conducting with a sham of a trial, and against people you call your own countrymen. By *God*, sir, it's no wonder we still clamor for our freedom. If you consider us countrymen and yet withhold all access to basic British law in these mock trials, how can you expect the Irish not to rebel?"

The Brigadier read the emblazoned headline across the top of the paper Tom had thrown onto the desk. "BRITISH EXECUTIONS CONTINUE" it read, accompanied by a four-column picture of several coffins lined up with mourners in various states of wailing grief.

The brigadier looked up at Tom. "Sir, I was led to believe that you are an American, as is your son."

Tom had acquired a semblance of control over his temper and smiled at the brigadier. "Sir, I am an Irishman, and as God is my witness, I will be an Irishman the day I die. Now, sir. Is it the telephone, or shall I see my son?" he asked calmly.

⁂

The service tray had been uncovered and the two hotel waiters were departing the room as PJ came out of the bathroom suite, his hair still wet and his robe loosely tied about his waist. Seamus sat in the corner, waiting, as Tom pulled two more chairs around the small table next to the food tray.

"Ah, Dad, that's the first bath I've had in over six weeks, if you don't count the hosing. It was a stifling hell hole they had us in."

Tom didn't respond and simply nodded toward the food. "Seamus, join us," Tom said.

As the three men ate, Tom silently took stock of his son. He'd lost weight, but was not in any physical danger. It actually seemed as if he'd toned his frame during his absence. When PJ finished eating, Tom poured himself a cup of coffee and moved to sit on the divan. He pulled his watch chain and noted the time, each action calm and deliberate. PJ recognized the manner. The three Callahan kids used to call it "the calm before the storm."

"PJ," Tom said softly, "start at the beginning."

PJ rose from his seat next to the food tray and sat in a leather chair adjacent to the divan. Seamus returned to his corner seat near the window and sipped at his coffee. They were all silent for a few moments, watching PJ, who seemed unsure how to proceed.

"Dad . . ." he said, his head lowered toward the rug. The silence returned momentarily, then PJ stood and stepped to stand in front of his father. "Dad, we're *Irish*," he said firmly.

Time spent renewing Tom's acquaintance with his remaining brothers and sisters took up the remainder of the week. His visit to Tipperary, to his mother and father's cemetery plots, and even a talk with his boyhood friend and fellow miscreant, Tony Leonard, and his wife, Jo, filled Tom with nostalgia. Tony's spirited declaration of the need to once and for all rid the countryside of the Brits brought to Tom's mind the deep-seated hatred most rural Irish felt for their uninvited guests.

The train ride to Cork where they were to meet the steamer also reminded Tom of his walk through the same countryside, the week he had scurried from Tipperary one step ahead of the law. The night before departure, Seamus, who had accompanied Tom and PJ during most of their stay, suggested they visit the pub for a while before turning in for the evening. Accepting Tom's younger brother's suggestion, the three men left the hotel and walked several blocks to McHanrahan's, the very same pub Tom had frequented during his sojourn in Cork so long ago. The pub was full of men. Consuming a requisite pint or two before going home to face the wife was a ritual of their everyday life.

The three Callahans sat at a rear table, but not fifteen minutes had passed before Seamus stood and headed for the toilet. He returned a few minutes later and motioned with his head for Tom to follow. Tom rose and PJ followed, both men trailing Seamus.

"Is this to be a family outing to the toilet," Tom laughed as they closed the water closet door and were alone in the small room.

Seamus smiled, opened the stall door, and reached behind the ceramic toilet bowl to knock on the wall. A three-quarter door opened in the wall, and Seamus stepped over the toilet bowl and went through the opening. Tom and PJ followed.

The door closed behind them, and Tom found himself in a slightly larger room where three men were seated around a small table.

"Ah, Mr. Callahan," one of the men said, rising. "*Three* Mr. Callahans to be exact," he smiled. "Thank you for joining us. We won't take but a moment of your time, if you'd be so kind as to indulge us."

Tom quickly understood he had unknowingly stepped into a meeting of the fledgling Irish Republican Army. Formed from multiple groups of disaffected Irishmen, dating back to well before the unsuccessful Fenian uprising in 1867, they had banded together as a result of the Easter Rising fiasco. Forced by English repression, some unity was finally coming to the forces that opposed the British occupation of Ireland.

"Please, be seated," the man said. "Mr. Callahan, my name is Michael Collins, and this is my associate, Robert Lynn. I have been asked to meet with you before your departure."

"And who did the asking?" Tom interrupted.

"Ah, yes. Who's in charge? Well, we're still working on that, Mr. Callahan, but you can rest assured that we are all headed in the same direction, finally. It's good to see your lad fared well."

"Did he now?" Tom said. "And did he fare well when someone saw the need to get him in this mess in the first place?"

"He saw his duty, Mr. Callahan. His family . . . I mean, young Seamus there, explained to PJ the abuses we've had to tolerate while some were, shall we say, comfortably established elsewhere."

"I make no apologies, Mr. Collins, either for leaving Ireland or for my, as you say, *comforts*."

"Indeed, and none are required, Mr. Callahan. But then there are those of us who remained to continue the struggle, so you see. To finish what our Da's and their Da's began."

"I've heard it all before, Mr. Collins. Get to your point."

Collins nodded. "I appreciate directness, Mr. Callahan.

Well, then, here it is. No matter where we live, we are always Irish. *We've* stayed to fight. But *you* can be of just as valuable a service, if you've a mind."

"I see," Tom said, looking at each of the men around the table. "This particular Irishman fights his way through the bank, is that it, Mr. Collins?"

"Aye. That and possibly through his connections to Mr. Browning's company in Ogden."

"I don't control John Browning's weapons company, Mr. Collins."

"No, certainly not. But you do hold a significant portion of his loans, and his weapons are, as we have been told, of the finest quality."

"So, I provide the money and the weapons, and you provide the troops."

"Aye. There you have it, Thomas Callahan of County Tipperary. You buy the gloves, and we'll bloody the Brits' nose. The time has come, Tom," he said, his voice more conciliatory. "It'll still be a struggle and might even take a few more years, but the fever's high now, and we're ready."

Tom looked at PJ, barely eighteen and already in and out of a British jail. PJ looked up at his father, seeking approval of what he had done and the course he had taken. Tom stepped closer to Seamus who had remained quiet during the conversation.

"Well, me baby brother . . ." Tom said, grabbing his sibling, "I can't say I'm pleased with how you've welcomed your nephew to Ireland, but given the way it turned out, it seems ye may need to travel to America occasionally to make your acquaintance with the rest of the family. What d'ya say?"

"Aye, Tom. Aye," he said, his face beaming.

Tom turned back to Collins. "Mr. Collins, we'll be off

tomorrow, but send young Seamus to visit his family in about a month. I'll see what can be done."

"Welcome aboard, Tom," Collins said.

"It's not quite that easy, Mr. Collins. I've only been here just over a week, but I don't feel the unity quite so strongly as you make it appear."

Collins nodded agreement. "Aye, but we've a good start. We just need to be able to show support from beyond the farms and the hillside. It's hard to take on the village constabulary with pitchforks, or have ye forgotten?" he smiled.

"Aye," Tom said, extending his hand. "Send young Seamus over. And now, is there some bloody way out of this place without crawling back over the toilet?" Tom laughed.

16

Sister Mary sat patiently, a tender smile on her old, wrinkled face as the young girl fidgeted and mumbled platitudes, trying her best to avoid getting to the point. Finally, Teresa looked directly at Sister Mary and a broad smile crossed Teresa's face as the old nun gave one of her well-known, "All right! Out with it," looks.

"You're worse than my Mom," she laughed out loud.

"Teresa, I've known you every bit as long as your Mom has, lass. I should have learned something about your habits by now," Sister Mary replied.

"And you knew Mom back then, too, didn't you?"

"Back then?"

"I mean back when she met Dad."

Sister Mary Theophane, approaching seventy-eight, nodded.

Her smile gone and her hesitancy returned, Teresa continued, but in a more serious tone of voice. Sister Mary knew the subject that was about to be broached.

"Sister Mary, did you, uh, did you know Mom, *before* she married Dad?" Teresa asked, unable to continue to meet Sister Mary's eyes.

"Not well, Teresa, but yes, I knew your Mother then. I first met her after your father had gone to Alaska."

"Then you knew she was married before?"

Sister Mary thought for a few moments before answering, and then asked, "Have you spoken to your mother about this, Teresa?"

"I didn't know anything about it," she blurted out. "It all came out a few months ago when *he* came."

"He?"

"Seby, or Sebastian Antonio. Oh, I don't know *what* his name is. He seems to have several. But when he came, it all came rolling out, and I . . ." Teresa stopped talking, lowered her head again, and clasped her hands, rubbing her fingers together.

"Teresa, have you and your mother had a disagreement?"

Teresa looked up briefly, the tears just on the verge of flowing. "I've been so mean to Mom, Sister Mary," she cried. "I just yelled at her and told her to leave my room, and I haven't spoken to her for weeks. I couldn't go back to the sorority house, I was so embarrassed. She was a *polygamist*, Sister Mary. And I'm . . . I don't know what I am. After Dad left to get PJ in Ireland, the house was dead silent for two weeks. Now, Dad's coming home, PJ's safe, and I . . ."

"It was quite a shock, my dear, wasn't it?" the elderly woman said.

"Of course! I mean, wouldn't you be shocked if your mother told you she'd been married before and in a polygamous marriage?"

Sister Mary placed her hands on her knees and pushed herself to her feet. She came to sit on the couch next to Teresa and put her arm around the young girl.

"Maybe there's a bit more to the story than you know, Teresa. Let me tell you some of what I understand. Your mother is actually an exceptional woman. I'm certain you thought of her that way before this new revelation."

Teresa acknowledged this with a nod of the head and a sniffle.

"So then," Sister Mary exhaled, "where can I begin?" she said, pursing her lips and rubbing her chin.

An hour later, darkness had nearly enveloped the small room where Sister Mary and Teresa sat. The time had been profitably spent. The young woman's tears had dried, and under Sister Mary's skillful prodding, her laughter had returned.

Sister Mary had taken the time to help Teresa understand her mother's dilemma. Forced to choose between two suitors, Katrina had chosen the one who shared her religious beliefs, only to find that she had been deceived. She was unwittingly made a party to a polygamous relationship that she would never have approved. After the death of her first husband, she had entered into an honorable marriage with Tom, the real love of her life. Teresa's mother had done nothing to be ashamed of. It may have been wiser to have told the children, Sister Mary conceded. "But when," she asked, "would have been a good time to do that?"

It was a contrite Teresa who hugged Sister Mary and thanked her for helping her understand. But instead of leaving, the young woman stood fidgeting near her chair.

The old Catholic nun paused in the doorway and glanced back at Teresa, giving the young woman another of her looks.

"There is one more thing, Sister Mary," Teresa mumbled.

"Aye," the older woman said, pursing her lips and nodding again. "You like this new young man, don't you?"

Teresa's eyes grew wide and she tried, but failed, to keep the smile from forming on her face. "How do you do it, Sister Mary?" she laughed.

"Experience, lass. Experience."

⸻

Tom entered the double doors of the Church Office Building and informed the receptionist that he had an appointment with Elder David O. McKay. The young man asked him to be seated and went to advise Elder McKay that Tom had arrived. Sitting in the busy foyer, Tom was amazed at the number of people coming and going. It was his first visit to Church headquarters, and he quickly gained the impression that it was more like a corporate office than an ecclesiastical headquarters.

After a few moments, D.O. appeared and greeted Tom warmly. Together, they climbed the stairs to Elder McKay's office where Tom was offered a seat on one of two soft leather chairs in front of an ornate wooden desk.

"I hear you've been to Europe, Tom."

"I have, D.O. My son, PJ, got into a bit of a scrape over there. Actually, he's the reason I've come. I don't want to take too much of your time, so I'll get right to the point."

The young Apostle, his shock of brown wavy hair beginning to turn slightly gray at the temples, leaned back in his chair, crossed his legs, and smiled at Tom.

"I hope there never comes a day when a visit with you will take up too much of my time, Tom. I've valued our friendship ever since we met."

Tom laughed. "I remember that day, D.O. If you hadn't grabbed me out of the way, that horse would have made short work of me."

"Yes, well, that was an exciting day, wasn't it? Statehood

for Utah, a new friendship. And how is Sister Callahan these days?"

"She's fine, D.O., but to be truthful, it's been tough. Even though it's been four years, there's still an emptiness. She doesn't say much, but . . ."

"Of course. And that's to be expected. Actually, Tom, I ran into Sister Callahan one evening after choir practice over on Temple Square. We sat on a bench for a few minutes and had a chat about the loss of your Benjamin. *That* is a remarkable woman you married, Mr. Callahan."

"Aye. One of my better decisions, that."

Elder McKay leaned forward and rested his hands on his desk. "So, how can I be of assistance with, uh, PJ, was it?"

"Right. I'm worried about him, D.O. Let me give you a little background.

"We . . . actually, *I* thought it would be good for him to visit Ireland, you know, to sort of get in touch with his roots. I can't say Katrina was wild about the idea, what with the war in Europe and all, but we sent him over there for a look around and to meet some of my family."

"PJ is how old now, Tom, nearly twenty?" McKay asked.

"He's just coming on eighteen. I've got a younger brother, Seamus, who is only a couple of years older than PJ, and the two of them hit it off. But my brother, fool that he is, got the two of them mixed up in the Easter week uprising. PJ ended up in a British jail, and if it hadn't been for some quick intervention by my brother-in-law, Anders, and by President Wilson, there's no telling what might have happened to PJ."

"And he's safe and well now?"

Tom nodded. "He's home, back working at the bank. But I'm concerned about him, D.O. He's gotten the notion that the Irish need to finish this struggle once and for all. I'm afraid he might just head back over there."

"I see," D.O. replied, waiting patiently.

"He's known you most of his life, D.O. He respects you and has a strong belief in Mormon teachings. I thought that perhaps if you could speak with him—you could persuade him to avoid the conflict."

"Do you think he's wrong, Tom?"

Tom smiled at Elder McKay. "That's another kettle of fish, D.O. The Irish have had the short end of the stick for centuries. Perhaps it *is* time for their view to be heard internationally."

"And you'll assist?"

Tom cocked his head slightly, and raised an eyebrow. "I'd rather not say, D.O., not meaning to be impolite. But whatever *I* do, I'd like to keep PJ out of it."

McKay reached for his calendar, studied it for a moment, then said, "If PJ is free, I could see him Wednesday morning about nine."

"That's fine. Thank you. I know he admires you. Sometimes . . . well, you know, kids get tired of listening to their parents."

"Don't I know it?" McKay smiled, shaking his head.

Tom started to stand. "Well, thank you for your time. I know you're busy, D.O. Or should I say, '*Elder McKay*'?"

Laughing, McKay motioned for Tom to sit. "Some of the older fellows around here wouldn't like it, I suppose, but I hope I never get so pious that one of my friends can't call me by my name."

The young Apostle leaned forward. He said nothing, but looked intently into Tom's eyes. Finally, he spoke.

"Tom, you've been in Salt Lake and around the Church for a good many years now. I've seen you in conference quite regularly. Has anything besides your wife's lovely music pen-etrated that thick Irish skull?"

Tom shifted in his seat. "I listen, D.O.," he said. "My Catholicism aside, don't ever underestimate the impact *you've* had on my family. Hardly a week goes by without one of the kids or my wife quoting something you've said—usu-ally to contradict something I've tried to get them to do or some household issue," he added, smiling.

McKay smiled back but said, "I hope I haven't been the source of any contention, Tom. I've often wondered how you and Katrina have managed your religious differences."

Tom didn't answer for a few moments. When he spoke, it was in a tired voice.

"I'll be honest with you, D.O., it hasn't been easy. We've managed mostly by ignoring the subject. I agreed before we got married that she could raise the kids as Mormons, and I've kept that commitment. But I also promised my mother, before I ever left Ireland, that I wouldn't forsake our Catholic faith. We've been Catholic in our family for gen-erations. Maybe you've noticed," he smiled, "being Irish and Catholic sort of go together."

"I understand, Tom. And I hope you won't be offended by my saying so, but its obvious you and Katrina are unequally yoked in this regard. I can only imagine how dif-ficult that is for both of you. Katrina is too noble a woman to say so, but in the few conversations I've had with her, it's been evident that she yearns for a unity the two of you have not enjoyed, with regard to religion."

Tom sat staring off into space. After a time, he raised his eyes to look at McKay. "I don't know what to do," he said. "I agree with many of the things your church teaches, espe-cially the part about children being innocent. When Benjamin died, I couldn't even think about what might happen to him according to Catholic dogma." Tom turned in his chair and took a deep breath.

"I'd like to have an answer, D.O. But I don't. I've envied you and Bishop Scanlan and my friend and partner, Robert Thurston, for your faith. You all seem so sure."

"Brother Thurston is a fine man, Tom. Bishop Scanlan's passing last year was a great loss to our community. I admired him and considered him a friend. But the truth is, Tom, theologically, the two churches are at odds. No disrespect, but we can't *both* be right. I think you know that."

They sat without speaking for a long moment. The Apostle broke the silence.

"Tom, would you do something for me?"

"If it's within my power, D.O., just ask."

"Oh, it's within your power," he said, turning to a bookshelf behind him.

"I'd like you to read this." He held a blue bound book in his hands. "You know Elder Talmage, one of the Twelve, of course. He's just published *Jesus the Christ*. It's a powerful study of the Savior's life and teachings. I'd like you to have it," he said, handing the book across the desk. "I think you'll find it interesting, and it will answer many of your questions."

Tom accepted the book. "In all these years, D.O., I've never known you to proselyte me," he smiled.

McKay returned the smile. "Tom, you've not needed to hear *my* words. We have an understanding, you and I. It's the Lord's words you're seeking. I think, my friend, that you are perhaps not as confused as you assume. You're a good man, and you've had a wonderful influence in this town and in your family. Many a Mormon woman has given up on a man who couldn't take her to the temple. Katrina is a wonder, but it says a lot about *you* that she's been willing to wait, trusting that the two of you can reach a permanent accord."

"Hmmm. Thank you, D.O. Your respect means a lot. I'll see what I can find in Elder Talmage's words."

Rising and coming around the desk, the Apostle put his hand on Tom's shoulder and walked him to the door.

"I'll look forward to speaking with young PJ. And, Tom," he said, "if I can ever be of assistance to *you*, I hope you'll let me know."

———— ❦ ————

Just over five weeks later, PJ burst into the bank, dashing straight past the teller windows and barging into Tom's office without knocking. Tom sat behind his desk, and Robert Thurston sat on the other side, with Mark Thurston on the couch.

"Dad, I got a letter from the Church," he said, waving an envelope.

"What do you mean, a letter from the church?" Tom asked.

"I mean . . . well, here, see for yourself. It's from 'Box B,' Salt Lake City."

Robert and Mark exchanged knowing looks.

"And I bet you can't guess what it says?" PJ blurted out, sounding more like he was twelve than eighteen.

"Well," Tom said, rising and coming around the desk, "I think you're here to tell us."

PJ opened the envelope, already torn from repeated entry. "Dear Elder Callahan," he read, "Having been found worthy . . ." he stopped and took a deep breath, dropping the hand holding the letter to his side. "Dad, I've been called on a mission to New Zealand. I'm going to the South Pacific."

"*New Zealand,*" Tom exclaimed. "Why that's . . . that's farther than Ireland. Why in the world would the Church send anyone to *New Zealand?*" Tom asked.

"Dad, the Church sends missionaries all over the world. Think of it, Dad, I'm going all the way to New Zealand."

Tom looked at Robert.

"Don't look at me," Robert exclaimed. "You know that Mark went to England, and that I went to Scotland some years ago, even before Elder McKay. But this isn't any of my doing. The Church calls those whom it feels can serve the Lord. It seems that young PJ has just lost his job at the bank," Thurston said. "My heartiest congratulations, Elder Callahan," he said, reaching for PJ's hand. Mark joined in the congratulations.

"Does your mother know?" Tom asked.

"No, she's gone to Ogden with Tess to visit Aunt Sophie."

"Well, this'll put a bee in her bonnet."

"*Dad,* Mom'll be thrilled."

"Sure. One son is in Washington, D.C., going to college, a daughter becoming a society or sorority snob at another college, and now her oldest son is sent, what, thousands of miles, off to some remote Pacific island full of aborigines."

"C'mon, Dad, get with it. That's Australia. New Zealand is populated by native Maori's and English, Irish, and Scottish emigrants."

Tom's eyebrow went up. "And how do you know that?"

"I looked in our encyclopedia before I came here."

"Well, gentlemen, I think our meeting is over," Tom grinned. "We need to find this young lad's wayward mother and inform her of the newest Callahan departure. Let's call Aunt Sophie up in Ogden," Tom thought out loud. "Maybe we can drive up there and meet them for dinner. Then you can tell the whole family about this new development."

"Meeting adjourned, then?" Robert laughed.

"I think we were through anyway, Robert. Mark, you arrange to meet with the Marwick & Mitchell people. I'd like to retain their accounting firm to audit the mine records and, in fact, the bank could do with a good housekeeping review."

"You're sure you want that firm?" Mark queried. "They're new."

"Absolutely. I met Mr. Marwick in New York last year and was suitably impressed. He's had a going accounting firm in London and New York since before the turn of the century. They just did an audit of Sweet Candy, here in Salt Lake."

"All right, Tom, I'll get right on it. My best to you, PJ," Mark said, turning to the excited young man. "It's an exciting adventure you're about."

"Thank you, Mark. Let's go, Dad, I want to see Mom's face when I tell her."

"Aye. But you'd better bring a couple of handkerchiefs, PJ. She's easily moved."

Katrina *was* moved. In fact she remained speechless for some moments. When she finally recovered from her shock, she simply hugged her eldest son and the tears flowed.

"Mom, it's great news," PJ declared.

"Of course it is, PJ," she stammered, "but it also means that you're becoming a man. My baby is gone."

"Aw, Mom. I'm a foot taller than you, and I haven't been your baby since—"

"Well, then," Tom intervened. Suppose we all head for a fine, celebratory dinner, what say?"

Tess joined her mother in hugging PJ and Tom stood by, watching as his family shared in the news of PJ's missionary calling. Finally, Katrina extracted herself from PJ's reluctant embrace, and turned to Tom.

"Thomas Callahan, I will have your word right here and now, that when PJ completes his mission, we will go to New Zealand, wherever *that* is," she said, shaking her head in confusion, "and see where he has served the Lord."

"Katrina, that's waaaaayyyyy down in the South Pacific."

"Thomassssss . . ." she said, tilting her head and looking at him askew.

"All right, all right. I promise."

"Me too, Dad," Tess squealed.

Tom let out a big sigh. "Why don't we *all* just go on PJ's mission with him?"

"Because, Thomas," Katrina said lifting her chin, "*you'd* have to be baptized first. PJ could do it before he leaves, if you're of a mind."

Tom's smile broadened, ear to ear, and he shook his head, holding both hands up in surrender.

"Enough of that. Let's go eat."

Fidgeting would put it mildly. If she had been a nail biter, her fingers would have been bleeding as Teresa stood on the street corner, across from Utah Trust Bank. At least six times she had decided it was a fool's errand and had determined to leave. Within half a block she had turned around and come back. When some of her friends from school had driven by, stopped, and offered a ride, she had even gotten in the car to go with them, but had changed her mind once away and made them bring her back to her appointed spot.

Teresa had done her homework. On the pretext of retrieving something she had left in his office, she had convinced the head teller to let her into Tom's office a few days before. Checking his daily calendar, she found the "Stromberg purchase," listed for five o'clock, Thursday evening. It was nearly quarter to five, and still Seby hadn't appeared.

She hid around the corner as Mark Thurston left the bank, got into his car, and drove away. At twenty-six, Mark had completed college, served a mission to England, and was already well on his way to becoming a partner in her father's bank. He had expressed an interest in Teresa, notwithstanding the difference in their ages, but she had not responded. It wasn't that Mark wasn't an okay suitor. He was in fact, every woman's dream. It was just that young men held no particular interest for her. She was kept plenty busy by school, her riding, and her friends in the sorority at the university.

Then Seby came into her life.

From the moment he had entered the parlor when she had been listening to the music, she had lost the ability to be ambivalent toward him. There was something intriguing about his self-assured but polite manner. His olive skin, dark hair, and blue eyes were a handsome combination. When Seby was revealed to be the long-lost son of her mother's best friend, from her mother's plural marriage, Teresa's world came apart. Yet, even then she was unable to dismiss him from her mind. Her caustic and thoroughly rude treatment of him on the day they went riding, was, she now realized, a reaction to the feelings he stirred in her. It both infuriated and fascinated her that Seby had remained a complete gentleman, refusing to retaliate. When he had finally spoken abruptly to her in the stables, she had bristled, but admired his refusal to knuckle under to her tantrum.

At quarter-past-five, Seby arrived, parked across the street, and entered the bank. Again she fidgeted, made several decisions to leave—this time out of fear—but finally gained control and committed herself to her plan.

Forty-five minutes later, October darkness beginning to settle over the valley, Seby exited the front of the bank, and the head teller locked the door behind him. He crossed the street, heading for the parking lot. She had moved from her original position to the street corner, next to the parked cars. Without noticing who she was, Seby tipped his hat, said, "Good evening," and walked on by her.

Two steps further, recognition dawning, he stopped, but didn't immediately turn around. Teresa gathered up her few shreds of remaining courage, now fully committed, and stepped to his side.

"Mr. Stromberg," she began.

"*Si, Señorita,*" he replied, removing his hat.

"I . . . I have come to offer my apology to you, Mr. Stromberg, for my inexcusable behavior in March."

Seby was silent.

"Seby, *please,*" she said.

"*Señorita* Callahan, I think it is not *I* who deserve your apology, but rather your mother."

She nodded. "And she has it, Seby," Teresa said.

And she did. Following her meeting with Sister Mary, Teresa had given ample thought to the issue and had prayed for guidance, all the while knowing what was needed. When she finally found the courage to broach the subject with her mother, Katrina listened to only a few words before pulling

288

her daughter into her arms. Both women collapsed immediately into tears. Katrina had held Teresa for some time and refused to let her daughter say anything more than, "Oh, Momma, I've been such a brat."

Although Teresa had not yet found the opportune moment to complete the process with her father, she could tell from his actions toward her that Katrina had told him about the reconciliation. Her father's renewed kindness and expressions of love for her convinced Teresa that he was willing to forgive her, but in her heart she knew it was a bridge yet to be crossed.

Meeting with Seby had been another matter. Teresa had tried to find occasions to see him throughout the summer. When she learned that he was in the process of buying the Stromberg ranch in Draper, she was delighted. That meant that Seby would remain in Salt Lake. By the time fall term began at the university, she knew she needed to talk not only to her father, but to Seby. She couldn't rest until she had made her apologies to both men. With regard to Seby, it wasn't so much a matter of closing a door as it was opening one.

"You have spoken with your mother?" Seby asked.

"I was a fool, Seby. A young fool. Perhaps I still am, but I'm getting wiser all the time," she said, trying to laugh.

Seby stood his ground quietly and Teresa wondered if he was going to do anything to make this easier for her. She knew she had one thing going for her. From the time she was a little girl, Teresa had been aware that she was beautiful. She had inherited that from her mother, along with the ability to be downright charming whenever that was needed to get her own way. Now that the initial embarrassment of making the first move was over, it was time to put her skills to work.

"Seby," she said, laying her hand on his forearm, "I made

a hasty judgment, and I offended you when you had no thought other than to accept my parent's hospitality. It's true that I was startled by the revelations that night, but *you're* not to blame for any of that. I can see now that my mother drew upon her courage and her faith in order to save you both. She candidly admits that if it hadn't been for the sense of responsibility she felt for you, as a young infant, she wouldn't have survived the ordeal. Therefore," she smiled brightly at him, squeezing his forearm and tilting her head coyly, "I have *you* to thank for me having such a wonderful mother."

The speech came out fluidly and clearly—much more so than during her earlier attempts in front of the mirror. Her coy facial expressions, so calculated to convey her sincerity, came easily to her, the products of frequent practice and a determination to convince this young man that she had seen the light.

Seby listened to her speech patiently, then lifted her hand from his arm.

"I am happy for you, *Señorita*. You are fortunate to have such a mother. And I am most grateful that you have taken the time to tell me these things."

"They are true, Seby," she smiled. "I am truly sorry for any hurt I have caused you."

"*Si, Señorita*," he said, his face as yet unrevealing.

"*Seby*," she pleaded, her voice shakier. "I really mean it."

"I understand. I am certain that this meeting was not easy for you to have considered. Obviously you have given much thought to what might happen—to what you would *say*," he smiled. "Your expression lacks only one thing."

"Yes?" Teresa said, now cautious and instantly afraid of being rebuked.

"You are a beautiful young woman, Teresa. You have your father's lustrous dark hair, and your mother's brilliant green eyes, *Señorita,* but I think it will be some time yet before you acquire your mother's depth. It is good that you have spoken to her and offered your apology. And I appreciate your coming to talk with me. Perhaps we will meet again some time."

His abrupt dismissal shocked her. Control of the meeting had changed hands without Teresa realizing what had happened. In an instant, Seby had taken the situation in hand, leaving Teresa speechless. Stunned and embarrassed, she struggled to retain some semblance of pride.

"You don't offer a person much latitude, Mr. Stromberg," Teresa said, her voice now cold.

"Perhaps," he nodded. "My grandfather often told me something you might consider: *We have little control over how life treats us,* Señorita, *but we have complete control over how we respond and how we treat others.* Fortunately, you have good parents, and, God willing, time may provide you the opportunity to meet their expectations—to develop, perhaps, your own expectations for yourself."

"My, aren't *we* the self-righteous one?" Teresa mocked.

Seby smiled. "I hope not, *Señorita* Callahan. And I wish you the very best. Good day," he said, replacing his hat and turning to walk toward his car.

"Mr. Stromberg!" she called out after him.

Seby stopped and turned to face her.

Quickly subduing her anger, Teresa smiled politely. "Congratulations on the reunion with your great-grandfather. I wish you the very best with your cattle ranch. Perhaps we shall meet again," she said, waving and turning to walk away.

"It will be a pleasure, *Señorita,*" Seby called out, his smile returning. *Already you are learning, little one,* he thought as he got into his car.

17

Finding a seat on the train was not as difficult as Tommy had anticipated. The initial contingent of recruits, including young Tommy Callahan, had boarded in Washington, D.C., picking up additional men at several stops on their trip south. He'd left a short note for Uncle Anders, after having decided against a face-to-face explanation of his plans.

April 27, 1917

Dear Uncle Andy,

I am most grateful for your hospitality and for your understanding of my problems with my father. Perhaps running away from my troubles in Salt Lake to attend college at Georgetown University wasn't the bravest thing I've ever done, but I hope to rectify that.

The president has called for America's youth to stand forth and save the world for democracy. You would understand that, Uncle Andy, because, although you have never discussed it with me, I know something of your bravery in Cuba so many years ago. Now, it is my turn and I must do this thing.

When you read this, I will be traveling south to the

293

new Marine Corps training site in South Carolina. I ask you most sincerely, Uncle Andy, please do not use your congressional office to intervene or to have me recalled. There has already been enough family involvement in my life's decisions. This time, I need to stand alone. I know you will understand.

Please give my love to Aunt Sarah and thank her for me for all her kindnesses during my stay in your home.

Sincerely, your nephew, Tommy

"But, Thomas, he's barely seventeen."

"Aye, Katie, but he's made his choice. Now he'll have to live with it."

"Thomas . . ." Katrina pleaded as they lay in their bed, the telegram from Anders having arrived earlier in the day, " . . . we're at war. He may *die* as a result of this choice."

"He's a man now, Katie, or at least he's trying to be. I'll give him that."

"Oh, Thomas, I'm frightened for him," Katrina whimpered.

"Aye. You and a million other mothers, I'd say."

Traveling with several hundred other young men scattered throughout the train, Tommy sat by the window, lulled into reflective thought by the clickity-clack of the train wheels. He watched the lush Virginia landscape roll by as the train approached North Carolina and thought of the beautiful Uintah Mountains and the fishing trips he had taken there with PJ and their father. After a time, he fell into a restless sleep, in which he was constantly disturbed by the rocking of the train and the movement and snoring of the other men, all headed for an uncertain future. Just before dawn, he awoke abruptly when a man fell against him while returning to his seat.

"Sorry," the lad said.

"Not to worry," Tommy yawned, stretching his arms above his head. "Where are we?" he asked, looking out the window at the early light filtering through the trees to the east.

"The conductor says we're about thirty minutes out."

Tommy nodded. "Is the, uh. . . ?" he indicated with his thumb.

"Yeah," the man replied. "Back toward the end of the car, but there's a line."

Tommy smiled as he stood. "From what I hear, that will be the norm from now on."

"Waiting in line will be the least of our worries, I think."

Fifteen minutes later, Tommy returned to his seat to find the other man arranging his few possessions in a small suitcase. "Tommy Callahan," he said, sticking his hand out.

"Good to meet you, Tommy," the young man replied, grasping his hand. "I'm Francis Borello. Just call me Frank. I'm from Staten Island, New York. And you?"

Tommy figured Frank to be about twenty-four—somewhat older than most of the recruits on the train.

"Well, lately, I've been living with my uncle in Washington, D.C. My family lives in Salt Lake City."

"That would make you a Mormon, then," Frank said.

Tommy looked out the window briefly. "Not so you'd notice," he replied.

Frank nodded and looked around the train car, where most of the men were beginning to stir and assemble their possessions. "I guess we come from all over the country," Frank said.

"Yep, and in about an hour, we're gonna be Marines," Tom smiled.

"Oh, no, Tommy. Not yet," Frank laughed. "There's a long road before they'll let us call ourselves Marines."

"What do you mean?"

"Well, my dad was a Marine in the Philippines during the Spanish-American War. He warned me what to expect. They're gonna chop us up first, Tommy. Dad said we'd be like a piece of clay and that they're gonna mold us just how they want us. And then maybe, just maybe, they'll let us call ourselves Marines."

"What's the big deal? We'll put on the uniform and be Private Callahan and Private Borello."

Frank shook his head then bent to slide his suitcase back under the seat. He looked out the window for a moment before answering. "My dad won a couple of medals in the Philippines and turned them into a pretty good job when he came home. He's kind of anxious, if you know what I mean, that I should be a good Marine."

They were sitting facing each other as the train began to slow, preparing to enter the station. Tommy leaned forward and slapped Frank on the knee. "We'll *both* be good Marines, Frank. Maybe we've *each* got something to prove."

———

Most of the men were standing, clutching their bags before the train had come to a complete stop. Waiting to receive them on the train platform as the car rolled to a halt were about a dozen men in uniform, wearing their campaign hats slanted down over their eyes with the leather strap fastened tightly below the crown on the back of their heads.

The bottoms of their uniform trousers were wrapped with leggings, and they all wore a white, web belt with small cartridge packets attached on each side and in the rear. They were not smiling. Before any of the young recruits could get off the train, one of the uniformed men came aboard. He had three stripes on his sleeve, and he banged what appeared to be a police baton on the back of the first seat he came to.

"All right!" he bellowed, in a deep gravelly voice. "My name is Sergeant Ryker. *This* is the Marine Corps Training Center, Parris Island. You *will* keep your mouth shut. You *will* exit this train in an orderly fashion. And you *will* board *my* trucks quietly and quickly. And you will NOT, I repeat, you will NOT refer to yourselves as United States Marines. *I* am a Marine. *You*, on the other hand, are a disgusting pile of mush-for-brains, gutter dwellers until I say otherwise. *Is that clear?*"

A couple of men nodded their heads or mumbled their acknowledgment.

"You *will* respond," he bellowed again, "'*Sir, yes, sir!*' Now, I said, IS THAT CLEAR?"

About half the men weakly voiced, "Sir, yes, sir."

"I can't *hear* you, ladies," the uniformed man said. "*Is— that—*CLEAR?"

"SIR, YES, SIR!" they shouted in response.

"Now, get off this train and get on *my* trucks. And your mouth *will—be—shut!*"

Frank shouted "Sir, yes, sir" and gave Tommy a quick grin. "*That* is a Marine," he whispered as he quickly moved past Tommy toward the back of the car.

The ride to the training facility took about forty minutes and immediately upon their arrival the two hundred or so men were herded off the trucks amid constant shouting and shoving from other Marine noncommissioned officers wearing uniforms similar to Sergeant Ryker's. The recruits entered a cavernous building where about a dozen other Marines were standing.

Yellow footprints were painted on the concrete floor, and the first men through the door were roughly grabbed and shoved toward the first several pair of footprints. The others quickly got the idea and began to line up on the footprints, which resulted in a four-deep formation of men on one side of the room. On the floor in front of each pair of painted footprints, lay what looked like a pair of folded, white hospital pajamas.

"You maggots will strip your cheap civilian clothing, *now!* You will put on your military clothing issue, and you will return to the position of attention. Now, do it!"

In seconds the two hundred men were disrobing and climbing into the sameness of the white, cotton garments. Within three minutes all of the recruits were outfitted in a one-size-fits-all uniform, some of the smaller men holding up their pants by bunching them at the waist. One of the men raised his hand and called out. "My pants don't fit."

Instantly, three of the sergeants were standing inches from the man's face, one to his front and one on either side, glowering at him. The sergeant in front leaned into the man, his lips scant inches from the man's eyes.

"You—will—keep—your—mouth—SHUT! Is that clear?" he said, spittle flecking off his lips onto the man's face.

"Sir, yes, sir," the man responded meekly.

The sergeant turned to one of the other sergeants standing immediately next to the small recruit. "I think we've found our first house-mouse."

The other man nodded. "Always one or two in every platoon."

The sergeant standing in front turned his gaze back to the young recruit. He stood even closer, until his nose nearly touched the man's nose. "Do you want to be my house-mouse, maggot?" the sergeant whispered.

"I don't know what you mean, sir?"

"YOU? Do I look like a ewe, maggot."

"Sir?"

"I said, do I look like a ewe? A ewe is a female sheep, boot. Do I look like a sheep?"

"Sir, no, sir," the terrified youngster mumbled.

"When I speak beyond the comprehension of your pea-sized brain, the response will be, 'Sir, the recruit does not understand the drill instructor, sir.' Now, get this pathetic scum out of my sight," the sergeant bellowed. The sergeant took one pace backward and turned to walk along the front line of recruits, stopping in the middle of the room.

"I am Senior Drill Instructor, Staff Sergeant Holloman. I will be your mother. I will be your father. I will be your priest, and I will be your favorite schoolteacher all rolled into one. I will tuck you in at night like good little boys. I will ever-so-gently roust you out in the morning. And I *will* put you back on that train and send you home to Momma the minute you fail me. IS THAT CLEAR?"

"Sir, yes, sir," the assembled men voiced in unison.

Sergeant Holloman cocked his ear toward the frightened young men. "I can't *hear* you, ladies."

"SIR, YES, SIR," they shouted even louder.

"Hopeless! Absolutely hopeless," he said as he shook his head. Addressing the other sergeants in the room, he continued to shake his head. "If we get even *ten* Marines out of this worthless pile of garbage, I'll be amazed. The recruiters scraped the bottom of the barrel to find this putrid lot."

He stood silently in front of the men for a few moments, surveying the room. Finally he came to a position of attention and barked his orders.

"Platoon leaders! Move 'em out!"

Four sergeants moved to the front, each standing forward of a portion of the body of men. One of the sergeants stepped between two rows of recruits who were lined up four deep, back to front, with about fifty men across each file. He raised his arm and motioned down the four-deep row.

"From here over," he shouted, "First Platoon, riiiiight face!"

About half of the men he had indicated turned to face the right, and slowly the others caught on and also turned. The sergeant then moved to the front of the first file, walking backwards to continue facing the troops. "By columns of one, Forwaaaaard, Harch!" When no one moved, he grabbed the first man in line and dragged him forward. Then the others stumbled to stay in line as the first platoon moved out, one file at a time. Guided through the far entrance by another sergeant, approximately fifty men departed the building before a second sergeant stepped in between the next two groups of men.

"Second Platoon," he barked. "Riiiiight face!" This time, a greater number of men understood the order and immediately turned to their right, shuffling off in single file as the following command to march was given. When the second body of men arrived at the next building, they lined up behind the first platoon and waited. Each man was forced to stand close enough for his chest to touch the back of the man in front.

Tommy and Frank had fallen in with the group that became the Third Platoon, and as their turn came to enter the next building, dressed in their white pajamas, they saw the next communal ritual. Eight barbers stood behind a long, wooden bench, their electric shears humming continuously. On the floor were mounds of multicolored hair shorn from the First and Second Platoons.

In less than forty-five minutes, the two hundred men in 42nd Company, Second Recruit Battalion, had been unceremoniously stripped of their clothing and shorn of their hair. As they exited the shearing pen, another recruit, picked at random from the First Platoon, stood with a bottle of iodine and a cotton applicator. Each recruit was instructed to bow his head, and a number was painted on the top of his now nearly bald scalp. By noon, the men in 42nd Company had completed their in-processing, having acquired haircuts, medical exams, vaccinations, and initial uniform issue. Reassembled in the original hall on the same yellow footprints, the beleaguered recruits were once again addressed by Sergeant Holloman.

"We are fortunate to have with us today, Congressman Edwin Denby who will address you. Congressman," he said, stepping back.

Congressman Denby, a diminutive fellow attired in a suit and carrying a cane, spent the next fifteen minutes orating on the history of the Corps, the patriotism inherent in service to one's country, and the evils of drink, desertion, and venereal disease. At the conclusion of his remarks, 42nd Company marched outside under the command of four platoon leaders and two assistant drill instructors for each platoon, heading for the mess hall and their first Marine Corps meal.

The psychological effect of the previous five hours had transformed the two hundred cocky recruits in 42nd Company into a semi-organized group of uncertain, frightened young men. Most were afraid to speak, having witnessed the instant descent of three or four shouting drill instructors on any unfortunate recruit who dared to ask a question. By dusk, the four platoons had been assigned to their individual platoon areas, which, in each case, consisted of a series of six large tents. Each tent housed twelve to fourteen men and was arranged with the others symmetrically around a larger tent, which they soon discovered was the main assembly area and instructional facility. A smaller tent in the compound comprised the drill instructor's office and was designated by a hand painted, wooden plaque as company headquarters.

Tommy and Frank had remained together throughout the morning and now became double-bunk mates in the Third Platoon training area. At nine o'clock sharp, a drill instructor walked through the tent, and one by one, pulled the chains dangling beneath the three bare bulbs that provided the only light in the tent.

"Good night, ladies," he said, bending to exit through the tent flap.

All was silent for a few moments as the recruits of the First Squad, Third Platoon, 42nd Company, Second Recruit Battalion, were left alone with their thoughts and fears. While some had contemplated what Marine training would be like, and some, as in Frank's case, had family members who had tried to explain it, the abusive treatment and instant control achieved by the drill instructors left no doubt in their minds that they belonged, mind, body, and soul, to the three drill instructors assigned to their respective platoons. Most were asleep in five minutes, but in the quiet of the night, a few sniffles could be heard from those who were unprepared for the shock treatment that had accompanied their arrival.

"Frank? You awake?" Tommy asked of his upper bunk mate.

"Yeah, Tommy."

"I'm still determined to be a good Marine, Frank," Tommy whispered.

"Then there'll be two of us, Tommy," he said, turning over, fluffing his thin pillow, and instantly falling asleep.

18

The first Maori *Haka* that Elder Callahan ever saw, at the beginning of New Zealand's summer in November 1916, left him astonished. The energy expended by the native dancers made him tired just watching. Only three weeks in New Zealand, his initial assignment to the Hawke's Bay region, on the east coast of the North Island, and a rural community outside of Napier, quickly confirmed to young Patrick James Callahan that his life of luxury and creature comforts was over. Of course, the mission president had told him exactly that during his arrival interview.

When James Lambert interviewed PJ and the other two newly arrived missionaries, the mission president had made sure the three understood that New Zealand was at war, and had been for over two years. Food supplies were short, and wool, which was otherwise plentiful in New Zealand, had been allocated for Commonwealth uniforms. Petrol was rationed, and the population as a whole was sacrificing, all economic classes included.

After living for a time among the Maori people, Elder Callahan had surrendered to their simpler way of life. In an early letter from his mother, she had acknowledged that it was going to be difficult adjusting to the loss of his wealthy and comfortable upbringing. She had said she was sure the sacrifice he would be called upon to endure was worth it. She also said she would be praying for him, and somehow, the vision of her kneeling in his behalf touched his heart. He would be a good missionary, if only for her sake. The changes required of those he would teach were far greater than those he would need to endure for the term of his service. Following his first convert baptism, Elder Callahan quickly accepted his mother's admonition. Three months spent in Napier, including his first Christmas away from home, brought PJ a literal sense of mission and instilled in him some of the direction he sensed his father had always felt was missing.

PJ's letters home were full of new discoveries: tales of hardships endured by the Maori people, their extraordinary faith, and the kindness and love that they showed to him and his companion. In his January, 1917, letter to Tess, he asked her to inform his parents that he had been given a reassignment and would be going to the South Island.

"We've been instructed to open a new area in the sheep farming country, up in the mountains southwest of Christchurch. I'm told it's prime land and full of Irish and English immigrants. Perhaps the Lord thinks I need a reminder of who I am," he had written.

He had also written about one of the senior elders in his area, an outstanding missionary who had already been in New Zealand for over two years. "One of our elders, Matthew Cowley, has such a knack for the Maori language. It astonishes the other elders how fluent he is and how the Lord has blessed him in his missionary work. I was present at a Maori gathering the other day when Elder Cowley was asked to bless a baby who was blind. I still find it amazing, but Elder Cowley laid his hands on that baby and promised, in the name of the Lord, that the child would eventually see. To have such faith is clearly a gift from the Lord. I would be frightened to declare such a blessing."

On a Saturday morning, Cathedral Square in Christchurch, New Zealand, was full of bustle, crowded with people out for some relief from their weekday routines. The Square had become a gathering place for soapbox proponents of all sorts of ideas. All that was required was the pluck to stand up in front of a group of people and voice one's opinion. Political candidates, antiwar proponents, and amateur theatricals were typical performers in the Square.

Elder Callahan and three other Mormon missionaries had claimed their station in one corner of the quadrant, attempting (mostly unsuccessfully) to lure passersby into taking an interest in their message. PJ had heard stories of the missionaries taking their turn in Hyde Park, London, and being harassed or soundly booed for their efforts. The "Kiwis" were perhaps more polite than their British cousins, but as a group they weren't any more receptive. They sat or stood silently and listened for a bit before moving on to see what the next group of speakers had to say.

Christchurch had been settled by the English. The first four ships of the founding colony had arrived in 1850, and the community had quickly taken on the appearance and atmosphere of a proper English village. Located in a favorable place, on the ocean with a natural harbor close by and proximate to the central plains of Canterbury, Christchurch grew rapidly beyond the village stage. By the time PJ Callahan arrived, in 1917, Christchurch had become a full-fledged city.

To the west, within easy sight, lay the magnificent

Southern Alps—a range of snow-covered mountains that PJ wished desperately to visit. Their towering splendor reminded him of the Wasatch Mountains east of Salt Lake City. Now, in the southern hemisphere, in late June, winter was hard upon New Zealand, although Christchurch's location on the ocean kept the climate moderate. The mountains, however, were another story. Rising in places to nearly 14,000 feet, they were continually snowcapped. In fact the missionaries had planned a trip to the west coast, intending to survey the area for possible missionary work, but the road across Arthur's Pass to Greymouth had been snowbound for three days.

PJ had learned that the Irish had settled much of the west coast. "*Coasters*," they were called by the locals. They lived there somewhat as PJ's father had explained the Irish did in western Ireland. Although the Gaelic language was not present in the western part of the South Island of New Zealand, other old Irish traditions still existed, and PJ wanted to see it for himself. He had come to view himself as Irish, and he occasionally wondered what was happening with "*The Cause*," in Ireland. Christchurch papers carried current news, of course, but PJ felt it had a British slant.

On one occasion, the Elders had traveled by train down to Dunedin, about 200 miles south of Christchurch. The Scots had settled Dunedin, and the accent of the people varied markedly from that of Christchurch. After laboring three months in Napier among primarily Maori, spending five months in Christchurch, and paying visits to several outlying communities, PJ was impressed by the diversity of the population. His letters home were full of praise and wonder at the strength of a people whose rugged ancestors had come to these two relatively small islands, located deep in the South Pacific Ocean.

When President Lambert had visited the six Elders in Christchurch, suggesting that two of them travel inland through the smaller communities and sheep stations, Elder Callahan and Elder George Armitage, a young Englishman from Huddersfield, Yorkshire, in the northwest of England, quickly jumped at the chance. The trip would be hard, the President had warned them, for they would be on foot and have to find board where they could. They would, he had said, be itinerant missionaries and would need to depend on the kindness of the local residents.

So, after spending five months in Christchurch, in August, 1917, as spring made an early appearance, Elders Callahan and Armitage began their trek west toward the Southern Alps, turning south and paralleling the mountains. PJ instantly took a liking to the countryside and the people they met. He and George Armitage got along well. Each of them had a brother in the war, and that helped them form an instant bond. Elder Armitage had been rejected for service with His Majesty's armed forces due to color blindness, and no amount of pleading on his part had been able to convince the authorities to allow him to enlist with his brother.

The people in the central South Island were indeed friendly and helpful, and the elders spent only a few nights in the open. PJ hardly minded having to do so. The night sky over New Zealand was magnificent. The formations of stars were not the same as those visible in the northern hemisphere, and among the billions of tiny lights was the famous constellation called the Southern Cross. Lying out in the open air, gazing upward, the two young men marveled at the immensity of space and were awed by the handiwork of God. Being out also reminded PJ of the times when he, his father, Tommy, and less often, Tess, had spent time camping together in the mountains of Utah. Remembering, PJ experienced a spate of nostalgia and homesickness that was bittersweet to him. Still, he was content to be in a great country and grateful to be involved in a good cause.

Tom sat dumbfounded. In fact, his facial expression actually betrayed his disbelief, surprising Robert Thurston. Tom had always had the ability to put on a "poker face" in negotiations and face-to-face confrontations. It was an ability Thurston had always admired in his friend and business partner.

"Robert, one of the biggest deals we've ever done is coming to fruition in the next six months. I *need* you."

"Tom, how long have we been in the bank together?" the older man asked softly, crossing his legs as he sat in one of the leather chairs in front of Tom's desk.

"I don't know," Tom dodged. "Over twenty years, probably."

"Twenty-one years, Tom. And we've done more *big* deals together than you can count. *This* is a big deal, too, to me."

"Well, who does McKay think he is?" Tom stammered. "They've already got my *son*. In Ireland it's tradition to give only *one* son to the priesthood. They can't have the *president* of my bank, too," Tom smiled thinly, knowing his partner had already made up his mind.

"And how *is* PJ?" Robert asked.

"His letters are . . . he's engrossed. That's the only term I can use."

Robert nodded his head. "It was the same with Mark. Tom . . . there's something else . . ." he said, staring across the desk at him as he had that first day when Tom had returned from Alaska and asked Robert to consider heading up the new bank Tom intended to start. "In these twenty years I've not pressed you for understanding about my church. I've always known that you have as good an understanding of what we believe as most of the men in my ward. And so," he continued, rising and walking to the window, where he looked out for a couple of silent moments, and then turned back to face Tom, "I knew you'd eventually come to terms with my decision. You've got a great staff here in the bank. And, if I do say so myself, Mark has taken hold of his job and is running full speed. The bank won't skip a beat."

Tom looked over the top of his reading glasses at his partner, who had moved back to stand behind his chair in front of Tom's desk. "I guess you're right. The only things you've brought to UTB are hard work, integrity, and sound business judgment. We'll get along fine without those." Tom allowed a smile to betray his feelings and continued. "Seriously, I'm happy for you, Robert. I know it's a great honor to be called as a mission president. You'll do great."

"Thank you, Tom. Your support means a lot. My thoughts, and, you should know, my prayers, have so often been with you and your family. Losing young Benjamin was like losing one of my own. But now, Tom, seeing I'm leaving so soon, and for several years, I have one duty that I've put off far too long."

Tom held Robert's eyes silently for a few moments. "Yes, President?" Tom grinned.

"I'm not joking, Tom. Please, hear me out. This is something you can't ignore any longer. For over five years I've watched as you've wrestled with your feelings for Tommy. He's in the Marines now and as surely as it snows in Utah in the winter, he's going to war. You've *got* to put your heart right about this matter. Tommy has always loved you, and whether you know it or not, he has sought your love and your approval all of his life. When I was his bishop, he and I spoke several times of the conflict between you two. I was acutely aware of his need for you. Yet you've held him at arm's length when he's needed his father's love."

"Robert, that's—"

"Just listen to me, Tom. You may *never* have another chance to make it right with the boy. Like it or not, he will, or maybe he already has, become a man. Fathers and sons tend to drift apart and avoid the things that are important in life—like fathers telling their sons that they love them. We get engrossed in our work. Like these *big* deals we do in the bank. I don't make light of our efforts and the good living it has brought both your family and mine, but in the overall scheme of things, Tom, none of that matters. It truly . . . doesn't . . . matter. We'll take none of this with us when our time comes. When you see Benjamin again, and as God is my witness, you *will* see him again, he won't ask, "How'd things go at the bank, Dad?" Do you understand that, Tom?"

Tom looked up at Robert and said nothing. Robert came forward to stand against the front of Tom's desk and waited. Tom took a deep breath and exhaled slowly, looking down toward the floor and then back up at Robert.

Tom's face betrayed his feelings once again. This time it was pain.

"You're right, of course, Robert." He removed his glasses and sighed, rubbing his eye sockets with the heels of his hands. "I've been angry at him for years, and I know it's broken Katrina's heart."

"Why, Tom? Have you truly thought it through? What was there to be angry about for that many years?"

"For a long time, I blamed Tommy for Benjamin's death—for letting go of his brother's hand and letting him

310

get away on . . . on the ship. Nursing those feelings made it easy to blame him for a lot of other things and pretty soon we weren't able to talk anymore. We just learned to stay out of each other's way and became strangers."

"It wasn't Tommy's fault that Benjamin drowned," Robert said.

"I know that," Tom said. "I figured it out a long time ago. I wasn't mad at Tommy, I was mad at myself—for sending Katrina and the kids off to Europe, for not being there to help when they needed me. *I* was the one who failed, not him. I eventually understood that, but the way things had gone, I didn't know how to fix it. What can I do? He hates me. How can I tell Tommy that I'm sorry and that I love him?"

"Just—like—that," Robert said. "I'm sorry, and I love you, son."

"Would he want to hear that, Robert? Isn't it too late, after the way we've hurt each other?"

Robert stood up and prepared to leave. He looked across the desk at Tom, who for the first time since Robert had known him had tears in his eyes.

"You know the answer to that, my friend. Take care of it."

Robert gathered up his briefcase and walked to the door. Before he could leave, Tom called out after him.

"Do you know where you're going to be assigned?"

"Not yet. In a couple of weeks I'll be advised. It really doesn't matter, though. Alice and I will be happy to serve wherever we're asked."

Tom came around his desk and across the office. He extended his hand and the two men shook.

"There is one other thing you might like to take care of, Tom," Robert said. "The next step, following repentance, is baptism. As my first official act as a missionary, I'd be happy to help you take care of that," he grinned.

"One step at a time, President Thurston," Tom smiled back. He hesitated for just a moment, and then wrapped his arms around his friend and partner, a physical demonstration of affection Tom had never previously shown. Stepping back, Tom said, "I'll tell you what, though, you're going to be one heck of a mission president."

⸺⸺

On a bright Thursday morning, the third week in August 1917, one hundred and eight-two members of 42nd Company, 2nd Recruit Battalion, United States Marine Corps, proudly marched the mile and a half from their training area to the "Grinder," the name affectionately given to the half-mile square, close-order-drill, parade ground. Hastily assembled grandstands stood off to one side of the parade ground and several hundred guests, parents, and well-wishers were in attendance.

For eleven weeks the recruits had slogged through dirt and mud, learning to assemble and disassemble their weapons under the most trying conditions, and perhaps, more importantly, learning to obey orders without question. Their physical conditioning had gone on nearly the entire sixteen hours they were awake, and while they were trying to sleep, the sand fleas and mosquitoes mounted another assault on them.

In the second week, squad leaders were chosen for the four squads in each platoon, and Tommy Callahan and Frank Borello were both selected for two of those positions. In the fourth week, Frank was chosen to carry the platoon guidon, and he assumed his position to the right-front of the fourth squad, marching alone to the forefront of the platoon. Tommy had retained his position as first squad leader from the second week right though training.

By a third of the way through basic training, the recruits had been fully indoctrinated to the Marine Corps' most important job: that of a rifleman. For a full week, they were subjected to "snapping-in," the process of assuming the positions necessary to accurately fire their rifle from standing, sitting, and prone positions. Through the entire process, not one shot had been fired however. Each evening, the recruits went to bed with new muscles aching from the contorted positions they were required to assume. By the end of the week, when they finally commenced live-fire exercises, their muscles had adjusted, and they were able to assume the various positions with ease, and able to hold the weapon rock-steady during the final seconds of sighting the target. Both Frank and Tommy qualified "expert" on the first qualification day, and thereafter they assisted others in subsequent attempts.

Tommy received several letters from his Uncle Anders and, after a few weeks, also from his mother and Tess. No communication was forthcoming from his father, and Tommy had sent none as well. He did not explain to his mother that his impetuous decision to join the Marines was based on his deep-seated need to demonstrate to his father that he was not the coward his father thought. Perhaps even he did not yet fully understand his motive.

His friendship with Frank Borello grew. Each young man found in the other a person who understood the need to somehow establish a bond of sorts with his father. However, in Frank's case, it was to please a father who wanted his son to be a good Marine and to follow in his footsteps. For Tommy, it was simply a matter of trying to overcome what he had seen for years as his father's rejection.

Attired in dress greens, the four platoons marched in perfect unison. Staff Sergeant Holloman, Company First Sergeant, watched them pass in review before the gathered guests. To a man, they stood taller than when they had first arrived. To a man, they reflected the pride of having completed the toughest training course that could be found within the United States military establishment. To a man, their hair was a full quarter-inch longer than the day they had been shorn as a flock of sheep. And to a man, they all waited for the one word with which Staff Sergeant Holloman would address them.

Every heel hit the ground at precisely the same instant. Their column movements were orchestrated to maintain a proper interval between the man to the front and the man to the side. Their heads moved in unison, a far cry from the bobbing and weaving evident in their close-order drills of the first several weeks of training. Their rifle movements were also precise, with one crisp sound emanating from each platoon as their drill instructors gave the execution commands.

In four columns, ten or eleven ranks deep, each platoon assumed its respective place in echelon as the company formed for review. To the fore of each platoon stood one single recruit, positioned to the right, in front of the fourth squad. This platoon member, referred to as the Guidon, carried the platoon banner with which he performed a series of crisp maneuvers, raising and presenting the flag with each platoon movement. Immediately behind him stood the four squad leaders, each heading his respective column. Behind them stood the forty to forty-eight remaining members of each platoon.

Forty-second Company had dropped eighteen men since that day they arrived, were shorn of their hair, and stripped of their dignity. Two broken legs, seven cases of shin splints, four heat prostration's, and five "I-can't-take-it-anymores," had reduced the original complement to the one hundred and eighty-two men now assembled.

Sergeant Holloman stood forward of the review, between the four platoons and the podium, on which sat several senior officers and distinguished civilians. As the four platoons reached their final positions and came to a halt, Sergeant Holloman did a sharp about-face, and stood at attention, facing the podium. Colonel Albertus Catlin rose from his seat and stood at attention alongside the podium. Sergeant Holloman snapped a crisp salute, holding his fingers parallel to the corner of his right eye, his right arm perfectly perpendicular.

"Sir," he barked, "42nd Company, all present or accounted for, sir."

Colonel Catlin returned the salute. "Carry on, Sergeant."

"Aye, aye, sir," Holloman replied, sharply dropping his salute to his side. He placed his right foot exactly twelve inches behind the left, his toe touching the ground, and, pivoting on the ball of his left foot and the toe of his right, executed a precise about-face.

"Companeeeeeee," he called.

Instantly, the four senior platoon drill instructors echoed the command to their respective platoons. "Plaaaatooooon."

"Orderrrrrr, arms!" Holloman cried.

As one, the men in the four platoons executed the three-point movement, coming from right-shoulder-arms to the position of "order arms," with the rifle resting lightly on its butt end, standing alongside each man's right leg.

Observing the movement, Holloman waited several seconds, then continued. "Paraaaaaaade, rest," he concluded.

Again, one hundred and eight-two left arms snapped to, with the back of the left hand laid tightly against the small of the back and the left leg and foot extended about eight inches to the left, widening the base of support for the men who would be required to stand in this one position for an extended period. While called "parade rest," the position was no less formal than "attention," requiring the person to stand rigid and immobile. Still, the small extension of width provided to the feet allowed the person leeway to imperceptibly shift weight between legs, facilitating blood flow and preventing restricted circulation, which would cause unconsciousness.

Sergeant Holloman again performed an about-face, and came himself to the position of parade rest, both hands clasped behind his back, since he was not in possession of a rifle. Colonel Catlin immediately stepped behind the podium to address the guests and assembled troops.

"Ladies and gentlemen, it is my honor to address you today, August 16, 1917. Assembled before you is one of the earliest companies of Marines recruited, trained, and prepared for embarkation since the president's call for Americans to stand forth. They are an honorable group of men. I have personally observed their training, their intensity, and their rise to manhood as they have assumed the mantle of a United States Marine. I am proud of them, as is Staff Sergeant Holloman and the various drill instructors who have brought these young men to this point. But they have further to go, ladies and gentlemen. Soon, they will join the great conflict on the European continent. I am confident they will acquit themselves well, and that they will uphold the highest traditions of the Marine Corps and the United States of America.

"We are greatly honored today to have with us, two

distinguished representatives of the Congress. Representative Denby, long a proponent of the Marine Corps, and Congressman Anders Hansen of Utah, who served with a medical detachment nearly twenty years ago in the Spanish-American War. We will first hear from Congressman Hansen, and then, in conclusion, from Congressman Denby. Congressman Hansen?" he said, turning and offering the podium to Anders, who rose and took up his position behind the lectern. The empty left sleeve of his suit jacket was neatly folded and pinned to his shoulder. Tommy's eyes grew large with the realization that his Uncle Anders was to be a speaker at the graduation ceremony.

"Ladies and gentlemen, honored guests, and Marines . . ." he said, looking over the lectern at the assembled troops " . . . history is nothing, if not prophetic. Several times each century it becomes necessary to assemble the brightest, the strongest, and the bravest of America's youth, and to stand them on the wall to defend us. The cause for which these wars are fought is often lost in the chaos of battle, but I have learned one thing certain in my brief life: wars are *not* fought for political reasons. Oh, I understand that old men such as Congressman Denby and myself voice all these platitudes about '*just cause*,' and the '*honor of the nation*,' but once the battle commences, it is fought by each man in support of his comrades. It is fought to preserve life—the most sacred gift that God has given us. And when honor reaches its highest plane, it is fought to preserve the life of someone other than ourselves. For as God has told us, 'Greater love hath no man, than he lay down his life for his friend.'" Anders paused, and glanced back at Sarah, sitting alongside his empty seat and smiling at him, her hands folded in her lap.

As Tommy stood in the sun, his thoughts segueing over

the past several months, he only partially heard Uncle Anders's remarks. He began to think of Utah and the 4th of July, followed by the Pioneer Day celebrations and the massive fireworks displays over the lake at Nibley Park Resort. How his family had loved the patriotic enthusiasm and the picnics his Mom had prepared for an all-day-in-the-park occasion. Now, with these men standing alongside him, men he had shared three months of intense discomfort with, he felt part of that patriotic fervor. For a time, Tommy had wondered if he would make the grade, actually become a Marine, and have something to contribute to the country. But, gradually, he and the others had come along. They had reached the point where they looked with disdain on the incoming raw recruits. During the final week of their training, even the Drill Instructors had begun to treat Tommy and his class with a grudging measure of respect. They were becoming Marines.

Nearing the conclusion of his remarks, Congressman Hansen softened. "Now let me add one more thought: it is inevitable in any war, that some will give their all. Say what we will about duty and honor and glory, the truth is, my young friends, that each of you will likely leave behind on the field of battle some of your dearest comrades—you must *never* forget those with whom you serve.

"Now," he smiled and surveyed the troops standing before the podium, "may the same God who guided the Israelites through the wilderness, preserve, protect, and defend you as you follow Him in righteousness. And may He who also sacrificed His all, go with you on this sacred mission. God bless you."

As Anders sat down, the several hundred guests applauded his remarks. Moving to the lectern, Congressman

Denby waited for the applause to subside, then began his address.

"Marines, you have heard this day the voice of one who served his country by serving others first. When Congressman Hansen went to Cuba in 1898, to serve with a hospital detachment, he was not part of a military contingent. Little did he know that he would be called upon to crawl through enemy fire to rescue wounded troopers. But he did, and in that service he lost his arm. I have seen the plaque of commendation that hangs in his congressional office, signed by President Theodore Roosevelt, who also participated in that earlier conflict. I am proud to serve in the United States House of Representatives with such a man, and I am privileged to call him my friend.

"This current conflict in Europe has been called 'The Great War.' But can *any* war be great . . . ?"

Again, Tommy's thoughts drifted far from the confines of Parris Island Marine Corps Training Center, thinking perhaps of the last words Uncle Anders had said. *Some give their all.* Was it his turn to die, and how many of them, Tommy thought, as his peripheral vision took in a half-dozen of his platoon mates, would not come home from this war? For the first time since the exciting venture began, Tommy Callahan felt a twinge of fear.

" . . . if this war is 'great,'" Denby continued, "then it is great because of the valor of men such as yourselves. May you uphold the honorable traditions of those proud Marines who have gone before you, and as Congressman Hansen has said, may God go with you on the journey."

Congressman Denby received another round of applause and retook his seat. Colonel Catlin rose to stand alongside the podium once again, and Sergeant Holloman, immediately below and to the front of the reviewing stand, came to attention.

"Sergeant, dismiss your Marines," Catlin commanded.

"Aye, aye, sir," Holloman replied, performing another about-face.

"Companeeeeeee."

"Platooooooon," the drill instructors echoed.

"Attennnnn hut!" Holloman barked. "Right shoulder—Harms!"

Tommy snapped his rifle off the ground, and in another precisely executed three-point maneuver, brought it to rest on his right shoulder. Out of the corner of his eye, he watched Frank perform a similar maneuver with the Guidon pole, raising it high above his shoulder before bringing it smartly to carry position. And then they waited for the moment that would culminate their eleven weeks of training—the moment when they would be accepted as full-fledged members of the elite of the United States military establishment.

Holloman looked left and then right, once again appraising the troops assembled before him. And then he took a deep breath, filling his lungs with the power to properly give the command they all awaited.

"MARINES," he trumpeted, "disssssss-missed!"

As a single voice, the sound reverberating across the parade ground, one hundred and eight-two young men replied, "AYE, AYE, SIR! SEMPER FI!"

19

Frank Borello's burly, loud-voiced father was everything Tommy had expected. Frank's mother was quiet and demur, her pride in her son reflected by the more loquacious father.

"So, they made you Guidon? You didn't tell us that in your letters."

"Well, Pop, I wasn't sure I'd keep it."

"Nonsense. They recognized your qualities, wouldn't you say, Tommy?" he laughed.

"Yes, sir. Frank was the best among us," Tommy smiled.

"There. You see, Frank. Even your platoon mates saw it. Good for you, son. Good for you."

"If you'll excuse me, Mr. and Mrs. Borello, I'd better see if I can find my uncle. It was nice to meet you. I've heard wonderful things about you from Frank. Frank, I'll find you later at the mess hall about seventeen-hundred."

"Good, Tommy. Thanks for meeting my parents."

Tommy nodded and started to turn.

"Stick with my Frank, son," Mr. Borello said. "He'll see you through."

Tommy and Frank exchanged brief looks, and Tommy could see the embarrassment in Frank's eyes.

"He already has, Mr. Borello, just getting me through

boot camp. When we get to France, I'll stay closer than his knapsack. You can bet on that. See you all later."

Tommy turned and left the Borellos, searching through the crowd for Uncle Anders and Aunt Sarah. Hundreds of parents, friends, and relatives were fawning over their newly graduated Marines. Tommy caught a quick glimpse of one of his squad mates being admired by his parents and a shy, lovely girl who Tommy could see wanted to hug her new Marine, but, in the presence of his parents, was too timid.

Angling through a cluster of well-wishers, Tommy spotted Uncle Anders, speaking with Colonel Catlin and several of the Training Center officers. He hesitated, content to wait until Uncle Anders was free, not wanting to interfere in their conversation, but Anders spotted him and called out.

"Tommy, ah, there you are, lad. Come and join us," Anders beckoned, waving his arm. Not wanting to enter the cluster of officers, Tommy thought for an instant to pretend he didn't hear Anders, but Colonel Catlin briefly caught his eye and Tommy noticed an almost imperceptible nod of approval from the Colonel. Tommy walked up to the group and immediately came to attention.

"Sir, good morning to the Colonel," Tommy said, rendering a crisp salute.

"And to you, Private Callahan," the Colonel said, reading his nametag and returning Tommy's salute.

Aunt Sarah gently placed a quick kiss on his cheek, which Tommy endured silently in the presence of the officers.

"So, Tommy," Anders said, "now you not only wear the uniform, but you carry the title as well. We're all very proud of you, son. And I'm sure your mother and father are also," he quickly added. "Colonel," Anders said, turning to Catlin, "would there be any objection to my nephew joining us for lunch?"

Colonel Catlin glanced at Tommy, aware that the private was in an awkward position. "Congressman Hansen, I think that on this special occasion, we can permit Private Callahan entrance to the Officers' Mess. Captain," he said, looking toward one of the younger officers, "please arrange a separate dining facility for, uh, let's see," he paused, looking around the group, "eight, I make it."

"Aye, aye, sir," the captain replied.

Colonel Catlin hesitated another moment, thinking of a way to make Tommy's participation somewhat easier. "Captain, make that nine, and see to it that Sergeant Holloman is invited to join our group."

"Aye, aye, sir," he replied again, glancing briefly at the other captain before departing, a raised eyebrow reflecting his chagrin.

All through this exchange, Tommy had stood at attention, aware that his uncle had broken protocol in asking that a junior enlisted man join the senior party in the Officers' Mess. He was caught, however, in an awkward position. It was not his to object or to offer unsolicited advice. Had he been asked, Tommy would have politely suggested to his uncle that they meet somewhere on the grounds following his luncheon with the Colonel and Congressman Denby.

In the Officer's Mess, seated next to his uncle, Tommy slid his chair back and stood to attention when Staff Sergeant Holloman entered the small dining area.

"Ah, Sergeant Holloman," Colonel Catlin said. "Thank you for coming. "Let me introduce you to Congressman and Mrs. Denby, Congressman and Mrs. Hansen, and of course, you already know Captains Ericksen and Palmer."

Holloman nodded acknowledgment to each of the congressional parties and the two captains.

"And of course you already know Private Callahan," Colonel Catlin concluded.

"Yes, sir," Holloman answered.

"Fine, then. Take a seat here, Sergeant, next to me. Private Callahan, resume your seat."

"Thank you, sir" Holloman replied, taking his seat. His eyes locked momentarily with Tommy and Tommy tried to facially explain his own ignorance of how this unusual event came to be. Holloman's brief wink almost caused Tommy to drop the napkin he was unfolding in his lap, but it put him at ease temporarily.

"We are honored, gentlemen," Colonel Catlin said to the two congressmen, "to have such distinguished guests at our first commencement. As I said earlier, there are nine companies in training at the moment—nearly two thousand young men desperately waiting for graduation day to rescue them from Sergeant Holloman's peers, who are equally tenacious in their training regimen. Tell us, Private Callahan, did you find the training program rigorous?"

Tommy was completely surprised to be addressed by the Colonel. He had assumed, perhaps wished, he would be allowed to eat his lunch quietly and depart without attracting any notice in the gathering. He looked directly at Sergeant Holloman who offered a hint of a smile.

"Sir, I believe the training provided was appropriate for our conditioning."

"Come now, Private," Catlin laughed. "Surely there was more discussion of the training than *that*. Why do you think the non-comms were so forceful in seeing to it you and the others finished the course? After all, it was the first such training program the Corps has developed so thoroughly."

This time, Tommy noticed a slight nod from Sergeant Holloman, an encouragement perhaps to speak his mind—within limits, of course, Tommy instinctively understood.

"Sir, Private Borello, Guidon of the Third Platoon, and I did discuss the training on several occasions. It is our belief, sir, that Sergeant Holloman and the other drill instructors had but one motive. They wanted us to learn all we could about combat, discipline, and the chain of command so that should we, uh . . . *when* we become engaged in this conflict, we would all be able to come home, sir. They wanted us all to survive."

The group sat silent for a moment, the two captains nodding slightly at Tommy's answer. Sergeant Holloman held Tommy's eyes, silently expressing his approval of the young man's response.

"Well said, Private Callahan. If you're not careful, Congressman Hansen, you may find another Utahn taking aim at your congressional seat some day," he laughed, as did Anders Hansen and the others around the table.

"Do you think your fellows in 42nd Company share your understanding, Private?"

Again, Tommy thought for a moment. "Sir, I can't speak to their collective understanding of course, but there was one young man in my squad who perhaps understood better than I, what has happened to us here. If I can recall his words, he wrote home to his parents, if I may paraphrase: *The first day I was at camp, I was afraid I was going to die. The next two weeks my sole fear was that I wasn't going to die. And after that, I knew I'd never die, because I'd become so hard that nothing could kill me.*"

"I see," Colonel Catlin said. "So the confidence level of these young men has been raised.

"That, sir, and their trust in their leaders."

"There you have it, gentlemen. The voice of one of our newest Marines. Captains Ericksen and Palmer, you should not soon forget what this young private has said. If your men trust in you, then you will be victorious. But you must earn that trust, as quite obviously, Sergeant Holloman and his drill instructors have done." Catlin stood and reached for his glass. "Ladies, and gentlemen, I give you a toast to the Corps and . . ." he said, raising his glass to Tommy who was now also on his feet, " . . . to the thousands of new privates who will carry its banner. To the Corps, and to the Fifth Marines, now on French soil," he said, raising his glass to his lips.

"To the Corps," the assembled guests replied. Holloman winked again at young Tommy Callahan as the party resumed their seats.

After lunch, Anders, Sarah, and Tommy strolled a short distance around the training grounds, exchanging news of home and talking of everything except the growing conflict in Europe. Finally, Anders looked at his pocket watch and shook his head.

"Look at the time. I'm sorry, Tommy. Your Aunt Sarah and I have to catch the four o'clock train back to Washington. It's been splendid seeing you again, son. You're looking mighty fit," he smiled.

"Thank you both for coming," he said, reaching to hug Aunt Sarah, whose tears were just beginning to form.

"What's next for you?" Anders asked.

"I'm not sure, Uncle Anders. Scuttlebutt has it that most of the company will be sent over to France as replacements for the Fifth Marines. Frank and I are hoping for that."

Anders nodded. "Well, Private Callahan," he grinned, "whatever comes your way, I'm certain you'll do your best.

Aunt Sarah and I will be in Utah for Christmas, and we'll see your parents. Would you like me to deliver a message?" he asked, placing his hand on Tommy's shoulder.

Tommy pursed his lips. "No, Uncle Andy. I think you know the trouble I have communicating with my father. Thanks, but I'll just write to Mom and Tess."

"It, uh . . . well, it may be some time before you see your father again, Tommy," Anders said.

"Aye."

Anders smiled. "Perhaps neither of you realizes how very much alike you are."

"Maybe so, Uncle Andy. But the part of him he sees in me, he doesn't seem to like very much."

"I know it seems that way, Tommy, but I've spoken to him on a different level. He very much loves you."

"I suppose there are many kinds of love, Uncle Andy. I would have liked for ours to be different than it is."

"Give it time, son. Just give it time."

Tommy thought for a moment, then held his hand out to shake Anders'. "I hope we have enough time, Uncle Andy. But if I don't . . ." he hesitated, looking down at the ground.

"Yes, Tommy?"

Private Thomas M. Callahan looked up at his uncle and then smiled at his aunt, before looking back toward Anders. "If I don't . . . have the time, I mean, please tell my father that I am sincerely sorry that I disappointed him, and that . . . and that I love him."

Anders wrapped his one arm around Tommy and hugged him for a silent moment. Tommy struggled to keep the tears from flowing as he pulled away and turned to give his aunt a kiss.

"God be with you, Tommy," Aunt Sarah said, hugging him closer.

Tears standing in his eyes, Tommy stood back and smiled at both of them. "Have a safe trip home," he said. "And thanks again for coming," he added, before turning and quickly walking away across the parade ground, joining the other Marines heading back to the Company training area, their liberty expiring at seventeen hundred hours.

As the train pulled out of the station and headed north, Sarah snuggled up to Anders. "He's become a fine young man," she said.

"Yah, that he has. But he does come from good Norwegian stock," Anders smiled.

"And his Irish side?" she smiled.

"Well, he'll have to overcome that," Anders laughed.

"Anders," she laughed, "what a thing to say about your brother-in-law."

They rode in silence for the next several minutes, looking out the window at the fading daylight and long shadows that were enveloping the passing countryside.

"Anders, have you ever figured out why the Lord did not see fit to bless us with children?"

When Anders did not answer for some moments, Sarah linked her arm in his and lay her head on his shoulder, riding that way for several minutes until she could tell that he had fallen into a light sleep. She looked up at his handsome face, somewhat sagging as his chin bobbed gently against his chest.

She thought of the long, childless years she had borne, and of the hundreds of mothers who had given birth to the hundreds of young men they had just seen graduate—other women's children, who were now going to war. She wondered what it might be like for those mothers—sending their precious sons away into an uncertain future. The pain of being childless was momentarily assuaged by the relief that one of hers would not be in harm's way. Then she thought again of Tommy.

"As thou would, Lord," she silently prayed. "As thou would."

After evening mess call, Frank and Tommy walked back toward their platoon area, twenty minutes ahead of the time when Frank had advised Tommy they had an appointment with Sergeant Holloman.

"And he didn't say what he wanted?"

"No," Frank replied. "In fact he didn't deliver the message himself. Sergeant Ryker told me that Sergeant Holloman wanted to see us."

"Well, that was before I was invited . . . or ordered, to have lunch with Colonel Catlin. So it can't be about that."

"We'll find out soon enough. There he is now, going in the command tent."

Tommy and Frank entered their sleeping tent and quickly brushed their shoes, adding a bit of polish and checking each other's uniform for "ropes," as Marines called the tiny slivers of thread that often came loose from seams or buttons.

"I suppose he can't bust us back now," Tommy laughed. "And sending us to France is what we want, so there's nothing to be worried about, right?"

"Just stand tall, Private Callahan," Frank said formally. "We'll find out shortly."

The two new Marines approached the command tent, and Frank wrapped three sharp knocks on the wooden post set in the ground outside the tent flap. As he finished his knock, he called out. "Sir, Private Borello and Private Callahan reporting to the Senior Drill Instructor as ordered, sir."

"Enter," boomed a voice from within.

The two ducked under the tent flap, quickly standing tall and approaching the desk, coming to a stop exactly eighteen inches from the front of the desk. Their eyes were focused well above Sergeant Holloman who sat behind the desk. They concentrated instead on a small placard mounted on the pole behind the sergeant, which read, "Eyes Here."

Holloman stood up behind the desk, his face now on their level. "Stand at ease," he commanded.

"Aye, aye, sir," they both replied, coming to a modified "Parade Rest," but retaining their formality.

"As you know, at twenty hundred hours, the Company will assemble in the main training area to receive orders. Most, as the scuttlebutt has indicated, will embark immediately for detachment to the Fifth Marines in France. Most, except you, Private Borello and you, Private Callahan. And a few others from the other platoons in the Company.

Frank and Tommy maintained a straight face, masking their surprise and disappointment at the news.

"No comment?" Holloman asked.

Frank and Tommy remained silent.

"Speak your minds, Privates."

"Sir," Tommy commenced.

"Private Callahan, you are now an accepted member of the Corps. Officers are referred to as 'Sir.' Noncommissioned officers are referred to as corporal or sergeant. Your training phase is over.

"Yes, sir . . . er, yes, Sergeant. Sergeant Holloman,"

Tommy continued, "may the Private ask the reason for his omission from the Company movement?"

"I need you, son."

"Sir?" Tommy replied.

Holloman smiled at both men—a facial expression they had not witnessed or thought possible in Holloman during their eleven weeks of training.

"Borello—Callahan—have a seat, both of you," he said, gesturing to a couple of orange crates stacked against the side of the tent wall.

"You go by Frank and Tommy, is that right?"

"Yes, Sergeant," Frank replied.

"Well, then I repeat, Frank. I need you two. You've both performed well during recruit training, and the Corps has been stripped of many of our experienced noncomms to go with the Fifth Marines to France. Before long, we will have thousands more recruits here at Parris Island. We've got to be able to train these men. I've conferred with the other drill instructors, and they have selected eight men from the company whom we feel can aid us in the job. For every one new private, we can place that additional non-comm with another new platoon. Each platoon needs three drill instructors, and each of you will be the third man on those training teams."

"Sergeant, we had hoped—" Frank started.

"We had *all* hoped, son. This job is every bit as important as assignment to the Fifth Marines. Those are your orders. Get used to it. Tomorrow, you'll move your equipment into the instructors' barracks. Oh, and to make the job a little easier, a stripe goes with the assignment. So, Private First Class Borello, and Private First Class Callahan, report to the Barracks NCO at oh nine hundred, sharp."

Both men stood, understanding they had been dismissed.

"Aye, aye, Sergeant," Tommy responded.

They performed an about-face and commenced to leave the tent.

"PFC Callahan," Holloman called out. "Hold one."

Frank exited the tent and Tommy turned back around and came to attention.

"At ease, Tommy," Holloman said, coming to stand in front of him. "I know how uncomfortable it was at lunch this morning, but rest assured, PFC Callahan, Colonel Catlin was most impressed with your comments. And one more thing, lest you let your mind run away with you. Congressman Hansen had nothing to do with your new assignment. In fact, Colonel Catlin made sure he didn't know of the orders."

"Thank you, Sergeant," Tommy said.

"Give me two training cycles, Private, with your best effort, and I'll see what I can do to arrange a transfer. Two cycles—until February."

"Aye, aye, Sergeant." Tommy came to attention and stood in place for a moment, waiting to be dismissed.

"That will be all, PFC Callahan."

"Aye, aye, Sergeant. And Sergeant," he added. "I meant everything I said to Colonel Catlin. I will never forget the things you taught me and the purpose behind your methods."

Holloman was taken aback for a moment, but quickly regained his composure. "EWE? Do I look like a sheep, Private?"

"No, Sergeant," Tommy replied straight-faced. "You look like a Marine."

"Dismissed, Private," Holloman said, a small smile creasing his leathery face.

"Aye, aye, Sergeant," Tommy smiled, completed an about-face, and departed the tent.

In the platoon tent, Frank was gathering his gear and beginning to pack it in his duffel bag. Tommy entered and smiled at Frank.

"So, France will have to wait awhile, eh?" Frank said.

"To tell you the truth, Frank, the closer it gets, the more I wonder why we've been so anxious to go to war."

"Because it's there, Tommy. And because we're Marines."

"Aye. We're Marines all right. And now we're going to do what we can to transform another bunch of . . . what was it Sergeant Ryker always called us, '*worthless, mush-for-brains, gutter dwellers*,' into Marines."

"Semper Fi, Tommy."

"Semper Fi, Frank," Tommy replied and they both started laughing.

The sheep station wasn't large by sheep station standards, comprising perhaps only sixteen hundred hectares, or roughly four thousand acres, but it was set in some of the most beautiful country PJ had ever seen. Even Elder Armitage, who spoke often about the beauty of Hawke's Bay, admitted to PJ in an unguarded moment that Shenandoah Station was situated magnificently.

For the past week, as they were making their way south along the foothills of the Southern Alps, residents of the area had told the two transient elders that another Callahan lived further up the road. PJ had thought nothing particular about the name, since Irish names were common in the

South Island, especially the further west one went. Still, his curiosity was aroused as they neared Shenandoah Station.

Walking up the long, dusty approach road, Elders Callahan and Armitage took note of the signs of a well-kept station. Now, in late November, spring lambing had been completed, and the station gave all the signs of full activity.

Noticeably absent were the groups of young men usually found on such a station. Instead, the operation was manned by an older group, the result, PJ considered, of the war and the need to send the young men to more immediate wartime tasks. At an outshed, about a mile from the main house, the elders stopped for a drink of water. Two leathery-skinned Maori were tending to saddle repairs. Elder Armitage greeted them with a traditional *"Kia Ora,"* and asked for some water. Without speaking, one of them pointed to a can standing in the back of a nearby, dilapidated, open truck.

"You boys know where we can find John Callahan?" Armitage asked.

Again, the older of the two just pointed toward the main house, further up the dirt road.

Their thirst quenched and some of the road dust brushed off their clothes, the two young men walked the short distance remaining to the main house. A pretty young woman, about eighteen, sat on the covered porch that surrounded the house, a verandah overhanging all four sides that provided some welcome shade. She was wearing a light colored, sleeveless dress and no shoes, and she had a bowl in her lap and was rocking slowly in her chair as she shelled peas. She shaded her eyes from the glare of the sun, trying to see who was approaching as the two elders reached the house.

"Good morning," Elder Armitage said. "Might we find a John Callahan hereabouts?"

"Shouldn't expect him till about dinner time," the young woman said.

"I see. And Mrs. Callahan?"

The woman looked up the road for a minute, past the elders, and then looked back at Elder Armitage. "Mrs. Callahan died two years ago. I'm John Callahan's daughter, Emily. Can I be of some assistance?"

Armitage glanced at PJ who nodded. "If you'd be so kind, ma'am, we'd like to stay nearby and wait for your father. We just want to talk to him for a few minutes if possible."

Continuing to shell the peas, Emily watched Elder Armitage intently as he spoke. Finally, she put the bowl aside and walked to the corner of the porch, looking down at the Elders who remained in the dirt yard in front of the house.

"If you hike over that rise," she pointed, again shading her eyes from the sun's glare, "and continue on about eight miles to the water well, it's likely you'll find him. Dad's out repairing it right about now." She turned and smiled at George Armitage. "Or, you could have a seat over on the shady side of the house, and I'll fetch you a cool drink and a couple of Lamington's. He'll be back after a while."

George Armitage's face lit up, and he turned to PJ. "Seems an easy choice to me, Elder. How about you?" he laughed.

One of the first things Elder Callahan had learned to appreciate after arriving in New Zealand was the moist, coconut sprinkled cake that the Kiwi's called "Lamington's."

"You're senior, Elder," PJ grinned. "I'd really rather walk another eight miles, but I guess I better follow your lead."

The elders stepped up onto the porch, and walked around to the shady side of the building, where they took seats in a couple of weathered, wooden chairs set against the house.

The young woman returned in a few minutes with a tray that held two glasses of a red-colored punch and a large plate of Lamington's.

"This is kind of you, Miss Callahan. We very much appreciate your hospitality," Armitage said.

"I would say, sir, that you have the advantage," Emily smiled brightly.

Armitage choked slightly on the first Lamington he was tasting and quickly coughed, to clear his throat.

"I'm very sorry, Miss Callahan. I completely forgot my manners. I am Elder George Armitage, and this is my companion, Elder Patrick Callahan. We usually go by our church title, 'Elder.'"

At the name *Callahan*, Emily turned a steady gaze upon PJ for the first time since the two men had arrived. "Callahan, is it, then?" she smiled.

"Aye. PJ Callahan," PJ replied, affecting an Irish brogue.

"Would you be knowing my father?" she asked.

"I don't think so, ma'am. We are missionaries from The Church of Jesus Christ of Latter-day Saints. We've been walking through the countryside, meeting people, and telling them about our religion."

Emily nodded her head. "*You're* the two. I thought as much when I saw you approach. Word had it that you were headed this way."

Armitage smiled and wiped his lips to clear the remaining Lamington crumbs. "We've learned it's a pretty fair 'bush telegraph' in this part of the South Island," he said.

"If it's my father you're after, you'd do just as well to

finish your cake and be on your way," she said, no indication of anger in her voice. "Dad'd be the last one to listen to two missionaries, I'm afraid." She pronounced it "mishunries."

"And would that make you the first?" Armitage grinned.

Without responding, Emily walked around to the front of the house, retrieved her bowl and a new bag of peas, and returned to where the elders were seated. She pulled one of the chairs from the wall and sat down, adjusting the bowl in her lap.

"A little conversation never hurt anyone, Mr., uh, Armitage," she smiled. "Now Elder Armitage here has a Pomy accent, Elder Callahan, but yours is rather American, I should think, or Canadian, in spite of your attempt at the Irish," she said.

"I'm afraid you've got me," PJ laughed. "American, with an Irish heritage."

"How do you like New Zealand lamb, Elder Callahan?"

PJ exhaled. "The way I've had it cooked here in South Island, Miss Callahan, I like it just fine."

"Good. We'll be having lamb stew, with new peas of course," she laughed, gesturing to the bowl in her lap. "I suppose Dad won't be having any objections to a couple more plates on the table."

"That's very kind of you, Miss Callahan. Very kind, indeed," George Armitage said.

"And you, Elder Armitage, you're from . .?"

"Yorkshire, ma'am. Huddersfield, to be exact."

"As I thought, another POM," she said, clicking her tongue and shaking her head in mock disdain. "Well, a good dose of South Island cooking will fix that."

Emily Callahan had the table set, candles in place, and a delicious aroma coming from the kitchen that brought both elders closer to the kitchen door from their meandering around the house. John Callahan's arrival, shortly before Emily called the men to dinner, barely gave the elders time to introduce themselves before he went to wash up.

Not to question his daughter's invitation to the two men, John Callahan quietly accepted his two guests and as all sat down to dinner, he sat quietly for a moment while Emily completed the serving then took her seat at his side.

"We've heard a couple of mishunries were covering the countryside. You are welcome in my home, gentlemen. I've no need for religion, mind you, but you are welcome nonetheless. I'd be pleased if you'd say grace. It's rare enough we take such pains."

"Certainly, Mr. Callahan. Thank you for the privilege."

Elder Armitage expressed gratitude for the food, and light conversation commenced while the meal was consumed. PJ noticed that Emily continued to watch George whenever his companion was preoccupied with his meal or turned to converse with her father. She busied herself with up and down chores otherwise, and PJ didn't think that his senior companion had any idea that the lovely young woman had taken an interest.

"We don't see many Callahan's around these parts," John said. "Where did you say your family came from originally?"

"I was born in Salt Lake City, Utah, Mr. Callahan, but my father comes from Ireland. Tipperary to be more precise."

John nodded. "Yep, there'd be plenty of Callahan's from that neck of Ireland, topped only by the Ryans I should think. Do you know your grandparents' names?" he asked, reaching for another bread roll.

"Yes, sir. I believe Dad has a complete genealogy of the

family. My grandfather was also Thomas Matthew Callahan, and his wife was Margaret Donohue. They both died some years ago."

John halted instantly, his butter knife stuck in his bread roll. "And your father's name again?"

"Thomas, sir. Thomas Matthew Callahan," PJ said, aware of the look of surprise on Mr. Callahan's face.

"Son, do you by any chance have a picture of your father?" the elder Callahan asked.

"I do, sir, and my mother as well."

John Callahan stood and came around the table to take the picture from PJ then moved closer to the light fixture attached to the wall.

"By all the saints, man," John exclaimed.

"Sir?" PJ questioned.

"You're the oldest you say?"

"Yes, sir. I have a younger brother and sister, Thomas and Teresa, twins they are, and my youngest brother, Benjamin, died when he was just seven."

"Elder Callahan . . ." John smiled, "unless the coincidence of these events is misleading us, I believe that I would be your Uncle John—your father's oldest brother. And you would be my nephew." He reached his arm around Emily and pulled her close. "And Emily here, would be your cousin."

"Sir, I don't . . . I don't actually know what to say."

"Well, I do, son. Welcome to your New Zealand home."

20

The night before their ship sailed for New Zealand, with a four-day stop scheduled in Hawaii where Katrina had told Tom she wanted to visit the new temple under construction, Tom and Katrina attended the opera in San Francisco. They were staying in the same hotel they had used the week they were married. October, 1897, seemed so long ago and Katrina actually blanched as they spoke of their impending twentieth anniversary, now just months away.

Tess had accompanied them to San Francisco and was looking forward to the trip to New Zealand, but she had been invited to spend two days in Half Moon Bay with one of her sorority sisters, and was planning to join her parents at the dock the morning of their departure.

"*Twenty years*. It can't be, Thomas," she teased.

"Aye, but it can, and it is, Katie m'darlin'," he insisted. "That would make you, let's see . . ."

"Thomas, stop it right now," she laughed as they rode in the taxi back to the hotel.

"But, Katie, you don't look any different than when we were last here," he soft-peddled, kissing the back of her hand.

"You know, Thomas, my father may have been right

about the Irish. One can never be sure that they're telling the truth, can one?"

"Why, Katie, I'm astonished that you'd doubt me on something so important," he said, his face set in a mock scowl.

"Thomas Matthew Callahan, I have my oldest son on a mission in New Zealand, my youngest son in the United States Marine Corps, heading for a war zone at the moment, and my only daughter intent on attending acting school in New York City. Now you tell me, sir, does that sound like a young girl to you?"

"Ah, Katie, you missed the point," he countered, teasing, "it's not how old the *children* are, it's how old we *act*. And as for me, I *feel* no older than they *are*. And that's the truth of it."

"Keep telling yourself that, Mr. Callahan, and I'll keep plucking those small, silver hairs that have been insidiously appearing on the side of your head," she said, reaching to run her fingers through his hair.

"Nothing a few days in the Hawaiian sun can't cure, I'm told. Plus a long ocean voyage into the South Pacific."

"*Three weeks.* That *is* a long voyage. Are you getting excited, Thomas?"

"About what, Mrs. Callahan?" Tom said with a leer.

Trying not to smile, Katrina gave him a disgusted look and hit him lightly on the shoulder with her fist. "Thomas, *really!*"

Tom laughed and pulled her close, kissing her cheek. "Katie, it's been twenty-five years since I've seen John. I don't know what we'll have in common."

"Rubbish. You're brothers, Thomas. You'll grab him and wrap your arms around him. That's what you'll do, and the twenty-five years will be gone, just like that," she said, snapping her fingers.

"I wish I had your confidence," Tom replied.

"Mr. Callahan, sometimes you are a complete mystery to me," Katrina laughed. "I don't know a living soul with more confidence. It'll work out fine. You'll see."

"PJ was excited to find his uncle, wasn't he?" Tom said.

"That was really something—running into your brother in a far-off place like that. I keep thinking what a surprise it must have been when they finally made the connection."

"I remember before I left Ireland," Tom continued, "that we'd heard a rumor John had taken a ship for New Zealand or Australia, but not one letter ever came during those next few years. And then Mor never said anything about where he was after I came to America."

"Maybe he never wrote to them, Thomas. It wouldn't be all that unusual. Surely they would have told you where he was if they had known."

"I suppose. In a few weeks we'll have the chance to find out, I guess."

They exited the taxi and entered the hotel, where they checked for messages and then took the elevator to their room. While Tom was getting undressed and into bed, Katrina slipped out of her dress, removed her jewelry, and put on her nightgown. She then sat in front of the mirror and let her hair down. She never went to bed without brushing it, and Tom had never tired of watching her nightly ritual.

"Have you thought about Tess, Katie?" he asked.

"What do you mean?"

"Well, I've never been comfortable with the interest she's taken in drama. Ever since that fawning critic at the *Tribune* took a liking to her and gave her such rave reviews, she's had her head in the clouds. I really don't approve of this acting bit."

Katrina rose from the dressing table and came to the bed. Sitting down, she removed her slippers and slid under the covers. "Well, you told her she'd have to wait till next year, so she'll be almost twenty before she goes. I think she'll do all right."

"What do you mean? You approve of this nonsense?"

"No, I didn't say I approved. I said, she'll do all right. She's a fine young woman, Thomas. We can be proud of her."

"Yeah, well, I've been to New York, and I can tell you it's no place for a nineteen-year-old, single girl," Tom said.

"We've got six months to figure it out, Thomas. Perhaps you can arrange somewhere for her to stay. With, or under the supervision of, some of your banking friends."

"That's all we need. Some rich banker's kid chasing after her."

Katrina laughed. "She *is* a rich banker's kid, Mr. Callahan."

"Well, if I can find a way out of it, I will," he stated, half-heartedly. "And I'll need your support," he added.

"You have it," she said, reaching to turn out the light. "But she is her father's daughter. You won't find it so easy to dissuade her."

They lay there in the dark for several minutes, each lost in thought.

"Katie," Tom voiced tentatively, "Do you realize we've been married more than half our lives?" After a moment, he asked, "Have I been a good husband to you?"

"Oh, Thomas, you Irish larrikin," she laughed softly, "you've made my life one whirlwind of excitement and adventure. I do *so* love you, Mr. Callahan."

He turned over on his side and laced his fingers through her hair, pulling in short, gentle tugs at her golden tresses. "I've nearly completed reading *Jesus the Christ*," he added.

"And?"

"It's so much to think about, Katie. And it's so different from what I've been taught."

"It's between you and the Savior, Thomas. No one else."

"That's what Elder Talmage says, basically."

"You'll know what's right," she said. "Just know that I love you and that tomorrow we're off on another adventure. Our little family has taken on a true international flair, Thomas. There's no telling what the next three months will bring."

"It seems so unfair, Katie. Here we're off on an extended vacation to Hawaii and New Zealand, and Tommy is, he's . . ."

"Have you written to him?"

"No."

"Well, I write to him twice a week," Katrina said, "and I tell him that we *both* love him."

"Do you think he understands that?"

"Whether he does or not, he needs *you* to tell him, Thomas. Robert *was* right, you know. As much as it frightens me, Tommy has an uncertain future. We have to face that."

"But to write to him now, Katie, after all that's gone by—he'd just think I was doing it because I thought he might . . . he, well, you know, he might be injured, or worse."

"And what do you suppose he'll think if you *don't* write?"

"I know, Katie, I know."

On February 8, 1918, Private First Class Thomas
Callahan and Private First Class Francis Borello stood to the
front of their respective platoons with the small cadre of
drill instructors, as the 98th Company, 2nd Recruit
Battalion formed up for their graduation. Tommy had seen
two complete platoons through their training and had
gained an even greater appreciation for the noncommissioned officers with whom he served. And, he admitted to
himself, he had gained a measure of pride in the work he
had done. Ninety-seven Marines that he had personally
trained, in two platoons, proudly wore the uniform and
claimed the title United States Marine. Tommy had been
part of their indoctrination, from the "sheep-shearing," to
the polishing of brass for the graduation ceremony.

Immediately following the graduation, Sergeant
Holloman sought out Tommy and Frank. Seeing him
approach, Tommy nudged Frank and they both came to
attention.

"Sixteen hundred hours, Colonel Catlin's office,"
Sergeant Holloman said. Remain in your dress greens."

"Aye, aye, Sergeant," they replied as Holloman walked
away.

"Now what?" Tommy exhaled. "Another two training
cycles?"

"Man, I'm proud of what we've done, but this thing's
gonna be over before we see any action."

Tommy laughed. "Still gotta show the old man, eh?"

"You want to go, too, and you know it."

"Aye, that I do, Private Borello, that I do."

"That's Private *First Class* to you," Frank corrected him.

At eight minutes to four, Tommy and Frank were

standing outside the command post where Colonel Catlin's office was located. As Sergeant Holloman approached, they came to attention and at the wave of his hand, followed him into the building.

Holloman approached the desk outside the Colonel's office.

"Staff Sergeant Holloman, Private First Class Callahan, and Private First Class Borello to see the Commander," he said to the Corporal behind the desk.

"Aye, Sergeant. I'll let him know you're here," the young man said, stepping to the Colonel's door. He rapped his knuckles three times on the door, opening it without waiting for a response. Standing in the doorway, the Corporal said, "Sir, Sergeant Holloman and two PFC's are reporting as ordered."

Catlin grunted and waved his hand. "Send 'em in, Corporal."

"Aye, aye, sir." He turned to the men. "The Colonel will see you now, Sergeant."

"Thank you, Corporal," Holloman said. Inclining his head in the direction of the door, Holloman entered the Colonel's office, followed by Tommy and Frank. All three men came to attention immediately in front of Colonel Catlin's desk, Sergeant Holloman on the right.

"Sir," Holloman voiced, "Sergeant Holloman and Privates Callahan and Borello reporting as ordered."

"At ease," Catlin said, looking up from behind his desk. "I'll make it short and sweet. The Commandant has formed another regiment—the 6th Marines. The Regiment has been assembling at Quantico for some weeks. I've been given command of the 6th Marines." Colonel Catlin lifted a brown envelope from his desk and spilled the contents out.

One set of gunnery sergeant's stripes and two sets of corporal's chevrons overlapped on the desk.

"Gunnery Sergeant Holloman, take these two new Corporals and see that they're outfitted properly. Clear all base obligations and report to the Command Post, Quantico, at oh-seven-hundred hours on the tenth. That's the day after tomorrow. Most of this regiment is being formed from existing units with trained Marines. Therefore, it is my intention to embark as quickly as possible. General Pershing is forming the 4th Marine Brigade from the 5th and 6th Marine Regiments, as a complement to the 2nd Army Division. I intend to have the 6th in France by the time those regimental assignments are developed. Is that clear?"

"Yes, sir," Holloman replied.

"That'll be all. Dismissed."

"Aye, aye, sir," Holloman replied. "About-face," he said, and the three men crisply executed the turn, leaving the Colonel's office less than two minutes after entering it. Passing the Corporal's desk outside Catlin's office, they were handed typed orders, instructing each man to prepare for reassignment to the 6th Marine Regiment, headquartered at Quantico, Virginia. They were also given promotion orders: Staff Sergeant Holloman to gunnery sergeant and Privates First Class Callahan and Borello, both to corporal. Outside the building, Holloman stopped and turned to face the two men.

"Did you understand all that?"

"I believe so, Gunny," Tommy smiled, eliciting a smile from Holloman. "Congratulations."

"And to you, Corporal. To both of you. Well deserved. As Colonel Catlin said, clear all base obligations, laundry and so forth, draw a complete new uniform issue including

348

web gear, and then pack your kit. When that's done I don't want to see either of you until sixteen hundred hours tomorrow at the train station. We'll catch the night train to Quantico. That will get us in about oh-five-hundred the next morning. We will then report in and become part of the 6th Marine Regiment. You'll each be platoon Corporals and expected to act like it. Now, you're dismissed."

"Aye, aye, Gunny."

"And gentlemen. Don't let this shake your confidence when it sinks in, but the 6th is going to war."

Tommy looked at Frank and they both came to attention, smiling at Gunnery Sergeant Holloman.

"Semper Fi, Gunny," Tommy said.

"Get moving," Holloman barked.

⸻ ◦∞◦ ⸻

Corporal Callahan had never seen anything like it before. The grounds outside the Brooklyn Navy Yard were completely filled with New Yorkers come to see the new Marine regiment embark for France. Two bands outside the Yard, plus the Navy Band inside the Brooklyn Navy Yard, struggled to be heard over the cacophony of cheers and shouts of jubilation directed at the departing troops. The whole nation was caught up in war fever and people were anxious to send American troops "over there." Not since his graduation day had Tommy felt so proud of himself, the men who marched beside him—and the Marine Corps. Mothers, fathers, little children, sweethearts, and New Yorkers of all walks of life held signs aloft and cheered as over two thousand Marines marched in cadence through the gates of the Brooklyn Navy Yard. Inside the compound, specially opened to the public for the embarkation to engender public spirit and support for the war, thousands of people lined the dockside as the troop ship belched smoke from the forward of her two stacks.

By platoons, the men were filing aboard the troopship, also filling with nearly five thousand Army replacements for the 2nd Infantry Division. As Tommy stood alongside his platoon, prepared to give the order to board by columns of one, he saw a Marine Major approach with a civilian in tow. Tommy came to attention as the major approached.

"Platoon. At ease," he commanded. He then turned to face the approaching men, and saluted the Major.

"Corporal Callahan?" the Major asked.

"Yes, sir." Tommy said.

"Congressman Hansen would like a word with you for a moment. Place someone in charge of your platoon and speak with the congressman. Ten minutes, Corporal. We don't want to be late for the war."

"Yes, sir . . . I mean, no, sir. Thank you, sir," Tommy replied and saluted again. He turned back toward his platoon.

"Corporal Winters. Fall out."

"Aye," came the reply. Corporal Winters stepped lively to Tommy and stopped in front of him. "Johnny, take over for a few moments, will you? I'll be right back."

"Sure thing, Tommy," he said, nodding a silent greeting to the well-dressed, one-armed man standing behind Tommy.

Anders and Tommy walked a few steps away from the formed platoons, but remained distant, as best they could, from the cheering crowds and the noise of the band.

"I wasn't sure I could make it, Tommy. I'm glad I caught you."

"I am too, Uncle Andy. How's Aunt Sarah?"

"She's fine, Tommy. We decided it would be good for her

to go out and see your parents before they left for New Zealand. I think you know they're going down to meet your father's older brother. They should be almost there now."

Tommy smiled and nodded. "Tess sent me a couple of letters and told me about PJ finding Uncle John."

"So, you got your wish and you're off with the 6th Marines. A hastily formed, but as I understand it, very proud regiment."

"We've yet to earn our colors, Uncle Andy, but from what I can tell in a week, we've developed the *esprit de corps*."

"I've seen them for only thirty minutes and it's evident to me," the congressman agreed. "Tommy," Anders said, looking him in the eye, "I won't detain you from your duties long. I wanted you to know that I spoke with your father and your mother in Utah at Christmas. If it's any consolation, she will never forgive him until he reconciles with you over this unfortunate misunderstanding."

Tommy lowered his head and shifted his feet. Looking up again, he spoke. "Uncle Andy, I've begun to think recently that perhaps Pop is right. I've learned a lot about duty over the past months. I had responsibility for Benjamin. Mom trusted me to take care of him and I failed her—*and* Benjamin. When I've let it get to me, I've wondered if it might not have been better for all of us if I had gone down with the *Titanic* also."

Anders reached his hand out and took Tommy's shoulder. "Tom, now you listen to me and you listen very carefully," he said, his voice now stern. "You can't go off to war with that attitude. I see about fifty men standing there who need your guidance. I voted for the appropriations to send your regiment to France. The United States government has placed them in your hands. These boys'll need every ounce of your energy and strength. You've got to put this family tragedy behind you. It was a twelve-year-old boy who became separated from his seven-year-old brother in a situation of mass confusion. Over one thousand, five hundred people died that night, Tommy. You *cannot* carry that burden for the rest of your life.

"Your father is wrong, and I believe that he's beginning to see that too. His bloody Irish temper, and stubborn refusal to see past his loss, has in fact caused him to lose another of his sons, for far too long. The fact is, Tommy, your father blames himself and has for many years."

Tommy looked up into his uncle's eyes. "I don't understand," he said.

"He insisted, against your mother's wishes, that she and you children accompany your grandparents to Norway. He feels that *he* should have been on that ship. It was *his* responsibility to protect his family. You've only been a scapegoat for that guilt. I believe he understands that now and one day he will swallow his pride sufficiently to plead for your forgiveness. Do you understand that?"

"As much as I would like to believe you, Uncle Andy, I still think that perhaps he's right. Oh, he certainly made it hard on a young boy and for a while I came to hate him, but at its root, he's right. I let my brother die that night."

Anders shook his head and squeezed Tommy's shoulder. "Tommy, let me ask you a serious question. Have you ever asked God if you needed forgiveness?"

"No," was all he replied, his eyes again downcast.

"Many a soldier has found his God while clinging to the dirt of the earth, Tommy. Don't make Him wait that long," Anders pleaded.

The movement of the platoon ahead of Tommy's, beginning their boarding process, interrupted the conversation

352

and Anders could see that Tommy was anxious to return to his platoon and to end the conversation.

"Uncle Andy, I—"

"Corporal Callahan," Anders addressed Tommy, "you are now a Marine noncommissioned officer going in harm's way. Whatever the Lord has in store for you, may His will be done. But if you want His advice, you've got to ask Him, Tommy. And because you feel the way you do, it might not hurt to explain to your father that his rejection has been no harder to bear than your own feelings of guilt. As wise as your father is about most things, I don't think he understands that fact about you."

Tommy smiled thinly at Anders. "Uncle Andy, I have always loved you and Aunt Sarah. I want to thank you for all you've done. Please understand, I *will* think about what you've said. I've not had much to do with the Church. I don't know if that will change," he said, shaking his head. "But I love my family, including my father," he said, a glistening in his eye. "I promise you one thing: I *will* write to my father before we are sent forward."

"That's good, Tommy. But don't promise *me*. Promise yourself. Because I have a feeling that you will be unable to write, or even to forgive your father for his actions, until you've forgiven yourself."

Anders smiled broadly and reached to shake Tommy's hand. "Corporal Callahan, as I said at your graduation, may God go with you."

"Thank you, Uncle Andy."

Tommy stepped smartly back to his platoon and stood beside Corporal Winters. "I'll take over now, Johnny. Thanks."

"Sure thing, Tommy," he said, resuming his place in line.

"First Platoon—Ten-hut." Tommy watched as the final

file of the platoon in front of them moved off, up the gangway of the troopship, and then bellowed his command.

"Platoon: in columns of one, by route step—forward, harch."

Thirty minutes later as thousands of troops jammed the port side railings, Tommy stood side by side with Frank, watching the dock hands single up all lines. Smoke belched from both stacks now, and the tugs began to pull at the great ship, her single fore and aft moorage lines dropping away, one after the other.

On the dock, the Navy band struck up, "*Over There*," and the crowd began singing with all their fervor, waving small American flags. The words ran silently through Tommy's mind and the reality of their relocation began to sink in. *Over there. Over there. Send the word, send the word, over there. That the Yanks are coming, the Yanks are coming, and we won't be back till it's over, over there.*

Some of the troops were singing along with the crowd, straining shoulder to shoulder with their platoon mates to catch one final glimpse of their loved ones. Tommy was unable to see Uncle Anders in the crowd, although both of them could see Frank's father, waving his flag and wearing his old campaign hat from the Spanish-American War and the Marine expedition to the Philippines.

"It's kind of overwhelming, isn't it, Frank?" Tommy shouted over the din.

"Everyone loves a hero, Tommy. Even an untried hero."

"Aye. But can we measure up?"

"We're the 6th Marines, Corporal Callahan. And not a man-jack of 'em will let us down."

"And us? You and me?"

"It's just as the Gunny told us. We've got a job to do. We

can't let *them* down either, or some of them are going to die."

"Frank, some of us are going to die in any event."

"Aye, Tommy," Frank nodded. "But if we do our best, then we will have fulfilled our responsibility."

"Do you believe that, Frank?" Tommy asked, watching the scene on the dock recede into the distance as the ship pulled away and the strains of the Navy band faded.

Frank stared at Tommy for a long moment, his face unsmiling and intense. "Tommy, I've been meaning to say something to you for a long time, and I guess now's as good a time as any. You've got some ghosts harbored in your soul. I've known that for some months. But I'll tell you this. *I* need you, and every standing Marine in the First Platoon needs you. Exorcise that ghost, Tommy, and concentrate on the job at hand. We're all depending on each other. The day we met and you told me your family was from Salt Lake, I asked you if you were a Mormon—you remember? On the train? You said, '*not so's you'd notice.*' Well, I'm Catholic, as you know. It's not important that *I* notice if you're a Mormon or not, Tommy. It is important that *you* notice.

"We've both been indoctrinated with the confidence that training and reflex actions bring, but that's not enough. You've got to have faith in yourself. And if you can identify what you believe, you've got to have faith in your God. I have a feeling that we're going to come mighty close to Him in the next while, and I want Him to know that I care. And that I need Him, too."

Tommy looked at Frank for a moment. "I've never heard you talk religion before, Frank."

Frank shook his head. "I don't know as I have. But I think a lot of us will come face-to-face with things we haven't consciously addressed."

"Frank," Tommy said, his expression serious, "you *have* become my brother these past few months. I *will* be there for you."

"And I for you, Tommy," he smiled.

"Right. Let's go see that these guys have a place to sleep," Tommy said.

They looked back at the Brooklyn Navy Yard and the crowd of people still waving and cheering, their sounds now lost in the expanse of water between the ship and the dock.

"Do you think they'll be cheering when we come home?" Tommy asked.

"I don't know, Tommy. Let's just see that we *do* come home."

21

The *Pacific Princess* crossed just to seaward of Banks Peninsula, the bulge of land on which Christchurch was founded. It then skirted Taylor's Mistake, named for a cartographic error made by one of Captain James Cook's crew, and entered the inlet toward the Port of Lyttleton. The Port Hills passed slowly off her starboard side as she made her way up the channel. Even though it was early March, autumn had not yet chilled the air, and the day was crystal bright. *Aotearoa,* the Maori name for New Zealand, which means "Land of the Long White Cloud," presented herself that morning with not a cloud in the sky, providing for those passengers who chose to make the entrance while on deck, a view of land, sea, and sky that was infinite. It was New Zealand at its most brilliant, and Tom, Katrina, and Teresa absorbed the view with admiration.

Once berthed, luggage arranged for, and good-byes said to the crew who had served them for nearly three weeks, the threesome departed the ship, scanning the waiting crowd for signs of PJ. He quickly appeared, threading his way through the crowd, grabbing his mother as she stepped off the gangway, and twirling her around in his arms.

"*PJ,*" she squealed. Tom stood by and laughed at his

son's open display of affection. Next came Teresa, and PJ repeated the greeting to her equally enthusiastic response. Tom was content to accept a handshake and a brisk hug from his son before following him back through the gathered people to where a man and a young woman stood waiting, smiling as they watched the reunion.

"Dad," PJ said, "this—"

"Tommy," the man said, reaching out his hand and grabbing Tom by the forearm. "By all the saints, man, it's good to see you. Who could have guessed that we would meet, two runaway Irish lads, halfway around the world, twenty-five years later?"

Though their greeting was a bit more reserved than those PJ had presented to his mother and sister, it was nonetheless evident that Tom and his older brother, John, were pleased to see each other.

Luggage was loaded onto the sheep station's town truck, driven by one of the station hands, while the family loaded into two other vehicles, one driven by John and the other by PJ. The entourage immediately started the trip back to Shenandoah Station.

Tom and Katrina rode with John and Emily, the men in front and the women in the backseat. Tess, PJ, and Elder Onekawa, his Maori missionary companion for the final three days of PJ's mission, rode together in the second car. The drive took several hours. With John in the right-hand driver's seat and cars whipping by on "the wrong side of the road," it took the Americans time to get used to the backward driving convention. Katrina, in fact, gasped when John made his first turn into what she thought was the wrong lane.

"We do things differently here," he laughed.

The vehicles began the gentle climb up the eastern

slope of the Southern Alps, toward the higher sheep country and the increasingly magnificent scenery that unfolded with each mile. Tess and PJ talked the whole while, reacquainting themselves with current news, including recent communications from Corporal Thomas Callahan, United States Marine Corps.

"Tommy's actually in France, then?" PJ asked.

"That was what his last letter said, sent from New York just before they left," Teresa answered.

"I hope this war ends soon," PJ said, "Uncle John has suffered too much already."

"Did he fight, too?"

PJ shook his head as the car rounded a curve on the mountain road. "He lost both his sons, Tess. One at Gallipoli in 1915, and the other the next year in France. Neither one was twenty yet."

"Oh, my goodness," Tess exclaimed. "Does Mom or Dad know?"

"I don't see how. Uncle John hasn't written to Dad, I don't think. He'll probably tell them while they're here though."

"How did his wife take it, PJ?"

Again, PJ shook his head slowly. "She passed away six months after her second son was killed. Uncle John said she died of a broken heart."

"Oh, how sad," Tess said.

"So, what do you think of New Zealand, Tess?" PJ asked, changing the subject.

"It's remarkable, PJ. Truly remarkable. A person could get lost in these mountains," she said.

After a drive of several hours, the cars crested a rise in the road and descended into a broad valley that opened up before them. Farther on, they came to the entrance road to

Shenandoah Station. In John's car, the conversation had been primarily about John and Tom's flight from Ireland so many years prior. When John heard of Tom's adventure in Alaska and of their Uncle John's death during the blizzard, he turned sad.

"Uncle John was the only reason I stayed in Ireland as long as I did, Tom. You know Da named me after him, back when they were still friends. Uncle John tried to get me to understand Da, but it was no use. Before John left for America, there were a few times when I thought he was going to kill Da himself, for the way he treated Mor."

"He seemed happy in Alaska," Tom said.

"It sounds as though the year in the wilds did wonders for you, too, baby brother," John said, once again light-hearted.

"Aye," Tom laughed back, "it seems all those years we thought the little folk hid their gold in County Kerry, they were actually stashing it in Alaska."

"You'd be right there, Mate," John laughed loudly. "Well, here she be—Shenandoah Station. Not as big as some, but bigger'n others."

"Why 'Shenandoah,' John?" Katrina asked.

"We named it for Margaret's childhood home, in the Shenandoah Mountains, toward the top of the South Island. Margaret pulled me out of the doldrums and made something of me," he said. "For the first couple of years I was here, I was drinking, gambling, and getting thrown in jail. For some fool reason, Margaret saw beyond that. But she was no fool," he laughed again. "She let me fall in love with her, and then told me to get lost unless I straightened out. Her Pa liked to have killed me once, when I came out to his place drunk."

"What happened?" Katrina asked, her eyes bright.

"Margaret stepped between us and stood nose-to-nose with her Pa. She said, 'I'm going to marry this man, Pa, if he doesn't kill himself first.' I stood behind her and smiled over her shoulder at him, kind of smug. Then she turned and looked at me, her hands on her hips. She said, 'I want you off my father's land, John Callahan, and I don't want to see you again until you're determined to remain sober. I will not marry an Irish drunkard. If you come back sober within one year, can show me you've got one hundred pounds in the bank, and you've had a job for most of that year, *then*, I'll marry you.'"

"Wow," Katrina exclaimed, "that's some woman."

"Aye," John said, turning his car into the entrance road and pulling to the side of the road and stopping. "From here you can see the main house, down there in the valley. The first time we walked these hills, Margaret and me, she said we'd build our sheep station right here. And we did. And it was a heaven on earth, Tom, until the war came."

"Aye," Tom replied. "It seems few are going to escape unharmed."

John looked over at Tom, sitting on the left-hand passenger side of the car, with Katrina and Emily in the back seat. "Both boys, Tom," he shook his head. "Both of 'em, killed by this bloody war. The Brits used us like cannon fodder at Gallipoli. It was an outright slaughter, with Kiwi's and Aussies, even our Maori boys, carrying the can for the bloody Brits."

"John, I didn't know. I'm sorry," Tom said.

John nodded his head, sitting motionless, holding the steering wheel in both hands. PJ had pulled his car to a stop behind, just off the road and was waiting for John to continue.

"And then Margaret just gave up. She just died, Tom. I

guess her heart was broken by the loss of her sons. She's a victim of this bloody war every bit as much as the boys— and the thousands of other Kiwi boys that are never gonna come home."

Emily reached from the back seat and laid her hand on her father's shoulder.

"If it weren't for Emily," he said, turning slightly to smile at his daughter, "I don't know if I'd have made it." John exhaled forcefully and pointed off in the distance. "There's part of the flock. Did you know we've got nigh on twenty million sheep in New Zealand? And nearly a million of 'em think they're people!" John laughed loudly before anyone else got the joke, and as quickly as it had disappeared, his joyous mood returned. He started the car down the incline toward the main house, driving past a large flock of sheep.

"Watch this, Katrina," John cried. He repeatedly pressed his hand on the car's horn button and the sheep immediately bolted in all directions, running full tilt to escape the surprising sound.

"Never fails," he laughed. "Sheep'r dumber than a rock."

"Even dumber than an Irishman?" Tom laughed.

"Well, I dunno know about *that*, Tom," John smiled.

Nearly three weeks passed while John hosted his brother and his family. The bond that John and Tom had shared during their childhood, united in purpose against their abusive father, returned almost instantly, as Katrina had predicted.

At night, as they lay in their room, Tom and Katrina talked of the reunion as if the twenty-five years had simply evaporated. Katrina's one fear, having come face-to-face with John's loss of both sons to the war, was that Tommy would, by now, be in France facing similar danger.

With most of his family gone, John's plan—to sell

Shenandoah Station and return to Ireland for his final years—seemed sad to Tom, whose life in Utah had provided much more happiness than John had been able to obtain in New Zealand.

Still, as John had explained it, New Zealand had been a wonderful home. The thing was, those he loved and cared for, other than Emily, were gone. With tears in her eyes she had told her dad she wanted to remain in New Zealand. He knew she would eventually marry, and he would be left alone on the station. The last thing he wanted, as he explained it to Tom, was that Emily *not* marry so that she could stay and care for him as he got older. It was not a happy prospect either way one looked at it. At least in Ireland he had brothers and sisters and lots of family still living. Besides, though he couldn't explain it, something was drawing him back to the old sod.

Toward the end of the first week of their visit, Teresa and PJ, who was now officially released from his mission, established the routine of saddling a couple of Uncle John's horses and riding off into the hills to watch the sunset from a promontory overlooking a small valley to the west of Shenandoah Station. That other valley, Uncle John said, contained another twenty thousand acres of prime grazing land and ran adjacent to Shenandoah's western edge. Some years earlier, John had taken an option to buy the land, when its owner had retired and moved back to Christchurch. But that was before the war and during a time when John thought that his boys would marry and participate in the station. Soon, the option to buy would expire, and, according to the owner, others had expressed recent interest in the property.

Three days before their scheduled departure date, brother and sister cantered their horses over the hills, scattering sheep before them. With the horses nibbling at clumps of dried grass, they sat in the saddle, close enough to talk softly while watching the sun set behind the western peaks of the Southern Alps. To the southwest they could just make out the top of Mt. Cook, which at nearly four thousand meters is New Zealand's highest peak. A three-day trip right after PJ's mission release had taken the two families down to Queenstown, circling Mt. Cook and the ever-present snowcapped peaks of the rugged range. South-western New Zealand, with its rocky fjords, was a perfect likeness of the west coast of Norway—something that delighted Katrina enormously.

This evening, as had become their custom, they sat silently, but Tess watched PJ closely, her mind racing with the thoughts that had been ruminating in her head for the past several days. PJ had not spoken openly, but Tess, in quiet and confident understanding of her older brother, had reached certain conclusions about PJ and his feelings for New Zealand. She stared at him for awhile, the breeze blow-ing her hair across her face and the horses sniffing the southerly wind.

Eventually, PJ looked toward Tess, his smile acknowl-edging that her stare had finally aroused his curiosity.

"Well, baby sister, let's have it," he laughed.

"Yes, I think Dad will understand," she said, calmly.

"What do you mean?" PJ asked.

"I mean, big brother, that Mom and Dad will not be *pleased* with your decision, but they'll understand."

"What decision?" he smiled, beginning to comprehend.

"You know very well what decision, Patrick James. You've chosen to stay in this beautiful country, haven't you?"

PJ watched the last tip of the sun disappear behind the

mountains to the west and nodded. "I don't know as I've admitted it to myself yet. I know how much Dad has wanted me to come into the bank, but—"

"Dad has plans or hopes for all of us, PJ. But he also loves us, and knows we need to find our own way. That's why he agreed to let me go to New York next year."

"And Mom?" PJ asked.

Teresa laughed. "She wants her grandchildren near home."

PJ nodded again. "New York's closer than New Zealand."

"Aye, as Dad would say," Teresa said, bursting out laughing. "Truly, PJ, this is a magnificent country. I can understand why you have fallen in love with it. What will you do here?"

"Ah, the big question. That part of my plan will be the weak point in my discussion with Dad. All of this, Tess," he said, sweeping his arm across the vast expanse that rolled before them toward the western mountains, "all this is Uncle John's sheep station, and over that rise, into the next valley, is another twenty thousand acres just waiting to be bought. Uncle John says it can be one of the most productive sheep stations in all of New Zealand."

"Have you learned about sheep ranching?" Teresa asked.

PJ smiled. "Only about the smell," he said. "But Uncle John said he'd stay on through the next year, and my earlier companion, I told you about him, George Armitage, has worked sheep ranches in Yorkshire. He intends to stay in New Zealand too. I think Emily has taken a liking to him, and I think I can get him to come out and work the station with me. I could learn, Tess."

"It seems a great opportunity, PJ. But it's a *long* way from Salt Lake."

"Will you support me when I talk to them?"

"Of course, PJ. If it weren't for you, Tommy would have broken my neck a dozen times over the years," she laughed.

By the following morning when PJ asked to speak with Tom, Teresa had already spoken with their mother, and Katrina, as dutiful mother and intermediary, had already briefed her husband. Tom could tell it was difficult for PJ, coming hat in hand to his father, but he didn't make it easy for his nervous son.

"So," Tom said, after PJ had finished his presentation, "you want me to loan you the down payment to buy Shenandoah Station from your Uncle John, so you can get married, have children, and live eight thousand miles from your mother? Is that correct?"

"*Dad*," Tess interrupted.

"You be silent, Tess," Tom said firmly. Katrina and Tess sat quietly as the two men began to discuss the financial arrangements that would enable PJ to remain in New Zealand and to acquire ownership of John Callahan's sheep station.

"What makes you think you can make a go of it here, PJ?" Tom asked.

"Dad, first of all, I've said nothing about getting married."

"We can all assume that will come in due course, son," Tom smiled. "There's bound to be a young woman in New Zealand at least *half* as pretty as your mother."

"Well, Dad, Uncle John did very well with the sheep station until his sons went away to war. It's good land, I'm told. I've asked around a bit, during the last part of my mission. Most folks in the South Island know about Shenandoah Station. Uncle John's agreed to stay for a year, cousin Emily wants to stay on in New Zealand, and George

Armitage will likely come in on the deal. He knows sheep, too. A lot of people are willing to help, Dad. And if you're honest, you'll remember that you didn't know much about mining or banking. I'm a Callahan, remember," he laughed, playing to his father's pride.

"I see. You've gained a bit of wisdom on your mission 'down under,' Mr. Callahan. Katie, would *you* like to inform your son, or should I?"

"You're doing just fine, Thomas," Katrina smiled.

"Tell me *what*, Dad?" PJ asked.

"Tess, even though you're the youngest, I'm going to allow you to remain while I explain something to PJ. Perhaps it's time to tell you both about certain plans your mother and I made some years ago for the financial security of our children. I must ask, however, that you keep what I'm going to tell you to yourselves until we're able to inform Tommy. Is that agreed?"

Tess nodded and PJ remained silent.

"PJ, in their ever-present feminine wisdom, your mother and your sister somehow came to a knowledge of what was in your mind. They both quickly saw how you love this place. And" Tom said, looking toward his son, "I must admit, I saw nothing other than how beautiful it is, but I understand, PJ. It's your right to find your own way in the world—to seek out and establish your domain. I admire you for that, son, truly," Tom nodded. "Don't misunderstand me. I don't *want* you so far away, and when your children start appearing, I can see I'll spend half my life on a boat bringing your mother down here to see them. But I do understand.

"Many years ago, when you were each very young, your mother and I put some money in trust for our children, to be accessed only when you were of an age to use it responsibly. We both feel that you are now entitled to that money,

PJ. It should assure that you can get started here in New Zealand without having to scrape by for so many years with a high mortgage over your head, and of course, Uncle John will have the money he needs to return to Ireland and establish himself. Tess, I don't mean to be harsh, but I think that you—"

"Don't worry, Dad," she smiled, "I'm not ready yet, I know that. Just keep investing my share, and pay my bills in New York," she laughed.

"You might not have anything left after that, Tess," Tom said.

"What are we talking about, Dad?" PJ asked, "I never heard of any money."

"I know. That was the idea," Tom said. "PJ, and you, too, Tess," Tom grew solemn, "your trust accounts, the last time I checked, had just over three million dollars in liquid assets, and about one and a half million in UTB stock holdings."

"Dad, I can't possibly—"

"PJ," Katrina spoke up, "you're not accepting anything. Your father has very wisely provided for each of us, including me, I might add, should anything happen to him. These funds are not gifts to you, or me, for that matter. It's *our* money that he invested many years ago for our security. You need feel no reservation about accepting control of your own trust fund. You have most certainly become a man and will have the means to establish your future. It's no different than your father coming back from Alaska laden with gold and sharing it with me, even if he *didn't* tell me until after we were married," she said, with a look toward Tom.

Teresa rose from her seat and went to her father. She sat on the arm of his chair and wrapped her arms around his neck. "Thank you, Dad. Thank you for providing for us so well."

"Just be happy, Tess. That's all your mother and I want. Now, PJ," Tom grew serious again, "John tells me that to make this station what it *could* be, you need to acquire the land across the mountain. He still holds an option to buy, and if you act quickly, you can make Shenandoah Station one of the biggest in New Zealand."

"That's what I think too, Dad."

PJ and Tom both stood, son embracing father.

"Do well, PJ. If you find a good woman, like I did," he said, pulling Katrina to him, "you'll make it fine."

The Tuesday following, on the dock in Lyttleton, the scene was one of sad parting as Tom, Katrina, and Tess prepared to leave New Zealand. PJ, John, and Emily, stood in a group as the time for boarding grew closer.

"And one other thing, PJ," Katrina said.

"Yes, Mom?"

"*Every* baby!"

"Mom?" PJ said, confused for a moment. Then he began to laugh. "Right, Mom. You have my word. But don't hold your breath. I've got a lot of work to do first."

"I'm sure the work will get done, but I want to see *every* baby."

"I promise, Mom. Dad, may I talk to you for a minute?" PJ said, taking hold of Tom's elbow and stepping away from the group.

"What is it, PJ?"

"I may never have the opportunity again to say this to you, and I *have* to tell you how I feel. My mission has brought a lot of things into focus for me. Dad, Mormonism

369

is true. When I left home, I didn't know that the way I know it now. But, it's true—everything—Joseph Smith, the Book of Mormon, the priesthood, the Restoration. The Church provides a way for families—our family, Dad—to be together in the Celestial Kingdom. I want that for our family, and Mom wants it, too. But we can't get there without you."

Listening to this lecture and looking into PJ's eyes, Tom suddenly had a moment where he wondered if he had ever really *looked* at his son. The features were all familiar, but in a way, it was a face he had never seen. The message also wasn't one he wanted to hear. Being counseled by his son wasn't something he was used to, and he was uncomfortable.

"PJ, I don't think—"

"Dad, please, let me finish. I need to tell you. In her heart, Mom longs desperately for the blessings that are given in the temple. You *must* know that. I know how long this has been an issue for you, and how supportive you have always been of everything we've done in the Church. But when I saw Mom in the temple when I was getting ready to go on my mission, well, . . . it was *very* hard to watch her."

Tom had always thought of his inability to accept the Mormon religion in terms of his own limitations. He knew of course that it was a huge issue for Katrina, but it struck him now in a way it never had before. PJ's description of Katie being in the temple—alone—made him sad. He had failed her. It wasn't something he could do anything about, but clearly, he had failed her. The realization hurt.

"Can you find it in your heart, Dad, to fill this one empty piece of Mom's life? Of her *eternal* life?"

"PJ, I'll tell you honestly, my private prayers have *always* been for the Lord to show me the way."

PJ put his hands on his father's shoulders and smiled at

him. "Can't you see what He's *already* shown you—in your own family—in Tess, me, and even Tommy? Mom has loved you all these years and never asked you to choose."

Tom nodded his head. "I promise you this, PJ. I *will* ask Him again, to show me the way. But, long ago, when I was about your age, my mother made me promise—"

"I know, Dad. Mom told us all years ago. But you *have* to follow your heart."

Uncomfortable having this conversation and anxious to bring it to a close, Tom said, "I haven't been a very demonstrative father, but I love you, PJ. Never forget that," Tom smiled, trying to lighten the mood and moving to rejoin the others.

"Dad, if you can find it in your heart to say the same thing to Tommy, a great burden will be lifted from your shoulders. I give you my solemn witness on that."

"Thank you, son. I guess it's hard for a parent to take advice from his children, but I suppose that the Lord bestows wisdom in His own way, and not according to age. Well," he said, looking toward the ship, "I guess it's time to get your mother and sister on board."

Tom took Katrina's arm and began to nudge her toward the gangplank. She didn't even make an effort to hide her tears as she hugged PJ, then John and Emily.

"The world's growing smaller every day, Katie," Tom said. "The trip is certainly long, but one day we'll just jump on one of these new-fangled airplanes and soar through the islands to visit PJ and his Kiwi brood." He shook John's hand, hugged Emily again, and took PJ in his arms once more. "Remember where we are, should you need us, son."

They stood on the deck, waving and watching the people grow smaller as the ship pulled away from the pier. The long white cloud had returned to New Zealand, covering the bay in Lyttleton, and the sun was shaded from their view.

"Tom, I don't think I'll pluck those silver hairs from your head anymore," Katrina said.

"Excuse me?" he replied, looking down at her.

Katrina snuggled closer to her husband, looking up into his eyes as the ship slowly turned around in Lyttleton harbor. "They look more dignified on a grandfather, don't you think?"

"It's a little bit early, wouldn't you say?" Tom said defiantly.

"PJ will find a good young woman soon. I know it in my heart. And we, Mr. Callahan, are moving into the next phase of life. It's time you looked the part."

"I see," he laughed. "And you?"

"Oh, I'm *far* too young to be a grandmother, Mr. Callahan. But I'll pretend."

"No matter, Mrs. Callahan. You'll always be, '*Katie m'darlin*' to me."

"I know that," she said, her voice taking on a serious tone. "I've *always* known that. But I want something more. I want it to be Katie, 'm *eternal* darlin'," she said, looking deeply into his eyes. "I've given you my youth, Thomas, and my love for twenty years—and four beautiful children. Now I'm asking for my due. I want a temple marriage. It's that simple, Thomas. I want you reconciled with Tommy, and I want a temple marriage. And I tell you here and now, that if you can't find it in your heart to listen to the Lord who's been speaking to you in so many ways all these years, then I intend to come back here to New Zealand—this beautiful land—and live with PJ and my future grandchildren."

Tom stood stunned, staring at his wife. "Katie, you've never demanded—"

"No, I haven't. Perhaps I should have, many years ago. But I am now, Thomas, I am now," she said, turning to wave at the pier once more as the great liner slowly turned into the Lyttleton Harbor channel.

⌘

April 25, 1918
Canterbury, New Zealand

Dear Mom and Dad,

You hadn't been gone two weeks when I received a hearty "Yeah, brother," from George Armitage. He had just taken a job in one of the factories on the North Island, and was thrilled at the prospect of venturing with me.

I believe I told you that when George was my companion and we first met Uncle John, I could see that Emily was interested in him. He is (in spite of being English), a very handsome lad. Within a couple of weeks of arriving back in Canterbury, he asked Uncle John for permission to marry Emily. She has accepted his proposal and has asked me to baptize her. They are to be married in Christchurch in September.

Emily is a fine young woman, very strong and resourceful. The death of her mother on top of the loss of her two brothers would have destroyed a lesser person. She is a Callahan, through and through (even though she'll have to sign her name as Armitage from now on). She was ready to hear and understand our message, although I could see from the start that her initial interest was not in the gospel but in George Armitage. Uncle John is staying until the wedding, and then he'll depart for Ireland.

Please know that I love you both and that I pray for our family, especially Tommy, every day. I had a short letter from him about a week ago. He's training with French army units at present but has not been in combat, thank the Lord. The Lord will protect him, Mom. Please don't worry.

I know the gospel is true, and that the work I've been doing in New Zealand is His will. The Church, as you saw, is very small here in the South Island, but with men like George Armitage, the Lord will work wonders. Thank you for the opportunity you've given me to serve Him.

Uncle John was right—sheep are the dumbest creatures on earth. He told me that sheep only know two things: where not to go and how not to get back.

I love you both.
Yours, sheepishly,

PJ

22

Three months spent in the French countryside and two training exercises later, the 6th Marines had experienced the rigors of trench living and night-fire hostile engagements. Even without enemy fire to consider, the conditions were appalling, and many of the newly arrived Marines had succumbed to dysentery, chills, and fever. As was the case so many years earlier in Cuba, some died as a result of illness, never having seen the enemy in combat. While not spoken of directly, the Marines quickly became aware of the cost of the war in terms of French, British, and German troops killed over the previous three and a half years. The living reminders, those who had spent months and in some cases, years, at the front, were wretched creatures. Their hollow eyes, loss of spirit, and often uncontrolled shaking, was the evidence that the war had indeed taken an immense human toll.

The newspapers had begun to refer to the huge numbers of the eighteen- to twenty-eight-year-old men who had died the "Lost Generation." Each side tried to downplay the number of their dead, but most governments agreed that well over five million men had died in the barbaric stalemate. Like most soldiers, the members of 6th Marines gave little thought to the prospect of personally adding to that toll, but to those in command, who knew their turn was coming, it seemed inevitable that some or many Americans would be added to the rosters of the dead.

On Sunday, May 30, Corporals Callahan and Borello were conducting a cursory inspection of platoon weapons when a French lorry sloshed along a rutted, muddy path being used for a road and came to a stop. A bedraggled French officer stepped out, wading through the mud toward the command tent.

"That's not encouraging," Frank said, nodding toward the officer.

"Ummm," Tommy replied, thrusting the weapon he was inspecting back toward the private. "Clean it again, Bartoskiwitz," he growled.

For six weeks, 9th Company, 6th Marines, had been bivouacked in a field, fifteen miles from the battlefield. Noncommissioned officers had rotated through "no-man's-land," observing French troops and conditions along the line. But Colonel Catlin had yet to fully commit the 6th to any direct action, and General "Blackjack" Pershing, Commander of United States forces, had struggled to integrate the 4th Marine Brigade into the Army 2nd Division. Each unit was reluctant to serve under opposite service officers, and so whenever a French or British officer showed, it was rumored to indicate that the Marines were going to be separated from exclusively U.S. command and seconded to foreign command.

Indeed, French General Jean Degoutte, commander of the French XXI Corps, had sought deployment of the Marine Brigade to his control, but General Pershing, who had served as a young lieutenant under Teddy Roosevelt in Cuba, had held firm that U.S. troops would only fight as a unit, and only under American command.

Twenty minutes after the French officer arrived, he left

the command tent, returned to his lorry, and departed. Gunnery Sergeant Holloman, now serving as Company Sergeant-Major, was close behind him, and as he passed the First Platoon area, Tommy moved to cross his path.

"Liberty in Paris this week, Gunny?" he laughed.

"Saddle 'em up, Corporal. We're pulling out in two hours."

"Where to, Gunny?"

"South. Toward Paris," he said. "But don't shine your boots yet, Corporal. We're gonna join the French Sixth Army. Some place called Chateau-Thierry."

"Where's that?"

"I dunno. And I don't care. Get 'em ready, Corporal," he said, continuing on past the First toward Corporal Borello's Second Platoon.

"Aye, aye, Gunny."

Before noon, the bulk of the 6th Marines were riding south in a long convoy of French lorries, confusion their constant companion. Road signs, language barriers, and even resentment over their presence dogged the Marines as scuttlebutt ran rampant that they were finally on their way to their first engagement. By dusk, they had received deployment orders, in reserve of the French forces at the front lines. Within forty-eight hours, most of the United States 2nd Division was deployed along the Paris-Metz highway, preparing to support the French Sixth Army, now engaged in a locked battle with the Germans who were advancing toward Paris. Refugees were streaming along the highway, intermingled with French army troops from scattered units, all trying desperately to outrun the advancing Germans. So many people moving toward Paris added to the confusion of American and French reserve forces, who were advancing in the opposite direction to meet the assault.

On June 2, the main German thrust began and French forces quickly began to crumble, retreating through the advancing Marines and the remainder of the U.S. Army, 2nd Division, ordered to stand in support of the retreating French troops. The 4th Marine Brigade assumed its position, holding a line north of the Paris-Metz highway. One French company grade officer passed by Tommy's company commander, suggesting in the exchange that the Marines pull out with the French.

Tommy stood nearby and watched as Captain Williams stood up in his open vehicle, surveying the mass of French troops and refugees streaming back past the Marines. The captain spit on the ground and replied to the exhausted French officer, "Retreat, hell! We just got here."

Within a matter of hours, the 6th Marines, assigned in reserve to support the French Sixth Army, found themselves instead the troops in the foremost front line, awaiting the onslaught of the German Army. Well directed by their officers and noncomms, the Marines dug in, positioned their weapons and prepared for their first major engagement. It was not long in coming.

Long-range marksmanship and automatic weapons positioned to ensure overlapping fields of fire rapidly turned the tide of the attack in favor of the U.S. forces. Stunned by unexpected resistance, the German advance first stumbled then ground to a halt. For two days a stalemate ensued, with Marines repulsing any forward movement by the German forces. Finally, French General Degoutte, seizing on the initiative of the moment, ordered the 2nd U.S. Division, including the 6th Marines, supported by the French 167th Division, to attack the German emplacements. The battle of Belleau Wood had begun.

For most of the month of June 1918, Marines and

American Army troops fought for pieces of ground that changed hands several times during the course of action. The first casualty in Tommy's platoon occurred the first time they went "over the top," out of the trenches, to begin an assault across open ground. The private ahead of Tommy climbed the ladder to the top of the trench, but before cresting the top rung, he took a direct hit in the forehead and fell back against Tommy, knocking him off the ladder. Gunny Holloman pulled the private's body aside and for a brief moment, without words, stared Corporal Callahan in the face and then gestured his head in an "up we go" motion toward the ladder. Tommy hesitated for only a split second as Holloman made for the ladder.

By the end of the day, seven First Platoon Marines had been killed, including the Platoon Sergeant. That evening Gunny Holloman was making his rounds and stopped at Tommy's corner of the trench, where a right angle led back toward the command area. He flopped down on the ground, his back against the mud wall, and took a long pull from his canteen. Both men were silent for a few minutes.

"How'd you know I'd follow you up the ladder, Gunny?" Tommy finally asked.

Holloman shook his head slowly. "I didn't, kid. Each man decides that for himself."

"But—"

"Listen, kid," Holloman voiced softly, trying not to draw others into the conversation. "If I'd been alone in the trench, maybe I wouldn't have gone either. We don't do it for ourselves. You followed me up that ladder because I needed you, and you knew it. Without you, I might have died. Without me, you might have died. That's why we do it, kid. For each other. There's no glory in it. Look at this place," he said, gesturing up and down the trench at the

Marines who were sitting, standing, and in some cases lying in various stages of exhaustion in the mud. "Is there anything here worth dying for," he paused, "except each other?"

Tommy remained quiet. Holloman stood. "If it's any consolation, kid," he smiled, "I knew you'd come. You're a Marine!"

Tommy looked up at Holloman and gave a small grin. "It's a long way from the parade ground at Parris Island."

"No, it's not, kid," he said, his face serious. "This *is* PI. *You* are PI," he added, rapping his knuckles on Tommy's steel helmet. "Well, I'd better get over to the Second Platoon. Borello lost four today, including his lieutenant. Oh, and by the way," he said, crouching to avoid showing above the top of the lower areas of the trench, "the captain said to tell you you're the new platoon sergeant."

"But, Gunny, I don't want—"

"Nobody asked ya, kid. Besides, I gotta tell Borello he's now the platoon lieutenant. Captain Williams got approval from Colonel Catlin to give him a field commission."

Tommy crouched next to Gunny Holloman. "Now that's the smartest thing I've seen come out of the command tent," Tommy smiled.

"Watch your mouth, kid," Holloman grinned. "Borello ain't gonna like it any more than you did," he laughed again, starting to walk away.

"Hey, Gunny," Tommy called after him.

Holloman halted and looked back.

"Some of my boys are still out there," Tommy said, rolling his eyes toward the battlefield beyond the trench.

Holloman nodded and rubbed the stubble on his chin. "I know, kid. God's got 'em now. We'll try to recover the rest later." He watched for a moment as Tommy struggled with the loss of men under his command. "See to the ones you can still help, Sergeant Callahan."

Tommy looked up again. "Aye, Gunny."

October 5, 1918
Somewhere in France

Dear Pop,

Always the sky. Blue sky above and the memories of our fishing trips in the Uintas. For over six months we've lived in this hell hole, our feet rotting, our clothes tattered and mingled with dirt and the blood of our friends—and our enemies. But in the silence of my own thoughts, I lay down in the mud at the bottom of our trench and look at the sky. It seems so peaceful, and I am able to pretend, if only for a moment, that I am once again in the Utah mountains and that life is good.

Pop, I've not yet found it within myself to speak with God as Uncle Andy suggested, and in fact, I've broken my promise to him that I would write to you before we went forward. For several months, we have been almost constantly engaged in one action or another, as you have probably read in the dispatches. Now, rumor runs wild that some end to this mess is in sight, but we've heard all that before.

It's turning gray now, as fall once again approaches. I don't think the men can stand another winter under these conditions. What keeps most of us from complaining is the knowledge that the French and British have been here for three winters. It's impossible to imagine. Already many of our regiment have succumbed to the elements after having survived the fire storm of the enemy. How difficult it is to write to parents and loved ones and tell them that their son or husband died of pneumonia or typhoid as a result of deplorable living conditions. What heroic statement can be made of such a wasted loss of human life?

I've written this letter hundreds of times in my mind, Pop. It all eludes me now. But here I've learned that life is short. I've not yet turned nineteen, yet I've seen older men die. I've even seen younger men—boys really—die. As Benjamin died. These young men who have died in this war will be nineteen forever in the hearts and minds of their loved ones, permanently enshrined behind a piece of dusty glass in a brown, leather frame on someone's dresser.

You told me once that our days are numbered. And I read somewhere that Joseph Smith said "they shall not be made less." If this is true, then perhaps my life may not be much longer than Benjamin's. When I came over here, I had the feeling that God would take my life, and that the war would be my trial by fire. He may still make that judgment, but I've also learned that it is His to make. Not mine and not yours. I don't know why I failed to keep Benjamin safe. I have blamed myself for years, and perhaps that is why your anger so affected me. I believed what you said was true. I had killed my brother. I no longer believe that, Pop. I'm sorry if that offends you. If you still feel that way, you will have to come to terms with it. I thought for many years that I would have to ask your forgiveness—to seek your permission to rejoin the family. But if my failure to watch over my brother was indeed the cause of his death, then it is his forgiveness I need, Pop. Not yours.

If you are still of a mind to hold me accountable, then

I will understand. For my own part, I will go forward with the remaining days God has allotted for my life. And if I survive this war—this desolation—then I will seek to accomplish something. I like the Marine Corps. Once again I am responsible for other men's lives. And I have failed some of them, Pop. As I failed Benjamin. But there are others I have not failed, and they will live to come home. And I must keep trying for their sakes.

I do not ask your forgiveness for Benjamin. But I ask your consideration, as my father, to accept me once again as your son. I have always loved you, Pop, and have admired the way you and Mom made your way in life. What I do apologize for is my anger toward you. I didn't understand, in my youth, that parents have a right to expect certain standards from their children. But children have the same right to expect certain standards from their parents. I offer my solemn promise that, should I survive, I will seek to maintain the standard you have set, for I agree with it, and I agree with the necessity of establishing standards for our lives.

Under the worst of conditions there is always a blue sky somewhere. I will never see the sky in the same light again, nor will I ever take it for granted. Lovingly, your son,

Tommy

P.S. Happy 43rd birthday, Pop. I hope this letter finds you, Mom, Tess, and PJ all in good health.

The "plop" sound was as familiar to the men in the trench as any everyday sound of life. Only this sound carried with it the ring of death. Some were sleeping, but most were simply too exhausted to sleep at the time the German grenade rolled into the muddy trench and landed amidst the silence of the late afternoon. In the following moments, several men scrambled away, around the right angle cut into the trench specifically to limit the impact of such an incident. Sleeping soundly against the wall, his rifle and kit standing loosely against the wooden framing, Sergeant Callahan never even heard the sound.

Lieutenant Borello's action was immediate. He saw the grenade come over the top of the trench even before the other Marines heard the sound as it landed. He glanced at the sleeping Tommy Callahan and knew there would be no time to awaken or to drag his friend around the corner to safety. As Borello instinctively leaped toward the lethal device, his father's face flashed into his mind, and he heard again the older Borello's parting thoughts on the dock in New York. "God be with you, my son. Make us proud," the former Marine had said.

Diving on the grenade and clutching it between his legs as he fumbled to grab it, Lieutenant Borello saw several Marines scrambling to reach the safety of the right angle trench. For an instant, he looked toward Sergeant Callahan, whose eyes opened momentarily and locked with those of Borello. The explosion lifted Frank Borello's body and threw him against Tommy Callahan. Pieces of shrapnel flew in all directions, but the bulk of the blast was absorbed by Frank's legs, as it ripped and tore at the bone and flesh in his knees and thighs.

Tommy wasn't even aware of what had happened in that instant. The concussion from the exploding grenade rendered him unconscious, and he remained in that state for several days. When he finally awoke in the hospital facility, his world was dark and he was totally disoriented. He actually woke screaming, and the nurses who rushed to his bedside, along with several male orderlies, worked to restrain him while trying to explain to him that he was safe, in an American military hospital, and that he would be all right. He had been unconscious for eight days, they said, and his sight was, at least temporarily, gone.

Six weeks passed before he learned of the details of the incident and the extent of the horrific injuries to Lieutenant Borello. His friend had lost both legs, they told him, high above the knee. The bones had been shattered and the flesh shredded. Gangrene had set in and in spite of the double amputation, an infection had developed which continued to plague Frank's recovery. When Corporal Broderick described Lieutenant Borello's selfless actions, Tommy had wept. Aided by the sight of another patient, Tommy had visited Frank in his hospital ward, but Frank remained comatose, and Tommy was never able to speak with him.

The hospital troop ship sailed from Brest in March, 1919, with both Tommy and Frank on board, and made the crossing in eleven days. But Lieutenant Borello traveled only part of the way. His death at sea from complications related to infection and heart failure, resulted in his burial at sea, along with two other Marines who had not survived their wounds. Sergeant Callahan's eyesight had returned, as the doctors had said it would, and his relatively minor injuries were well on the way to being healed. When Tommy inquired, he was informed that the continuing infection had raised Frank's temperature, reaching for, and finally finding, the young lieutenant's vital organs.

During the final few days of the crossing, his eyesight restored and his vision improving, Tommy spent most of his daylight and many night hours, standing on deck, his thoughts focused on the vagaries of life and the sacrifice

Frank had made in Tommy's behalf. When New York harbor appeared one misty morning, the ship was met by harbor tugs and escorted toward the Brooklyn Navy Yard, berthing not far from where their troop ship had sailed, barely a year earlier.

Tommy leaned against the railing as the ship moored, watching dock crews secure the lines and position boarding platforms fore and aft. Hundreds of people lined the dock, restrained by wooden fence lines as the returning troops began to disembark. No bands were present, and the crowd was silent, with no flags waving. Tommy watched the wounded descend the gangplank, in many cases aided by those more ambulatory. He was joined by a ship's officer who had occasionally stood and talked with Tommy during the crossing when his shift coincided with Tommy's nocturnal meanderings. They stood together, silently watching the injured and maimed men returning home. He thought of Frank who had once asked, *Will they be here to greet us when we come home?*

The slightly crippled led the blind down the ramp. The more severely injured were carried on stretchers. The sounds of crying, occasional screaming, and the constant low moan collectively escaping the individual families in the crowd as they found their loved ones, haunted the scene, filling Tommy's mind with the faces of those comrades he had left behind in France.

He uttered a silent prayer of thanks that no one had come to meet him, and that his family did not have to suffer through the agony of waiting to see the condition of a loved one. Slowly, the hospital ship disgorged it's cargo of mutilated young men, returned from their generation's effort to preserve what President Woodrow Wilson had called "World Democracy."

Tommy understood the silence from the assembled

crowd and their individual need to wait for their particular loved one, frightened by thoughts of the moment when they would actually see him. But something about the assembled families continued to confuse Tommy. There was something wrong with the scene on the dock below, and for the better part of an hour, Tommy stood, side by side with the ship's officer, as they watched the tragedy unfold before them.

And then suddenly, one young woman behind the railings fainted, overcome perhaps by the press of the crowd or the vision of yet another young man who, crippled, blind, or even insane, had lost his future. The reaction of the crowd was instantaneous, and, as if by instinct, Tommy immediately understood what was wrong. Waiting as each man descended the ramp—walking, led, or carried—the crowd collectively leaned forward, seeking fearfully to identify their loved one. Not seeing him, the relief on their faces was evident, but fleeting. Unable to endure the agony of yet another family's trauma—almost as a body, they turned their faces away.

Sergeant Callahan continued to observe the bitter aftermath of "The Great War" for some hours, as the crowd slowly thinned, filtering away to who knows where. Periodically throughout the ordeal, tears unashamedly streamed down his face. From that moment on, young Thomas Callahan, barely nineteen, would never be the same.

———— ∞ ————

"Sergeant Thomas Callahan, United States Marine Corps, reporting for orders," Tommy announced to the Naval Corpsman in the hospital administrative office.

"Callahan, Callahan," the corpsman said, riffling through a stack of papers. "Ah, here it is, Sergeant. You're to report to Major Kendrick at the War Department. You can catch a ride with the courier outside in about twenty minutes. Here are your hospital discharge papers."

"Thank you, Corpsman," Tommy replied.

Major Kendrick's office wasn't easy to find, especially since the corpsman had not indicated Kendrick's branch of service and because the War Department in Washington, D.C. was a busy facility. Finally locating his office, Tommy entered and approached the corporal at the desk.

"Sergeant Callahan. I'm supposed to see Major Kendrick."

Again, the corporal thumbed through a stack of papers on his desk, extracting one and standing. "Have a seat, Sergeant. Major Kendrick will see you shortly."

"Right," Tommy said, looking around the room, which was furnished only with a couple of wooden chairs. Even before Tommy sat, the corporal returned.

"The Major will see you now, Sergeant."

Tommy stepped into the office and was pleased to see a Marine Corps uniform behind the desk, gold oak leaves on the shoulders of the dress greens.

"Sergeant Thomas Callahan, sir. Reporting as ordered."

"Stand at ease, Sergeant." The major looked at Tommy briefly and began to peruse the file in front of him. "Hmmm, three meritorious service awards, promotion to sergeant. Two French awards for valor, and let's see, recommended for a field commission before you were wounded," he voiced quietly as if reading to himself. He looked up again at Tommy whose eyebrows had raised. "So, they didn't tell you that in the hospital, did they?"

"Sir?"

"The field commission? They didn't advise you of that, did they?"

"Sir, I'm unaware of . . ."

"Right, right, right," the major interrupted. "So what are your plans, Sergeant?"

"Sir?" Tommy asked again, somewhat confused.

"Are you planning to muster out? Go back home?"

"Sir, I've only been in the Corps just under two years. I hadn't actually, I mean, well, sir, I hadn't thought about it yet."

"Well, you've got about three minutes, son, to decide. I'm supposed to sort through this pile of returning Marines, wounded and," he paused, placing his hands on another stack of files, "otherwise,' he said softly. "These poor Marines have had their choices taken away, however," he said, leaving Tommy to assume they were deceased.

"Well, here you have it, son, in a nutshell. You can apply for immediate discharge or," again he paused, once more looking at Tommy's service record, "given the nature of your record I have been empowered to offer you one of fifty slots the Corps has been given in the next class at Annapolis." He looked up to gauge Tommy's reaction.

"Sir?" Tommy asked.

"Sergeant Callahan," Major Kendrick said, rising from his chair and coming around to the front of his desk. "The Corps has learned some hard lessons in this brief but disastrous escapade in France. We need seasoned, combat experienced professionals to build a cadre of officers who can further the needs of the Corps. The war's over, so we'll probably be gutted again, and if Congress has their way, our manpower will be reduced, but the Commandant has seen the wisdom of plucking out the best of the best. Your service record and the recommendation of your company commander, says that's you. So, what's it to be? Mr. Callahan, or *Midshipman* Callahan, United States Naval Service, class of, let's see, uh, Class of 1923 it will be."

"How much time do I have, sir?"

Kendrick looked at his watch. "Sergeant, I'm having lunch with the Commandant's adjutant in fifteen minutes. I'll be back here at precisely one-thirty. By one-thirty-three, you will either be on your way to Annapolis for entry into the summer program in May, or I'll send you down the hall where you can turn in your dress greens. That's all you have, son. An hour. If you want a piece of advice, this is a rare opportunity. I've already filled thirty-eight of my fifty appointments and congressmen are calling me every day, trying to slip their favorite candidate into one of my slots. But the Commandant is adamant. Marine war veterans with exemplary records are to have first shot. Think about it, son, and if you know anyone in this town who you can contact for advice, I'd use the next hour wisely. One-thirty," he said again, gesturing to his watch. "Don't be late."

"Aye, aye, sir," Tommy said, coming to attention as Major Kendrick left the office, leaving Tommy standing alone in front of his desk.

⁂

April 3, 1919

Mr. Thomas Callahan
Chairman of the Board
Utah Trust Bank
Salt Lake City, Utah

Unable to return Utah as planned—Stop—Assigned Quantico, 6th Marines Training Unit—Stop—Enter United States Naval Academy in May as Midshipman—Stop—Tell Mom I'm sorry—Stop—Love, Tommy.

23

Tom sat on the granite bench, his hands chilled by the coolness of the stone. With winter reluctant to release its hold, the buds on the rose bushes had yet to show green. He picked a few dead twigs off the ground and tidied a couple of loose odds and ends, more from the need to feel he was doing something than from the actual gardening required.

He looked again at the marble headstone, the edges of the lettering still sharp from the engraver's chisel.

Sister Mary Theophane
Born 3 October 1839
Waterford, Ireland
Died 11 April 1919
Salt Lake City, Utah

ALL SHE HAD, SHE GAVE

Katrina's telephone call the night before his departure from Maryland, informing him of Sister Mary's death, had made the train trip to Utah a long, somber journey. In the face of the worldwide influenza epidemic, Sister Mary had continued to disregard her own health, and her chronically weakened condition from recurring malaria made her a prime target for the flu. Over the protests of her co-workers, she had continued to spend extensive hours at Holy Cross Hospital, caring tirelessly for the unfortunate victims of the rampant, and often fatal, epidemic.

The only good thought from Tom's trip to Washington, D.C., and Maryland, was that he and Tommy had at last been reconciled. They had met by arrangement just outside the reception center at Annapolis. It would be the first time they had seen each other in nearly three years, and Tom paced nervously while waiting for Tommy to arrive. He had gone over in his mind the words he planned to say, discarding one approach and then another, and finally, despairing to know what to say at all.

When Tommy appeared, Tom had at first glance not recognized him. The man who strode toward him so purposefully was tall, ramrod straight, and resplendent in his Marine dress greens.

But as he approached, the Marine slowed his pace, then stopped altogether, standing a few feet away from his visitor—a look of uncertainty on his face. They had stood for a few moments, looking at each other, before Tom began to speak.

"Tommy, I know . . ."

Before he could utter another word, and in full view of the other young men passing by, Tommy stepped quickly to his father and the two fell into each other's arms—each of them unable to speak.

They had spent time together the rest of that day and into the evening, eating dinner in a nearby hotel and conversing afterward in a way they never had before—about feelings, fears, and hopes. They had gotten finally to the event that had separated them for so many years. When young Tom described for his father the heartbreak he had experienced when he heard Tom condemn him for his cowardice that morning in the hotel in New York, following the loss of Benjamin, Tom could only shake his head and lower his eyes in shame. After a time he expressed his sorrow and apologized for the pain he had so needlessly inflicted on his son.

That Tommy had become a man was no longer in question, and that Tommy had accepted his father's apology made Tom's heart soar.

"Tommy, it's been hard for me to accept, much less to say, but I have never really been angry at you. I was angry at myself," Tom said. "I was the one who should have been on that ship—I should have taken care of my family. There's no excuse, Tommy, but you were the only male I could blame. Your mother has understood my misdirected anger, but she has continued to love me anyway. I can't tell you how sorry I am."

But in spite of all that and Tom's plea for his son to come home and take up his rightful place at Utah Trust Bank, Sergeant Callahan remained adamant about his decision to accept appointment to the United States Naval Academy, and they had parted amicably. Once again, father and son.

His mind now at ease and the long-standing burden lifted, Tom's thoughts on the train had turned to the events in his life in which Sister Mary had participated. Not much he had done, he decided, had *not* undergone her scrutiny. He had benefited in untold ways by her words of wisdom. That he loved her was as certain as the solid granite underneath him. That she had loved all with whom she had come in contact was also just as certain.

"Ah, Sister," he said softly, sitting on the bench and reverting to the Irish dialect they had always shared, "what are we goin' to do without you? You were the very soul of the hospital. It's me own self that'll be needin' you—as I always have. If you'd been me own dear mother, I'd not have loved you more."

Tom lowered his head, reluctant to depart, content to remain on the bench. Katrina had said death had come reverently for Sister Mary, as she slept. She was taken by the angels, as it were, Katrina had said. And rightfully so.

"I'm only ten years younger than you were when I first came, Sister Mary, cap in hand, looking for work and a place to lay me head. And you gave unto me, as I watched you give all your life to those in need. The world has changed so much, Sister Mary. Values we took for granted are challenged and youngsters are finding life's choices more difficult. My children have all grown now, and started their own lives, but I have far too few answers for them, Sister—few words of wisdom, other than those you taught me, and now, I can't tell them to 'go see Sister Mary.'"

Tom stood and wiped his hand across the top of the headstone, clearing some imaginary dust.

"Sure now, and you'll be havin' a grand reunion with Father Scanlan, bless his soul. I suppose it's a strange thing to be askin' you, but if you should happen upon me mother, would you be asking her to understand that I need to go against her wishes, and that I mean her no disrespect? I pray that she'll understand, as you always have. Father Scanlan's gone, me dear Mor's been gone too all these years, and now, well, now Sister Mary, you've earned your reward too." He paused for a moment, looking up at the gray, overcast skies, then looking back at the inscription. "Remember, I'll not be far, Sister, should you be need'n me. I still live just down the road."

He turned to leave the gravesite, fresh with soft,

mounded earth, as yet uncovered by the spring grass. He turned once more, several feet from the grave, and removed his hat, looking back toward the headstone.

"God's blessings on you, Moira Molloy. I loved you truly."

Notes

1. During the Civil War, the United States Government had asked the Sisters of the Holy Cross to establish a hospital to care for Union soldiers. This hospital was established at Mt. Cairo, Illinois. In 1898, the Sisters were again asked by the government to operate a field hospital in Cuba during the Spanish-American War and immediately complied.

2. The First Volunteer Calvary Regiment included a unit known as the Rough Riders, under the command of Lieutenant Colonel Theodore Roosevelt. The Brigade also included the 10th Calvary, a Negro outfit, commanded by Lieutenant Jack Pershing, later to become commanding general during "The Great War" (World War I).

3. As is often the case in history, the site of what later came to be called "The Charge up San Juan Hill," actually took place on a nearby smaller knoll called Kettle Hill. Colonel Roosevelt's Rough Riders had been required to leave most of their horses in Florida for lack of transportation, and fought, for the most part, on foot as dismounted cavalry.

4. William Randolph Hearst, a strong proponent of the war against Spain, was present during the assault and assigned

his chief correspondent, Frederick Remington, to cover the war in Cuba. Steven Crane, author of *The Red Badge of Courage*, was also part of the correspondent corps.

5. For some years after the turn of the century, general conference for The Church of Jesus Christ of Latter-day Saints was held mid-week, moving to a weekend format later in the twentieth century as the Church grew.

6. Upon the promotion of Colonel Leonard Wood, Theodore Roosevelt, Wood's second-in-command, was also promoted to command the First Volunteer Calvary Regiment, visiting the wounded in Tampa, Florida, on his return from Cuba.

7. In *The Salt Lake Tribune*, circa 1905, Sister M. Bartholomew, an early leader of Holy Cross Hospital, is quoted as speaking out at a meeting of the State Medical Society, accusing physicians of contributing to the rising costs of hospital care by the exorbitant increases in their fees.

8. The author has taken the literary license to place this factual episode twelve months earlier than it actually occurred. Greek miners on strike held a standoff with police and government officials in September 1912. Greek Orthodox Priest, Father Vasilios Lambrides, actually mediated and helped to bring the situation under control.

9. On two previously recorded occasions, smaller vessels had been drawn toward a passing larger vessel by the turbulent action of the water. As vessels increased in size, ignorance still prevailed as to the effect of passage by such vessels, and on this occasion, in the minds of the investigators, it was still undetermined that the

larger vessel had indeed caused the *New York* to break free of her mooring lines.

10. The facts surrounding the sinking of the *Titanic* have, over the intervening eighty-five years, been confused with press accounts and fable, perpetuated by thirdhand accounts of the disaster. It was common practice at the turn of the century for oceangoing vessels to carry insufficient lifeboats, on the premise that with wireless radios, sealed compartment construction, and rapid transit available to those ships within reasonable distance, rescue vessels would be on the scene before the full complement of passengers and crew would find it necessary to abandon ship. The *Titanic*, touted as unsinkable in the press following her launching, gave everyone aboard the false notion that to remain aboard was infinitely wiser than to put out into a cold Atlantic sea, in a small, wooden lifeboat.

11. There are several recorded incidents of wives determined to stay with their husbands on the *Titanic*.

12. Upon receiving the *Titanic's* call for help, the *Carpathia* wired "Coming hard," and raced fifty-eight miles through ice-infested waters, firing flares enroute to encourage the *Titanic*, arriving just before dawn at the scene. The *Titanic* was long gone, but as dawn broke, lifeboats and debris could be seen stretched over a four-mile radius. The *Californian*, her wireless shut down for the night and her crew confused by the flares they had observed, had lain a mere nineteen miles away, oblivious to the tragedy occurring within sight.

13. Eamon de Valera (1882–1975) escaped execution after the 1916 Easter Rising as a result of his American citizenship. He rose to become prime minister of the Irish

Free State, which achieved full sovereignty in 1937. He served as the president of the Republic of Ireland from 1959–1973.